3/98

THE
STALKING-HORSE

THE
STALKING-HORSE

Miriam Grace Monfredo

BERKLEY PRIME CRIME, NEW YORK

THE STALKING-HORSE

A Berkley Prime Crime Book
Published by The Berkley Publishing Group
A member of Penguin Putnam Inc.
200 Madison Avenue, New York, NY 10016

The Putnam Berkley World Wide Web site address is
http://www.berkley.com

First Edition: March 1998

Library of Congress Cataloging-in-Publication Data

Monfredo, Miriam Grace.
    The stalking horse / Miriam Grace Monfredo.
        p.   cm.
    ISBN 0-425-15783-0
    1. United States—History—Civil War, 1861–1865—Fiction.
I. Title.
PS3563.05234S7   1998
813'.54—dc21   97-21547
                                                           CIP

Printed in the United States of America

10 9 8 7 6 5 4 3 2 1

For Rachel and David

DOUBLE HAPPINESS

ACKNOWLEDGMENTS

—m—

Mary Ann Neeley, director of the Landmarks Foundation of Montgomery, Alabama, whose generosity, energy, and knowledge of Montgomery history—along with her breathtaking, whirlwind private tour—made my time in her beautiful city a joy.

Joseph Maguire, Maryland Historical Society in Baltimore

Victor Nielson, Alabama Archives and History

Tracey McKether, Montgomery Area Chamber of Commerce

Peter Lester, Chesapeake Bay Maritime Museum

Carol Sandler, director of The Strong Museum Library

Bill Watson, gentleman sailor who gave assistance on sailing the Chesapeake

Dave Miller, sailor, friend, and zenith hour rescuer

David Minor, of Eagles Byte Historical Research, for his superb chronologies

Kathy Stewart, for many and essential sundries; and Mark Stewart, who, after *The Stalking-Horse* fatally trampled two computers, found and installed a third that was hoof-proof

Frank Monfredo, for perpetual encouragement and problem-solving assistance, and for being what every author needs most: a thoughtful and relentlessly honest critic

Rachel Monfredo Gee, daughter par excellence, for enthusiastic assistance despite The Big Event, and new son-in-law David Gee for providing the Horse-vs-Dissertation race to Armageddon; and to both for providing me with Much Happiness

And to my father, H. J. Heinicke, M.D., medical consultant and sailor, who designed the *Cascade* and suggested its course just weeks before his death: Thank you, Daddy. Rest in peace.

AUTHOR'S NOTE

—m—

The Stalking-Horse is fiction based on an actual historic event. Those who regularly read the Historical Notes section *before* they read the text itself should be warned that the notes contain details pertinent to the solution of the mystery. Thus, for those who enjoy the enigmatic: beware.

He uses his folly like a stalking-horse.

—Shakespeare, *As You Like It*

Stalking-horse . . . n 1: *a horse or a figure of a horse behind which a hunter hides in stalking game* 2: *something used to cover up a secret project: MASK; PRETENSE . . .*

—*Webster's Third New International Dictionary*

PROLOGUE

·~~~·

I heard the bells on Christmas Day
Their old familiar carols play,
*   And wild and sweet*
*   The words repeat*
Of peace on earth, good-will to men!

—Henry Wadsworth Longfellow

1860
Seneca Falls

*C*louds bearing western New York's first winter snowfall had come at midday, blanketed the village of Seneca Falls, then swung north. Now a dull-brass December sun sat low on the horizon. Glynis Tryon stepped out of her library and into long purple shadows just as a man astride a Morgan horse turned the corner onto Fall Street. Constable Cullen Stuart lifted his hand in response to the librarian's wave, and smiling at her over his shoulder, he continued riding up the wide main road that ran through the center of town. To either side of Fall Street, shop and office doors were hung with red-berried holly wreaths now glittering with fresh snow. Plump virgin drifts flattened silently beneath the Morgan's hooves.

Glynis Tryon turned to lock the door of her library set between the road above and the Seneca River below. From the distance came a jingle of harness bells on horse-drawn sleighs, and from the frozen Seneca and Cayuga Canal section of the river came the shouts of skaters. After she climbed the few shallow steps to Fall Street, Glynis paused at the top to catch the last rays of sun. While she stood gazing at flame-streaked clouds twixt earth and sky, bells in the village church steeples began to toll, calling worshippers to early service, and reminding her that it was Christmas Eve.

She suddenly realized her teeth were chattering. Although an earlier wind had died, the air held a knife-sharp chill that drove straight to the bone; raising the hood of her wool cloak and pulling the garment securely around herself, she set off in what had swiftly become twilight. Christmas Eve. The night which had brought the Prince of Peace. But under the star in the east this night hung the threat of war.

The bitterly contested national election of a month before gave the Presidency to the Republican candidate, but gave it by only a narrow margin. At the conclusion of the four-man race, Abraham Lincoln's opponents tallied, together, more votes than he. Lincoln's came from the western states and every northern state save New Jersey. Since the election, the southern states' call for secession had created such thunder it all but drowned the President-elect's call for compromise.

Even there in western New York, far above the Mason-Dixon line, the ranks of local militia companies had begun to swell. Of late, Glynis found herself wakened mornings by the drums that accompanied marching men in the nearby fairgrounds. The new recruits were mostly young, with no memory of war to blunt their eagerness; but surely, Glynis told herself as she trudged up Cayuga Street, there were thousands of men, both North and South, old enough to remember the Mexican War. And a few remained who had fought in 1812. So where was their witness to war's bloodshed and carnage, and where were their demands for restraint? And the women? The women of the South could no more want war than those of the North. Yet without a vote, without a political voice, they were powerless. The women of America must simply watch while the men in Congress brought them and those they loved ever closer to the brink of catastrophe. The drums of war beat more ominously each day as the Horsemen of the Apocalypse trampled what few voices of reason remained in their path.

In a mood of despondency, Glynis reached her white-framed boardinghouse at 33 Cayuga Street, but as she climbed the porch steps, her spirits lifted somewhat. The glow of candles on a balsam fir was visible through the front parlor window, and when she opened the door, she could smell bayberry and freshly cut evergreen boughs. From the kitchen down the hall came the aroma of roasting goose and chestnut stuffing, candied sweet potatoes, onions simmering in cream, plumcakes, and mincemeat pies.

For a few moments, Glynis stood there in the fragrance of Christmas, recalling a child's excited anticipation, regretting its inevitable loss, and taking comfort in the shelter of tradition.

After slipping off her cloak, she started down the hall and met her landlady coming through the kitchen doorway. Smiling broadly, Harriet Peartree gestured toward the front of the house, and Glynis then noticed the rising voices from the street outside. She went back to the door, opening it to a dozen or more carolers illuminated under a full winter-solstice moon, cheeks ruddy beneath tasseled stocking caps and chins tucked into long, fringed mufflers. Memories of Christmas past, a long unbroken procession of family and friends gathering year after year for the same carol singing, brought to her a surge of hope. And it was hope, she thought, that ever had been the true face of Christmas.

While Harriet bustled back into the kitchen for cookies and hot mulled cider, Glynis stood in the doorway to listen.

Snow crunched under the carolers' shifting boots, and chill air frosted their breath, but the song they raised came warm and clear:

> *Silent night, holy night,*
> *All is calm, all is bright . . .*

Sleep in heavenly peace.

I

The ages of gold, of silver, of brass, and iron, as described by the poets, are past. The present is the age of steam. By steam the commerce of the world is carried on. By steam we travel over sea and land. Steam has turned manufacturer, farmer, cook (although it must be acknowledged it makes a sorry business of this last). Latterly, steam and the fine arts have scraped acquaintance. The real and the ideal have smoked pipes together. The iron horse and Pegasus have trotted side by side in double harness, puffing in unison, like a well-trained pair.

—New Harper's Monthly, June 1859

1

Cast a cold eye,
On life, on death.
Horseman, pass by!

—William Butler Yeats

1861
Chicago

The young woman knew she was being watched. She stood at a glazed window, and even with her back to the room, she could feel the man's shrewd eyes appraising her, inspecting her to see if she qualified for his perverse demands.

The window, on the second floor of a building at Washington and Dearborn Streets, looked out on the heart of a noisy, hustling prairie city. The young woman gazed down at the cobblestone street covered with snow, where scores of horse-drawn omnibuses and carriages plowed gamely through drifts of white. A January storm had peaked some hours ago, and the snow fell more lightly now. Through its translucent veil, she could see in the distance a blur of grain elevators lining the shores of Lake Michigan; they waited for wheat that arrived in mile-long columns of wagons, some two hundred freighters, and the mighty Illinois Central and Rock Island railroad lines. If the man asked, she could tell him this: *the Illinois Central and the Rock Island.*

She stood quietly, hands clasped before her, making herself appear composed, calm, unruffled to the bearded man watching from behind his office desk. To accomplish this deception—her heart knocking against her chest wall—she tried to calculate how many individual grains of wheat might be needed to fill one of those elevators. Not a fruitful task.

She didn't like keeping her back to this man. When the telegram arrived for him, she had turned to the window out of a courtesy she now saw as misguided. He must have long since finished reading the wire, yet had said not one single word. He was using her courtesy to make her sweat. And at any moment, the smoke from his cigar would force her to choke, if not actually retch. It would not bode well if she vomited in his office. Why didn't he *say* something?

"Jane!"

At the gruff voice she whirled. From the way his eyes narrowed, she realized he had been testing her; seeing how quickly she would respond to a name not her own. And now he looked satisfied, at least as satisfied as he ever did. She felt rather satisfied herself; she had long suspected—although he would swear otherwise—that he did *not* know everything! In this instance, he didn't know that he could have called her James, or John, or Joe; that she had reacted so fast simply because he had startled her.

By the same logic, she could not know what the man had thought while he sat assessing her. Couldn't know that he thought her coiled but wind-blown red hair against falling snow would be unforgettable to any who saw it; and would make men picture that hair loosed from its coil, fanned like fire over white sheets. He thought that despite her long full skirt, the hint of what rounded just below the bow at the back of her waist would also be unforgettable. Even he, who had little inclination toward things carnal, doubted he would forget.

She could not know, but would have feared, that he had not even begun to count her other liabilities; the worst being her reckless disregard for discipline. To send this particular woman south could likely be the most foolish thing he would ever do. He would regret it, he could feel it in his bones. But he owed a favor. And he paid his debts.

And now *she* stood watching *him*, and she waited. At last, after removing the cigar, and with a sigh that sounded more like a groan, he nodded. Once.

She tried not to reveal her relief; pretended to listen while he went through the litany yet again. "You will be playing a role, and must act it out completely," he intoned, just like she imagined Moses must have sounded—in which case it was hardly a wonder that no one had listened.

"Remember too," he went on, as if he had not said this before a hundred times, "that the ends justify the means, if the ends are for the accomplishment of justice."

But the young woman, for all that she tried to look attentive, was already at the railroad station, riding an Illinois Central iron horse to the South. *The South.* It had, in these exciting times, an exotic, slightly dangerous overtone.

She could not have known *how* dangerous.

Baltimore

The old year had ended with unseasonably mild weather, but now, two weeks into the new, the city shivered in bitter cold.

On this particular night, the streets were nearly deserted, a wind slicing off the Chesapeake keeping even the most predatory of Baltimore toughs—the Plug-Uglies, Blood-Tubs, Rip-Raps, and Rough-Skins gangs—off the streets.

Which was a damned good thing, thought the sturdily built man who hurried up South Street, cursing himself for not spending three cents on an omnibus. He struggled to keep his footing on the ice-glazed cobblestones, but then, buffeted by a sudden blast of wind off the harbor, found himself forced to grab the nearest gaslight pole to wait out the gust. It was with considerable irritation that he finally, and tardily, reached the swinging door of Barr's Saloon. Once through it, he searched a haze of cigar smoke for the three men he sought. He found them grouped at the far end of the bar.

"Sorry to be late," he offered, removing a flawlessly tailored, knee-length overcoat. He offhandedly tossed the coat over his arm, although it was clear to anyone who bothered to watch that he meant to conceal its near-threadbare lapels and cuffs.

One of the three men, thin and sharp-featured, the sly look of a weasel about him, pointed to an empty booth at the back of the barroom. "Grab a beer, Seagram!"

Guy Seagram ordered a lager beer and joined Weasel, now seated with the others in a corner booth and isolated from their nearest neighbors by a shoulder-high wooden partition.

"The Horseman may not show tonight," Weasel announced.

"Thought you said he'd be here." Seagram raised his beer and took several swallows to cover his frustration.

"Horseman's a busy man. After that damn meeting last night there's work to be done 'fore the secession meetin' in

Montgomery next month. A lotta work." Weasel shot Seagram a cunning grin. "Our bastard governor oughta be lynched."

Seagram took another swallow of beer. The smoke made his eyes smart, and the smell of sweat was rank in the close booth. But one tavern was much like another.

He'd gone to the Union meeting the night before. As expected by the immense crowd there, the secession of South Carolina had been formally condemned. And the position of Maryland's Governor Thomas Hicks had been to vigorously oppose the secession of *his* state.

"The Captain will be along though," Weasel added now.

The newcomer assumed "the Captain" referred to Cypriano Ferrandini, whose barber shop was located in the granite basement of Barnum's Hotel on Fayette Street.

"So what do we-all do while we're waitin'?" ventured one of the other men, impatience making his voice loud.

Weasel silenced him with a look. "We wait, that's what!"

By happy coincidence, one of Baltimore's ladies of the evening was approaching and provided some diversion. A few minutes later, a tall man with thick brown hair, obviously freshly trimmed, made his way across the room. "Evenin', gentlemen!"

The Baltimore police chief, Marshal George Kane, blew on his reddened hands cupped around a whiskey glass. "Mighty cold out there. Got some news, though, that'll make y'all madder than hell, and that oughta warm things up some!"

Kane put his whiskey glass on the table, fondled the lady with familiarity, and sent her off with a resounding slap on her roundly padded rump. Then he pulled up a chair at the end of the booth, swinging immediately to Seagram. "I know you?"

"We've met a few times."

The police chief nodded, but gave Seagram a long look before he turned to Weasel, who quickly said, "He's O.K., Chief. And he wants in."

Seagram forced a smile, saying, "Is this it, then? All of the group?"

"Hell, no!" Weasel burst out, then, at a look from Kane, lowered his voice. "We got two squads worth—foot soldiers and cavalry."

How could any plan remain secret, thought Seagram, with that many men involved? A loose tongue here, a drunken boast there—the Trojan horse unmasked from within before it even entered the gates.

The police chief tossed back the shot of whiskey. "S'pect y'all want to hear the news."

But he wasn't going to give it until he was damn good and ready, Seagram decided, mildly amused at the Chief's theatrics, although he knew full well that theatrics were an effective tool in Kane's powerful grip on Baltimore politics. And as went Baltimore, so went the entire state of Maryland. Or so said conventional wisdom.

"Yes, sir, we sure do want to hear," Weasel agreed, his eagerness that of the experienced flunky.

"Get me another whiskey."

The whiskey appeared, and after disposing of it the way he had the first, Kane settled his ham-like shoulders against the chair. "Well, my boys," he said at last, "seems as if t'morrow we're goin' to have some important visitors to our fair city. These here visitors, three United States artillery companies, are from Fort Leavenworth—"

The erupting jeers only temporarily interrupted Kane.

"—and these troops are goin' to be taking up residence in our very own harbor. At Fort McHenry, right under the ole Star-Spangled Banner. That's to protect it, y'all understand, from some so-called ugly threats. Now isn't that just the most neighborly thing y'all ever did hear?"

"President Buchanan ordered that?" Weasel snarled. "He leaves office next month and he sends troops here now?"

"Buchanan's already said he'll provision the federal troops in Charleston Harbor," Seagram answered, "but nobody knows what *Lincoln* will do." He didn't add that Abraham Lincoln hadn't disagreed with Buchanan, at least not publicly; but then, Lincoln knew nothing about military tactics.

"Hell," Weasel said, "them Carolinians will never let the federals near Fort Sumter—they got the harbor ringed with guns."

"No!" The forceful voice came from directly behind Seagram. He swung around to see a slim, rather short, and extremely handsome man whose intensity flashed like heat lightning. "We don't worry about a fort! We got more important things to do, and we got to do them fast!"

"You have that right, Captain," Kane replied in a tone of surprising deference, as Cypriano Ferrandini rounded the table. "First thing tomorrow, I write the Washington mayor that these 'ugly threats' are Yankee rumors to discredit this fine city. The *i-dea*! Now I ask y'all: how could anyone doubt our loyalty to the goddamned Union!"

Laughter followed, but it did not, Seagram noted, include any from Cypriano Ferrandini. The man pulled up a chair and straddled it, his arms crossed on its back. He fixed each man there in turn with a near-hypnotic gaze, and said, "Marshal Kane and me, we got to plan. Now!"

The other men rose immediately from the table, almost in one body, as if yanked by a puppeteer manipulating a single string, and Seagram found himself reluctantly following them out of the barroom. He had heard of the power, the eerie magnetism of Ferrandini. And just then, however briefly, he had felt it himself.

This puppet master, Seagram concluded, could be a very dangerous man.

2

*And Montgomery, how exciting it all was there. So
many clever men and women congregated from
every part of the South.*

—Mary Chesnut, *A Diary from Dixie*

FEBRUARY 1861
Montgomery

*S*martly uniformed drummers of four militia companies
beat an insistent *rata-tat-tat . . . a-rata-tat-tat* as the parade
moved down the wide, sloping street. The young woman
who called herself Jane Dowling stood at the crowd's edge.
She decided that what made her uneasy wasn't the noisy celebration, or even the sword-bearing men on horseback, but
the snare drums' relentless, unvaried cadence. The surest relief might be to concentrate elsewhere. Since she was herself
a good rider, the horsemen and their superbly trained
mounts would be worth watching. Their response to command was swift and certain; the manes of the horses tossing
over arched necks, and the muscled flanks gleaming in wa-
tery sunshine, all made for an impressive spectacle. As did
the uniforms of the militia men, pressed and fringed and
spangled, with high black boots polished for the occasion to
a fare-thee-well.

After a gust of warm wind had passed, Jane leaned down

to shake her long skirts and petticoats free of the gritty dirt that had been raised by hundreds of iron-shod hooves pounding the unpaved Market Street thoroughfare. Their thunderous noise temporarily muffled that of the fireworks exploding behind the Georgian-style Capitol building on Goat Hill. Yet even in the face of this competition, the drummers persisted in their monotonous beat, as though determined that if they could not surpass, they could at least outlast every other sound in the state of Alabama.

At the foot of the hill, near an ornamental iron fence encircling the artesian basin whose wells once supplied all the city's water, Jane gave her skirts one last brisk snap before she straightened and returned her attention to the passing parade. When she looked back on this day, what she would most remember were the horses: the white and chestnut, the sorrel and bay, the roan and black and gray and piebald, all prancing in liveried splendor up and down Market Street. And the steam-chuffing iron horses of the Alabama railroad, whose clattering wheels every hour brought more politicians and celebrants into the already crowded streets of the new nation's capital. Cradle of the Confederacy, Montgomery was being called on this, the Confederate States of America's baptismal day. Thus, while the dusty streets held more people than the city had ever before hosted, and produced more noise than the young Jane Dowling would have believed possible, it was the red and white rosettes bobbing on the bridles of horses, the red and white ribbons streaming from the funnel stacks of locomotives, that to her most emphatically proclaimed: secession. The States of America were no longer United.

Jane pulled a handkerchief from her purse to blot the perspiration beading her face. She wasn't accustomed to this weather, not in February, although those around her caught up in the general euphoria didn't seem to notice the heat. It was as if a long-awaited party had at last begun and everyone in the state of Alabama felt compelled to attend. Banners waved the red and white Confederate colors, as did the ribbons on hoop-skirted dresses and frock coats, the fringes on parasols, even the collars on panting coonhounds, and they swirled together like spinning barber poles. Jane's own wide-brimmed bonnet, crimson silk trimmed with white cabbage roses, made obvious her Southern sympathies.

Three young boys suddenly raced past her, vaulted the iron fence, and leaped into the artesian basin. Sunlit water flew in rainbowed sprays. Slave women nearby, with buckets balanced on their kerchief-wrapped heads, concealed their grins as elegantly gowned white matrons frantically dabbed the splotches on their silk dresses. Jane's own smile dissolved when trumpets blared directly behind her, but when she tried to move away, she found herself carried along with the crowd. Managing to break loose, she made for the large front window of the *Weekly Advertiser,* where a handful of people stood waiting for bulletins to appear. In contrast to the spirit of the street, the mood of those in front of the newspaper office seemed apprehensive, and their troubled faces, Jane thought, more nearly reflected the reality of the moment. For beneath the noisy carnival atmosphere ran a silent, but unmistakable, current of foreboding.

She recognized one of the two men now emerging from the newspaper office as *Harper's Monthly* reporter Cormac Quinn, his squashed hat shoved back to reveal a thatch of bright orange-red hair. Her own hair, conspicuously red though it was, must pale in comparison with that of Quinn. Somewhere she'd heard that the reporter also free-lanced for the Baltimore *Sun* and the Philadelphia dailies, which would explain why he had been so much in evidence the past few days.

Meanwhile, those grouped around the *Advertiser* window

grew eerily quiet as the second man pinned up a bulletin which read: "DELEGATES VOTE TO FORM PROVISIONAL GOVERNMENT TO BE KNOWN AS THE CONFEDERATE STATES OF AMERICA."

A roar of sound behind Jane made her whirl in alarm before she realized the news must have reached the streets, and what she heard was the boom of cannons. The exuberance of the crowd now began to resemble delirium. Shouting and jostling their way forward, people pressed against the window to see the bulletin for themselves, despite the fact that it merely reported what had taken place just up the street on Goat Hill. Nor should the announcement come as a surprise. Not when pro-secession delegates from six slave states—Alabama, South Carolina, Mississippi, Florida, Georgia, and Louisiana—had gathered in Montgomery for the express purpose of establishing a Southern Confederacy.

Jane managed to elbow her way through to the far side of the street, her ears ringing from the cannons, which fired salvo after salvo. Then, suddenly, they stopped. Relative quiet began to descend as a trill of trumpets announced the first bars of "Dixie." The frenetic movement around Jane slowed as here and there, one by one, people began to sing. The solitary voices gradually swelled to many until the entire street seem to throb. ". . . *in Dixie Land, I'll take my stand, / To live and die in Dixie. / A-way, a-way, a-way down south . . . in Dixie!*"

Trumpet calls and cheering erupted at the final strains of the unpretentious little song; it had first appeared the previous year in a minstrel show, composed by a Northerner—or so the story went—one snowy afternoon in New York State. Its incongruous beginnings had not slowed the momentum favoring "Dixie" as a Confederate anthem; but then, although Jane had learned this odd bit of irony several weeks before, the origin of the song probably was not general knowledge.

The crowd, following behind the Montgomery Brass Band and their leader Dan Emmett, flowed down the street with Jane unwillingly carried along with it. She escaped by forcing her way through to the bricked front of Phister's Cigar and Tobacco Shop, where in its window a swinging brass pendulum had caught her eye. She craned forward to see the time. Nearly four-fifteen. She was already late. The message she'd been handed earlier read: *"My hotel—four o'clock."*

The band had begun the "Confederate Marseillaise" as she zigzagged through those packed along the storefronts, but by the time she reached the end of the block, the crowd had thinned. When she turned the corner onto Washington Street and saw, several blocks ahead, the weatherboarded Dillehay House hotel, there were fewer than a dozen people on the street. Nor was the noise of firecrackers and bands anywhere near as loud.

One block from the hotel she became aware of footsteps keeping time with her own; a quick sideways glance revealed a man of medium height on the far side of the street, walking at the same pace as herself. Jane recognized him immediately, but gave no indication. As she passed a small alley and went toward the entrance stairs of the Dillehay House, she heard the man's footsteps slow. He would need to cross the wide road to reach the hotel, and he must have been waiting for her to first climb the stairs.

Jane raised the hem of her skirt and started up the steps. She had nearly reached the top when she heard a deafening hammer of hooves. Thinking it part of the celebration, she didn't pay much attention. But at the fierce *crack* of a whip, she turned to see a team of horses, harnessed to a heavy Concord coach, galloping toward the hotel. The man below her had just reached the middle of the road, but now he paused, no doubt gauging the path of the horses. He must have decided there was enough space for the team to pass him safely on the far side—and it looked that way to Jane, too—because he continued across.

At the last moment, though, the team appeared to swerve and head directly toward the man. He looked around with a fleeting expression of surprise. Then, as Jane watched in mute horror, the horses and carriage were upon him, knocking him to the road. Without so much as a cry, he disappeared beneath the heavy, spoked wheels.

Jane had run halfway down the stairs before she realized the carriage had continued on at its breakneck pace. Was it possible the driver hadn't seen the man?

By the time she reached the broken body of Arthur Kelly, others were running into the road from stores and offices, their voices shrill with shock. Jane, after one quick look at what remained of the dead man, turned back toward the hotel and began to walk rapidly away. A male voice stopped her with, "Miss! Please wait a minute there, miss."

She pivoted slowly, giving herself time for a deep breath. "Were you speaking to me?"

"Yes, ma'am, I surely was," a thin, spectacled man answered. "Did you see what-all happened here?"

Others on the road turned to stare at her, and she lowered her head to let the wide-brimmed hat conceal her face. "No. No, I didn't see it." She allowed a weepy tremor into her voice. "I . . . I'm afraid I'm going to be ill. You must excuse me."

Not waiting for a response, she dashed to the hotel, and while she hurried up the steps, she heard behind her a dismayed chorus of voices. She didn't turn to look back, but rushed through the hotel entrance and into the lobby. A stylishly dressed woman, waiting by a window, came toward her.

"Jane! What happened to Arthur?" the woman whispered while taking Jane's arm and steering her into a small unoccupied parlor.

"I don't know—exactly." Jane, too, whispered.

"What do you mean, '*exactly*'? It was an accident, wasn't it?"

"I don't know. I guess it must have been. Didn't you see it from the window?"

"No, I was waiting for you in here. I only went to look out when I heard the commotion in the street." The woman showed no sign of distress—if, indeed, she even felt any—and Jane, attempting to cover her own, walked with studied deliberation to a flowered-chintz sofa. She sank into it wordlessly.

Something came back to her; a brief memory that until that moment must have been blotted out by shock. "I couldn't see the coach driver very clearly," she mused aloud. "He had on a large hat—one of those Texan things—and all I could see was the lower part of his face. He had sharp features, a pointed nose . . ." Her voice trailed off while she wondered uneasily if the driver had seen *her*.

The woman dropped beside her onto the loveseat. "But there's no delegation from Texas here in Montgomery. Are you *sure* you saw a Texan's hat?"

"No, I'm not sure. Maybe I imagined the whole thing. Could be I'm simply losing my mind, which would hardly be a surprise, would it?"

The woman's fingers closed tightly around Jane's wrist as her glance swept the room. "Quiet, girl! Get control of yourself."

Jane folded her hands in a deliberate gesture. "Sorry,

Anna. Nothing to worry about. But why did you want to see me?"

"Actually, it was Arthur wanted to see you—wanted to see us both. He passed me earlier in the crowd by the Capitol building—said under his breath that he'd recognized someone. Wouldn't say whom, not then, but he thought you and I should know about it."

"Did he say why?"

The sound of footsteps in the hall outside interrupted whatever the woman called Anna Clark had been about to say. She glanced toward the parlor door, whispering, "Someone's coming. We shouldn't be seen together here." She rose without haste, saying, "Wait a minute or two now, before you leave. And be careful!"

With that, Anna Clark drew in her wide, taffeta skirt and swept through the doorway. Jane Dowling slumped back against the sofa cushions and stared at the ceiling. This was not turning out as she had expected.

The sharp jab of anger that followed this thought startled her. She got to her feet and followed the other woman out of the hotel.

". . . in Dixie Land, I'll take my stand, / To live and die in Dixie . . ."

The closed door could not completely drown out the ebullient masculine voices coming from the barroom of Beauregard's Tavern. The singing bounced off the ceiling beams and vibrated the walls. Nonetheless, three men seated around a table in the back office paused in their conversation only when a crash in the barroom beyond was followed by the sound of shattering glass.

"Damn fools!" growled one, a heavyset man, bringing his own glass down on the table with a thump and sloshing dark bourbon over its rim. "They think this is all there is to

it? Just say 'So long, y'all' *to the Union and that's it? Fools!" He scowled at the puddle inching over the scarred tabletop.*

"C'mon, let's not get sidetracked here," a second man said quietly. Stroking his neatly trimmed beard he added, "They want to celebrate—so let 'em. They'll sober up quick enough, they come face to face with a Yankee regiment. And by the way," he asked a third man, "where's Seagram?"

The third man, of average height and unremarkable features, got up and went to the window facing the street, where he stood watching thin fog that curled above the Alabama River. "Seagram'll be along. Got held up in a meeting with the Maryland delegation—said he'd get here when he could."

"He's an odd one. You sure about him?"

"No reason not to be," the man at the window said absently, his mind clearly elsewhere. "So now—you understand where it's going to happen?"

"North of Washington," the bearded man answered, "and I have no quarrel with that. And then isolate the city. It's easy enough to cut the telegraph lines, but the railroad . . . well, that's another matter. And the railroad's the key."

"Take a fair amount of planning, all that will," said the other seated at the table.

"Planning's almost done," responded the man at the window. Suddenly he gripped the sill and leaned forward. "Who the hell . . . ?"

The two men at the table quickly got up and went to stand behind him. All three peered out into the misty night.

"That woman . . . across the street there!" The man at the window jerked his head toward the steps of a weatherboarded hotel opposite the tavern, where gaslights along the road showed a hoop-skirted figure descending the steps.

"Damn! That should have been taken care of! Thought Weasel had.*"*

"I thought so, too," said the one beside him. *"Wait a minute—there's two of them. Which one d'you mean?"*

"That one," the other pointed, his eyes narrowing. *"Likely she can identify me. We can't afford to take that chance at this stage—it's got to be dealt with."*

He turned to the others, while uneasy comprehension crossed both their faces.

The bearded man said harshly, *"I don't like it."*

"You don't have to like *it. Just do it."*

"When?"

The man at the window looked thoughtful. *"Sooner the better. In the meantime, keep an eye on her—she contacts anybody we can't account for, don't wait!"*

From the barroom, voices raised in drunken abandon sang loudly, and badly, off-key: *"Look a-way . . . look a-way . . . look a-way . . . Dixie Land!"*

3

Our true policy is peace and the freest trade which our necessities will permit. Obstacles may retard, they cannot long prevent the progress of a movement sanctified by its justice, and sustained by a virtuous people. . . . We may hopefully look forward to success, to peace, and to prosperity.

—Jefferson Davis, February 8, 1861

Jane Dowling, following the last strains of a Viennese waltz, swept her hoop skirt across the polished floor of Montgomery's Concert Hall Ballroom; it was one of many such ballrooms in which the city was celebrating that day's election of the Confederacy's first president, Jefferson Davis. If only she were free to enjoy the music. Not that she particularly liked dancing. Far more fun to be riding a horse. But one glance at her white satin gown with its voluminous, multitiered skirt, and the thought of mounting a horse in *that,* brought a short-lived smile; short because her escort, catching it, looked down at her with obvious satisfaction. Jane would love to tell this man that her smile had nothing whatsoever to do with him. He wouldn't, of course, believe it. He was as vain as were many born to wealth, and would naturally assume himself to be the source of every expression that crossed her face.

She said nothing, but since her need was to charm, she

tilted her chin to give him another smile, this one more ador-
ing and designed to buttress his vanity.

"My dear Miss Dowling," he murmured, while his eyes
slid over her fashionably revealing neckline, "I believe I
hear a Virginia reel—would you care to dance again?"

She glanced at the towering, brass-weight-driven clock
which dominated a far wall. "I think not—not just now,
thank you. I'd prefer another glass of punch, if you would be
so kind?"

She should be very careful. The bourbon punch, decep-
tively smooth, packed a wallop. However, she'd eaten vast
quantities of the mild Gulf oysters brought by steamship
from Mobile, hoping they would dilute the bourbon. If not,
she would have simply achieved a stomach roiling with
pickled shellfish.

Jane caught a telling expression on her escort's ordinarily
bland face—another serving of punch and she'd be putty in
his hands—and she smiled again. When he turned away, she
scanned the room for Anna Clark. The woman had been
there a short while earlier; gowned in filmy, white chiffon
silk, she had been gliding across the ballroom with a uniformed South Carolinian whose braid-decorated sleeves indicated an officer. It was now close to midnight. Anna
undoubtedly waited in the ladies' parlor, as they'd hastily
arranged earlier. Jane had no idea why the woman wanted to
see her tonight, but Anna had been insistent. She had also
been uncharacteristically anxious.

How, Jane wondered, to safely rid herself of her escort?
Her escort with the unlikely name of Falconer—Jules Falconer. This sounded to Jane like something plucked from
the lurid new Dime Novels that her aunt so thoroughly disliked. But it was not an uncommon Southern name, she had
learned, and certainly not in Montgomery; she'd earlier been
informed by her escort that his late, illustrious relation, one

John Falconer, had been the city's first postmaster. But a Falconer worthy of the name, Jane imagined, should have sharp blue eyes, long leather gauntlets, and chain-linked mail over stalwart shoulders. This Falconer's black-suited shoulders were nothing special. The eyes were river-mud brown. The most significant item of substance about the man—indeed, the reason Jane agreed to his company this evening—was his father's lavish investments in Southern railroads. These Jane had dutifully committed to memory: two Alabama and Florida lines, the Atlantic and Gulf, and the Central Georgia. Other than this, Jules Falconer looked like many another man whose family had money: well-groomed, well-mannered, and very well-tailored.

Still and all, while Jane needed to disappear to meet Anna, she had better take care; Falconer might be somewhat tedious, but she suspected he was not stupid.

Jane looked around, noted a sheen on nearby faces, and decided the heat of the ballroom would serve nicely. She moved toward the table to catch Falconer's eye. That she caught other eyes as well, she was aware, thus for the benefit of any who might be curious, she mimed patting her nose with a powder puff. Falconer, with a nod of understanding, waved her toward the spacious stairway, and Jane raised the heavy white satin skirt to hurry up the winding steps. Now to find the ladies' parlor.

Pausing at the top of the stairs to get her bearings, with her skirt brushing the knee-high railing, she gazed at the scene presented to her: crystal chandeliers lit by hundreds of candles flickered above a candy-cane swirl of red and white gowns. Hoops of immense circumference kept at arm's length the black swallowtail evening suits and the uniforms of various Southern state militia companies.

Strains of a lively quadrille all at once reminded Jane of Falconer's dance invitation. She leaned over the railing, and though she looked for him, he wasn't distinguishable from any of the other men below. In fact, Jane couldn't even recall whether his hair was black or dark brown.

She heard the murmur of feminine voices, as soft a sound as a cat's purr, coming from an archway beyond. When she followed the voices down a broad corridor, open windows to the street showed a brilliant moon. The warmth of the night air felt to Jane like that of a late-spring day in the North. She'd been told that summers here were unbearably hot, but no matter; she wouldn't be in Alabama long enough to find out.

A few turns down the corridor brought her to clusters of chatting women, begowned and bejeweled in the latest designer fashions. Their enormously wide hoop-skirts kept them some distance apart, and they necessarily perched on the edge of their chairs as if posing for portraits. The couture displayed made it clear that Montgomery had become a more sophisticated city than generally credited.

Jane found another half-dozen women on velvet lounges in the rose-colored parlor. She and Anna would never be able to talk privately, but a quick scan of the room didn't disclose her, anyway. It must not be quite midnight. To give herself something to do, Jane took a moist towel handed to her by a honey-skinned slave girl—hardly more than a child—then stood waiting her turn at the long, gilt-framed mirrors, smoothing her gown and fiddling with her hair as long as she could without drawing unwanted attention. As it was, she saw a few curious looks directed her way. Probably her hair! By now she was grudgingly willing to admit that Anna Clark might have been right when she'd proposed dyeing it. Too late now. Jane tried to ignore this reminder that on more than one occasion, her concessions came too late.

She turned from the mirror, colliding with another young

woman who had bent down to smooth her skirt over its hoop-frame petticoat. "I'm so sorry," Jane said, while grasping the other's arm to keep them both on their feet.

A pair of violet eyes flashed at her, and a throaty voice held humor. "No, please don't apologize—it's these hoops!"

Jane, nodding, released the woman's arm. "They're awkward." Awkward nothing; they were downright disabling. But Jane thought that this observation, in light of the present flock of hoops, should be kept to herself.

The other's shoulders moved in an attractive shrug. "Personally, I think we're all mad to wear them. But who would dare not to?" She smiled. "I'm certainly not brave enough to defy the fashionable."

Jane returned the smile. "Nor I."

"Please pardon my asking, but are you from up north? Your accent sounds like it."

"Ah, well . . . I spent some time in the North, yes," answered Jane, furious at her slip. She'd been caught off guard, and now her carelessness made it impossible to deny.

"I thought perhaps—" the young woman with violet eyes laughed "—that y'all Northern women had more freedom than we from the rules of King Fashion." She gave Jane what looked very much like a wink before she moved away toward the mirror.

Jane glanced over the room again, listening with half an ear to the strands of conversation winding loosely around her. Much of it involved secession, and she was struck by how keenly most of these women supported it. Only a very few sounded doubtful. Although one woman in particular was saying now that she had reservations about the course taken by the new Confederacy.

"Why, Mrs. Chesnut, I am *surprised* at you," another woman responded. "And here your husband helped draft the secession ordinance. Surely, you are not questioning his judgment?"

Jane shifted cautiously to look at "Mrs. Chesnut," assuming the dark-haired woman must be the wife of Senator James Chesnut from South Carolina. Former senator, that was; Chesnut had resigned his seat immediately upon Lincoln's election, and had since been in the forefront of the secession movement.

A woman in rich green velvet gown reached out to touch Mrs. Chesnut's hand. "Mary, dear,"—her voice held a whispery sweetness—"perhaps this is not the time."

"I admit that I feel a certain nervousness, Mrs. Pollard," answered Mary Chesnut, addressing the first woman and obviously not in agreement with Green Velvet. "I have a dread at this break with so great a power as the United States of America. Not that I am unwilling. The Southern Confederacy *must* be supported against that ogre Lincoln—him and his Black Republicanism. Still, I am no lover of slavery."

Her friend in green velvet drew in a breath with a quick glance around her. "Mary, dear, I should think," she said, her voice clearly audible for all of its sweetness, "that you might be more circumspect in public."

"But why?" Mary Chesnut said, her question rhetorical, as she added, "I believe most white women of the South are abolitionists in their hearts."

"You cannot speak for all, Mrs. Chesnut," interrupted Mrs. Pollard, although her tone remained determinedly cordial.

Mary Chesnut, while not appearing the least chastised, inclined her head ever so slightly.

"The most important thing now," continued the Pollard woman, "is that *all* Southerners present a united front." She gave Mary Chesnut a look that was unmistakable. "We must show the Yankees that we are determined to stand our ground. I have no doubt that the North expects us to cower in the face of their bullying, and to tiptoe back to the Union with abject apologies for our absence."

"I agree, of course, Mrs. Pollard," replied Mary Chesnut, though not quite as quickly as the other woman appeared to expect, "if only because no one in the North believes we are in earnest. I think when they see that we are, they will allow us to go in peace. But, Mrs. Knox," she added, and turned to the velvet-gowned woman who had spoken earlier, "your point is well taken about caution in conversation. Everywhere, it seems, political intrigue is as rife as it was in Washington."

Mrs. Knox, as well as Mrs. Pollard, nodded and appeared to be satisfied, both smiling warmly. But although the conversation then took a lighter turn, Jane Dowling had the sense that Mrs. James Chesnut would have liked to say more. But if what she *had said* was her honest view, then why did she and her husband continue to live on a vast plantation run by slave labor? Jane asked herself this with irritation, having some time ago decided that no issue was worth sending the country into its present furor. Worse still, a war would interfere with everything she had planned.

None of this was her concern. She needed to find Anna Clark.

She began slipping in and out of the archways that faced the main corridor. When she neared the staircase, she caught sight of a man in black evening dress, who stood near the top of the stairs, stroking a neatly trimmed beard. He appeared to be looking for someone. Had she seen him somewhere before? Montgomery, though, was filled to overflowing with men—it might have been anywhere in the past few days. What interested her was his faintly furtive air, the way his eyes continued to dart up and down the stairs. There was nothing casual about his observation. Then, for no apparent reason, he abruptly wheeled and made for the corridor. Moments later, another man in evening dress, who'd just dashed up the steps two at a time, paused at the top to flick the ashes of his narrow cigar into a large copper spittoon. Then, with an almost imperceptible nod, he followed the first, bearded man. They moved silently into an archway. It seemed peculiar that they didn't greet each other, didn't say a word, just glanced quickly around. If their manner hadn't been so surreptitious, Jane was to recall later, she wouldn't have paid them any further attention. But since she had to wait for Anna anyway. . . . Keeping an eye on the staircase, she drifted after the two men.

Moonlight coming through a corridor window showed her where they'd stopped, both of them with their backs to the wall as if watching for someone—or not wanting to be overheard. This piqued Jane's curiosity still more, and she edged along the corridor until she could hear a low-pitched murmur. She slipped into the nearest archway.

". . . and meet with the Horseman." This voice bore a deep, not unpleasant rumble. Some further muttered words were exchanged which Jane couldn't hear.

"Or because it's too dangerous," a different voice said quietly.

Too dangerous? Jane craned her neck around the arch, ear cocked to hear the words.

"Everyone needs to be discreet in what he says, and where he says it," answered the deeper voice. "Washington's crawling with spies."

Hadn't Mrs. James Chesnut just said much the same thing?

"Yes, and so's every other city in the South," the other agreed; the pitch of his voice sounded forced. "Do you have any sense at this point," he asked, "which way Maryland's going to go?"

"Not yet. The factions are still too far apart for . . ."

The words became inaudible; maybe the men had shifted position. Obviously they were discussing whether the Maryland state delegation would vote to leave the Union. It could be crucial—even Jane, despite her political indifference, knew that—because if war broke out, and Maryland joined the Confederacy, the city of Washington would be isolated. The capital of the Union would stand alone in the midst of secessionist territory.

The deeper voice, which had paused midsentence—to re-light the cigar?—resumed with, ". . . then we agree that we need to meet again in . . ."

Jane nearly tumbled into the corridor to hear his next words, but just then several women strolled by; she was forced to stand nonchalantly against the archway, fanning herself in barely contained frustration. As soon as the women were past, she cocked her ear again, inching as close to the men as she dared.

One was saying, ". . . then we've possibly four weeks until Equus begins the run to Armageddon. And a bloody end to it!"

Equus. Jane mentally scrambled after her hated, secondary-school Latin. She had heard the word as "*Ek-wis,*" the emphasis on the first syllable; still, if it hadn't been for the context, she never would have known for certain what she heard. Moonlight from a window polished her gown as she leaned forward slightly.

"I agree," the deeper of the two voices answered. "And where . . ."

For some reason there now came a lengthy pause. Jane shifted her feet uneasily, but then the same voice continued, "Perhaps we'd best join the others before we're missed."

Jane heard the murmur of assent. She rushed to the railing, where she stood and determinedly stared down at the ballroom with what she hoped looked like profound interest. At the same time she watched from the tail of her eye for the men to appear. They would have to go down the stairs, she reasoned, if they planned to "join the others."

But as luck would have it, several Confederate officers walked past, smiling with appreciation at Jane, but inconsiderately blocking any view she might have had of the Equus men. By the time the officers had passed, the stairs were empty.

Jane now felt the chill she'd suppressed while she eavesdropped. Any fool could tell that something malevolent had been discussed: a "*bloody end.*" And "*Armageddon?*" What could that possibly mean other than destruction and death? Could the "Equus run" mean the beginning of war? She needed to commit the dialogue to memory, word for word before she forgot it. Anna Clark would insist on accuracy.

Anna . . . ? What with all the traffic on the stairs, they must have missed each other, and the other woman most likely had returned to the ballroom. Before starting down the steps herself, Jane looked over the railing not just for Anna, but for the two men. Even though she'd seen them only briefly, she thought she could identify the one with the cigar—by smell if no other way. From where she stood now, though, the men below all looked alike. Then, as she started down the steps, Jane saw someone that might have been Anna, heading toward the orchestra on the far side of the room; in the ubiquitous red and white dresses, however, every dark-haired woman looked pretty much like every other. In any case, Jane would now have to jostle her way across the dance floor.

"My dear Miss Dowling," came a voice at her elbow the moment she set foot on the last step. Jules Falconer took hold of her arm as if he feared she might bolt, and she seriously considered doing it. But when he steered her toward a handful of men, she stifled her protest abruptly: the cigar-smoker was there, standing next to Cormac Quinn.

Before she reached them, she fixed a smile in place. Falconer introduced her, reeling off their names which ran together without significance as she concentrated on the smoker, one Guy Seagram of the Maryland delegation. Then, since they all seemed to expect something from her, she offered, "Did I hear y'all talking about railroads just now?" Don't overdo the drawl, she reminded herself.

"Are you a Southerner, Miss Dowling?" one man asked. "I thought I'd heard otherwise?"

"Just by birth, I'm afraid, sir. I've spent most of the years since in the North, as you can no doubt hear in my speech."

Jane, again warning herself to be careful, became aware that Guy Seagram was watching her closely. But then, so were the rest of the men, including Cormac Quinn. The reporter swayed on the balls of his feet, and his eyes—red, but not so bloodshot that they rivaled the color of his hair—meandered over her with unmistakable intent; that was, when his glance wasn't darting over the room. She felt uneasy, the hair at the back of her neck prickling, as if she were about to be drawn into a net. But short of feigning a swoon—which she had never resorted to in her life and which, in any event, would make her even more vulnerable—all she could do was to keep her voice steady while she lied her way through this conversation.

Luckily, Jules Falconer apparently felt called upon to spare her the rigors of speech. "Miss Dowling's a Southerner not only by birth, but by sympathy," he announced.

"And how are you fortunate enough to be in Montgomery at this propitious time?" Guy Seagram asked, heavy-lidded eyes never leaving her.

Jane turned slightly, wondering if he meant to trap her, although she might be overly distrustful here. He couldn't possibly know who she was, or the answer to his uncomfortably pointed question. But he did seem unduly attentive, observing her with sleepy, hooded eyes through his spiraling cigar smoke. He was attractive in a reptilian sort of way, with a wide mouth and lips that curved upward at the corners; she speculated whether his tongue could trap small unwary creatures, since his transparent interest in her resembled hunger. That alone didn't worry her—some men reacted to her that way. It had nothing to do, she reminded herself, with where she was born, or why she was in Montgomery, Alabama. Still, his question would require an answer.

Again Jules Falconer's conceit came to her aid. "Miss Dowling's father is a railroad investor," was supplied by her interpreter. "He's a stockholder in the Montgomery and West Point line, for one." Falconer glanced around, saying to her, "Your father didn't decide to come after all, did he?"

"What Mr. Falconer is referring to," explained Jane in response to the too-knowing smiles Falconer received, "is that Papa was feeling a bit peaky earlier. He allowed as how he might have to miss the festivities tonight, the poor darlin'."

Seagram shot her an enigmatic look. She knew she was overdoing it, but couldn't seem to help herself. It must be the heat . . . the bourbon punch . . . Seagram's intense scrutiny. If she weren't cautious, next she'd be yelling at him, "*What is Equus?*" since his voice was definitely the deeper of the two she'd overheard.

And he would then, with everyone there nodding in understanding, suggest that she might be under the influence of too much bourbon. Should perhaps be taken back to her hotel. He would be happy to assist . . .

She wondered if Anna Clark was watching this farce from a distance. In which case, why wasn't she intervening?

Clenching her hands against her sides, Jane gave them all the most naive, doll-like smile she could muster.

"Ah, then your poor old daddy's . . . illness is why you are in the lovin' care of ole Jules here?" Cormac Quinn's words slurred, although his tone was suggestive.

The slurring troubled her. Jane had seen Quinn off and on all evening, and he'd never even held a glass in his hand. His eyes looked red—but maybe they always were, or it might be he tossed his liquor down secretly. Or his besottedness might be an act. And just now there appeared to be altogether too many actors on this crowded stage.

A white-coated Negro had approached them with a tray of punch glasses, and Seagram, reaching over to take Jane's empty one, let his fingers intentionally brush hers. Then, handing her a full glass from the tray, he asked, "Does your father invest only in Southern railroads?—No, wait, Falconer! The young lady's capable of speech—let *her* answer!"

While she improvised, Jane forced herself to smile at this provocative man. Jules Falconer's smile also seemed strained, and apparently put off by Seagram's tone, he wandered away into the crowd.

"No," Jane said carefully, as Seagram watched her, "not only in Southern roads, sir—but those, naturally, are the ones that most concern Father right now. As you might imagine, all this dreadful talk of war is so worrisome."

That seemed safe enough to say, if glaringly obvious. For once, Seagram didn't seem to react, just continued to look at her with that sleepy expression. Which didn't for a second deceive her into thinking he wasn't paying attention to every single word. Jane began to feel strangely as if the alarm of a ticking clock were about to go off.

"I think your father can safely assume," Seagram began

casually, "that the possibility of war is worrisome to every-one . . ."

He stopped to look up at the railing of the balcony over-head, where some kind of commotion had broken out. From where Jane stood, she couldn't see much of anything, at least not distinctly, and at first hoped it might be nothing more than a drunken squabble. But she began to feel an ap-prehension stronger than her earlier uneasiness.

Even so, she was unprepared for the terrible, high-pitched scream from the balcony. And for the twisting, falling figure whose outstretched wings of filmy white fluttered limply as it hurtled downward. The sound when it struck was some-thing never to be forgotten.

A stunned silence followed. Jane, without any clear in-tent, began to move toward the crumpled heap. Vaguely aware of rising voices, she ignored them and kept moving forward to where she dreaded that a woman, a woman known to her, was lying inside a silken gown. She was within several paces when she felt her upper arm gripped in a vise, and then Guy Seagram was thrusting her aside and moving to obstruct her view. People began to crowd for-ward. Jane heard their voices, grown loud enough to pene-trate her shock, and with a sudden jerk, she wrenched herself free of Seagram's grip.

The crowd surged and eddied around them, and since Seagram now seemed to have forgotten about her, again Jane edged her way forward. Again his hand shot out to grab her.

"Stay back!"

Jane twisted away and thrust herself past him.

A woman lay on the polished floor. Cormac Quinn was kneeling beside Anna Clark's still form, holding her slim, flaccid wrist from which a silken sleeve dropped away in graceful folds. Quinn repeated several times, "But there's no pulse, there's no pulse."

All Jane felt now was an overwhelming need to get away. She took a step backward and turned to run, but found her path blocked. Flailing at those who stood between her and the door, she again felt powerful fingers grip her arms, pinning them to her side.

Next to her ear, Guy Seagram's voice came in a whisper as intense as a shout. "You're being stupid! Shut up, and don't draw more attention to yourself. Now, come along with me."

She shook her head, gritting her teeth against a swelling fear. Determined not to give in to it, she tried to jerk away from him. It seemed ridiculously unfair that he seemed to know something about all of this that she didn't. She aimed a kick at him. Hobbled by her hoop skirt, she stumbled, and his grip only tightened.

"Give it up," he said, "you can't possibly get away, you little liar."

He shifted, grasped her wrists with one hand and ran the other up her spine. His fingers did something to the base of her neck, and Jane felt her bones turn to water. The last thing she would remember was swirling white silk that wound itself round and round her throat like the tangled reins of a running horse. *Equus.*

4

Glynis Tryon, seated behind her desk in the Seneca Falls Library, studied the front page of the *Seneca County Courier* and concluded that the unthinkable had finally happened: the entire country—and everyone in it—had lost its mind. All at the same time.

She tossed the newspaper aside and stared toward the tall, leaded windows that faced the canal. What had gone wrong with whatever in the past had kept this simultaneous mass insanity from occurring? There really was no way other than mass insanity to account for current events: a massacre by the United States Army of an entire Indian village in a western territory; twenty-thousand well-paid male shoemakers arbitrarily on strike in New England, while, at the same time, the collapse of a defectively built textile factory in Massachusetts killed seventy-some women and children laboring for a pittance; riders of the new Pony Express service being shot willy-nilly by outlaws and renegades simply for carrying the mail; passenger steamers inexplicably sinking with all on board in the Great Lakes; and a man crossing Niagara Falls on a tightrope, while at the same time doing his laundry with some sort of washing machine!

And it wasn't only the United States. Italy was in upheaval because of someone with the melodious if implausible name of Giuseppe Garibaldi; French and British troops were burning down the Summer Palace in Peking; New Zealanders were slaughtering the native Maoris; and Australia was being crossed from south to north—for no discernible reason—by an expedition mounted on camels. *Camels!*

Closer to home was the imminent inauguration of the Confederate president Jefferson Davis, and the secession of yet another Southern state; this accompanied by savage vilification of President-elect Abraham Lincoln. Glynis, who had lived for a year at her brother's home in Springfield, Illinois, just down Eighth Street from the Lincoln family, found it incomprehensible that anyone could believe this honorable and intelligent, if on occasion melancholy, man meant to assume a dictatorship, much less intend to maliciously damage his country. And he hadn't even as yet been inaugurated.

Her eyes moved from the library windows to a letter lying beside the newspaper. And then there was her niece, Bronwen Llyr. Bronwen, who was sending cryptic letters from Montgomery, Alabama, that were making Glynis in western New York all but frantic. And who was doing Lord-knows-what under the assumed name of Jane Dowling.

With a prolonged sigh, Glynis picked up the letter and caught a startled glance from her assistant Jonathan Quant at his desk across the room. He had apparently surmised that her sigh was directed at his current reading matter. Its title in vivid scarlet could be seen a mile away: *"The Lament of a Maiden Betrayed."* And while Glynis supposed it was not altogether inappropriate that Jonathan had become Seneca Falls's resident expert on romantic novels, his recently developed passion for the dreadful new Beadle & Adams "Dime Novels" left her dumbfounded. But there was nothing to be done for it. She couldn't very well discourage him reading them—not when a sizable number of library patrons also found them irresistible.

She sent him a shake of her head, stared at Bronwen's letter, and sighed again. Her niece's decisions might seem to be unfathomable ones, but however misguided, they were not of Glynis's doing. She reminded herself of this frequently. She reminded her sister Gwen—Bronwen's mother—almost as frequently. Gwen, however, seemed to believe Glynis responsible for Bronwen's current pursuit, causing a rift to develop between the sisters that, until recently, would have seemed impossible.

"I think you've encouraged Bronwen," Gwen had accused her. "You've had more influence than anyone else, certainly more than Owen and I"—Owen being Gwen's husband and Bronwen's father—"and look what it's brought."

"I think," Glynis had protested, "that Bronwen has never been much influenced by anyone. If you recall, she's always been headstrong—and downright pigheaded at times." She'd been stopped by Gwen's yelp, and her own realization that she could have phrased it more subtly. Nonetheless, it was true.

She pushed away from her desk and walked to one of the windows, crossing her arms to lean on the sill. Below the slope behind the library, ice-skaters glided over the frozen Seneca River, their bright hats and scarves the only splashes of color in a landscape of somber February-gray. From Fall

Street came the jingle of harness bells—more sleighfuls of skaters heading for the river.

Glynis could still remember the winter day on which Bronwen, visiting with her family from their home in Rochester, had unnerved the entire population of Seneca Falls. The weather had turned mild, the river ice become suspect, but Bronwen ventured onto it anyway. The fact that she'd been warned off meant nothing. She was determined to learn to skate. Fortunately, someone had been watching when she broke through the ice. When frantic family members got there, they found Bronwen, not drowned or even faint with shock, but seated confidently on the riverbank. She had somehow managed to swim there. No one, Glynis recalled, even knew Bronwen *could* swim, and where she'd learned remained a mystery; stubborn in the face of her father's most dire threats, she refused to say. Her parents speculated it had been at the boys' swimming hole—from which, of course, she had also been forbidden. But the thing Glynis remembered most about the episode was the disgust with which Bronwen had greeted her family's anxiety. "Of c-c-course I'm all r-right," she'd told them between chattering teeth and with a furious scowl. "Do you think a little c-c-cold water will hurt me?"

As Glynis and her brother-in-law had walked back up the slope that winter day, Owen turned to her, saying in a voice more distraught than angry, "Bronwen's never going to learn, is she?"

"Learn?"

"The rules. And that when they're ignored, there are consequences. What will happen to her, Glynis, if Bronwen doesn't learn that? What will her life be like?"

Probably not like yours, Glynis could have said, but did not.

Now, through the window, she saw a black Morgan with

Cullen Stuart astride it, picking its way down the slope. Ah, yes, she suddenly recalled: The Great Horse Race Debacle. Had it been only three years ago—the summer Bronwen spent several weeks in Seneca Falls? Glynis always suspected the visit had less to do with her niece's affection for her than with the chance to escape her family.

The horse race had always been a high point of the annual Seneca County Agricultural Fair. Although Bronwen had spent a great deal of time that summer at Cullen Stuart's sheep farm, which also had several Morgan horses, Glynis never suspected what her niece had in mind. She should have: Bronwen talked endlessly about Cullen's new two-year-old stallion. Came the fair day, men and their horses lined up for the race, everyone wondering who might be the slim boy seated on the handsome young Morgan; the boy with a sombrero that covered his head and hid most of his face. When the starting gun roared, the Morgan took off and proceeded to hurtle over the obstacle course, the rider so adept that he seemed incidental, a mere fly on the horse's back. When the galloping horses entered the woods on the last leg of the course, the Morgan was ahead by several lengths. It emerged from the trees less than five minutes later to race over the finish line a full two furlongs ahead of the pack. But somewhere along the way the rider's hat had blown off, and a tangled mass of flaming red hair streamed behind one now revealed, unmistakably, to be a girl.

When Bronwen leapt from the Morgan and went forward grinning from ear to ear to receive the prize, Glynis held her breath. Sure enough, a furious mayor and fellow competitors shouted "Outrageous! Absolutely not!" A female wasn't allowed to compete—much less win! On this occasion Glynis found herself almost as angry as her niece. And when Bronwen frantically turned for support to Cullen

Stuart—after all, it *was* his horse that had won—he said simply: "I warned you this would happen."

For one awful moment Glynis feared the girl would haul off and strike the town constable. And the mayor. That she didn't, but merely stumbled away, eyes brimming with tearful fury, said to her aunt that Bronwen *had* learned something about consequences. The only one of the men who congratulated her, other than Cullen, was his young assistant deputy, Liam Cleary, who coming in second this time, had won the race the previous two years; and who, if he'd been asked, Glynis guessed, would have yielded Bronwen the prize. No one asked. No prize at all had been awarded that year.

Now, with a glance at Jonathan's head buried in *The Lament,* Glynis returned to her desk. She hoped Bronwen had written her parents, as not only did Gwen blame her sister for Bronwen's departure from western New York, but she complained that Glynis received many more letters. Which might be the truth. She had no intention of reproaching her niece for the path she'd chosen—and only to herself did Glynis admit to being somewhat envious of Bronwen's spirit.

Later that afternoon, lawyer Jeremiah Merrycoyf came into the library accompanied by chief deputy Zephaniah Waters. Both men, Glynis was heartened to see, looked down their noses at Jonathan's choice of reading material. Zeph's face, the color of dark buckwheat honey, assumed its customary scowl as he said, "Quant, your brain will rot if you keep reading that stuff."

To which Jonathan nodded, and smiled in vague fashion at what would appear to be welcome news, clearly eager to return to the lamenting maiden.

"Can I help you two?" Glynis asked, more from habit

than anything else, since both men were frequently in the library.

"No, we just need to settle an argument," Merrycoyf said, settling his spectacles back on his nose and lumbering off to the bookshelves.

"Another one? What is it this time?"

Zeph gave her a level look. "The man thinks he knows more than I do about guns—can you imagine that?"

No, she couldn't, but Merrycoyf was by nature contentious. So, for that matter, was Zeph. Yet they seemed to spend a fair amount of time together, the young black deputy and the elderly white attorney. All they would appear to have in common was their mutual regard for books—and bonds had been forged on far less than that, Glynis decided.

Minutes later, she heard a whoop of triumph from Zeph, and looked to see Merrycoyf's expression of indignation as they stood side by side over an open volume. No need to ask. The subject of their argument, though, reminded her of another incident involving Bronwen. It had happened about a year ago when Bronwen again came to Seneca Falls, this time strangely mysterious as to *why* she was there. It hadn't been a holiday, or summer vacation; she'd arrived by train with no warning and with suspiciously sweetened disposition. And again she spent time with Cullen. Glynis wondered what new mischief her niece was about; when Bronwen chose, she could charm the birds right out of the trees, but on those occasions she usually had an underlying reason. Not that it was necessary to charm Cullen. He'd taken a shine to Bronwen years ago, even before the horse race.

When Glynis questioned him, Cullen's response had been evasive. He'd finally relented enough to say that he had convinced Bronwen to stay in school.

"You mean she doesn't *want* to?"

"That shouldn't be hard to understand—she's bored. And she's smart. You know she's not one to find excitement in books—she wants to get it in person."

That certainly sounded like Bronwen. Glynis waited for more explanation, which didn't come, at least not to her satisfaction. Cullen just muttered something about not worrying, and that Bronwen would probably now finish school.

"What makes you think so, Cullen?"

"Oh, just that we had made a bargain. But I can't tell you what, so don't ask."

She did of course ask, and got nowhere. A day or two later, though, Glynis found herself fearing the worst. Upon hearing familiar voices, she'd looked out the library window to see her niece standing on the library slope with Cullen and Zeph and Liam. The four *each* held a rifle.

Glynis had rushed outside. "What is it you think you're going to shoot?"

"Just targets," Bronwen declared gravely.

At least Liam Cleary had the good grace to appear sheepish—the other two only grinned.

The maple stock of the Remington that Bronwen held looked too smooth. The barrel looked too shiny. In a word, the rifle looked *new*. Glynis bit her tongue, and didn't ask. She told herself she didn't want to know, not if it was a bribe on Cullen's part. But a diploma in exchange for a Remington rifle?

Dear Lord, she thought now: if only it *had* been that!

However, on that day, Glynis had watched in disbelief while the men and Bronwen hoisted the rifles to their shoulders, aiming at the rooster weather vane atop the library. "Wait! Why that?" Glynis had protested.

"Why not that?" answered Bronwen. "Besides, Aunt Glyn, you won't come after us if we damage it."

"I won't?"

"We'll replace it," said Cullen quickly, although Glynis saw the don't-say-any-more look he threw Bronwen.

"Don't worry about it, Miss Tryon," Zeph assured her, "the only one with a chance of hitting that bird is either the constable or me—" he gave Bronwen a sideways glance "—or maybe Liam."

"You think so," Bronwen said evenly. "How much you want to wager on that?"

"Bronwen!" But Glynis directed her black look at Cullen. Who shrugged and looked away.

Zeph's expression was untypically jovial. "You'll never hit it, not in a million years," he chortled. "I'll wager anything you want."

"A new pair of boots?" proposed Bronwen with an innocent air of the true hustler. "The brown leather ones in the window of Jackson's Tack Shop?"

Zeph nodded, grinning in spite of himself. Glynis would have thought he knew Bronwen better than that. But then, this was a girl, and in Zeph's eyes, *only* a girl.

Despite his every attempt to distract or intimidate her, Bronwen hit the weather vane rooster almost every shot. Only Cullen managed to better her—he hit the hapless bird's beak a few more times. Glynis had had to smile. She could still see the girl that day, marching Zeph off to collect her boots at Jackson's Tack Shop.

The last few times she'd seen her, Bronwen had no longer been a girl. Gone was the straight, stringy body; yet even when stringy, Bronwen had never been gawky, never awkward, the long arms and legs always under control. Her thick red hair had become *somewhat* less wild. Smooth pale skin stretched over sharp cheekbones and pointed chin, freckles peppered a nose too small to be classically beautiful, but the eyes were as brilliant a gold-green as those of a Maine coon cat. In truth, somewhere along the way, Bronwen had acquired a feline's graceful sensuality. She seemed artlessly at ease with this, making it all the more powerful. Most women sensed it immediately and tended at first to distrust her. Most men reacted true to form. As Glynis would have predicted, this unsettled her sister.

"You know," Gwen had said to her, just before their rift widened, "Bronwen was such a hoyden that I'd just about reconciled myself to her becoming one . . . one of those mannish kinds of women. Not, I suppose, that there's any harm in that."

"I'm glad to hear you say it," Glynis murmured, having found the type of woman just described to be among those she liked most in Seneca Falls.

"Anyway," her sister added, "now I don't think that's going to happen."

Glynis smiled. "I'd say it has practically no chance at all of happening, Gwen." Not that Bronwen particularly liked men, not on the whole. Nonetheless, she clearly responded to them.

"I really wish, Glynis, that you found this slightly less amusing. I'm worried about my daughter!"

"I know you are. But Bronwen is very effective at taking care of herself. None better."

That had been then. Today, Glynis now thought, she would give a great deal to retract that confident assessment. Brought back to the present by the sensation of someone looking over her shoulder, she found Zeph staring at the envelope that had held Bronwen's letter.

"You know somebody in Alabama?"

"I'm afraid so. My niece."

Zeph's look was knowing. "The red-haired one."

A statement, not a question. Though she had other nieces. "Yes, Zeph. It's from Bronwen."

"What's she doing down there? Not a good place to be right now, not for a Northerner, anyway."

He was right, of course. Not that the threat of war would greatly concern Bronwen.

Perhaps, Glynis thought, she was worrying unnecessarily. She unfolded the rumpled pages that had arrived earlier that day and scanned Bronwen's large, scrawled script: ". . . and here in the South, things move a lot slower than in the North. It's the heat—it makes everybody feel wrung out. The Southerners I've met are the most gracious people you can imagine, even to me, a Yankee. But it's hard to just sit around waiting for something to happen—like waiting for grass to grow, it is. I've become very impatient (guess that won't surprise *you!*). Well, that's all for now. I'll write again soon, when the red fox does more than just sleep in the sun."

Glynis shook her head at the wildlife reference. *Red fox*, being Bronwen herself, was part of the code she'd devised before she left: "So you'll be the only one to know what I mean, Aunt Glyn. That's in case my letters are intercepted."

"Intercepted by whom?"

"That's the whole point," said Bronwen, "because we won't know, will we?"

The fox sleeping meant all was well; simple enough. Glynis could hardly bear to think about more complicated messages arriving. She had Bronwen's elaborate decoding key, about which she'd been cautioned: "It's the only one there is, Aunt Glyn. Guard it with your life!"

This had brought to Glynis recurrent images of herself stretched on a rack, while an inquisitor stood over her with unspeakable ways to make her produce the priceless, one-of-a-kind key.

She refrained from sighing again, and decided to leave for home. Jeremiah Merrycoyf waited for her while she went through the elaborate bundling up that western New York winters required. Bronwen had no business complaining about the Southern heat.

Braced against the sharp wind off the river, she and Merrycoyf crossed Fall Street. Before Glynis turned onto Cayuga, she said, "Is it as colorless in this town as I sometimes think it is, Jeremiah?"

He peered at her over spectacles propped on his plump, cold-reddened cheeks. "What brought that on?"

Glynis grabbed at the ends of the scarf the wind sent whipping across her face. "Probably just my age. My aging, I should say. And the dark of endless winter . . . the talk of war . . . I don't know. I can't imagine, though, why Bronwen corresponds so regularly with a middle-aged spinster aunt."

"Couldn't possibly be she admires you."

"Me? Why on earth should she?"

"Surely you don't think it escaped your niece's notice that you once defied your entire family to attend college. That you deduced a half-score of nefarious doings in this town while everyone else stood around completely flummoxed. While also serving in the capacity of a 'middle-aged spinster aunt.'"

Until the blowing scarf blinded her, Glynis stared at Merrycoyf. She didn't like hearing this from him. Because she wasn't Bronwen's parent, didn't even live in the same town, any sway she might have had on her niece, as implied by Gwen, she'd freely discounted. She wasn't at all sure she wanted to count it now, not with her sister's anxious face swimming before her in reproach.

She undoubtedly looked troubled, because Merrycoyf leaned forward, apparently to examine her more closely. He narrowed his eyes before saying, "Cod-liver oil."

"Excuse me?"

"You need cod-liver oil. And more fresh air. Need I remind you that every winter—and I've known you for many—you enter into this state of brooding. While I, for one, thank God it *is* colorless in this town! No one's even been murdered of late—or is that something you miss?"

"Jeremiah! I feel out-of-sorts is all. Restless, I guess is the word."

"Then go south like your niece—for whom I suspect you harbor more than a touch of envy—and see how much you enjoy the 'color' of a potential war zone. Even though I believe you enjoy excitement—while not as overtly, or as much, as does young Bronwen—I'll wager you won't be able to return here fast enough! And do *not* complain about being a spinster—whose decision, I ask, was *that?* Most assuredly you were not forced into it—indeed, quite the contrary, from my observations. Now, my dear lady, I'm getting to be an old man, and my feet are frozen. Kindly let me return to my fireplace."

As she trudged up Cayuga Street with the wind rattling bare elm branches overhead, Glynis thought that Merrycoyf, while she loved him dearly, had been overly harsh. And the last thing on earth she wanted was to "go south." Not on your life, Jeremiah. Not these days, when everything below the Mason and Dixon line should be labeled: *Abandon hope, all ye who enter here.*

Bronwen, unfortunately, had never been much of a reader.

5

A devoted part of the sex—devoted for the salvation of the rest.

—Mary Wollstonecraft

"Fre-ash fi-ush! Get yo' fre-ash fi-ush! Ah got plenty oystahs! Oystahs straight from Mobile this ver-ee mo'nin'! Mah-ty good! Y'all get yo' fre-ash fi-ush heah!"

When the singsong baritone of a fishmonger on the street outside penetrated her uneasy sleep, Bronwen Llyr opened her eyes to the grime-darkened walls of an unfamiliar room. Pale light came through a bare window, shadowy, as if it were not quite dawn. Her head felt bulky, her stomach queasy. But she couldn't have been drinking *all* night. Where *was* she? And what was that odd, musky odor?

Lying flat on her back, she pushed hair out of her eyes and cautiously rolled her head to one side, discovering a sagging, discolored mattress. By the time she'd scrambled to a half-seated position, she had seen the man sprawled in the chair opposite her. "What are *you* doing here? And where *am* I?"

Guy Seagram responded with a level gaze. "Suppose you start by telling me who you are, since you're not Jane Dowling. And why you're *really* here in Montgomery—notice I said *really.*"

While he was talking, Bronwen struggled to pull a tattered and stained coverlet over her naked legs. She'd been stripped of shoes, stockings, petticoats, gown—all but her sleeveless chemise and her drawers. While she grappled with the implications of this, Seagram's questions scarcely registered. No, he couldn't have . . .

"What have you *done* to me?" she flared, thankful that her voice held more rage than the fright she expected.

"Answer my questions."

"Not until you give me my clothes." She could see them flung over a chair—he had no doubt searched them—but they were too far away to reach without abandoning the coverlet, inadequate and revoltingly dirty though it was. Gradually her head was beginning to clear, memory flickering.

His eyes ran over her with an expression of impatience. "You'll get your clothes when you cooperate. And since you're apparently so worried about it, your virtue is still intact." He stopped and smiled. "At least it is if you started with any."

"You're a real gentleman, Seagram!" Bronwen snapped, hoping this would be sarcastic and worldly enough to sound as if she didn't much care about her virtue one way or the other. "Besides, I don't believe you."

Seagram continued to smile. "So don't believe me, but I've never made a habit of ravishing girls. I like my women a little more seasoned—and conscious. Of course, if you insist, I suppose I can make an exception."

"Really, Seagram, you are a rotten man." Oddly enough, she actually hadn't believed he had raped her. She still wore her drawers, and she would have expected at least some soreness. On the other hand, she didn't trust him. She repeated coldly, "A rotten man!"

When he still smiled, she yanked the coverlet upward, which sent it flying over her head. With as much presence as she could muster, she retrieved and wrapped it around herself, then sat on the edge of the bed. "What am I doing here in this hellhole?"

"You know, Red, I'm getting a tad tired of your ingratitude. Here I remove you from harm's way, keep you from making a damn fool of yourself, maybe worse, and all you can do is complain about the company and the accommodations."

In the course of the past minutes, the previous evening had come back to her full force. "What did you do to my neck?"

"Nothing much. Quieted you down, though, didn't it? That and all the bourbon punch you'd drunk—in addition to a reckless streak, you've got a hollow leg. But now I want some answers."

"I told you and your cronies last night—by the way, what happened to Jules Falconer?"

He shrugged. "When I carried you off for my fiendish pleasures, I didn't see him. Some gallant protector *he* turned out to be. Admittedly, there was plenty of confusion, what with the woman's death. About which, of course, *you* know absolutely nothing! Right? Now, once again, who are you? Because you're not Jane Dowling. Not by a long shot."

"Who says I'm not?"

"I say so." Seagram got up from the chair and came to stand in front of her. "Fun's over, Red. I want some answers about why you're here in Montgomery, sneaking around under a false name and spying on conversations that don't concern you."

In spite of herself, Bronwen's breath caught. It was enough. Until then—she saw it in his eyes—he hadn't been sure.

Seagram grabbed hold of her upper arms and yanked her upright. "The next time you decide to eavesdrop, don't wear a shiny dress that reflects moonlight. Once I'd spotted you there, I figured I'd stay around and find out what you were up to. That song-and-dance routine about being a railroad investor's daughter is pure fiction. As it happens, I know Thaddeus Dowling. And his daughter's got black hair."

"I dyed it."

Seagram, still gripping both arms, shook her hard. "Talk!"

"All right, all right! What's Equus?"

His face instantly went blank, so completely devoid of expression it had to have been a rehearsed response. Then he dropped her arms and she thought he meant to hit her. Instead he pushed her backward onto the bed. "So you *did* hear that."

He gazed down at her, his expression no longer blank, but still unreadable. And for the first time Bronwen felt a twinge of real fear. It *had* meant something important, then, what she had overheard. Not that she'd doubted it. *Armageddon?*

Seagram turned away and walked to the open window, where he stood looking out. From the distance came the bass notes of a fog horn, and water slapping against piers, so they were near the river, probably somewhere on Water Street. The sky outside the window, what Bronwen could see of it, was dark gray, and she could hear the spatter of rain against the dirt-streaked upper pane.

Seated there in only scanty underclothes, she felt too vulnerable and cautiously inched off the bed, hoping she could reach her gown before he turned back to her. At the same time, she didn't intend to leave just yet; she seemed to be in no immediate danger from him, and she wanted to know what Equus meant. Seagram obviously believed she knew more than she actually did. Why else would he have brought her here? Clearly not for the usual purpose—for that he'd already had more than enough opportunity.

Then, suddenly, there was a sharp rap at the door. Seagram whirled and, before Bronwen could react, grabbed her and dragged her back onto the bed. She struggled beneath him, but he was much stronger than she would have guessed, and in a split second he had straddled her body, pinning her to the mattress.

"Keep your mouth shut!" he breathed in her ear.

She could hear the door begin to creak open. Seagram brought his mouth down hard on hers, stifling any cry she might have attempted. She felt his body move against hers.

A masculine laugh came from the direction of the door. Bronwen felt Seagram tense still more, and his hand clamped over her mouth before he raised his head to mutter, "What the hell . . . ?"

"Hey, sorry to interrupt, mister," came an amused voice. "Just lookin' for a room. Y'all go right ahead with what you were doin'!" Again the laugh, and Bronwen heard the door close.

Seagram rolled off her. His breathing slowed, and he lay on his back, staring at the ceiling.

Bronwen lunged, and made it to the edge of the bed before he grabbed her again. "What're you doing?"

"What am *I* doing?" she retorted. "You want to tell me what that lewd assault was about? But first, if you're going to keep me here half-naked, I want to bolt the door."

"There is no bolt."

"No bolt! What kind of place *is* this?"

"My God, will you stop complaining!"

"Let go of my arm . . ." She paused as footsteps sounded in the corridor outside the room. "Seagram!" she demanded as he again yanked her toward him. "Seagram, what's going on? Where *are* we?" But by this time, she'd guessed.

The footsteps went on past the door, and Seagram released her. "We're in a whorehouse."

Bronwen intended to curse him, but he held his hand over her mouth. "This is the most anonymous place in the world to be," he laughed softly. "Now will you keep your voice down?"

She considered biting him, but remembered his strength and thought better of it. She nodded, and when he'd removed his hand, she said icily, "Just why do we need to be anonymous? And in a whorehouse, a place I can truthfully say I've never had a desire to visit?"

"Finally—some honesty from you! This place is a precaution. In case someone's following you."

"Me? It's more likely *you* who's being followed—abducting young women as you do."

"Could be, but I don't think so. No, stay put."

She had begun to get up, but Seagram hauled her back down beside him on the bed. Since he didn't do anything else, she decided to distrust him a little less. "Anyway, why would someone be following me?"

"Because you overheard what you weren't supposed to. Because you aren't who you say you are. Because these are dangerous times—how the hell should I know! But you better start looking over your shoulder."

He was just trying to scare her. Bronwen gazed at the cobwebs festooning the ceiling, while Seagram raised himself on one elbow to look down at her, his heavy-lidded eyes the brown of wet cedar. "You ready to give me some answers?"

"Do I have a choice?" She moved her eyes away from his, acutely aware of the masculine smell of cigars and whiskey, and his closeness that was beginning to disturb her. Focusing on his neck, she said, "If I answer you, will you tell me what Equus means?"

He shrugged. "Horse. Now, why . . ."

"I know *that!*"

". . . are you in Montgomery?"

"*What* horse? And why do you think I have some hidden

reason for being here? I'm not the only Yankee woman in Alabama."

"You're the only one who was seen in the company of Ann Clements—or whatever name she used this time around."

"How do you know her?"

"That doesn't concern you. So, what is it you're doing, and what's it got to do with railroads?"

"I'm . . . I'm working."

"That I gathered. Working at what? Spying? For Allan Pinkerton's Detective Agency, maybe—like the late Ann Clements?"

Bronwen twisted away from him and sat up. "You can believe whatever you want," she retorted, "but I'm not spying. And even if I were—I said *if*—I don't see what that has to do with Ann Clements." She stopped, as with a jolt she recalled Arthur Kelly's accident.

"You don't see that." His eyes had narrowed as if to watch her lie.

"No! I'm here with Thaddeus Dowling, who, as you must know, since you think you know everything else, is very nervous about the railroads. That they'll all be confiscated by the Confederate government. He wants to find out what's happening to his investments."

Since this part was true, she looked at Seagram to see if he believed her. He'd been lighting a cigarette and didn't even glance up. "Keep going."

"This trip," she went on, "was supposed to look like a family visit, while he just incidentally looked into his investments. But Dowling's a widower, and he didn't want his daughter involved if things got . . . well, you know, unpleasant down here. So I came instead. Now what's so sinister about that?"

"Well, at least you kept your story straight."

"It's the truth!"

"Right. You lie so easily—"

"And you *don't?*"

He didn't seem to hear her, just dragged on the cigarette, staring up at the ceiling. "For a Chicago agency," he said finally, "Pinkerton's is ranging pretty far afield—even though the clients *are* railroad investors, and owners, and whoever else can pay. That part I believe."

Bronwen glared at him, but said nothing.

"How," Seagram asked abruptly, "did you meet up with Jules Falconer?"

"That was explained last night."

"No, not exactly. Not by you. Explain it again."

Why was Seagram asking this? Although she didn't trust him, she decided to keep as close to the truth as possible; he might relax enough to let drop something about Equus. "Thaddeus Dowling met several times with Jules, who's representing his father. The senior Falconer is also worried about possible railroad confiscation."

"His railroads are in the Deep South—he doesn't have to worry, not now, anyway," Seagram argued.

"I'll tell him you said so—I imagine he'll be reassured."

"Don't get smart, Red."

"Then don't be ridiculous. Of course he has to worry. *All* the railroad lines will be important if there's war. Even you should be able to see that."

"Careful . . ."

"Seagram, look at a map of Northern and Southern railroads if you don't believe me! The North has many more trains and track to move men and weapons and supplies—the South will need every foot of track it can find. Or can snatch by confiscation."

Seagram gave her a lengthy stare. "Pinkerton made sure you learned your stuff, I grant that," he said at last. "But you can't tell me anything about railroads I don't already know—" he paused, then added bitterly "—and absolutely nothing about war."

He ground out his cigarette butt in a pail on the floor. "I don't believe your story, Red. Somebody was plenty worried about Ann Clements, and I want to know why a Pinkerton agent would be dangerous enough to get herself killed. Of course, it was supposed to *look* like an accident. That she just happened to have a little too much to drink and leaned over the railing too far."

"And you think *I* know what, or why it happened?" Bronwen was now fairly certain, since he hadn't mentioned it, that he didn't know about Kelly's death—Kelly, who was also a Pinkerton agent. Unless Seagram was trying to trap her. Or unless . . . No, Seagram had not been the driver of the carriage that killed Kelly. But that didn't mean he hadn't been involved.

"You know something, because you were seen with Clements," Seagram now said. "So we're back where we started. To who you are and why Pinkerton sent you down here."

Bronwen sighed, partly to cover her growing apprehension. And partly from exhaustion. He was like a bull terrier; he wouldn't let go and he knew about Pinkerton, so she couldn't lie about *that* anymore. "I told you who I am. But this is the first time I've done anything like this."

"Right. So why's Pinkerton sending a novice through the gates of hell?"

"That's dramatic, Seagram, but a little exaggerated. As far as Ann Clements goes, I didn't know her before I got here. Thaddeus Dowling was told she could help us. That she knew the territory."

"Right."

"It's the truth! There's nothing devious or underhanded or

illegal about finding out if and when the Confederate government is going to take over the railroads. Men like Dowling have a lot of money invested in rail lines."

"Right."

"Will you stop saying 'right'! A woman is dead. How right can it be? And I'm in a house of ill-repute with a man who may have designs on my person, and who keeps hammering me with questions. And who won't even tell me who he is!"

"You got some of it correct."

"Is Seagram your real name?"

"You tell me—and forget Jane Dowling."

"All right, it's Bronwen. Bronwen Llyr."

"All right, it's Guy Seagram."

How could she challenge that? And it might actually be true. "So, why are *you* in Montgomery?" she demanded, not that she expected an answer.

"You know why. I'm with the Maryland state delegation."

"Keeping your story straight, too?" But from what she'd overheard last night, he might not be lying. "What is Equus, then?"

He gave her another long look. "You don't want to know anything about Equus. Believe me." Then, almost as if to himself, he added, "But there's more I'd like to know."

"*You'd* like to know . . . Just how dumb do you think I am, Seagram? You were talking to that man about it."

"For various reasons, which are none of your business, that man assumed I knew more than I did. And I was just about to learn more, when you interfered. The question, of course, is why were *you* so interested in Equus?"

"I wasn't. Didn't know anything about it, not until I accidentally overheard you and that man." Bronwen saw Guy Seagram's shoulders relax very slightly. Maybe he believed her. Then she had an unpleasant thought. "Do you think he spotted me?"

"If *I* spotted you, it's possible he did too, but you'd better hope not. These people are not playing by the rules—in case you hadn't figured that out."

"You mean they—these people—killed Ann? Who *are* they?"

"That's enough. You already know too much. You're an inexperienced kid, in way over your head. You don't have any idea what you're dealing with. Now go on home and—"

"Other than abduct women, Seagram," she interrupted, "what is it that you *do* as a member of the Maryland delegation? If you *are* a member."

"Oh, a little of this, a little of that."

He wasn't going to tell her anything. Bronwen flounced off the bed. "Thanks for your candor. And for the charming accommodations. But I've had enough." She went to her shoes first and placed them on the floor beside her, then pulled her dress on over her head, and stepped into her hooped petticoat. She sat down to put on her stockings.

Seagram didn't try to stop her. He just lay on the bed, watching. "Maybe I was wrong about you, Red."

"Is that so!"

He swung his legs to the floor and stood up. "Maybe you're not too young after all. You're damned feisty, I'll say that." Grinning, he cocked his head and eyed her with an unequivocal expression. "Could be fun."

"Don't come near me," Bronwen said evenly. She yanked her high-laced shoes toward her and bent down, ostensibly to put them on.

"Better not give orders, Red—not when you don't have a weapon."

Her head snapped up. He had extracted from his trouser

pocket her short, leather-sheathed stiletto, and was tapping it with his index finger.

"You're still a rat, Seagram. So that's what was jabbing me on the bed a while ago," she said, reaching for it.

"You think so." Seagram laughed.

Bronwen came close to blushing, and jumped up to grab the stiletto. To her surprise Seagram let her, although he chuckled, "I suppose you'll tell me you know how to use that."

She glanced around her. "See that small dark spot on the far wall"—she pointed over his shoulder—"looks like a splashed drop of wine?"

In the time it took him to turn and find the spot, she'd whipped the knife from its sheath, raised her arm, and flung it. The blade entered the wall with a dull thud, the handle quivering directly over the wine-colored droplet.

An odd expression streaked across Seagram's face. He instantly suppressed it. "O.K., I'm impressed."

"You were supposed to be. A Seneca Indian taught me that. Name of Sundown. And you better hope, Seagram, that you never meet up with *him*." She went to the wall and withdrew the stiletto, returning it to the sheath, which she slipped inside her high-topped shoe. "Now, I assume I have permission to leave this place." Not a question.

"Feel free. If you think you'll survive."

He was trying to scare her again. "Survive? Why shouldn't I?"

"Even if what you overheard was accidental—and I'm still not sure I believe that—it doesn't matter. It's dangerous, Red, and I'd be worried if I were you. Don't forget your friend Ann Clements."

She studied him for a minute before stepping to the window. "There's nobody down there, is there?"

"Not that I can tell. Now listen to me—listen very carefully. I'm telling you the truth."

"You expect me to believe—"

"Listen! I don't know all of what Equus involves, not yet. I do know it has a very bad feel to it."

"I'm sure it does, Seagram. What with 'Armageddon' and 'bloody ends.' And it's already associated with death. But who else's death?"

He shrugged lightly. "Could be the death of the Union. Could be . . . could be a lot of things."

"And why are you suddenly so forthright?"

"Get out of Montgomery, you little fool! Get out of the South altogether. Go home, get married, have children. Be a nice, normal woman."

"I've been told that before. Many times."

Seagram didn't respond. Instead, he went to the window. "Go home. You could end up like Clements." He turned and held her eyes.

To her irritation, Bronwen felt a mixture of attraction and alarm, but succeeded in staring steadily back at him. "I'm staying in Montgomery for a while longer, Seagram. Until I finish what I'm being paid to do."

"Can you handle a gun?"

"*What?* Yes—I can."

"Now why doesn't that surprise me? O.K., get yourself one."

"They're bulky. I'm good with a stiletto, you saw that. There's only one person anywhere better—Sundown, who taught me. But I'll consider a gun."

"Good. You'll need it. Now get the hell out of here."

Bronwen opened the door and looked up and down the corridor before she stepped out of the room. Then she closed the door softly. And suddenly felt very much alone.

The door behind her flew open. She whirled around, half-expecting to face a revolver. Instead, Seagram said blandly, "Next time I see you, Red, it better not be in a whorehouse. And start looking over your shoulder. Now."

The door closed. Bronwen made for the stairs.

Guy Seagram stood watching her from the window. The shiny white satin made her hard to miss. She was a perfect target. He shouldn't have let her go alone. . . . No, damn it; he wasn't a nursemaid! She'd have to take care of herself. But what the hell was Allan Pinkerton thinking when he let this girl off a leash? She had more pluck than brains. Or maybe not. Well, Pinkerton would find out in a hurry. Because unless Seagram was very much mistaken, Bronwen Llyr was marked.

They might not kill her right away; maybe wait to see whom she tried to contact. But they would get her. The stakes were too high for the Equus conspirators to let live someone they'd see as a potential wild card. They'd proven that with Ann Clements. But what had she known? What had made Clements dangerous? Unless they thought she'd recognized one of them. They couldn't expose themselves to that risk. They'd already blundered once.

Seagram himself didn't like killing. Didn't even like thinking about it, but in his work he'd been forced to, if only in the abstract. And he'd be damned if he would have this girl on his conscience. He had warned her! Said as much as he could to scare her, and perhaps more than he should. She'd either listened to him or not. That was her decision.

Now he watched her turn onto Commerce Street, only a white blur in the distance. At least it had stopped raining. Precipitation, he mused; the great unknown. The bane of military campaigns: Henry sloshing around in Agincourt's rain-sodden fields; Napoleon undone by Russian snow; Washington nearly undone by Valley Forge sleet and hail.

Seagram allowed himself a brief, bitter smile.

And now he had to get moving. He should depart Montgomery before any more bungling took place. The Maryland delegation was splitting up. Its radical wing had been denied credentials by the new Confederacy; its members had been thought too extreme, too eager to use violent means. How true that was, Seagram thought. But could Jefferson Davis and like-minded, honorable men hold back the extremist tide? Not if more mistakes were made.

The other Maryland factions—the conservatives and moderates—were going their separate ways with their separate agendas. Back to Baltimore, most of them, to try to convince fellow politicians to vote for or against secession. There would not be much time left.

He took one last look down Water Street. The girl in white satin was gone.

6

―∞―

*Railroads . . . are positively the greatest blessing
that the ages have wrought out for us. They give
us wings; they annihilate the toil and dust of pil-
grimage; they spiritualize travel!*

―Nathaniel Hawthorne

*B*ronwen walked east on Madison Street as the seductive
blush of an Alabama sunrise began to clear the sky of clouds.
Because she felt so conspicuous in the white gown, she kept
Seagram's warning in mind. Every few steps she'd glance
over her shoulder. Otherwise, she would have enjoyed these
solitary moments; the first she'd had since arriving in
Montgomery.

Situated on a bend of the Alabama River, it was a graceful city which had spread quietly, and with the same gentil-
ity that characterized its residents, over seven low hills.
Some forty years before, the Alabama legislature had created it by consolidating the villages of New Philadelphia
and East Alabama, and had named it to honor the American
Revolutionary War hero, General Richard Montgomery.
Along its hard-packed dirt roads grew thickets of pine trees
dotted with the white of wild dogwood in bloom, and stands
of ancient elms and oaks that towered like silent sentinels.
The trees had probably been there since the time Creek Indians lived along the streams.

Sprawling under the trees were bright yellow swaths of daffodils; the heralds of spring, Bronwen thought with a small, unfamiliar pang of homesickness. Daffodils wouldn't appear in western New York for several months to come.

For the past few minutes, she'd been walking in a drowsy haze, but came wide-awake when she caught a slight movement from the corner of her eye. Just ahead rose the stately spire of St. John's Episcopal Church, and she could now hear the footsteps behind her. Following, keeping time with her own. Before she turned, she needed to get the stiletto from her shoe. Her worry was how fast she could withdraw it. The yards of satin and wretched hooped petticoat would slow her down.

She tried altering her pace, speeding it up, curbing it slightly, then pausing and listening. The footsteps behind her stopped. She bent down as if to retie her shoe, and reached for the stiletto.

"Lovely morning," called a cheerful voice. She spun around to see a pleasant-looking young man in white clerical collar just opening the gate of an iron fence surrounding the church. A discreet sign beside the gate told her this must be the Reverend Mr. John March Mitchell.

"Yes, lovely," she answered with a confused mix of relief and mostly embarrassment; since what must the Reverend Mr. Mitchell make of a lone woman, in a wrinkled satin ballgown, traipsing the streets at this ungodly hour? He probably thought she'd been working in a whorehouse!

She ducked her head and quickened her pace again, throwing a glance over her shoulder every few paces. When several minutes later she reached Commerce Street, and at last the Campbell House hotel, her heart beat as if she'd run all the way from Water Street. To avoid the lobby she went up the back stairs—always locate an alternative escape

route, she'd been drilled—to her second-story room. It was
just down the corridor from that of Thaddeus Dowling.

Once inside the room, which was cluttered with overstuffed furnishings, and in which miscellaneous floral designs had run riot on every inch of fabric, Bronwen threw
herself facedown across a delphinium-print coverlet on the
four-poster bed. Her head felt waterlogged and she desperately wanted some sleep. Instead, she needed to think. She
raised herself on an elbow to see the rose-painted porcelain
clock on the bedside table, and groaned. In one hour she had
to meet Dowling for breakfast; then accompany "her father"
when he met with several Southern railroad investors and a
British businessman. Jules Falconer, she thought with sudden dismay, would probably be there, too. She'd be forced
to concoct some story to explain her abrupt departure the
night before. With another groan, she rolled over and stared
at the whorls on the plaster ceiling. They made her think of
hoop skirts swirling in the steps of a Viennese waltz.
Women in red and white gowns.

Somehow she must get word of Ann Clements's death to
Pinkerton in Chicago. Although perhaps someone else had
already done it. On second thought, just who might that
someone be? Arthur Kelly was dead. Thaddeus Dowling
hadn't been at the ball, and even if he had, he didn't know
Ann Clements; he would have met "Anna Clark" for the
first time this morning. Since Bronwen was a novice, and
since Allan Pinkerton was fixated on security, she'd been
given the names of only two other operatives south of the
Mason and Dixon line. Neither operative was in Alabama.
The tightfisted Pinkerton had insisted that three agents in the
state would be sufficient to handle the railroad confiscation
reports. Hence, there was only herself left to wire him.

And when she did, he would undoubtedly order her back
North. This assignment, her first time out, was to have been

a "soft one," as Pinkerton had phrased it. "Simply to break you in, give you some small amount of experience in the field," he'd said, fingering his wiry beard and fixing Bronwen with the cool, grayish blue eyes that never left the face of the person to whom he was speaking. She'd waited in his office interminably, afraid he would never make the decision to send her South. And now, he would demand her return to Chicago, and the iron-willed Scot would tolerate no argument.

She couldn't go back. Detective work was what she wanted to do! She'd have to finagle a way to sidestep Pinkerton's orders. No; that would probably be impossible. From the start the man had had his doubts about her: that she was too young had been Pinkerton's biggest complaint. That she was not good at taking orders was right up there with her age. Also, her looks were too—how had he put it?—"unforgettable," although he *had* conceded that might be an advantage when dealing with certain men. But only if she were careful. And Pinkerton seemed to question whether careful was something she knew how to be: "reckless" was another of his favored epithets.

In fact, though he also conceded that over all her qualifications were equal if not superior to those he ordinarily required, Pinkerton didn't want to hire her. He wouldn't have but for Constable Cullen Stuart, who'd once worked for the detective. Cullen had persuaded Pinkerton, "called in his note" as he'd phrased it, to at least give Bronwen a trial run. This being it.

But now, if forced to abandon her first assignment, the stubborn Scotsman would use it as the excuse to get rid of her.

All right, she could not give Pinkerton that excuse. She wouldn't wire him about Ann Clements's death—not right away. Not until she'd found out what had caused it: accident or murder. In the meantime, she'd learn more about Equus. Her detective work might so impress him that he'd beg her on his knees to stay. Even raise her salary . . . Well, maybe not that, knowing Pinkerton. But he would at least continue to employ her. Treat her with the same regard he gave his other female operatives. And to grudgingly give the devil his due, he did hire women.

She rolled off the bed, fatigue too costly to indulge.

"A pox on all politicians!" Thaddeus Dowling brought his fist down on the Chippendale table in the Pollard mansion parlor, making teacups and whiskey glasses skitter across its polished surface.

"I could hardly agree more," said Lucas Osgood, giving the table a rap himself for good measure. Mrs. Charles Pollard eyed her Staffordshire china with concern.

Bronwen, upon her arrival, had immediately placed her hostess as the "Mrs. Pollard" of the ladies' parlor conversation the evening before. Virginia Scott Pollard now glanced at her husband with her eyebrows raised significantly. Her signal was missed, however; Colonel Charles Pollard, president of the Montgomery and West Point Railroad, was too engaged in studying Thaddeus Dowling with distinct reservation.

"It's politicians, backed by a handful of radical abolitionists in the North and secessionists in the South, who are fueling this tinderbox," Dowling went on. "I cannot believe most men in this country want war. Certainly not over slavery!"

The Alabamian Pollard frowned, but said nothing. Lucas Osgood seemed about to reply, hesitated briefly, then said, "Perhaps. It's true that most secessionists simply want to leave the Union quietly. They would like to believe the North will allow them to do that. I'm not so sure it will happen. Everything hinges on how the new President reacts. In any case, I agree the threat of war does not in any way help our railroad interests."

Bronwen watched for Jules Falconer's response. It puzzled her that he'd been unusually quiet during this discussion. Perhaps because it involved Alabama's Montgomery and West Point Railroad, in which Dowling and Osgood had invested; as well as the newly proposed railroads, designed to join the north and south sections of the state, in which the two men had planned to invest. The Falconer railroad interests lay elsewhere. But they *had* made a recent investment in the Baltimore and Ohio. Still, Bronwen recalled from Pinkerton's indoctrination, the Baltimore and Ohio ran west from Baltimore through the federal arsenal at Harper's Ferry. And all the way to the Ohio River. If war should come, the B & O would be a crucial link from the west to Washington and the Chesapeake Bay. She'd have thought Jules Falconer would be interested. Perhaps he was more of a dilettante than she'd guessed.

There had been an awkward moment earlier when she and Falconer had met at Osgood's. Beforehand, Bronwen had invented a case of nervous vapors to explain why she'd left the ball the night before.

"It was seeing that poor dead woman," she'd explained to him in suitably distressed tone. "I got so shaky . . . well, I couldn't bear to stay after that. I asked Mr. Seagram to get me a carriage"—that inspired addition was in case Falconer had seen them together—"and I looked for you, naturally, but there was such a crowd! Then I went straight back to my hotel."

She'd thought this a fairly plausible story, and expected to receive Falconer's sympathy and a "Please, my dear, don't think a thing of it." What she got was a stony stare. And finally a clipped "Yes." That was all.

The only grounds for this cold reaction that made any sense was if Falconer *had* seen her with Seagram; perhaps imagined she and Seagram had done more than just drive to the hotel. More, as in, "spent the night together." How insulting! How ironic! But there was nothing to be done for it now. Too much explanation could be worse than none, she had been warned. She'd also been warned that agents occasionally had to undergo "uncomfortable" things. No one had mentioned abduction to a whorehouse.

Bronwen covered a yawn with her hand. The two investors, Dowling and Osgood, had been talking for what seemed hours. And she, despite having become somewhat interested in railroads, was bored. She had called Pinkerton nasty things—under her breath, of course—when he demanded she learn more about rail lines than she thought she needed to know. But the forced education now stood her in good stead. Here, though, the investors' conversation was repetitious, while they tried to determine where the other stood—without actually asking outright. Thaddeus Dowling's concern was the loss of his investment if the Montgomery and West Point lines were confiscated. Bronwen knew for what Dowling was angling: an offer from the Southerner Osgood to buy him out. So far it hadn't happened.

All during this lengthy exchange, Charles Pollard had remained silent, his fingers steepled under a square, clean-shaven chin, his expression strangely aloof. And Falconer had gone to stand at the window.

"What do *you* think of politics and politicians, Miss Dowling?" This from the man seated beside her on a gold-velvet, arched-back sofa drawn up before the fireplace in Pollard's parlor. Until today, Bronwen wouldn't have imagined that extra heat in Alabama would ever be necessary. But when she and Thaddeus Dowling had arrived earlier, by way of an open surrey, there had been a definite chill in the air. She'd been grateful for the fire.

She turned to her sofa companion, an elegantly tailored Englishman. Either because of his nose, an imposing beak-like one, or the shiny black eyes, he resembled a large, rather dangerous bird. In spite of this predator cast, or perhaps because of it, he looked intriguing to her.

"What do *I* think of politicians, Colonel de Warde?" she repeated. "Quite honestly, I try not to think of them at all."

The man chuckled softly. "You are wise beyond your years, Miss Dowling. I believe Shakespeare's definition of a politician was: 'One that would circumvent God.' "

"That sounds like something my aunt might quote," Bronwen said, giving him a rare, thoroughly genuine smile. "My aunt's a librarian." That seemed safe enough to say— she had to make *some* conversation, and agents were limited as to what they could discuss. Reveal nothing personal, she'd been drilled again and again. But de Warde seemed a pleasant, educated man—certainly not someone who'd pose a threat.

Thus she was surprised to find him studying her rather intently, as if for some reason she had confused him. "Colonel de Warde?"

"Pardon me, Miss Dowling. But for a moment there, when you smiled, you greatly resembled someone I once knew. Although it was not so long ago that I can't remember the lady quite well."

"I trust the lady was worth remembering?"

"Yes, indeed." Colonel de Warde smiled. "A lovely and intelligent woman. And one quite wasted, in my opinion, in the small town in which she lives."

"It's a coincidence," Bronwen said, "but I've told my aunt, the one I just mentioned, the same thing and . . ." She paused as something odd streaked across the man's face. It was fleeting, and she might have been mistaken, but instinct buttressed by Pinkerton's training cautioned her. "On the other hand," she laughed and went on, "probably every niece feels that way about a favorite aunt."

"No doubt," he said, his expression enigmatic. Then he smiled and turned toward the others, as if something had been said that caught his attention.

"So what do you think, de Warde?" Thaddeus Dowling now asked in regard to a question Bronwen hadn't heard.

Apparently the colonel hadn't heard it either, as he apologized and asked Dowling to repeat himself.

"I asked your opinion on investing in the projected railroads right now," Dowling said.

De Warde answered quickly, "I shouldn't do it, if I were you. As you are aware, gentlemen, my country's concern is that nothing interrupt the flow of Southern cotton to the Atlantic ports, irrespective of political saber-rattling. Britain, as you are also aware, is vitally interested in seeing the South maintain its current rate of export if war *should* come to pass. By all means, transport cotton over your rail lines. But why build more of them? You'll never convince cavalry men to abandon their horses for trains."

De Warde might not be as smart as Bronwen thought; although, once again, she had to credit Pinkerton's force-fed instruction. And while she didn't know much about past wars, even she could see the new railroads would make a difference. The length of time it took horses to carry supplies and food—not to mention the troops themselves—held an army back. But not anymore; not when the iron horses could carry those same things so much faster.

But these particular four men were interested in business and trade. Those were the sole things in which they appeared to have interest. However, Allan Pinkerton could be right, much as Bronwen hated to admit it, when he said the face of war would be changed forever by steam. That was why he thought it dangerous, foolishly dangerous, that the capital could be approached by only a single line, the Washington branch of the Baltimore and Ohio. What if something were to happen to that rail line? Something catastrophic, anywhere along its hundreds of miles of track? Washington would then be totally isolated from the North.

Bronwen suddenly felt cold. For some inexplicable reason, some primitive instinct, she turned to look over her shoulder, and caught Colonel Dorian de Warde eyeing her speculatively. While suppressing a shiver, she edged closer to the fire.

7

I listened attentively to what she [Dorothea Dix] had to say. . . . The sum of it was, that there was an extensive and organized conspiracy through the South to seize upon Washington, with its archives and records, and then declare the Southern Confederacy de facto *the Government of the United States. At the same time they were to cut off all means of communication between Washington and the North, East, and West, and thus prevent the transportation of troops to wrest the Capital from the hands of the insurgents.*

—Samuel Morse Felton

For the second time in five minutes, the president of the Philadelphia, Wilmington and Baltimore Railroad left his desk and went to the office window. Samuel Morse Felton drummed his fingers on the sill as he watched the busy Philadelphia street below. Allan Pinkerton, noted for his punctuality, was already four minutes late. However, even while Felton stood there, a horse-drawn omnibus drew up before the office building and the thick-set, unsmiling Scotsman descended to the road. From between his lips, mostly concealed by a heavy beard, protruded an unlit cigar.

Felton went back to his desk. It was not the first time he had awaited Pinkerton. When the disturbing rumors had first come to Felton's attention, the detective had been summoned from Chicago, arriving at the railroad executive's office with, for all Felton knew, the very same cigar clenched between his teeth. Pinkerton never *had* lit it.

The rumors Felton had heard, but which so far he'd been unable to verify, said that Southern sympathizers were planning to sabotage the tunnels and bridges and rolling stock of his railroad.

"I discounted much of the early talk that came my way as overwrought gossip," Felton had told Pinkerton at that first meeting. "Then, several weeks ago, I had a visit from the philanthropist Dorothea Dix. Miss Dix presented in tangible and reliable shape what I had previously learned only in bits and pieces."

Pinkerton frowned. "I've heard of this woman as some sort of reformer," he said in a tone that implied her work was eccentric meddling, "so by what means did she come by such information?"

"She builds hospitals," Felton answered, "an activity that brings her into contact with men prominent in Southern politics. She said she's become familiar with the structure of Southern society, and with the workings of its political machinery. I've known Miss Dix for some time, Mr. Pinkerton, and I believe her report to be factual. And her concern of genuine importance."

The city of Philadelphia, Felton painstakingly pointed out to the detective, was the funnel into which poured all of the railroad lines covering New England, New York, and New Jersey. Felton's railroad provided the only direct route from Philadelphia to Baltimore, and thus to the Baltimore and Ohio Railroad's single track to Washington—the sole line connecting the capital with the North. If war should break out, and the new President were to order Federal troops to Washington, Baltimore would become the key military point of the North's rail system. And if the Philadelphia,

Wilmington and Baltimore Railroad were to be disrupted, the troops would be prevented from reaching the capital; an isolated capital if Maryland seceded as was increasingly feared.

Felton had explained all of this to Allan Pinkerton, even though he assumed the detective must be aware of the situation. Nonetheless, Pinkerton had patiently heard him out, then asked gruffly, "So you want me to investigate the rumors?"

"Yes; find out whether there is genuine basis for alarm. Or if I am concerned needlessly."

Pinkerton had agreed to make preliminary inquiries. He went back to Chicago, and from there wired Felton several days later; he had learned enough, the detective stated, to definitely justify a more thorough investigation. He would himself return to Philadelphia to hammer out their future tactics.

Felton now rose to meet the Scot as he came through the office door. Pinkerton gave him a perfunctory handshake and, with no effort at small talk, launched into his proposal. "Since we first met I have confirmed your suspicions about potential danger to your rail lines. My operatives in the South say these rumors are flying too thick to be ignored. Therefore, as time is of the essence, I propose to immediately send four of my best agents, disguised as Southern sympathizers, to various Delaware and Maryland towns along the P, W & B track. They will pursue the rumors to their source. If there *is* a plot to damage railroad property, they will unearth it."

"And then what?" Samuel Felton, despite the detective's apparent confidence, was now more worried than he wanted to admit.

"The agents will forward the information to me," Pinkerton answered briskly. "I myself intend to set up headquarters in Baltimore, where, once a threat is substantiated, the strategy to trace and thwart it can be designed. I presume that meets with your approval?"

Pinkerton's thick eyebrows had drawn together in an intense scowl, and Felton decided that if he didn't approve, he'd better keep it to himself. He nodded slowly.

Pinkerton's scowl eased. "Good. And now I need some additional information from you—the places where your railroad is most vulnerable to attack."

Felton got to his feet and indicated the large map hanging on the opposite wall. He and Pinkerton went to stand before it.

"There are two strategic danger spots," explained Felton, pointing to Maryland's Chesapeake Bay shoreline. "Ten miles north of Baltimore there's a wooden railroad bridge over the Gunpowder River. And some twenty miles north of that bridge, at Havre de Grace, Maryland, is where the Susquehanna River empties into the Chesapeake; the mouth of the river is too wide to bridge, so boats ferry the railroad cars across it. My master mechanic, William Stearns, tells me he's heard a rumor that the bridge and the ferries will be burned—or blown up by explosives."

The cold gray-blue eyes that Pinkerton had fastened on the other man held no expression. He merely stated, "I'll position agents at both those locations," and then started toward the door. "In the meantime," he added, "I'll be staying at the Howard House in Baltimore, under the name John H. Hutchinson, with another one of my operatives. Best way to pick up rumors is to mingle—in taverns and hotel lobbies, in barber shops and billiard rooms, so that's what we'll be doing. Don't contact me unless it's an emergency. I'll be in touch as soon as we get something definite."

Pinkerton left the office before Felton could voice any objections. Not that he had any significant ones. The detective agency had gained a national reputation for apprehending train robbers and protecting railroad property, and Pinkerton's rapid, explicit response had been impressive. If, Felton reasoned, a pro-Southern conspiracy threatening his railroad *did* exist, Pinkerton would undoubtedly find it, if anyone could.

The inauguration of the new president was scheduled for March 4. Abraham Lincoln would be leaving his home in Springfield, Illinois, in a matter of days to begin a two-week train tour to Washington, so if secessionist trouble were to erupt, it would probably be soon. But all he could do now was to trust in Pinkerton's judgment, and pray that the detective would live up to his reputation.

Samuel Felton had not become president of one of the most successful rail lines in the country by readily relinquishing control. But on this occasion, he decided he had very little choice. He just hoped the situation wasn't more volatile than Pinkerton had suggested. Or more ominous.

8

No one, not in my situation, can appreciate my feelings of sadness at this parting. To this place, and the kindness of these people, I owe everything. Here I have lived a quarter of a century, and have passed from a young to an old man. Here my children have been born, and one is buried. I now leave, not knowing when or whether ever I may return. . . .

— Abraham Lincoln, Springfield, Illinois,
   February 1861

 ary Lincoln watched icy morning rain spitting against her parlor window. The sleet only added to her misery, reflecting, as it did, her own dismal cast of mind. But the weather was appropriate; much as she disliked Mondays on principle, this one was particularly cruel. Springfield, home for so many years, would soon be left behind, as would her friends and her cherished house. That would have been hard enough, but at this very moment her husband was at the train station, leaving without her.

Her wide, smooth forehead furrowed with the angry memory. Those four men sent by the War Department, who had surrounded her husband ever since the election, had ordered—*ordered!*—that she and the boys would not travel with Mr. Lincoln (as she had *always* called him and always would) on the train to Washington, but would follow on another several days later. Moreover, a party of fifteen men *had* been permitted to ride. She'd bitterly protested being separated from her husband, but the end result, as usual, had been his acquiescing to their demands. "It will be all right, Molly," he'd said.

"It will *not* be all right, Mr. Lincoln!" she'd retorted, more in hurt than in anger—although she supposed that at the time it had sounded much the same. But then he had gazed at her with such misery that she stopped arguing and gave in. She knew her behavior made her look like a shrew, and she also knew that behind her back those men ridiculed her. But they didn't understand. He needed her, and she him. Without him, she would be afraid. She *was* afraid.

Last November she had thought to welcome this day; the euphoria of the election returns had made her giddy with joy, had made her feel strong again—for the first time, really, since little Eddie's death. But now the hour had arrived, she felt gripped by a dread she could hardly explain, even to herself. What had *happened* to her? Where was the strong young woman who had defied her Kentucky family to marry a man they thought too poor, too rough-hewn, and too far beneath their station? She'd had many, *many* suitors—why *him?* they had demanded and argued and harassed. And long before that, she had fought fiercely to attend an aristocratic French-run boarding school; although, she thought now, the battle had been won not so much by her as by her stepmother's dislike of her. Still, what had become of the girl considered to be one of the brightest and prettiest of Lexington's belles—even if she had also been considered too outspoken. But he, Mr. Lincoln, had liked that. He had liked her intelligence, that she was well-read, interested in politics, and able to argue with him. Oh, how they argued!

It had been little Eddie, she thought now, listening to the sleet drum on the window. It had been the helpless weeks of watching him suffer that had changed her. The child she had once carried safe within her own body, had nursed for much longer than necessary so he wouldn't contract milk fever, had protected and treasured—this beloved child had endured consumption for fifty-two days. Mary could remember every single one of them. Would never, ever, forget them. The doctors, after their blood-letting, their dosing with purgatives and emetics, had given up long before she did. Even if nothing she tried could help him. Not massaging his chest with balsam ointment, or giving him Wister's Wildcherry laced with opium, or bathing him with witch hazel four times a day to reduce the fever. Nothing had relieved his torment. Her prayers, her pleas to the Lord for mercy, went unanswered, and in the end she had lost him.

The grief—at times so overwhelming she could not stand upright, could barely draw breath except to beg for her own life to be taken—the grief, she believed now, was where the fear began. It brought her the certainty that she could never survive another such loss. And the fearsome thing she'd learned was how little control she had over the well-being of those she loved.

Now, when she left Springfield, she would lose even that small amount of control—over her own life, or that of her children or her husband.

Fear for him consumed her every waking moment. The reason for the separate trains had been security, and the War Department had sent the officers because there were already threats. *Already*—before he was even President. Not that she had any doubts there. Not about *him*. She never had. He would be a brilliant President, better than most of the country deserved. Certainly better than those wretched newspapers that portrayed him as a buffoon, mocking his frontier accent and ambling gait, saying he was nothing more than a hick lawyer who didn't know a salad fork from a pitchfork, a friend from a foe. Although to some degree *that* held truth: he *was* too trusting. And believing the best of people, when he was disappointed or betrayed, he was slow to act. He needed *her.*

She sighed, and smoothed the thick black velvet of her ribbon-trimmed, flounced, hooped skirt. It had cost her dearly, that and the rest of her new wardrobe, but she meant to show Washington a thing or two about style. *That* was something she *could* control. She suspected the capital anticipated some dowdy little Midwest matron—and they were in for a surprise! Not for nothing had she learned French; she subscribed to every available journal of French couture. Just the thought of Washington's astonishment began to make her feel better.

She looked through the window, past the iron fence to the corner of Eighth and Jackson Streets, where ruts puddled and overflowed with rainwater. The mud must be inches deep. But they shouldn't have made him leave for the station without her. For a terrible moment she couldn't even remember if she had said good-bye to him. How could she not remember *that?*

She rushed to the hall wardrobe, threw a cloak around herself, and called to the boys, "I'm going to the train station." Then she let herself out the door, nearly slipping on the wet wood of the front porch before hurrying down the steps and into the rain.

As she neared the small brick depot, sloshing as quickly as she could through the muddy streets, she could hear Springfield cheering him. Then the heel of her silk boot caught in a rut, and she went down in a tumble of petticoats. Struggling to her feet, her hair disheveled and streaming water, and her cloak heavy with mud, she heard a bell clang. Almost running now, she saw steam pouring from the stubby funnel of the locomotive smokestack, and then heard its long, plaintive whistle. As the train began to pull out, there must have been close to a thousand people standing in the station yard. She could never make her way through them in time.

She stopped at the edge of the crowd, and standing alone in the rain, she watched until the train rounded a curve of track, disappearing from sight.

He was gone. And now she remembered; she had not said good-bye.

9

—∿—

Who sees the lurking serpent steps aside.

—Shakespeare

Bronwen stood at the corner of Montgomery's Court and Commerce Streets, waiting for several Clydesdale-drawn coaches to thunder past, the white fetlock hair of the powerful draft horses shimmering like silk fringe. Directly behind her was the Winter Building, the second floor of which held the Southern Telegraph Company; she had just left there after checking what time of day it opened. Rumor had it that Alabama would soon sever itself from the federal postal service, so to wire Aunt Glynis tomorrow instead of writing a letter tonight made more sense. In a way, she regretted not having an excuse to visit again the Old Montgomery Theatre Building, where the post office was housed, and which, in less than a year, had already seen more than its share of grand moments. The theater had opened the previous October—Colonel Charles Pollard having been among its principal backers—and its premier performances, *Hamlet* and *Julius Caesar,* had starred John Wilkes Booth, the dashing younger brother of famed Shakespearean actor Edwin Booth. Recently, the brothers had performed there together in *Othello.* And a few days later, so the story went, a musician had on impulse scribbled the words to "Dixie" on one of the theater walls; thus the song's humble beginnings as a Confederate anthem.

As Bronwen crossed the street, she puzzled over the compelling urge to contact her aunt. After all, Pinkerton was the one to whom she *should* report. Perhaps it was because she felt so isolated; although, ironically, for some time she'd also half-suspected she was being followed. And while logic said this must be her imagination, the sense of an unseen shadow persisted.

It had begun when she and Thaddeus Dowling returned from the Pollard plantation. They'd stopped for oysters and lobster salad at Pizzala's Restaurant, run by one of the many Italian immigrant families in a city that, not surprisingly, bore an impressive array of Italianate architecture. Bronwen had glanced over Pizzala's other patrons because of a vague feeling that she was being watched. The restaurant had been crowded, though, and the tables placed close together, making it hard to conduct a search with only a casual look. She'd recognized no one. Later, after "father and daughter" had arrived at the Campbell House hotel, Dowling said he needed to do some paperwork and would see her next at breakfast. It then was still late afternoon. Bronwen dawdled in the hotel lobby, deliberating as to what an experienced Pinkerton operative would do—if there had been one left in Montgomery. Since there wasn't, this could be her opportunity to show Allan Pinkerton she could handle more than mere traveling around in trains with aging railroad investors.

When she had left the hotel, the sense of being followed became even stronger. On the way to the Winter Building she turned several times, but Commerce Street held a goodly amount of people, not one of whom appeared the least interested in her. She tried to shrug off her misgivings by conjecturing what Pinkerton would instruct. Undoubtedly he would tell her to first try to determine if she *was* being followed, and then by whom, and then, if possible, for what reason. Why would anyone spy on an innocent-looking, albeit falsely so, young woman? Discarding the obvious—she didn't think any Southern man would be so crude as to proposition her on a public street in broad daylight—the answer could be connected to the fate of the other Pinkerton agents, as Guy Seagram had insisted. Since that proved to be a thoroughly unpleasant line of reasoning, Bronwen bolstered her nerves by reminding herself that she was the only agent left to discover what really had happened to the others. And to learn what Equus meant. Thus earning Pinkerton's respect rather than a boot out the door of his agency.

She now continued on down Commerce, passing the grand Exchange Hotel, where the visiting politicians stayed, and the several bookstores beneath it, and on past the dozen or so of Montgomery's clothier shops. Although she glanced into plate-glass windows for the reflection of a follower, and spotted no one, her suspicion persisted.

Stepping into Giovanni's Confectionery, she stood just inside the door to look searchingly up and down the street until the smell of chocolate made her mouth water. As the gaze of the proprietor seemed to question her loitering in his shop, she felt obliged to purchase a small box of chocolate-covered pecans before she left. It was not exactly a hardship.

Although dusk had begun to gather, the city's gas lamps would soon give light, and determined to conquer her apprehension, Bronwen walked to the triangular area perversely called Court Square. The decorative iron fence surrounding the basin formed by the artesian wells shone with a coat of fresh black paint. The wells, she'd been told, had been there since the beginning of time. They supplied water to Creek Indians and Spaniards and French before the arrival of Virginians and Georgians and Carolinians joining the westward movement of the infant republic. And now, while no longer the main source of the city's water, they bubbled forth into the "Cradle of the Confederacy."

A scuffed dirt area next to the basin held the city's slave-auction block. Even when not in use it stood as a stark monument to the empire of King Cotton.

Across the street reared the facade of the Lehman Brothers store, whose several-story building stocked a complete line of dry goods. Henry, the oldest Lehman brother, had emigrated from Bavaria and was among the first Jewish settlers in the city. He'd come through the port of Mobile, set himself up with a wagonload of merchandise, and worked his way along the Alabama River to Montgomery, opening the Commerce Street dry goods store several years later. Joined by his two brothers, the Lehmans began bartering cotton-made goods for raw cotton, and were now among southern Alabama's largest cotton merchants. And had recently expanded their operations to New York City. Everyone, everywhere, it seemed, wanted Southern cotton.

Alabama's big plantations were in the southern part of the state within the broad band of dark rich soil known as the "black belt"; here grew what some said was the world's finest cotton. That morning, as the Dowling carriage had driven to the Osgood plantation, Bronwen had passed fields of homely, woody shrubs with spreading branches and broad, lobed leaves. Now, staring at the slave-auction block, she had to question whether these unimpressive-looking plants were reason enough to start a war. No matter how simpleminded that notion might appear to others—namely Southern politicians—to her it essentially rang true.

A murmur of voices behind her made her whirl to see several slavewomen toting buckets to the wells. The sight of the women brought her to consider what the Montgomery Negroes thought of secession; in this city of near nine thousand people, more than half were slaves. She imagined the irony of the immense flag fluttering from the alabaster dome of the Capitol building must not be lost on them: made by the white ladies of Montgomery, the flag showed a goddess of Liberty with a sword in her hand. The reverse side had the state seal, a cotton plant, and a rattlesnake.

"Are y'all sight-seein', or just ponderin' the state of the universe?"

The throaty-voiced question came from Bronwen's left. With a start of surprise, she spun to see the violet-eyed young woman she had met briefly in the Concert Hall ladies' parlor. The woman stood beside a three-legged wooden apparatus, and looped over her arm was what looked like a milliner's measuring tape.

"A little of both," Bronwen answered, the relief of seeing a familiar face bringing a spontaneous grin. "How nice to meet again. But what on earth is *that?*" She pointed to the three-legged object.

"Tripod. Holds a camera—when there's one around." The woman walked toward Bronwen and held out her hand, trailing the measuring tape behind her. "I'm Zoe Martin, and it's nice meetin' *you* again, even if y'are a Yankee." An impish smile warmed the qualification.

"And I'm Br— Excuse me," Bronwen said, coughing to cover her slip, although it seemed absurd to carry the impersonation into a chance meeting with someone she would likely never see again. But Allan Pinkerton's cold eyes flashed before her. She gave her name as *Jane Dowling.*

Then took a quick breath when Zoe Martin, looking around them, asked, "Are you with your railroad daddy?"

Bronwen shook her head, while her stomach clenched. How did this woman know that her "father" was in railroads—or know anything at all about her? And now she could visualize Pinkerton's scowling face.

"Guess you wonder how I know *that?*" Zoe said, laughing. Bronwen's expression must have been answer enough, because the young woman added, "In some ways, Montgomery's a very small town. Word gets 'round real fast when there's an allurin' Yankee woman to speculate on. I 'magine half the men in this city know who you are by this time."

She laughed again, and Bronwen felt her tension ease. "Well, you know more about me than I do you," she said. "May I ask what you're doing with that tripod thing?"

"Testing possible sites—what can be seen from where." Zoe lifted her arm with the looped tape measure. "And I'm measuring off some distances for a photographer—A. C. McIntyre. Heard of him?"

Bronwen shook her head. "Sorry, but I haven't been in Montgomery long. A. C. McIntyre you said?"

Zoe grinned. "The *A*'s for Archibald—I don't know what the *C* stands for, but maybe it's something just as bad. He's married to my cousin, and I'm doing some work for him. I'm hoping he'll hire me permanently when all the political to-do here is over. Not that a woman—a *white* woman—like me is supposed to be doing physical work. But this photography is so new, seems like nobody's yet figured out we females aren't strong enough, or smart enough, to do it." The ready, impish grin blossomed again.

The infectiousness of her good humor made Bronwen laugh, and she nodded. "Why do you need to measure?"

"Mostly it's to figure out distance and light—how close Mr. McIntyre needs to be to the subject. Inside his studio here on Market Street is one thing, but he wants to take more photographs of the Capitol building before President Davis's inauguration. I don't know what time of day he wants to use. 'Course I hope it'll be high noon, when the light's the best."

"And will you be allowed to assist?"

"Oh, I'll have the glamorous privilege of toting the equipment—bottles of chemicals, the precious box of glass plates,
probably this tripod . . ." Zoe broke off, then said, "Look,
I'm done here for now. Have to go to the Capitol itself
next—if you haven't seen it close up, why don't you come
with me?"

Why not? Bronwen realized she hadn't even thought of
her phantom follower since she'd so serendipitously met
Zoe Martin. Perhaps too serendipitously, in which case she
should try to find out more, so Pinkerton would say.

By the time they'd trudged up the slope of Market Street,
eating chocolate-covered pecans and lugging the unwieldy
tripod between them, Bronwen had not learned much more
about the woman. Except that Zoe Martin was clearly not a
typical Alabama female. And she talked not of herself, but
of photography—with passion. "Y'all have some women
photographers up north I hear of," she said as they climbed
the broad steps of the Capitol to its front portico. " 'Course
you have lots of things we don't have down here—by we, I
mean women."

"From what little I've seen, I'd guess that's true," Bronwen agreed slowly. She was still disturbed over her earlier
slip of the tongue, and intended to be cautious. Although she
intuitively liked Zoe Martin, she didn't quite trust her. Two
chance encounters with this attractive young woman within
twenty-four hours certainly might be coincidence, even if
Zoe's explanation of how she knew about Dowling seemed
a shade too pat. But it did make sense. Bronwen decided she
was becoming as skeptical as the rest of Pinkerton's agents.

And yet, she could almost see the bearded detective's nod
of approval when she reminded herself that *two of those
agents were dead.*

•   •   •

A half hour later, Bronwen took her leave of Zoe Martin and the graceful, chastely white Capitol. And by that time she'd learned that Zoe's uncle, Joshua Martin, had been the twelfth governor of Alabama, and the one to move the capital city from Tuscaloosa to Montgomery. Zoe herself had attended a boarding school in Maryland, where she had, as she put it, "picked up some abolitionist notions" that made her family rue their decision to send her north.

"Baltimore's probably not your idea of 'North,'" Zoe had said, "but believe me, compared to the Deep South of Alabama, it might as well be Hudson Bay."

When they'd headed back down Market Street, dusk darkening the sky, Zoe had offered to walk with Bronwen back to the Campbell House. But as night had fallen the city had lit up. Houses glowed from candles in holders tacked to window frames. The gas street lamps blazed. And in every quarter bonfires burned, kept aflame by men and boys who added wads of cotton and boxes and barrels of pine wood soaked in turpentine.

"Thank you, anyway," Bronwen told her, "but I can't possibly get lost."

Shadows concealed Zoe's face, but her voice sounded uncharacteristically grave when she said, "You'd best be careful, all the same. There's some here who're just spoilin' for trouble." She paused and seemed to consider something, then moved closer to Bronwen and added in a whisper, "You take care now, you hear? Watch you don't get caught in the middle of something you don't understand." She broke off, then gave Bronwen an odd, wistful half-smile before she walked away in the opposite direction.

From the Alabama River came the sudden, shrill blast of a steamboat whistle. Startled, Bronwen glanced around her, and again had the unsettling sensation that she was being observed. She exhaled sharply and decided weariness could be at least partly to blame for her skittishness. A good night's sleep would set her to rights.

She walked briskly toward the hotel, defying her phantoms and refusing to look back. When she arrived at the Campbell House, only a handful of men occupied the lobby. The South Carolinian proprietor, J. D. Campbell, was standing behind the desk, deep in conversation with reporter Cormac Quinn. Bronwen thought she heard the word "Baltimore" several times, and as she walked across the lobby, Campbell seemed to give her a more than cursory glance. Perhaps the comings and goings of Thaddeus Dowling and "his daughter" were creating speculation. With a sassy smile tossed at Campbell—let him think what he wished—she headed for the back staircase.

She was stopped by Campbell himself, who'd come out from behind the desk and now said loudly, "Miss Dowling, may I have a word?"

Oh, Lord; did the man think she'd been flirting with him? Bronwen sighed and struggled against fatigue, positioning a glassy noncommittal smile while Campbell approached her. Then, without warning, she was pushed aside by another man sprinting for the stairs. She didn't even have time to see his face before he dashed past.

After regaining her balance and staring in annoyance at the figure running up the stairs, she turned back to the hotel owner. "Yes, what is it, Mr. Campbell?"

"My dear Miss Dowling, your father has informed me— just now when he went out for his usual airing—that you'll both be leaving us tomorrow. What a shame you'll not be here for the pre-inaugural festivities."

Not only surprised to hear this, Bronwen also felt some irritation at not being informed of Dowling's change of plans. Since she didn't want Campbell to see it, she said quickly, "Yes, I'm disappointed, but Father has other business." As she spoke, Bronwen stifled a yawn and began to wonder why this sudden attention from the hotel owner. And what was that he'd said about Dowling going out "for his usual airing"? She hadn't been aware he'd been in the habit of leaving the hotel at night. Why would he?

Campbell seemed about to comment, but Bronwen interrupted him. "And now you must excuse me, Mr. Campbell. I've had such a long day, I really must get some rest. Good evening." Before he could say more, she smiled, turned, and went to the stairs.

When she reached the door at the top of the stairwell that opened onto the second-story corridor, she paused with her hand on the knob. "Always look around before you proceed!" Pinkerton had warned repeatedly. "Don't let yourself be surprised when you least expect it."

Most of the time Bronwen either forgot or ignored this, but tonight she paid attention: she'd heard the sound of a nearby door closing. When she cautiously peered into the corridor, all she saw was the back of a dark-haired man as he hurried down the hall, clutching a large wickerwork carry-all. Would that her own luggage were so lightweight, she thought, reaching into her purse for the brass room key.

Stepping from the warm corridor into her room, she felt an unexpected chill. The window must have been left open. When she crossed the room to check it, though, she found it latched securely. But before she lit the oil lamp on the bureau next to the bed, she pinched the wick, and found it still warm. Her earlier feeling of uneasiness returned. Then she looked toward the bed and sighed with relief; the maid must have just been there, to put a warming pan under the bedclothes. Bronwen could see its rounded hump beneath the coverlet.

She realized, again, how tired she was, and stripped off her clothes to wriggle into a flannel nightdress, then unlaced and removed her shoes. After washing in the porcelain basin on the commode—which also held a chamber pot—she began shivering with either cold or fatigue, and sank onto the edge of the bed. The top of the coverlet had been turned down, and she was just about to slide underneath to the waiting warmth, when she remembered the lamp. It was still burning on the bureau.

"Rats!" She jumped up, making the mattress bounce. It was then, out of the corner of her eye, that she saw the warming pan move. At least the hump it made had moved. Moved in a faint rippling motion.

No, she must have imagined it. That, or her eyes were playing tricks; she *was* exhausted. She took a firm step toward the bed, and stopped. The hump had moved *again,* and this time she was sure. But it wasn't possible.

While she stared fixedly at the coverlet, Bronwen bent down and pressed the foot of the bed, releasing it quickly to make the mattress bounce again. And then she heard it. An unmistakable buzzing sound, muffled somewhat by the coverlet but distinctive all the same.

She stood in rigid disbelief. But she'd heard the sound often enough, from the bridge over Rochester's Genesee River gorge. A gorge where at the bottom, sunning themselves on the warm rocks, lay hundreds of rattlesnakes.

For several seconds she just stood there, watching the bed, fear making her immobile. It couldn't be: a snake could *not* be in her bed. Not in a hotel room. The maid had just been there. Unless . . . Unless it had not been a maid. Very slowly, and carefully, she took a step toward her shoes with a mute curse at her carelessness. Because she'd been tired, she hadn't remembered to place the stiletto beside her pillow as she usually did, and she'd kicked her shoes under the bed.

When she began to bend down, the coverlet rippled again.

From beneath it thrust a scaly triangular head, slithering out over the pillows, the forked tip of its tongue darting in and out of its mouth. The dark, diamond-shaped blotches on its back were unfamiliar to her—the rattlesnakes of New York State had brown bands—but she had no doubt it was a rattler. At the moment the rattles were silent. Bronwen didn't know if this was a good sign or not.

She did know how fast a rattler could strike. And this one, still sliding out from under the coverlet in smooth serpentine motions, had already exposed a length of some four or five feet. One that big could move like lightning. And Bronwen had somewhere heard that the larger the snake the more venom it produced. She was afraid to shift a muscle, even to swallow the bile in her throat, and yet she couldn't just stand there. If the snake left the bed and started to slither toward her, she knew she couldn't bear to stand still. Somehow, she had to reach her stiletto.

She glanced down to where the toe of a shoe, she couldn't tell which one, protruded from under the bed. But it might be its mate that held the knife, and that one could be farther away. How much time would she have to search for it before the snake struck? Maybe she shouldn't do anything; simply wait to see if the creature would go back to the heat of the warming pan. But this did not seem likely, as it now undulated—all six feet or more of it—across the coverlet toward her.

Bronwen took a gulp of air, clenched her teeth and dove for the floor. On her hands and knees, she grabbed the closest shoe, her fingers fumbling for the stiletto. The shoe was empty. While she groped desperately under the bed for the other, she began to hear above her an ominous buzzing. The shoe—where *was* it? Then her outstretched fingertips brushed it. She lunged forward, plunged her hand into the shoe and yanked out the stiletto, snatching off the sheath.

But now she couldn't see the snake. She rolled toward the opposite wall and as she pulled herself into a crouch, the rattler's fanged head appeared, just above her at the foot of the bed. It had wound most of its length around the bedpost and now its head reared back, ready to strike.

Bronwen, precariously balanced with every muscle in her body straining, flung the stiletto as hard as she could, and fell backward against the wall.

The snake flailed furiously, the stiletto nailing its head to the bedpost. Its rattles vibrated louder than cracking bones. Breathing hard, Bronwen crawled toward the window and went up on her knees to open it, hoping the fresh air would keep her from vomiting. Her nausea gradually receded, sometime after the snake had stopped writhing. She tried to get to her feet and found that her legs refused to hold her.

When she was finally able to stand, she dragged the stuffed wing-back chair to the window, turning it so she wouldn't face the thing hanging from the bedpost. The rattler was as big around as a man's wrist and, in fact, since she'd had little time to aim the stiletto precisely, it was the snake's very size that had allowed her to hit it. Something that large must carry a deadly amount of poison.

She didn't want to speculate from where the snake might have come; although now, remembering the wickerwork carry-all that she'd seen being taken down the corridor, she didn't have to think too hard. All the same, she wished she could somehow convince herself it was coincidence; that the snake had somehow found its way into her room and into her bed by some strange accident.

She couldn't do it.

Without much imagination, anyone could see it had been staged. The room was cold when she had entered because, as she'd thought at the time, the window had recently been open, ensuring that when the snake was placed in the bed it would remain there, coiled around the warming pan. If she'd not forgotten to put out the lamp, she would have climbed under the coverlet completely unaware of what awaited her.

She considered going to the next room to tell Thaddeus Dowling. Then she recalled J. D. Campbell saying that Dowling had left the hotel, even though he had earlier told Bronwen he had work to do. Stop it right there, she told herself: Dowling couldn't possibly be involved in *this!* Why would he? And it had been Campbell who delayed her downstairs. Had it been just innocent chitchat, or had he been giving whoever was in her room time to get out, being warned by the man who had dashed up the stairs?

The safest course was probably to stay put. If she didn't leave the room, whoever was behind this might think the rattler had done its job. Then maybe she could make it through the night with relative safety. Maybe.

Bronwen peered around the chair at the snake's body. She had to reclaim her stiletto. There would be no sleep tonight, because after she worked up the nerve to pull the knife from the bedpost, she would sit in this chair, armed, until morning. Where was Pinkerton's "soft assignment"? She had not bargained for this! She'd had visions of tracking criminals, of bringing them to justice as Cullen Stuart did, but she had never considered that she herself might be the one hunted.

Gritting her teeth, she reluctantly sidled toward the bedpost. Only by tugging and twisting the stiletto—while the dead snake whipped around her arms—did she manage to retrieve it. The snake had meanwhile dropped to the floor, and she realized that she had to do something with it. She couldn't stand to leave it there all night. And even if she could, what about a poor unsuspecting maid that came in the morning to clean?

After she'd speared the snake with the stiletto, she carried it at arm's length to the window and, about to drop it to the street below, stopped. She wanted whoever had done this to think, at least until morning, that the venom had worked. No. Too bad. She could not stand the thought of spending the night with this thing. Besides, since a rattlesnake graced the state flag, it must not be a particularly rare sight in Alabama. So who cared if next morning the street sweepers got a nasty shock. She dropped the snake.

Next she struggled with the bureau, and finally succeeded in pushing it against the door. Then, lowering herself into the chair, she sat there rigidly, stiletto clenched in her hand.

Maybe in the morning she could see things more clearly. Figure out why someone would want to kill her or, at the very least, nearly frighten her to death. If she'd had any lingering doubts about the deaths of Arthur Kelly and Ann Clements, about whether they'd been accidents, the doubts had vanished. Two Pinkerton agents were dead. She herself apparently was a target. Guy Seagram had warned her to be careful, and the warning had been linked to the conversation she'd overheard about Equus. If she was being hunted because of it, she clearly needed to find out what Equus meant. And why knowledge of it was so dangerous. In the meantime, a long night lay ahead.

10

It was necessary to close up our home and abandon all we had watched over for years, before going to Montgomery; our library, which was very large and consisted of fine well-chosen English books, was the hardest to relinquish of all our possessions.

—Varina Howell Davis,
Jefferson Davis: A Memoir by His Wife

Although the night had proved to hold no further threat, the next morning at breakfast Bronwen's eyes burned from lack of sleep. Thaddeus Dowling, seated across the table with his head buried in a newspaper, didn't seem to notice. By daybreak she had begun to wonder if her sanguine trust in Dowling the night before might have been misplaced. And since she was supposed to travel with him to Atlanta, and then on to Chicago, it seemed foolhardy to ignore misgivings, no matter how preposterous they appeared.

She waited until he'd folded up the paper and reached for his coffee. "Did you enjoy the night air last evening?" Bronwen smiled, an unassuming, virtuous smile, she hoped. Subtlety had never been her strong suit.

Dowling's hand seemed to hesitate over his coffee cup before he picked it up, saying, "I worked until late—no night air for me."

"Oh, I thought Mr. Campbell said you'd gone out. He must have mistaken you for someone else."

Dowling looked at her obliquely. "Yes, he must have been mistaken. I was in my room all night."

Although she couldn't know for certain, she thought he was lying; it was the way his eyes slid away from hers when he'd spoken. Ordinarily, Thaddeus Dowling gave the impression of being a straightforward man. If deception was uncommon for him, then why had he adopted it now—especially when hers was such an innocuous question?

But obviously she'd get no explanation, and the smile she held was beginning to make her cheeks ache. She excused herself and pushed away from the table. When she started to rise, a voice from directly behind stopped her.

"Good morning, my dear, and you, Mr. Dowling. I was told I'd find you here at breakfast. May I have a word?"

Bronwen looked up into the sharp black eyes of Colonel Dorian de Warde. She glanced over at Dowling, who seemed surprised by de Warde's arrival, although he quickly gestured at an empty chair. "Of course, do sit down, Colonel. Sit down."

The look Dowling now sent Bronwen made it plain that she should tactfully fade away. Which was not going to happen. She was curious about de Warde, about what brought him here this morning, and she had no intention of leaving unless actually ordered to do so. Acting as if she hadn't seen Dowling's signal, she beckoned to the waiter for more coffee as de Warde seated himself. The waiter looked shocked. Another gaffe, Bronwen told herself; Southern women must not publicly beckon.

De Warde smiled pleasantly at Bronwen before remarking, "I'm told you are departing Montgomery today. In which case"—de Warde now turned to Thaddeus Dowling—"I'm delighted to have caught you before you left. I have a modest proposition which I hope you will consider."

Dowling's bushy eyebrows raised slightly. "By all means."

"I've been thinking about the conversation at Colonel Pollard's yesterday," the Englishman explained, "and it occurred to me that we might be able to do each other a favor, Mr. Dowling. Since I'm aware that your time is short, let me be direct. I should like to purchase your shares in the Montgomery and West Point Railroad."

"Really," said Thaddeus Dowling, clearly startled by this development. "How very interesting."

How very fortunate, thought Bronwen. Dowling had been more than troubled after yesterday's meeting, as he had fully anticipated a similar offer from Osgood. That Dowling hadn't received it was likely a fair indication that Lucas Osgood expected imminent confiscation of the railroad. But now, it seemed, Dowling was about to be delivered from such a substantial monetary blow. Fortunate, indeed. But why?

"I am concerned about your railroad—that it remain in operation," de Warde explained. "As you've no doubt realized, I represent commercial interests in Great Britain that are troubled by this threat of war and a potential interruption of cotton to British mills. As you may not know, my dear Mr. Dowling, last year most of the South's three and a half million bales of cotton were shipped to Liverpool. The railroad in question is a crucial link to the Atlantic ports, especially Charleston. Please permit me to be blunt, Mr. Dowling. British interests may well stand a better chance of negotiating with the Confederate States about this rail line's operation than do you, a Northerner."

And Dowling readily nodded his agreement. Bronwen had heard him try yesterday to convince Osgood of this same point, but the man seemed reluctant to accept it. Or, perhaps, the man was simply too worried about his own investment.

"I would be willing to consider an offer," Dowling said now. "A reasonable offer."

Bronwen marveled at the man's bravado, since he was, so to speak, over a barrel on this. But Thaddeus Dowling then proved that he was shrewder, if somewhat less patriotic, than she'd credited him.

"I'll also be blunt, Colonel de Warde," he went on. "I know the Confederate States desperately want their sovereignty recognized by Britain. Indeed, if it comes to war, they would no doubt want rather more than recognition. So the Montgomery and West Point Railroad could become very useful as a bargaining tool, could it not? The Confederate government, for example, might agree to allow the railroad exclusive, unlimited access to transport the cotton you and your countrymen need—in return for British arms. I think you follow what I'm saying."

Colonel de Warde didn't even blink. "I believe we understand each other, Mr. Dowling."

After a moment's silence, Bronwen realized that both men were giving her a look that said their negotiations required privacy. "If you gentlemen will excuse me," she murmured, rising from her chair and bringing them to their feet, "I need to finish packing and run some errands before we leave Montgomery."

"Train departs at eleven," Dowling stated. "Make sure you're back here at the hotel by ten."

"Perhaps it's best if I simply meet you at the train station," she told him. "I'll have my baggage sent on ahead." He seemed about to object, so Bronwen quickly added, "I'll be at the station in plenty of time." She said a hasty goodbye to Colonel de Warde, then walked briskly toward the lobby, grateful that she'd had the wits to give herself some additional time, as well as the opportunity *not* to leave Montgomery if she so chose. That choice would depend upon what she might learn now.

She'd seen J. D. Campbell standing near the front desk, talking with Cormac Quinn as he'd been the night before. Campbell faced the entrance door, and as Bronwen went through the lobby archway, she scanned the room to see how she could come up behind the two men unobserved. She swerved to stand behind a tall potted palm.

Their voices were low, and she could only catch an occasional innocuous-sounding word here and there; innocuous until Cormac Quinn said, ". . . wait and see *Baltimore* . . ."

His voice faded and Bronwen leaned forward, the palm fronds scratching her cheeks.

". . . not what the others said about it. But you're going to Atlanta *today?*" That had been J. D. Campbell.

And then words too low to hear until ". . . activities of the Maryland delegation and . . ." Cormac Quinn broke off as the palm fronds had apparently waved too strenuously.

Bronwen stepped forward quickly. "Good morning, Mr. Campbell," she said cheerily, "and to you, Mr. Quinn."

If either man was surprised to see her—see her alive, that was—he didn't show it, though she might already have been seen in the restaurant. That being the case, she wondered if she ran the risk of another species of local wildlife—a scorpion, say, or a venomous spider—being introduced into her baggage.

"Indeed, it's a fine morning," Cormac Quinn agreed. "We were just saying that the weather should permit good viewing of the parade tonight. Unfortunately, I am called elsewhere. As I hear you are yourself."

Why would a reporter leave now—at the height of the political season there in Montgomery?

J. D. Campbell, after glancing at Quinn and nodding, said, "Will you be checking out, Miss Dowling?"

"Yes, and I'll want some help with my baggage, Mr. Campbell, so please send someone up in thirty minutes. I'll need a carriage as well. Just put it on Mr. Dowling's bill," Bronwen finished airily, and headed for the stairs.

"Miss Dowling, a moment please?" Cormac Quinn had taken a few strides after her. Bronwen stopped for a deep breath. "I couldn't help seeing you," Quinn continued, "at the table in there with those gentlemen—" he bobbed his head toward the restaurant "—and wondered if railroads were being discussed. Your father is a large investor in rail companies, I understand. Anything interesting said?"

"Interesting, Mr. Quinn?"

"Yeah, you know—anything I can use. Something newsworthy."

"I have no idea what you would consider newsworthy," she answered. "I suggest, if you want information, that you ask *them*." She smiled sweetly and went on to the stairs. She could feel Quinn's eyes following her. So he was going to Atlanta, was he?

After opening the door to the second-floor corridor, she looked up and down the hall before starting for her room. But she froze in place when the room's door swung slowly open. Someone was inside.

With a cold surge of fury, Bronwen ducked back into the exit doorway. How *dare* they make another attempt—in broad daylight? The sheer arrogance of it wiped all else from her mind as she bent to her shoe. This time she would not accept it quietly. She straightened, ready to hurl the stiletto at whoever came through the door, and waited.

An elderly Negro woman emerged into the corridor, carrying towels and bed linen. Bronwen, sighing with relief, replaced the stiletto and went forward. "Excuse me," she said, approaching the woman, "but are you the one who put the warming pan in my bed last night?"

The woman's deeply lined, walnut-brown face immediately assumed a blank expression. She shook her head and stared at the floor. "No, ma'am, not me."

"Oh, I'm sorry," Bronwen said, too late recognizing her error, "if you think I'm blaming you for something. I'm not, please believe me. I just meant to thank you for your kindness—it was a cold night."

At this the woman raised her eyes slightly to focus on Bronwen's chin, and gave a brief nod. "Yes, ma'am."

"So you did bring the warming pan?"

"No, ma'am."

"Would you know who did?"

A shrug. "Maybe Lucy."

"Lucy—is she the night maid on this floor?"

"Sometimes."

"I see," Bronwen said, angry with herself for making the woman too frightened to tell her anything. "Do you know," she tried again, "if Lucy was working last night?"

Shaking her head, the woman took a step backward. Bronwen decided she wasn't getting anywhere with this, other than to further distress the woman. "I apologize if I startled you," she said, then added, "I'm just checking out."

As she anticipated, the woman's face showed unmistakable relief, and she nodded rapidly, almost as rapidly as she moved away.

Bronwen sighed, recognizing the hollow feeling she always had when dealing with slaves. She again told herself that slavery didn't concern her one way or the other. Besides, every white Southerner she'd met told her slaves were treated well, and that those who insisted otherwise were either ignorant or rabble-rousers. The Negroes in the South were content under slavery: they were fed, housed, and clothed far better than they would be otherwise.

Bronwen wanted to believe this. She hadn't joined Pinkerton's to involve herself in the abolition dispute. But she couldn't avoid asking why, if the slaves were contented, did so many try to escape? Rochester saw scores every year, running North with the help of the Underground Railroad. If they were treated so well, why did they often act dispirited, or frightened, like the hotel maid?

She wouldn't think about it. In a few hours she could leave Montgomery and, soon after that, leave the South altogether. Besides, she had worries greater than political ones. Someone had tried to kill her and could well try again. The only comforting aspect she could find lay in—as Pinkerton would put it—the *modus operandi*. A rattlesnake bite would've looked accidental, as with the Arthur Kelly and Ann Clements assaults. Which might mean she wouldn't be shot, strangled, or stabbed—not in public, at least. Not that this reasoning provided all that much comfort.

She looked up and down the corridor after readying the key. Turning back to the door, she began to insert it, only to have the door swing open on its own. It occurred to her that the maids might often forget to lock up after themselves, in which case anyone could gain entry. No wonder the one she'd just questioned acted frightened. She'd no doubt be punished if Bronwen complained. Of course complaining was out of the question; she didn't need any more attention drawn to herself. Better to just leave.

Stepping inside, she looked behind the door before scanning the rest of the room, her eyes coming to rest on the baggage she'd packed during the sleepless night. She looked at the lock again. Just what might have been added to her bags since she left for breakfast? Using a wooden coat hanger, she cautiously lifted the lids of her trunk and hatboxes.

When nothing slithered, crawled, or jumped out, and although she'd pretty much expected it—the obvious not being a signature of this killer—she sank into the wing chair with gratitude.

The soft knock instantly brought her to her feet. "Who is it?" she called, darting to the door and flattening herself against the wall behind it.

"Y'all wanted help?"

Stiletto ready, she inched the door open a crack, and felt only slightly foolish when it proved to be the man sent up for her baggage.

Bronwen shifted her feet impatiently while she waited in line at the Southern Telegraph Company. She'd had no idea there would be so many people sending wires from Montgomery, although she should have guessed given the political furor there. Glancing at the clock, she winced: ten-thirty. The train departed at eleven. She should abandon this now. Leave, and instead send a telegram from Atlanta. Provided she ever got to Atlanta. She was finding that she very much wanted to leave Montgomery. Looking at the clock again, she debated. All right, five more minutes.

The woman ahead of her in line abruptly backed up, the expanse of her hoop skirt forcing Bronwen to do the same, thus stepping directly into the person behind her. When she turned to apologize, the stony-faced, well-dressed man said nothing. He just stared coldly at some point over her head; the first time in Montgomery she'd been treated less than cordially. The man must be a Yankee.

Five minutes later the woman ahead of her finally reached the telegraph clerk. Another glance at the clock made Bronwen so anxious she could hardly stand still, muttering, "Hurry up!" under her breath. The clerk looked extremely boyish; if he was new to this, no wonder things were taking so long. But then her way was clear. She rushed forward to the harassed-looking clerk, saying, "A wire to Seneca Falls, New York," and leaned on the counter to write. Her pencil flew over the telegraph form, but when she'd finished the clerk took forever to figure the cost. And then he began to apologize for the delay.

"Yes, yes, it's all right," she told him, rooting in her purse for money.

She all but threw her coins to the clerk, then whirled toward the door, so intent on leaving she didn't see the man behind her spring forward. He brought his hand down flat on her telegram, holding it in place while he rapidly scanned the message. Then, without even a glance at the bewildered clerk, he swiftly moved away.

Before Bronwen hurried out of the telegraph office, she looked again at the time: ten forty-five. Fifteen minutes to reach the station. She dashed down the stairs of the Winter Building and out to the corner of Court Street. Looking frantically around for a hack, she thanked whatever premonition had made her send her baggage on ahead. Where were all the omnibuses that usually crowded the streets? It seemed inconceivable that not a single one was in sight!

She lifted her skirts and began to run down Court Street toward the railroad depot, searching wildly for a carriage and knowing full well that on foot she would never make the train in time. How could she have been so stubbornly stupid as to wait at the telegraph office? Pinkerton was probably right to think she would foul everything up. And now, besides feeling incompetent, she began to feel scared. As she fought a feeling of helplessness, one of Montgomery's many dogs, scratching itself in the road, sent a spray of dust into her face. Blinded, and forced to stop and wipe her eyes, Bronwen heard hoofbeats slow, then halt alongside her.

"Need a ride?" called a familiar voice. She turned to see

a Montgomery Omnibus Company hack. Smiling at her from behind the driver was Jules Falconer.

"Oh, yes; please!"

Falconer immediately jumped down when she added, "I need to reach the rail station by eleven!" Although the driver groaned, Falconer grabbed her by the waist and tossed her onto the carriage seat, then scrambled up beside her.

"An extra half-dollar," he shouted to the driver, "if you get us there in time!"

The offer clearly improving the driver's disposition, he nodded, cracked a whip over the horse, and they took off down Court Street, scattering dogs and chickens and every other living thing in their path.

"You know, it might be better," Falconer shouted over the clatter of wheels, "if you didn't wait until the last minute for these things—like I do."

Bronwen felt such relief she didn't even retort, but laughed and collapsed back against the seat. Then she realized what he'd said. "Are you taking the same train?" she asked. "The one to Atlanta?"

It occurred to her that perhaps she should be wary of him. No, that was absurd. She couldn't be suspicious of everyone. She should be grateful, not suspicious. Still, he had shown up very conveniently. And he never did answer her question.

In a matter of minutes they drew up in front of the two-story Montgomery and West Point depot, located on the bend of the Alabama River. An engine, hauling a six-wheel tender for wood and one passenger car, stood on a crude wooden track, engulfed in clouds of steam. On the nearby siding stood another car for baggage and mail. A small, brass-trimmed car—Bronwen assumed it belonged to rail-road president Colonel Charles Pollard—was being coupled to the passenger car. Thaddeus Dowling had probably insisted on riding in it. And if he had reached an agreement with Colonel de Warde, it would probably be his last ride.

Jules Falconer jumped from the hack and swung Bronwen down, then fished in his frock coat pocket for the driver's pay, while she shouted her thanks and hastened toward the depot. As she neared the entrance door, Thaddeus Dowling appeared, frowning fiercely and waving something at her.

"I have your baggage tickets," he grumbled as she reached him. "Where the devil have you been?"

Bronwen shook her head and apologized, then followed him to the train and, as she'd guessed, the president's car. When she climbed the steps to board, she looked back over her shoulder for Falconer, but a conductor hurried her on into the small, luxuriously appointed car before she could find him.

After a jolt that undoubtedly signaled the baggage car coupling, she settled herself in the wide leather seat for the eighty-some miles to West Point, Georgia. Although exhausted, she felt too keyed up to sleep, and the condition of the rickety wooden tracks made her nervous. Railroad accidents were all too common. But happily, from West Point to Atlanta the tracks would be iron, and in any event she would have to be mad to imagine that the Equus cabalists, just to get at her, would cause a train wreck.

Then, out of nowhere, a memory surfaced: the telegram she'd written. She couldn't remember how she had signed it, and had a blurry remembrance of writing her own name. She couldn't have! Yes, she could. She'd been in such a hurry that she hadn't concentrated on anything but the coded message. She might well have signed her own name. How could she have let herself become so rattled she'd do something that careless? That dangerous! On the other hand, who would see it? Just the clerk and telegraph operator, and they knew nothing about her. But it didn't excuse her error. She had been slack, and her lapse of caution further unsettled her.

She exhaled slowly, trying to loosen the knots in her neck. Glancing around her, she was startled to see Jules Falconer entering the car. Behind him was Cormac Quinn. And his departure still made no sense. Why would a newspaper reporter be leaving Montgomery *now?*

The engine whistle blew shrilly. And as the train slowly started to move forward, Bronwen suddenly spotted something that brought her bolt upright. A man had come rushing from the station and was now running toward the train's passenger car. Just as the engine's whistle shrieked, he put on a burst of speed, and Bronwen, face pressed against the glass, saw him grab for the step railing. Then he disappeared, presumably in the passenger car ahead. As she pulled back from the window, Bronwen felt a chill streak down her spine. She had identified him immediately as the same stony-faced man who had stood behind her at the telegraph office.

Cigar smoke filling the interior of the car made her turn reluctantly back toward the window. Large droplets began to splatter against the dirt-filmed glass; it must have just now begun to rain. Threatening black clouds billowed against the sky and looked as if they were about to descend upon the train like a shroud.

Bronwen burrowed back into her seat, restraining an urge to claw the leather like a trapped animal. She took several deep breaths, straightened her spine, and folded her hands in her lap, then stared out the window at the approaching squall. Reflected in dusky glass, the three men in the railroad car stared back.

She supposed she should at least be grateful that none of them was Guy Seagram. And that she could wire Pinkerton from Atlanta with the results—admittedly obscure—of her lone investigation: that she had uncovered a plot of un-known magnitude, code name Equus; that it likely had cost the lives of two operatives; and that it seemed to be linked, however remotely, to the city of Baltimore. It wasn't much, and Pinkerton would probably be justified in throwing the wire and her, in absentia, out of his office window, but she would send it, anyway.

When she looked toward the windowpane again, the men were still watching her.

II

I like to see it lap the Miles—
And lick the Valleys up—
And stop to feed itself at Tanks—
And then—prodigious step

Around a Pile of Mountains—
And supercilious peer
In Shanties—by the sides of Roads—
And then a Quarry pare

To fit its Ribs
And crawl between
Complaining all the while
In horrid—hooting stanza—
Then chase itself down Hill—

And neigh like Boanerges—
Then—punctual as a star
Stop—docile and omnipotent
At its own stable door—

—Emily Dickinson

11

The votes have been peaceably counted. You are elected.

—telegram to Abraham Lincoln, February 13, 1861

𝕸ary Lincoln watched the red, white, and blue bunting on the railroad car ripple in the morning wind. The colors of it to some, she imagined, might look like rivulets of blood streaked over snow and sky. She was standing on a platform with her husband at the rear of a freshly painted red caboose, listening to him give another speech, in another town, at yet another railroad station. Below them, and in spite of dark threatening clouds, several hundred people had gathered to witness the new President's departure. Mary glanced around at the station house sign to remind herself where they were: "COLUMBUS," it said. Still in Ohio.

The telegram that arrived in late afternoon of the previous day said the electoral vote had been "peaceable." But apparently, according to later wires, the peace had been maintained only by the hundreds of police officers patrolling Pennsylvania Avenue, armed with clubs and revolvers. They had managed to control the angry howling mob outside the Capitol by using their own bodies as flying wedges and moving into the crowd, then carting the ringleaders off to the nearest station house.

The bunting now tossed in a gust of wind. Mary withdrew

one hand from a beaver muff to pull her bright blue wool mantle more tightly around herself; the mantle, long and flared, with fur collar and wide, fringe-trimmed sleeves, was new, fashionable, and beautifully tailored from a design she'd seen in *Godey's Lady's Book*. It had cost a pretty penny. Well spent, however; when Mr. Lincoln had first seen her wearing it, he had raised his eyebrows with a smile of approval. She dressed to please him. And he always noticed. In contrast, he was wearing what he invariably did: his standard lawyer garb of sober black suit, white shirt, black scarf tie, tall silk hat, and boots.

As the wind gusted again, the ribbons of Mary's spoon bonnet whipped against her cheeks. She should have stayed inside the train with her sons, but she'd felt too confined in the passenger car. The air was so close, she had feared she might faint. She knew, though, that her presence on the platform irritated the omnipresent War Department officers surrounding Mr. Lincoln; their displeasure at her unexpected arrival on Tuesday had been all too evident. How dare a lowly *wife* interfere with official plans. Well, that was too bad! She could not be separated from him—she couldn't bear it. Right after his train had left the Springfield station on Monday, she'd rushed home and packed up the boys and the remainder of her own things, then hired a carriage to drive them to the station. The following morning, her train had pulled in directly behind his at the Indianapolis station.

"An inspired present, Molly," Mr. Lincoln had whispered to her. It had been his fifty-second birthday.

He had been so glad to see her, he hadn't even mentioned her defiance of the War Department orders. All he'd said to the four scowling officers was, "Mrs. Lincoln has her own ideas." And then, after he turned the boys over to Mr. Lamon, they'd had a night together in private at the Burnet House hotel. She had felt like a bride. She always did when they were alone. Their attraction for each other remained just as strong as when they'd been courting; the intensity of it had drawn them together, and despite all who tried to pry them apart, it bound them together still.

After that night, though, she had been constantly afraid. Near the Indiana state line, an engineer had spotted an obstruction just ahead on the track. It had been so placed that, if not seen in time, the train would have been derailed. Since then, as a precaution, a pilot locomotive preceded their own. Then, a short distance from Cincinnati, a hand grenade had been discovered on one of the passenger cars. Everyone, especially Mr. Lincoln, had tried to keep her from learning of this, but while she and the other passengers had been made to sit waiting, during what had at first appeared to be an inexplicable inspection of the train, she'd overheard a conversation between two of the War Department officers.

"Looks like somebody's after him," one had said.

"Maybe, but the question is *who?* A secessionist lunatic? Until we know that . . ." The voice had trailed away, but she had heard more than enough.

She demanded the truth from him. And because he never lied to her, he told her the truth, but with reluctance in his dark eyes.

He had ended with, "It's nothing, Molly."

"*Nothing?* You say it's *nothing?*"

He moved his shoulders in that half-shrug, smiling down at her. "Reckon there's some mule-stubborn secessionists rather see themselves hang than have a Republican President. But we can't let them hang themselves, can we?" He chuckled softly and she'd wanted to scream.

Her hands clenched at her sides, she had tried again. "Mr. Lincoln—"

"No more, Molly. We just go on, and we trust the men

who have the job of keeping me alive—foolish as that job may be."

He had reached down and cupped her chin in his large hand. She would get no further.

But this day could bring additional danger. One more stop in Ohio. Then, before they reached Pennsylvania, the train would have to cross a finger of land that belonged to the slave-holding state of Virginia.

Now, to the sound of muted cheers, her husband turned to take her arm and guide her once more inside the train. Back into the passenger car that had begun to resemble a coffin.

12

Any woman who is sure of her own wits is a match at any time for a man who is not sure of his own temper.

—Wilkie Collins, *The Woman in White*, 1860

Glynis Tryon climbed the library steps and turned east onto Fall Street to be met by a bitter wind gusting off the Seneca River. Now late afternoon, the street was almost deserted, and she understood why; the temperature had dropped like a stone in just the past hour. It must be well below freezing, and compared to the recent thaw it felt more like zero. Snowflakes darted in the air to mimic the flight of summer butterflies.

She'd been working alone—Jonathan at home with a cold, undoubtedly consoling himself with the latest Dime Novel—and she should have closed the library sooner. She had intended to, but that was before Zeph came by to drop off the mail. The odd expression he'd worn, when handing her a small package posted from St. Louis, made her place it unopened on her desk; the distinctive square lettering on the package clearly identified Jacques Sundown as the sender. Although Glynis could not quite understand why, Zeph didn't approve of the connection between herself and Jacques. His attitude couldn't stem from the fact that Jacques was Indian—rather, half-Seneca and half-French—

at least she didn't believe so. She'd have thought that, as a Negro, Zeph would have experienced enough bigotry in others to avoid it in himself. So, no; it wasn't that. It most likely involved a misguided loyalty to Cullen Stuart.

After Zeph had gone, she opened the package. There, wrapped in a Missouri newspaper, lay a carved wooden buffalo; small, but with the detail characteristic of Jacques's work. She searched through the wrapping, and found a note. He didn't always include one. Sometimes there would be only the carving: an eagle, a covered wagon, a wild pony, a tiny locomotive; something he'd seen on his treks into the western territories as guide for an occasional wagon train. More common of late, he'd been scouting for railroad companies and their surveyors.

The last time she and Jacques had been together—in the fall of '59, now more than a year ago—Glynis had said: "Please don't just vanish again. You leave for months at a time, and I don't even know whether you're . . . you're still alive. At least let me know *that!*"

He had looked at her for a long time with those gold eyes; eyes of his clan spirit, the wolf. Ordinarily his eyes appeared brown, and only she, he said, could lay bare the gold. As to her request, he'd given her a barely perceptible nod. She hadn't even been sure she'd really seen it, not until the first carving arrived. They came weeks and, on occasion, months apart. But they came.

The note this time had been as brief as usual; Jacques was laconic by nature, even in correspondence. It simply said he'd been hired by the president of the Ohio and Mississippi Railroad, a Major George McClellan, and would shortly be heading for the military installation at—of all places—Harper's Ferry, Virginia. He didn't say why.

A few minutes after she'd read Jacques's note, the telegram arrived.

Now, heading into the wind, Glynis tucked her head into the hooded collar of her green alpaca coat, thankful for the quilted lining made affordable by the new sewing machines. On the other hand, if she hadn't been so worried, she'd be home by now curled up in front of the fireplace with the intriguing new Wilkie Collins novel. Instead, there she was, trudging to Cullen Stuart's office to once again question him about Bronwen. Although Glynis's hands were plunged deep into her coat pockets, her right one could feel the telegram even through gloved fingers.

Abruptly the wind calmed, allowing her to raise her head as she passed the pale green shingles of a dress shop and scrolled black letters on a sign that read *EMMA'S*. It belonged to another of Glynis's nieces, Emma Tryon, daughter of Glynis's brother in Illinois. Emma, who, pursued with intense determination by young Seneca Falls attorney Adam MacAlistair, continued to insist that she didn't have time to marry.

Glynis pushed aside an impulse to stop. Her concern for Bronwen would be all too obvious, and she didn't want to hear Emma's standard comment: "My cousin Bronwen is crazy." This was invariably followed by something like: "Bronwen has always been crazy, Aunt Glynis, and it looks as if she always will be. So what has changed?"

Glynis didn't think Bronwen was crazy. She certainly was *different*, and as unlike the pragmatic Emma as . . . as snowflakes from butterflies. Nor was Bronwen like her soft-spoken older sister Kate. Glynis's three nieces, in fact, had little in common other than a pair of mutual grandparents.

When, after rounding the corner of Fall Street, she headed downhill toward the river, a near-arctic blast took her breath away. Not another storm, she prayed, sniffing the wind. Not again. Eight days before, a northeaster had dropped three feet of snow on the village and collapsed the roof of a church. *Why did anyone live in such a climate?*

Just ahead was the firehouse that held the lockup and the constable's office. When Glynis tugged open Cullen's door, the wind caught it, swinging it out to crash against the brick wall. She was forced to crouch there while the wind rocked her and the door banged into her again and again until Cullen came leaping through the doorway. He pulled Glynis into the office, and dragged the door closed behind them.

"And now you're going to ask why any sane person would live in this weather," he said, pulling out a chair for her opposite his desk.

"I know why, Cullen. It builds character. Or so I'm told, although I notice no one ever says what kind!"

He smiled, leaned back in his chair with hands behind his head, and hoisted his boots to the desktop. When he smiled like that, Glynis thought, he looked not much older than when they first met, years ago. Except for a few streaks of gray in the thick, sand-colored hair and mustache, and a few more lines in the rugged face, Cullen had changed very little. Women still smiled, patting their hair, when he passed.

Warmed by the fire in his cast-iron stove, and soothed by the smell of burning pine, Glynis smiled back at him. They were friends again. By unspoken accord, they never mentioned the darker moments of the past few years, and Glynis wondered if they ever would—or should. But she felt they'd at least regained some of their affection for each other. This did not mean they always saw eye to eye. They never had on some things, Bronwen being one of them.

Finally thawed enough to move without cracking, Glynis reached into her coat pocket. When she withdrew the telegram, Cullen's smile faded.

"Bronwen?"

"Yes, Cullen, and please don't tell me I'm overly concerned, or too imaginative, or whatever else you say when I'm worried about her. Take a look at this."

Handing him the wire, she sat biting her lip as he read it. She already knew it by heart: "RED FOX AWAKE IN SUN STOP MAYBE SHADOW STOP RIDING GRAY HORSE TO SEE ALICE AND GERALD STOP WIRE AGAIN AT NEW SUN STOP BRONWEN."

"Glynis, I hope you understand this better than I do. I assume it's in Bronwen's code—and about the only thing I can decipher is 'Red Fox.' "

"I had to use her decoding key to unravel it. Even then, there's something I don't understand—why did she sign it 'Bronwen'? Isn't she supposed to be posing as Thaddeus Dowling's daughter, Jane?"

"That's what Pinkerton told me. Maybe she just forgot— which, if she's getting careless, is not good. But, Glynis, how many times have I reassured you about her assignment? Pinkerton swore there was nothing to it—that Bronwen's just riding around on trains with Dowling. So why are you worried again? Although—what's this 'shadow' business?"

"It means Bronwen believes she's being followed— 'maybe,' she says."

"Why would she be followed?"

"Cullen! That's what I'm asking *you!* Did Pinkerton mention that he was having her watched to see how she performed?"

He shook his head. "But that doesn't mean he wouldn't do it. In fact, that's probably it exactly, and Pinkerton wants to know if Bronwen's alert enough to pick it up." Cullen looked at the wire again, and now smiled. "What's this 'gray horse' mean—the train?"

"Yes, the iron horse," Glynis sighed, "though the next bit is more obscure. According to Bronwen's decoding key— honestly, Cullen, she is so dramatic—after she uses the word *see*, she will always follow it with the first initial of a

city, and then the state. I'm assuming—because she and
Dowling must be heading north—that 'Alice' translates to
Atlanta, and—"

"And 'Gerald' to Georgia." Cullen grinned.

"I'm afraid I don't find this quite as amusing as you do."
Hadn't her own sister recently said the very same thing to
her? "At any rate, the last part means Bronwen will wire me
again within twenty-four hours."

"Then why worry? You'll hear from her tomorrow,
right?"

"I certainly hope so. What really makes me uneasy,
Cullen, is that 'shadow' reference. I don't believe Bronwen
would concern me without good cause, not knowingly, and
yet she *must* have known that wire would give me every reason to worry."

"You just pointed out yourself how dramatic she can be,"
Cullen responded, although not as quickly as Glynis would
have liked.

"You're worried too, then?"

"No! Not until tomorrow I'm not. Just wait—Bronwen
will wire you that the shadow turned out to be another
Pinkerton agent. Besides, Glynis, be realistic about this.
What could possibly happen to Bronwen when she's on a
train with Thaddeus Dowling? And probably right this
minute he's shepherding her back to Chicago—to deposit
her on the doorstep of the Pinkerton Agency."

Did Cullen really believe that what she wanted was
merely blind reassurance? Intuition told her that Bronwen
was in trouble, but she could imagine what Cullen would
say to *that.* And admittedly, intuition often proved unreliable.

Cullen groaned and swung his feet off the desk. "Look,
Glynis, I know you expect me to do something. Probably
wire Pinkerton, right? Well, I'm not going to do it, and

Bronwen wouldn't want me to, anyway. Pinkerton can't play nursemaid to his agents, and you shouldn't expect him to."

Glynis stifled a retort and instead concentrated on what she wanted to achieve—something she'd learned from the practical Emma. "All right, Cullen, but if I don't hear from Bronwen tomorrow, will you wire Pinkerton then? Please?"

"Glynis . . ." He groaned again.

The trouble was, she had another piece of information, but didn't want to tell Cullen from whom it had come; before he would act on it, though, he would want to know its source. Which was not unreasonable, she had to concede, but it would likely re-create between them more of the strain they had finally overcome.

"I'll try not to worry until tomorrow," she agreed.

"Good. Now, I'll walk you back to your boardinghouse— can't let the wind carry you away." He smiled at her easily, and got to his feet.

A fresh layer of white covered the village. The sky had cleared, and the wind had died, leaving the air crisp and fragrant with the smell of new snow. Two stars were held within the curve of a slim, horned moon.

"Beautiful night," Cullen said. "We'll stop at the livery, and I'll take you home in a sleigh."

Reminding Glynis that Cullen *liked* winter.

By six o'clock the next day, she knew no telegram would come, and she told him so when he came through the library door. "Bronwen *is* in trouble, and please don't dismiss this, Cullen."

"I still think you're alarmed without good cause. Don't you think we would have heard if something had happened to her? Pinkerton would have wired."

"What if Pinkerton doesn't know—and how could he? He's in Chicago."

"He has two other operatives in Montgomery—"

"Cullen," she interrupted, "there's something I haven't told you."

His face became wary. "Like what?"

"I've had a letter from Washington—with some disturbing information."

"I see," came his clipped response. "And I suppose this *letter* was from the Treasury? In any case," he went on, "I suggest you tell me about it."

As he had guessed—and Glynis knew he would—the letter had been sent to her by the head of the Treasury's Special Detective Unit. Rhys Bevan had written her frequently since they had first met, over a year before, when he'd investigated a counterfeiting ring in western New York. Cullen hadn't much liked Rhys Bevan then and, from the current look on his face, didn't like the Welshman any better now. She and Cullen had never discussed this before, and Glynis was certain this would not be a good time to start.

"So, what is it?" Cullen prodded.

"I've been told that a former acquaintance of ours—and one I'd hoped never to hear of again—has returned to America from England."

Cullen's face momentarily went blank. "Who . . . ? Not the Brit . . . not *de Warde!*"

"The same. Just what do you suppose he's up to now?"

"I have no idea. But what could it have to do with Bronwen? Or with you? Unless Treasury, as a matter of policy, routinely keeps you informed of all foreign espionage agents."

Glynis sighed, ignoring the sarcasm. But Bronwen's safety was too important to waste more time pussyfooting around. "Please hear me out, Cullen. Rhys Bevan says that Treasury has been watching Colonel de Warde since he arrived in Baltimore several weeks ago. The assumption, not an unlikely one, is that his arrival means nothing good. Furthermore, he left Baltimore just last week and has been traced to Montgomery, Alabama."

"And so?"

"And so? *Bronwen* is in Montgomery, as you are well aware!"

"Glynis, thousands of people are in Montgomery—as *you* are well aware. Why in hell would you think de Warde's and Bronwen's paths would cross? Even if by some coincidence they did, how could de Warde possibly connect her to you? She's Jane Dowling, remember?"

"The question is," Glynis replied, "does Bronwen remember? She signed her telegram with her own name. And if she simply forgot, as you suggested yesterday, there must have been some good reason for it. Either she was overtired, or in a terrible hurry, or frightened. None of those possibilities makes me any less concerned. Now, will you wire Pinkerton?"

"I'll wire him. But this is the last time, Glynis."

She decided not to tell him, not yet anyway, that she'd already sent her own wire—not to Pinkerton, who would no doubt ignore it, but to Rhys Bevan—asking for more information about Colonel de Warde's activities. She'd also wired two friends who lived below the Mason-Dixon line: Chantal Dupont in Richmond, Virginia, and Meg Fairfax in Dundalk, Maryland, southeast of Baltimore. Glynis had promised Bronwen that she could rely on either woman if she ever found herself in trouble.

Staring up at the familiar ceiling of her library, Glynis knew a decision could not be avoided. If Pinkerton's response to Cullen's wire didn't satisfy her, and if she heard nothing from Bronwen within the next two days, it would be unthinkable to just sit in Seneca Falls and twiddle her thumbs. To say nothing of facing her sister Gwen with this turn of events. No; she would go to Washington and enlist the help of Rhys Bevan's detective unit to locate her niece.

She suddenly found herself wondering how many miles Washington might be from Harper's Ferry.

13

Let us pray that a Caesar or a Napoleon may be sent us. That would be our best sign of success. But they still say no war. Peace let it be, kind Heaven!

—Mary Chesnut, *Diary from Dixie*, February 1861

When the train braked, Bronwen's head jerked violently and her eyes flew open. She had dozed off again. In the past two hours she'd done it several times; how she could possibly fall asleep when she felt so uneasy, and especially since the rickety tracks were jarring enough to topple an elephant? She would suspect she'd been drugged, but she hadn't even drunk any of the coffee offered. On the other hand, she did feel a peculiar security inside the railroad car; she might not trust her fellow passengers, but she didn't believe they could *all* be members of Equus! Thus, there was some safety in numbers. She *had* been exhausted, although this was not an excuse for sleeping that Pinkerton would accept.

She glanced toward the window, but all she could see was a curtain of rain falling over the glass. The murmur of men's voices continued as it had since they'd left Montgomery. It provided a soothing sound over the train clatter and acted much as an opiate. She straightened on the leather seat, determined to remain alert.

". . . and it's the South Carolina fanatics," Thaddeus

Dowling was saying to the others. "They rammed secession down the throats of all the other delegates in Montgomery."

"The delegates *voted* to secede, Mr. Dowling," Cormac Quinn answered, "and they didn't have guns aimed at their heads while they did it."

"But why the all-fired hurry?" Dowling objected. At least he stayed with the weapons metaphor; Bronwen told herself another pointless political debate would put her to sleep again. Then she remembered, the memory not pleasant, that Equus was undoubtedly a political creature. She had better pay attention.

"Why couldn't they go back to their home state legislatures and put it to a vote *there?*" Dowling continued. "Better still, elect delegates to address the issue at a later date—that's what Maryland has done. Those delegates in Montgomery weren't, for the most part, elected by anybody but other secessionist rabble-rousers. And given time, the Southern states might come to realize that Lincoln is not the threat they think he is. Why can't they wait and see what he does?"

"He's a Yankee Republican, isn't he?" The softly voiced question came from Jules Falconer. "Doesn't seem to be much doubt about his position on secession."

"Nobody knows that for certain," Dowling retorted, "so why not wait? Why let South Carolina pull all the strings? They're firebrands. Always have been. And they intimidated the rest of the slave-holding delegates into voting with them."

"It's done. It's over, Dowling," said Quinn. "And now, whether there's war or not depends largely on Lincoln. If he lets the South go in peace—which is all it says it wants . . ." He shrugged, then grimaced at the blast of the locomotive's steam whistle.

"Must be coming into the station, such as it is," Dowling

announced. He looked across the aisle at Bronwen. "Good, you're awake. The train will stop here for fuel and water—better stretch your legs before we head on to Atlanta. But the station house is primitive, you know."

Bronwen knew: that meant no inside privy. And much as she needed to use one, she wanted to remain on the train. When boarding, she'd seen a closet that must hold a commode; although, being designed to accommodate men, it would probably be a tight squeeze with her hoop skirt and petticoats. But that would be preferable to getting soaked in the rain to reach a dirty wooden shack behind the station house, now in view as the train rumbled its way into West Point, Georgia. They were just over the Georgia state line, eighty-eight miles northeast of Montgomery. Close to one hundred south of Atlanta, and another two to three hours travel at best.

As the engine ground to a stop, Bronwen shook her head at Dowling's beckoning gesture. "I'm fine here," she told him. "And I'd rather not get wet."

He seemed to hesitate, then turned toward the door. Bronwen caught the smiles of the three men as they started down the car steps and could imagine what they were thinking: *Just like a woman—afraid her hair will be ruined by a little rainwater*. Fine; let them think what they wanted. She wasn't getting off that car and into some unknown situation, not with the memory of rattlesnakes and two dead agents behind her.

She waited, peering through the window into the rain, until she could see the men, along with passengers from the other car, converging on a small, weatherboarded structure. Then she hurried toward the closet. When she opened its slatted door and saw the tiny space holding a wooden commode chair, she almost gave up. She'd never fit; not and remain as lady-like as the genuine Jane Dowling. Well, so be it. Glancing around to make certain she was alone, she swung her hoop up in an arc in front of her and squeezed backward through the doorway. Then, with her skirts bunched to her chin and the door only inches away, for some reason she thought of her aunt's complaint that women had no voting rights. *Who cares about the vote, Aunt Glyn—demand the right to get us out of these damn skirts!*

When she stood up, holding her petticoats from the floor, she heard footsteps apparently mounting the train stairs. She leaned forward with an eye pressed to the slatted door. The space between the slats was minuscule, allowing only the narrowest range of view, but she thought she saw the flash of metal. An object held in someone's hand? Like a knife, or a gun?

The footsteps came toward the door. Knowing the slightest movement would make her skirts rustle, she held herself still, not even daring to breathe, while her mind raced. In the confined cubicle there was no room to bend over for the stiletto in her shoe. And if she were to burst out the door, what would she meet? She wouldn't have a chance against a revolver, not at such close range. She twisted her head, squinting, and frantically tried to see more through the slim crack as the footsteps came closer.

Then, suddenly, coming from somewhere distant, she heard a shout. Followed by several more. The footsteps stopped. Bronwen heard a short intake of breath, and whoever it was began moving off. The footsteps quickly faded.

Bronwen waited as long as she could stand to, then carefully inched open the door while at the same time reaching for the stiletto. When she emerged from the closet, there was no one in the car. She started for the train steps, refusing to stay alone to be trapped again. Better the rain and the safety in numbers. But reaching the top of the steps she checked herself, hearing Pinkerton's gruff order: *Don't be reckless, Bronwen Llyr! Stop and think!*

Right. It would be nothing short of idiocy to go bounding down the steps in full view of the rattlesnake custodian—now armed with a knife or revolver. She took a quick step back inside the car, looking around for another way out. There had to be an alternative one; not all stations were on the same side of the tracks, were they? She decided they must be, as the only other means of exit, at least on *this* car, seemed to be from the rear platform.

She crept out onto the platform's wooden boards, wincing as they creaked, and looked down at the ground. If she had to jump, she'd probably tangle herself in the cursed skirt and petticoats. And break both legs. She thought a moment, then flipped up her dress skirt and, reaching under it, untied the strings around her waist that held the plain cotton petticoats and the one with a hoop. Stripping them off, she tossed them to the ground below, followed by her soft-brimmed bonnet. She hated it, anyway. Then, standing there for only a moment, she took a deep breath, and jumped into the heap of fabric.

After scrambling to her feet, Bronwen stuffed the petticoats and bonnet under the railroad car without a twinge of regret, and started walking, the train between herself and the station. She had no intention of boarding that train again; not the president's car, at least, and not as Jane Dowling. Her thought was to round the engine ahead. Then she could cross the tracks to the back of the station house. A fine drizzle sprinkled her face—at least it had stopped pouring—and the mist might help to conceal her. She could hear nothing but steam hissing from the engine—so the sudden tug on her sleeve made her heart leap to her throat. She whirled to find a young Negro boy at her side, gesturing for her to stop.

What did he want—or was he a runaway? Bronwen shook

her head to indicate lack of understanding, but the boy cut in front of her, saying loudly, "Please, missie, I got something for you. Please stop."

Bronwen stood there staring at him. Could he be setting her up for some kind of "accident"? She readied herself to grab her stiletto, thinking that, at this point, almost anything was preferable to an ignominious death on a closet commode in West Point, Georgia! Seized by an insane urge to laugh, she clenched her teeth and shook her head again. "Who sent you?" she asked the boy.

"White man sent me—said give this to you," he answered, hauling a scrap of brown paper from a denim trouser pocket.

Bronwen snatched it from him, and turned to shield it from the misty drizzle. Cupping her hand over the scrap she read: *Get the hell out of here. Your life isn't worth a tinker's damn on this train, Red. Head north and tell Pinkerton, look in Maryland for Equus conspirators and trains to Baltimo* The message ended in midword as if Seagram had been interrupted. It *must* have been Seagram—no one else had dared call her *Red* since she'd learned to shoot.

She spun back to the boy, but he'd run off. She saw him disappear around the locomotive. The rain, although light, had begun again, and glancing about, she guessed she had better "get the hell out of here." To where, she had no idea. If Seagram appeared and carted her off to the nearest whorehouse, it would almost be welcome. She couldn't remember ever feeling so alone.

She picked up her single limp skirt and ran down the track until she came alongside the baggage car. The question she wanted to ignore kept intruding: did Seagram warn her off the train so he could get to her himself? But his warning sounded genuine. So did the part about Equus.

Not more than a minute or two could have passed since

she'd read the note, and so far she had apparently avoided being spotted. Everyone else would assume she was still on the train. Everyone, she hoped, including whoever had boarded after the others left for the station house. Or had it *been* one of the others? Seagram must have been traveling in the passenger car and saw her board the president's car in Montgomery. If he'd been watching for her when they stopped here in West Point, maybe he had seen someone going up the steps after her. And he'd been the one who shouted. Not, she supposed, that it made any difference now. But it made her less distrustful of him. Then she remembered the unfinished word on the note. Had it been time or something more ominous that had kept Seagram from completing *"Baltimore"*?

She couldn't think about that now. Her focus should be to escape West Point and head north. If she could just reach Atlanta, she'd be able to conceal herself in the anonymous setting of a big city.

Bronwen crouched to look under the platform between the passenger and the baggage car. The wagon delivering firewood to the tender directly behind the locomotive had been unloaded, and it began to clatter back across the tracks. Railroad men were hauling the spout of a huge water tank away from the funnel. The engine belched clouds of steam, and through it passengers were returning to the cars. She didn't have much time to make a decision.

She couldn't stay in West Point; there might not be another train for twenty-four hours, and there was no telegraph office to wire Pinkerton. Nor could she ignore Seagram's warning. Even if she didn't completely trust him, she couldn't chance going back to the president's car. But surely Dowling wouldn't let the train leave without her; that was, unless he *knew* that her dead body would shortly be found in the closet. Otherwise, he'd hold the train.

This time the sense of aloneness came close to staggering her. There was only *her*. She knew, though, that if she kept dwelling on it she would paralyze herself with fear.

Stop and reason, Bronwen Llyr!

Biting her lip, she watched the station house and finally saw "her father" walking toward the train, deep in lively conversation with . . . Colonel Dorian de Warde! And strolling beside them—Bronwen gaped in disbelief—was the photographer's assistant, Zoe Martin.

Bronwen suddenly wondered if she were still dozing and sleep had turned to nightmare. The only encouraging aspect was that Dowling seemed to be so engrossed in conversation with de Warde and the young woman that he was walking toward the passenger car—where, of course, the Englishman must have been riding to unobtrusively check on his future investment. But why would Zoe Martin be with him?

Bronwen held her breath and prayed to a God she had never been too sure existed.

Yes; it was going to happen. Dowling, still talking, had begun to mount the steps behind the young woman and Colonel de Warde. It could be entirely possible that Thaddeus Dowling wouldn't know "his daughter" was not in the president's car where he had left her; not until the train pulled into Atlanta. And the others, Falconer and Quinn, would assume she was with Dowling.

Her decision made for her, she now had to find a way into the baggage car.

The sliding wooden door looked too heavy for her to move alone, except that she spotted a small opening where it didn't quite meet the wooden car slats. It was only a crack, but it might be enough.

At the foot of the door ran a narrow ledge. She climbed up onto it and, kneeling behind the door, tried to drag it open. She couldn't budge it—not an inch. At the same time, the train whistle shrieked, a bell clanged, and steam poured from the locomotive's funnel. The train clearly was about to leave. She could never cling to the ledge for a hundred miles. She would be swept under the huge iron wheels . . .

Fear pulled her upright to stand precariously on the ledge. The train vibrated violently under her feet. Then, with a jerk that nearly sent her plunging off, it began to move.

With wind and rain whipping her hair around her face, her fingernails dug into the wooden door as she desperately tried to pull it open. Her arms ached, and she could feel her feet slipping on the wet ledge. As the train gathered speed, she knew she couldn't hold on much longer. Repositioning both hands on the door, and with all the force she could gather, she tugged.

It shifted half an inch, and stuck; then grated just far enough for her to squeeze through and tumble head first into the car.

She dragged herself to a nearby pile of straw and lay there, breathing so hard her chest hurt. The floor of the baggage car shook underneath her, but she couldn't move, not if her life depended on it. And suddenly her life did, as a dark shape came hurtling from the car's inner gloom. For a split second she thought it was a piece of loose baggage, but then realized it kept moving, fingers digging into her arms as she was hauled to her feet.

She thrashed wildly, sure she would be thrown from the car. Her efforts were no match for whoever gripped her. In the dim light available from the door opening, Bronwen could make out intense dark eyes boring into her own. Struggling in terror, she saw her own fear reflected in the other's face. The fingers abruptly released her with a muscular gesture that sent her stumbling backward.

"You're a girl!" came a voice ripe with disgust. The voice sounded young enough—twenty maybe?—to slightly diminish her terror. The Equus cabal would likely be composed of older men. But why did she think that?

Bronwen forced herself to stand there, pushing strands of wet hair out of her eyes, while she tried to collect her wits. Making her tone as self-assured as possible, she said, "O.K., I'm a girl. And what are *you?*"

She didn't need to ask. The strength in the fingers gripping her arms had been unmistakably male. She could feel them still, bruises beginning to sting.

She got a grunt in reply as he moved to the door and slid it nearly shut as easily as if he had been pushing butter across a warm plate. He stood looking out through the remaining crack, and Bronwen craned her neck to see him more clearly. But he turned, the light behind him making it impossible to see his face, only a thin frame and shaggy, light-colored hair. Blue jean–cloth trousers and loose-woven yoked shirt. Scuffed boots that looked too costly to be those of a tramp.

"What d'you want?" he said, voiced more as a demand than a question.

It seemed to her an odd thing to say. Not, *Why did you fall into this baggage car?* or even, *Who are you and what are you doing here?* "What do I want? How about a name?"

"What for?"

"Well, if we're going to be in this car for one hundred miles, it—"

"Not quite a hundred." He shook his head and lowered himself to a crouch, again staring out through the door crack.

"Atlanta's the next stop, and it *is* a hundred miles, I assure you. Unless you're planning to leap off a moving train into a Georgia swamp somewhere."

While she said this, Bronwen sank to the straw, poking at her shoe to make certain the stiletto hadn't been lost in her battle with the door. It was still there. She hoped she wouldn't need it. Not that these were the most favorable conditions under which to judge someone, but he seemed an unlikely Equus conspirator. In fact, if he were, she would eat this straw! And she didn't care whatever else he might be, she was so relieved to be on the moving train, heading toward Atlanta. On the other hand, he was strong, much stronger than she.

Fear nudging her again, she glanced up to find him staring at her; not precisely a curious stare, it was more a look of irritation. As if she had invaded some territory to which he'd staked a claim.

"So"—she tried again, needing to get some sense of him—"do you have a name?" She attempted a smile. "An address, birth date, that kind of thing?"

He just kept staring at her. It occurred to her that he might be simpleminded, but she doubted it. An earlier glint of alertness in the dark eyes spoke intelligence. Even if he was surly!

Bronwen felt a cold pain throb through her feet, and realized she had soaked her shoes as well as her dress and hair. She glanced around at the piles of luggage and mail bags, looking for something in which to wrap herself. *He* just continued to crouch by the door like a caged animal waiting for a chance to break free.

"Ah, have you seen a blanket, or anything like that in here?" she asked, not that she expected a reply.

He stood up and stomped to the back of the car. A minute later, to her surprise, he emerged with a large wool blanket stamped PORT OF MOBILE in bold black letters. He tossed it to her, then moved off and sprawled against a pile of suitcases.

"Thank you," she said, still surprised. She wrapped the blanket around herself, leaving some free to towel her hair. All this time he said nothing.

"Is this yours?" she asked, gesturing at the blanket. "Are you from Alabama?"

"You ask a lot of questions."

"I was just curious . . ."

"That's for damn sure."

". . . because you don't have an Alabama accent."

He shrugged.

"Do you have some scruple about talking to strangers?"

"Look, I didn't ask you to get on this train. And I ain't inclined to answer a lot of questions that ain't none of your business."

It became Bronwen's turn to stare. It was his speech. Although "ain't" was unschooled, he mostly sounded like he had some education, and his accent seemed to be a Northern one. But why try to hide it?

The train's speed for some reason began to slow, the wheels grinding as if the engineer was braking. Bronwen felt a prickle of unease—why would they be stopping?—and her companion, admittedly a reluctant one, jumped to his feet and quickly went to the door opening. He posted himself behind the frame, and peered out with obvious caution. It suddenly struck her that he might be pursued. Chased, hunted, like an escaped criminal for instance? Is that why he wouldn't give his name?

Bronwen started to her feet, then collapsed back on the straw. He hadn't tried to hurt her. Had given her a blanket. And if he *was* being hunted? What about herself? Why else was she sitting in a dirty baggage car, soaking wet, scared, and alone. Well, not exactly alone, but she might as well be.

She needed to change that. If he was on the run, he could know quite a lot about trains—and more about the way North than she did. Because after she reached Atlanta, what then?

"Can you see something ahead?" she asked him. "Why is the train stopping?"

He said nothing for a time, then she saw his shoulders relax from their taut position. He shook his head and moved away from the door. "Just a steep grade to climb. You can feel it, the car tilting."

She did, but until then it hadn't registered. "Who are you running from?" she asked, keeping her tone even.

"I'm not running!"

"Yes, you are. I know when someone's running."

"I told you before, it's none of your business. Now stow the questions!"

Bronwen suppressed a retort. And looked at him with more interest. He wasn't at all bad-looking, or wouldn't be if he shaved off that stubble, had a bath and a haircut. She wondered, almost idly, if he'd been in jail. It didn't seem to matter particularly; she didn't feel threatened by him—not much, anyway—and after the train pulled into the station she would never see him again. But she needed to start thinking about what to do when she reached Atlanta. He might know if there was a telegraph office at the train station. And how she could avoid being seen.

"How can you tell?" he asked suddenly.

"*What* . . . tell what?"

"When someone's running, like you said."

"How do you think? You refused to give even a simple answer like your name. You tensed up when you thought the train might be stopping for no apparent reason. Besides, it was just a guess—but a good one, wasn't it?"

He shrugged again. "So what are *you* doing in a baggage car?" he said, watching her closely.

"I'm running like you. Well, maybe not like you—I haven't committed any crime."

"Neither have I!" His voice exploded in the enclosed space.

She tended to believe him, for no good reason other than he seemed so put out by her insinuation. Or maybe he was just a good actor. For all she knew, he'd axe-murdered his entire family—but he *had* given her a blanket.

"O.K., so you haven't," she said. "I really don't care. I've other things to worry about."

He snorted, as if her worries had to be negligible ones. Then he cocked his head to listen. "Slowing down," he muttered, and again went to peer around the door.

The train *was* slowing, and this time Bronwen could feel no elevation. She got to her feet, going to stand across from him. The drizzle had stopped and the sky had begun to clear, and she must be looking west, as she could see a weak sun straining through a few remaining gray clouds.

When the engine bell began clanging, he leaned toward her. "We're stopping. You got any idea why? They likely to start searching the train for you?"

"They might."

"Shit!"

"I agree. What do we do?"

"*We!* What'd you mean, *we?*"

"If they find me, mister, they find you, too. I assume that's something you want to avoid?"

He looked at her with contempt. "If you get me caught . . ."

"Apparently neither of us can afford to be caught. So why don't we stop arguing and think! Does it make sense to get off the train? Here?"

He pointed straight out the door. When Bronwen looked, all she could see on a slope below them were trees—hundreds of trees draped with ragged smoke-colored moss.

"You want to try wandering around through that?" His voice, although still harsh, had lost some of its hostility.

"It's just a woods, right? I can cope with woods."

The bell clanged again, and iron wheels screeched.

"There's no time to get off!" he said. "Not without being seen from the train. Anyway, Georgia woods are full of swamp holes and snakes . . ."

"We *don't* get off! Quick, what's there to hide behind in here?"

Glancing around, he shook his head. "They can unload all this stuff if they really want to look. But maybe . . ." His voice trailed off as he gazed upward.

"The roof?" Bronwen asked.

He slid the door open wider, and leaned out of the car. He looked in both directions. "Got maybe one minute before we stop. I'm going up," he pointed, "you can damn well do what you want."

He started to swing himself out. Bronwen grasped his shirt and held on. "I'm going with you." She saw the look he gave her and added, "If you don't help me get up there, I'll tell them where you are!"

She released his shirt, and stared at him, hard: she'd meant what she said. His eyes narrowed, and a strange expression crossed his face, then he grabbed her around the waist and lifted her through the door opening.

While he held her, her fingers scrabbled against the outer roof of the car, trying to find something to grasp, something to give her purchase. Finally, she felt a solid piece of wood like a low barrier or fence railing, some six inches high, that felt securely attached to the roof edge. It seemed to run around the roof perimeter, probably to keep baggage from sliding off. Every so often there were open circles in the barrier to let rainwater run out, Bronwen guessed.

"You find a hold?" he yelled above the shriek of the train brakes.

She nodded, needing all her breath to ready herself.

"So hoist yourself!"

"Give me a boost," she gasped.

She felt an upward thrust as his hands left her waist, tossing her over the wooden barrier like a sack of potatoes. She whacked her shins before rolling several times. Then, knees scraping the rough wood, Bronwen crawled back to where his head was appearing over the barrier edge. She'd heard the door bang shut; at least he was shrewd enough to do that! She pointed to the small openings like handholds. His knuckles whitened as he gripped the barrier, and his head disappeared. Then he was swinging up beside her.

"Move to the middle of the roof so they can't see you from the ground—the angle will be too steep. Get down, and *stay* down!" he ordered, as if she were a fool, and he were Pinkerton.

Nonetheless, Bronwen went down on all fours and crawled to the roof's midpoint, then flattened herself against it. He dropped on his belly alongside her, but kept his head raised to see the track below.

"*Stay down, yourself!*" she whispered, as a jolt signaled the train's halt.

"Just a minute—got to see what they're doing."

"No, you don't *got* to see," she mimicked. "I'll tell you what they're doing. They're looking for *me*."

"I figured that! Anybody looking for me's not on this train."

Bronwen could now hear voices coming from below, and they were growing louder. Who had discovered that she'd gone missing? Dowling, after returning to the president's car? Or the one who had first come into the train after her? At that time, she'd narrowed the list to Quinn or Falconer—

in addition to Dowling—but the later appearance of Colonel de Warde and Zoe Martin complicated the field. Or, she supposed, it could be someone who was a total stranger to her. One of the Maryland delegates. Maybe even a hired assassin. . . . Assassin! Could that be what Equus did?

Her thoughts were interrupted by his whisper next to her ear. "You know any of those voices?"

She listened; whispered back, "No. Can you tell where they are?"

"Getting closer. They're all on one side of the train. Only good thing is, they probably won't think of looking on the roof—I mean, how would you get up here?" A sudden, and unexpected, grin flashed. It not only erased the surliness, it changed his entire face. Then it vanished as he muttered, "Better shut up."

And now, directly below, Bronwen heard a voice that she recognized instantly.

14

All day the fire-steed flies over the country, stopping only that his master may rest, and I am awakened by his tramp and defiant snort at midnight. . . . He will reach his stall only with the morning star. . . .

—Thoreau, *Walden*

Bronwen heard Thaddeus Dowling say, "I can't imagine what could have become of her."

She listened to these words with mixed emotions. The man sounded genuinely worried, but it could be for one of two reasons: he was truly concerned about her welfare, or he was anxious because she had escaped him.

Another familiar voice said, "She must have been left at West Point"—it sounded like Cormac Quinn—"because when we checked in the other car just now, no one seems to have seen her since we stopped there."

"But why didn't you hold the train?" Dowling protested.

"We assumed she was with you," answered someone Bronwen guessed might be Jules Falconer, although she couldn't be certain.

She shifted on the hard wood, receiving a scowl from her roof-mate. He mouthed "Don't move" at her—as if she had a choice! Then she heard a rasp as the baggage car door opened and someone said, "Don't know why she'd be in there. Guess we'd better take a look all the same."

A flurry of footsteps in the car underneath, followed by the noise of baggage being shifted, made Bronwen recoil, scraping her cheek against the roof. Her involuntary intake of breath was followed by something heavy falling on her shoulders, and she realized her new companion had swung his arm over her.

"Shut up!" came the whisper in her ear, the order made explicit by the tightening of his arm. Since her face was now squashed into his side, she couldn't even nod. Despite the discomfort, at least the voices below were muffled by his body. And while he didn't look all too clean, and his shirt was damp with sweat, there was about him an unexpected fresh smell like that of line-dried sheets slapping in the wind.

"Hey, over here!"

The sudden shout from directly below made her start, and she felt the arm around her tense.

"Over here!" the voice repeated. "What about the roof?"

In the silence that followed, Bronwen felt her stomach cramp, and she rolled to her side and drew her knees to her chest. He must have thought she might do something in panic as he shook his head and tightened his arm. She gestured to her shoe and, before he could react, reached down and grabbed the stiletto sheath. For a brief moment his eyes widened, then he turned his head toward the roof edge as another voice said, "How could she be up on the roof? She'd need wings!"

That had sounded like Guy Seagram, but again, Bronwen couldn't be sure.

"Yeah, O.K.," came the response. The door to the car grated shut.

"The only explanation"—it was Dowling's voice again—

"is that she was left in West Point. . . ." His voice trailed away, and the other voices gradually faded, too.

Bronwen shifted her position again. Then she heard the low murmur of several new voices, the words indistinguishable until, ". . . and admit we lost her at least for now, damn it!"

This was followed by someone muttering, and she caught only ". . . the Horseman is raising hell. . . . She could blow the whole thing."

The voices abruptly became louder, as if the speakers thought they were now alone.

"Maybe she *is* back in West Point—good thing we left somebody there just in case. We can send a wire from Atlanta, and watch for her there . . . pick up her trail, because she'll have to go through the station. . . . Hope to hell she doesn't reach Pinker— Baltimore."

All at once the voices became ragged, as if the men had abruptly walked away.

Bronwen strained to catch more, but the next thing she heard was the roar of the steam engine.

"It's you they're after, all right," he said in a low voice, barely audible over the locomotive's noise. "What the hell did you *do?*" He eyed the stiletto. "You kill somebody with that?"

"As you said to me, it's not any of your business," she retorted, sliding the stiletto back into her shoe. "Why should I tell you anything? You won't even give me your *name!*"

"Marsh."

"*Marsh* . . . as in Marshall?"

"Marsh as in swamp. Sink holes, quicksand—" he paused, glancing at her sideways "—snakes. O.K.? Satisfied?" He withdrew his arm and wormed forward on his belly to look down the track.

She supposed it wasn't worth asking if that was his given

or his surname. But she'd be rid of him soon enough, and in the meantime, maybe she could make use of his considerable strength; it was odd, that, because he appeared lean almost to the point of gauntness. Maybe he'd done hard labor in prison.

With a raucous blast from the whistle, the train began to move. Her companion rose to a crouch, obviously making ready to climb back into the baggage car. Bronwen suddenly wondered if he meant to leave her up there.

"Ah . . . Marsh? How do we get back in the car with the door shut?"

"*I'm* going back in through the door *I'm* going to open. You can damn well stay up here and ask the moon a hundred of your questions for all I care."

"Wait!" Bronwen yelled, grabbing his shirt. "You go down there without me and I'll . . ."

"You'll what? Knife me in the back?"

Since that was precisely what she'd been about to threaten, the fact that he didn't seem overly concerned gave her a moment of real fear. He wrenched away with a ripping sound, and she was left holding a torn scrap of shirt. There was nothing to do but watch as he leaned over the barrier and slid his upper torso, head down, over the edge of the roof—probably gripping the baggage strap bar—and despite the clatter of the train wheels, she heard a faint sound when the door grated open. His legs began to slide forward, and she leaped to grab them.

"Goddammit, let go of me!" he shouted, as she braced herself to hold onto his ankles. The wind made it hard to maintain her balance, and for a moment she thought she would topple off, taking him with her.

"I'll let go," she yelled, "when you promise to help me down!"

She knew very well that it was a hollow bargain she proposed. Why should someone like him, undoubtedly an escaped convict, keep his word?

"O.K.! O.K., damn you—now let *go!*"

Between the force of the wind and the jolting train, she couldn't hold on longer anyway, not without sending them both over the side. She released his ankles, and he disappeared.

She waited. And waited. Dropping to her knees, she gripped the barrier railing and leaned over it.

"Marsh—get me *down!*" The edge of fear she heard in her voice infuriated her, and she leaned over farther to see how he had managed to swing into the car. It looked to be a long drop even for a gymnast. If only she were as tall as the wretch who had left her up there! She couldn't *stay* there, though, not for the remaining distance to be traveled. Even if the steadily lowering temperature didn't give her pneumonia, or the jolting train break every bone in her body, what would she do when they reached Atlanta? The station house was very likely to be two-storied; someone looking out a top-floor window could easily spot her on the roof, and from the last conversation she'd overheard, someone would definitely be looking.

Clearly, she had to get inside the car, and she hadn't heard the door close. She climbed over the barrier, gripping the edge fast as the train jolted her, and facing the car, she drew up her body, jamming her feet firmly against the side. Below her she could see that, yes, the door was at least one-third open. She cautiously let go one hand to search for the baggage strap carrier. Her fingers hit the protruding, U-shaped piece of metal and she grasped it tightly. She wanted to judge the distance from the carrier to the door opening, but since she *had* to get down it seemed better to just do it! She knew that if she thought about it much longer she'd lose her nerve completely.

She carefully moved her other hand to the carrier, and began to uncurl, walking her feet down the side of the car. Then the train rocked suddenly. She lost her foothold and swung out over the swiftly moving ground below.

Dangling in mid-air, she received another jolt from the accelerating train, wrenching her arms while pain shot through her shoulders. One of her hands slipped off the carrier, and she nearly lost her grip altogether. While hanging from the other hand, the swaying train smashed her against the car when she tried to hoist herself up to grab the carrier with both hands again. As her weight dragged her downward, the fingernails of her free hand clawed at the car, attempting to stretch her legs enough to dig the toes of her shoes into the top of the door. But the train rocked, and she found herself again swinging by one hand out over the track and the massive iron wheels.

Her wrist twisted, and she gasped in pain, fighting the urge to just let go. If she could only hold on long enough for the car to sway sideways, and propel her legs forward through the door opening. She didn't have to be what's-his-name Newton to know defying gravity was the goal here. So the drop would be dangerous but what choice did she have? Ahead she saw a curve of track which should make the train list to one side, then rock to the other. She could do it now. Glancing down toward the grinding wheels, she readied herself.

Suddenly arms shot out the open door and caught her calves, hauling her downward. She slammed against the car, fingernails of one hand clawing wildly for something to grasp, as with the other she tried to hold on to the baggage strap carrier. Then a jerk on her legs yanked her fingers off the metal and she plunged, only his grip between herself and the blur of steel below. His hands slid up her body and she knew he would drop her—just before she was hauled through the door opening, and dumped on the straw.

Bronwen just lay there, pulling in gulps of air and too exhausted to even look up. All she could see were his scuffed boots.

"You really are a lunatic!" he shouted. "Couldn't wait for two seconds, could you?"

"I waited," Bronwen panted. "You weren't going to help me. Besides, I *could* have done it myself."

"You waited because I was stacking baggage so you could *climb* down. But no—you had to be an acrobat! A damn fool!"

Bronwen sat up slowly, gaping at him. "I couldn't see you stacking—"

"I should've just let you drop!"

"Why didn't you?"

He hesitated as if he were asking himself that. "Because I'm not a murderer."

"And you think I *am?*" Bronwen snapped.

"I don't know *what* you are—'cept you're more trouble than you're worth." He turned away from her and threw himself down against the haphazardly piled baggage next to the door.

For some time the only sound was the rumble of the train. Bronwen sat with legs drawn up and her arms wrapped around them, head resting on her knees. Occasionally she reached up to rub her aching shoulders, and then her wrists would hurt, as well as her bruised shins from when he'd first heaved her over the railing. She wasn't aware of time passing until she was nearly knocked flat by a mighty jolt from the braking motion of the train. She felt it bump, slowing. "What *now?*" she groaned.

Marsh leapt to the door, and stood looking out. By the

time he turned and collapsed against the baggage again, the train had begun to accelerate. "Just a pig," he muttered.

"*What?*"

"A pig," he repeated. "Sleeping on the track. Cowcatcher pushed it off—still asleep from the looks of it."

Bronwen nearly grinned, but she was too tired. She started to put her head back down on her knees when, next to his boot, a glint of bright metal caught her eye.

"What's that?" She pointed. "There, by your foot."

He glanced down, looked away, then looked again. His fingers grasped a small disk of gold and pried it from where it had wedged between the floorboards. "Eagle," he said, bouncing it in the palm of his hand.

"Ten dollars? Where would that have come from?" Bronwen asked as, with a grimace for her complaining wrists, she crawled forward to see the coin.

He looked at the luggage. "Probably out of one of those"—he bent forward to look more carefully—"but none of them are open." He dropped the coin back onto the floorboards.

"What're you *doing?*" Bronwen yelped. "That's ten dollars!"

"It's not *your* ten dollars."

"Look, we just found it there. It doesn't belong to anybody," she argued. "You may be rich enough to pass it up, but not me. I'm in trouble and I'm going to need money to get me out of it. Even if *you* insist on being so bloody honorable, I don't. Now give it to me!"

He didn't move, just stared at her with something like disgust. But when Bronwen crawled forward to retrieve the coin, he didn't try to stop her. She snatched it from the floor, wondering what kind of criminal he *was*. Not a murderer; she believed this, as he hadn't been forced to help her into the car. Not someone who would even take advantage of a loose gold coin. What could he have done to be running from the law? He might be a rapist—but that didn't ring true either. He'd had plenty of opportunity to prove that.

"Ah, Marsh?" She made her tone as conciliatory as possible. "I'd like to know why you're on the run. I assumed that you'd escaped from jail—did you?"

"It's none of your—"

"Well, yes, it *is* my business," Bronwen interrupted. "You heard what those men said when we were on the roof. They're after me."

"Sure sounded that way," he conceded, his voice not quite so much of a growl. "Who are they?"

That was encouraging; his curiosity exceeded his churlishness.

"To be honest"—she winced slightly when he glanced toward the coin in her hand—"I'm not sure who they are. Really!" she protested as his skeptical look deepened. "They know I overheard something in Montgomery. They *don't* know I didn't hear much. So they think I have more information than I actually do."

"About what?" At this point his expression went beyond skepticism; he looked downright disbelieving.

Bronwen hesitated before answering, giving herself time to think. The truth sounded bizarre even to her. He would never accept it. On the other hand, she could use his help when they reached Atlanta, which would be in several hours. And since he already thought she was deceitful—at least about money—and no doubt crazy, what could she lose by trying the truth? At least some of it.

"Look, Marsh," she began, "I'll tell you something about myself, if you'll listen."

"Why should I?"

"Because we might be able to help each other. For instance, where are you heading?"

"North."

"Could you be a little more specific?"

"Why should I?"

In exasperation, Bronwen threw the coin at him. "Head to hell, then, for all I care. I was offering to maybe help you if I could. But forget it!" She fell back on the straw, flinched at the pain in her shoulders, and stared in silence at the baggage car roof.

"Why," he said at last, his tone cautious, "would you want to help me?"

Bronwen quickly pulled herself to a seated position, saying, "Actually, I *don't* want to help you. But I could use some myself and I thought we could work a trade-off. Mutual assistance, that sort of thing. If not, I can take care of myself!"

The snort was quick in coming. "From what I've seen, you don't do a great job of that. I could've killed you at least twice now, if I'd wanted. Hell, you almost killed yourself!"

"But you didn't kill me. You helped me, so now I trust you some. Not much," she added, "just more than I did. You *have* to trust someone, some of the time."

"Girl, you are a real innocent if you believe that."

"Well, I do believe it, and maybe it's because I *am* a girl—in case you forgot."

"Hard to forget." He seemed to almost smile. Almost. "But like I said," he went on, "I think you're more trouble than you're worth."

"Suit yourself." She added casually, "But I know people in the North who, if you're in trouble, might be able to help you. And don't bother saying 'Why should they?' "

He shrugged. "Why should they?"

"Because I'll ask them to," she snapped, "if you'll do one small thing. It's nothing much. You'd only have to send a couple of telegrams. You heard those men. They're going to be watching for me, and I can't just march into the Atlanta telegraph office so they can kill me."

"Let me get this straight. You want *me* to march into the telegraph office, so they can kill *me*."

"They won't kill *you*—they don't even know you."

"And then what? After—*if*—I send the wires."

"Then we head north on the railroad. I need to get to Baltimore, but I'm going to Richmond first—where I know somebody." She paused, then asked, for no particular reason she could think of, "Don't you even want to know my name?"

"What difference does your name make?"

"It makes no difference," she retorted. "No difference at all. Now, will you send the wires for me?"

"What do you plan to use for money?" He glanced down at the gold eagle shining on the floor.

"I have money. Not much," she said quickly, not trusting him enough, despite the coin episode, to leave herself open to robbery. "But I can afford to send two telegrams. One to Chicago, and one to Seneca Falls, New York. Will you do it? I'll write them out, and you can just hand them to the telegraph operator when we get to Atlanta."

"Telegraph office is at the rail station."

Bronwen mulled over this piece of news, deciding that perhaps she didn't need him after all. She had begun to think that *he* was more trouble than he was worth. If she could manage to remain concealed, and could wait until the station house emptied, then she could send the telegrams herself. After all, from what the Equus men had said, they wouldn't expect her to show up in Atlanta anytime soon. At the station she could also find out if trains ran directly to Richmond.

"You've changed my mind," she said. "I don't think I can trust you after all. What's to keep you from ignoring the telegrams and instead taking off with my money? I'll send the wires myself."

He said nothing, just put his hands behind his head and lay back against the baggage.

Bronwen sat there, trying to think through a plan of action; without one, so Allan Pinkerton claimed, disaster was almost guaranteed to occur. But first, she had to find pencil and paper to write out the telegrams. Just as important, she needed to disguise her appearance.

She eyed the pile of baggage.

15

When I hear the iron horse make the hills echo
with his snort like thunder, shaking the earth with
his feet, and breathing fire and smoke from his
nostrils . . . it seems as if the earth had got a race
now worthy to inhabit it.

—Thoreau

"About ten miles more to Atlanta," Marsh announced,
standing at the door sometime later. It was the first thing he
had said since Bronwen started breaking into the luggage,
although most of the time he'd been asleep.

"You've ridden this line before?"

"Once. The last time I escaped."

"You're very forthcoming all of a sudden," she commented. "Escaped from where?"

Marsh ignored her question as, by this time, she'd assumed he would. "You know, I'd gone three days without
sleep," he offered instead. "Now that I finally got some . . .
you should try it. Might sweeten your temper."

"I can't afford sleep." She tugged at the drooping bib over
her chest. The straps of it held up the blue cotton-wool
weave, jean-cloth overalls she'd found in a trunk after pry-
ing it open with her stiletto. The trunk held not only the
overalls, but a blousy, loose-woven, undyed cotton shirt, a
black wool vest, and a blue cap. Further rooting uncovered

a carefully wrapped round of cheese and a tin of biscuits, which—despite Marsh's silent but obvious disapproval of the break-in—the two of them devoured.

Otherwise, all he'd done was watch, never said a word when she disappeared behind a mound of mailbags to change. She had also extracted some coins from the flat purse tied around her thigh and put them in the trunk, along with her dress, before she closed the lid. Despite what she'd told Marsh, Pinkerton supplied his agents with a fair amount of money. He did this reluctantly, of course, and all of it that was spent had to be justified by a full accounting.

A small valise had yielded Bronwen paper and several pencils. Dropping to her knees she spread the paper over the valise and chewed the end of a pencil before writing swiftly:

To Miss Glynis Tryon—33 Cayuga Street—Seneca Falls—New York State. Message: Red fox running to see Rick versifying French song stop

The one to Pinkerton could be more straightforward. He would be alert to anything coming out of Atlanta, and she wouldn't have to identify herself by signing it. She didn't have at hand the elaborate code system Pinkerton had devised for reporting—she wasn't supposed to have *needed* it—and since she hadn't memorized it, she could only pray that the wire went through as written. She finally settled on:

To Pinkerton Detective Agency—89 Washington Street—Chicago, Illinois. Message: Urgent stop Baltimore danger stop Maybe assassins stop Code name Equus stop Suspect Maryland delegation stop Send name Baltimore contact to Richmond contact stop

Bronwen jumped, and realized the warm air she'd felt on the back of her neck came from Marsh, who stood looking over her shoulder.

"Holy Father!" he breathed. "What are you playing at?"

"It's not a game."

"No, I didn't think so. But why are you wiring a detective agency?"

"Because that's where I work. *Pinkerton's*—you heard of it?"

"Yeah. I thought it had to do with railroad robberies. Why would they hire *you?*"

Bronwen gave him what she hoped was a disdainful look, and disdained to answer. She bent her head to shake her hair out, sectioned it with her fingers, and began to braid.

"This Pinkerton's," he said, only slightly more cordially, "do they . . . do they ever look for missing persons?"

"Not ordinarily, why?"

He shook his head.

"Right," Bronwen said tartly, "it's none of my business. But if you're looking for someone, you could try asking Pinkerton—he knows just about everyone in law enforcement."

"I don't want the law!"

"But the law wants you? What for?"

Getting to his feet, he went to the door. After a glance outside, he stood leaning against the doorframe, watching while she braided.

"You'll never get all that hair under any cap," he stated.

"I have to hide it. Got a better idea?"

"Cut it off."

Bronwen, a curly strand of red hair gripped between her fingers, stared up at him. "Cut it *off? My hair?* I'd rather die."

She bit her lip as it occurred to her that dying was the possible alternative. "I *can't* cut it," she moaned, then blurted, "It's the only pretty thing about me." She drew in her breath, stunned. How could she have confided this feeling to a sullen stranger?

The expression of the sullen stranger changed, almost as if something pleasant were mistakenly crossing his mind. He agrees with me, Bronwen thought, her mortification complete.

Then he shrugged, and said, "It's your funeral."

She winced, and had to admit, though only to herself, that he might have a point. "Even if I did want to cut it, I don't have scissors."

He pointed to her shoe. "Knife would work. Or you could always break into another piece of baggage. Anyway, there's not time now—we'll be in Atlanta in a few minutes."

Bronwen piled the braids on top of her head, then tried to fit the cap over them. The braids slithered out. She went through this several times until he said, "Here!" and grabbed the cap. She didn't protest, but held the braids in place while with both hands he yanked the blue, visored cap down over her ears. Then he stood back and looked at her, a sudden grin flashing over even, white teeth.

Bronwen felt her face flush and swung away, but turned back to him when he asked, "You know this detective Pinkerton, then?"

"Of course I know him. I told you, I work for him."

He still looked skeptical. "For now I guess I have to believe you. O.K. I send your telegrams if you ask him to help me find somebody. Trade-off, right?"

"I can *ask* him," Bronwen said, not sure why she should agree to this. Did she really need him? She went to the door and peered out. And was unpleasantly surprised by the amount of light coming from a curl of moon, and from the gaslights on poles positioned like guards around the substantial brick station ahead. It could be she did need him. She had no idea how long the train would stop, or where she could hide until the station emptied. If, in fact, it ever did empty. The station house and the area around it looked much larger than she'd expected. Not as big as those in Chicago, but big enough to be dangerous. Even at this time of night, she could see people milling around three tall, arched entrances. Wagons and small carts rattled across vacant tracks. The terminal had multiple rails, some empty, some with idle freight trains being unloaded. Big.

She didn't dare to test the effectiveness of her disguise by coming face to face with a potential killer. Narrowing her eyes at Marsh, she agreed. "Trade-off."

"O.K., let's go. Better get off now, before we stop."

"Jump from a moving train?"

"It's not moving much. And somebody will come back here to unload as soon as we stop. C'mon, give me the telegrams."

Bronwen handed him the sheet of paper, then started to slip behind the mailbags to retrieve the purse tied on her thigh.

"What're you *doing?*"

"Getting money."

"There's no time! We're almost there!"

Bronwen reached down and snatched the gold eagle from the floorboards. "Here, and don't argue about it."

He shoved the coin into a pocket and jerked the door open. "Out!"

Bronwen, gaping down at the shifting ground and the spinning iron wheels, hesitated. A shove from behind sent her soaring through the opening. She hit the sandy ground, letting herself roll easily down a slight grade.

Then, with a dull thud, something landed just ahead of her.

Except for scraped knees and elbows, Bronwen found herself still in one piece. "Marsh?" she whispered, although the noise of the braking train made her caution more reflex than necessity.

"Yeah."

"I think"—she pointed—"we should head for those barrels over there."

He nodded and scrambled to his feet, then sprinted toward the station. Bronwen followed him at a run, slowing only to hop over the crossties of the tracks. Just in time, as a screech of wheels signaled that the locomotive was grinding to a stop.

Together they crouched behind the hoard of barrels stacked at the side of the Atlanta station house. Ten feet beyond stood a gas lamp post, and directly above them a window flickered with lantern light. Some yards away, directly behind the farthest pair of tracks, stood a white, two-story building that looked like a hotel and tavern. Gaslights glowed to either side of the entrance steps. A short distance from its wide front porch sat another building, so small in comparison that it resembled a hut. Its height looked to be not much more than the pricked ears of a sorrel horse that stood alongside.

"Telegraph office," Marsh whispered, following her gaze. "But you can't stay here while I'm sending the wires."

"Why not?" Bronwen answered her own question when she saw a wagon pulled by a mule team, its lanterns careening with each bump, coming slowly toward the barrels.

"Bushes—far side of the hotel porch," Marsh said, then eased out from behind the barrels to lope toward the telegraph office.

After checking that her hair remained concealed beneath the cap, Bronwen quickly glanced around her as she too edged out onto the rutted area between the gaslit station and the hotel. Light fell in uneven patches, which she managed to avoid, but then several times she nearly tripped over the tracks. The passengers on the train from West Point must have left it by now, but none of the scattered voices around her sounded familiar. She forced her eyes to remain on the ground in front of her, and adopted a shuffling gait that she hoped would look very unlike her normal one. Her aunt had once said that the surest way to identify people from a distance was by their walk. Dear Lord, if Aunt Glynis were to see her now!

Bronwen didn't even dare to glance at those nearby as she approached the hotel porch. And while she couldn't imagine that anyone would recognize her, she felt as if every eye in Atlanta were trained on her. After she came abreast of the porch, she continued shuffling on toward the rear of the hotel. Skirting several large open barrels, she fought the urge to retch as the smell of rotting garbage made her stomach toss. She rounded the building quickly.

Beside the hotel stood a planting of glossy-leaved camellia shrubs that stood in shadow. After a quick glance to make certain she was unobserved, Bronwen wedged herself between several of them amidst a shower of white petals. From there she could clearly see the well-lit telegraph office some yards away. A line of customers waited. Marsh stood among them, his gaze fixed with apparent concentration on the feet of the man ahead of him. Bronwen couldn't suppress a shiver when she recognized the man as Cormac Quinn.

She told herself it made perfect sense for a reporter to be sending telegrams. Who better? she thought, in an attempt at reassurance. Besides, why should Quinn even notice the young man standing behind him? Bronwen then nearly plunged headlong from the sheltering shrubs in her effort to see the man who stood behind Marsh. It was Thaddeus Dowling.

Her teeth started to chatter and she clenched them together. Again, it was perfectly natural for Dowling to be wiring someone. Probably about her own disappearance! He *did* appear anxious, his glance darting over those in the line and the surrounding area. Twice Bronwen held her breath when he seemed to look directly at the camellias. When he turned toward a gaslight to read something grasped in his hand, Bronwen crept forward to conceal herself behind the first shrub to see better some wanted posters she'd spotted, tacked on the side of the telegraph office.

Although she needed to squint to make them out, one in particular had caught her attention. Large block letters at the top of the poster said "MOBILE, ALABAMA."

She fought down a spasm of fear by telling herself it must be coincidence. There had to be all manner of wanted men from Mobile—it was, after all, a large port city. It couldn't be *Marsh* on that poster!

But what if it was? He would walk straight into the gaze of the telegraph operator, who had probably tacked up the poster himself.

The heads of those in the line swiveled toward the roundhouse, where a locomotive had just delivered itself of an extraordinarily loud belch of steam. Bronwen jerked the visor of her cap down and inched forward. She had to see that poster. Keeping her face averted from the lanterns on the hotel porch, she shuffled toward the side of the telegraph office. When she came within several yards of it, she needed only a glance. It indeed looked to be a sketch of Marsh's face glowering from the poster, at least a credible likeness. But she clutched at hope until a closer look brought confirmation: "TRISTAN MARSHALL—WANTED FOR MURDER."

She turned and, forcing herself to move slowly, shambled back to the shadows alongside the porch. Tristan? Murder? He was wanted for *murder?* Bronwen backed into the shrubs, her mind wheeling along a hundred different avenues of speculation, finally pausing at the one that said the poster could be mistaken; that he'd been falsely accused. She simply could not believe he was a killer. Or if he was, maybe it had been self-defense. He had no choice. Or, maybe he . . .

She stopped herself. There was no point in this. The most important thing was those telegrams, and they wouldn't be sent if Marsh were hauled off to jail. The fact that she had put him in just such danger she acknowledged, but she shouldn't feel much responsibility toward someone who had committed murder. If he had. If he hadn't . . . ?

Her mind seemed jammed, just when she needed to think fast. She looked at the telegraph office; there remained only one person to enter ahead of Cormac Quinn. Then, after Quinn, Marsh would unknowingly walk into almost certain disaster. Casting desperately about, Bronwen's eyes fell on the hotel's deserted hitching post. At the near end of it stood a bale of straw.

Bronwen hoisted herself to the wide railing of the porch, lowered herself to the porch floor, and stood a moment glancing around to make sure no one was watching. Then she carefully lifted a kerosene lantern from its hook. From the tail of her eye she could see Cormac Quinn just entering the telegraph office. Marsh waited on the threshold, and behind him Thaddeus Dowling continued to read. There was no time for caution. She allowed herself only one more quick glance around before hurling the lantern down onto the straw bale.

There was a tinkle of breaking glass, nothing more. What had gone wrong? Not enough kerosene? Could the bale have

been wet? Bronwen anxiously leaned forward—just as a
ploosh of sound came from the igniting straw. She forced
herself to wait for several more seconds until flames began
to lick at the bale.

"Fire! It's fire!" she yelled at the top of her voice, while
at the same time hurtling down the porch steps to run toward
the far side of the telegraph office.

The speed of reaction surprised even Bronwen, although
fire was the single worst catastrophe that could occur in a
city built primarily of wood. Behind her, people poured out
of the hotel as if from a pump that had been primed. Those
standing on the narrow strip of ground next to the tracks
jumped toward the hotel's watering trough as though
launched by cannon. Bronwen looked for, but could not see,
Thaddeus Dowling. He'd probably already joined the growing crowd at the hotel. She reached Marsh just as Cormac
Quinn and a man with a green visor erupted from the telegraph office, their attention drawn by the shouting throng
around the blazing straw.

Bronwen turned aside as the men ran past, then grabbed
Marsh's arm and tugged him backward. "You've got to get
out of here! Right now!"

He glanced toward the fire, then down at her and, to her
relief, followed her without a word.

Her intention was to head around to the back of the hotel,
which, from the looks of the crowd in front of it, would be
deserted. She had calculated wrong. Men were positioning a
hose leading from the hotel well to a pump cart. Running,
they wheeled it around the building. Bronwen and Marsh
shrank back into a stand of feathery pine trees beside the
next-door bakery shop.

He grabbed her upper arm. "You didn't have anything to
do with that fire, did you?"

His fingers dug into her flesh and Bronwen cringed, but

more from guilt than from pain. Then, suddenly, a billow of black smoke whooshed skyward, accompanied by a roar of cheers. Clouds of smoke spiraled as the cheering continued.

The acrid smell was making Bronwen's eyes water, but she said with relief, "The fire must be under control."

"No thanks to you, I bet. You set it, didn't you?"

"I had to create a diversion . . ."

"You're crazy!"

". . . to get you away from the telegraph office. Your face, *Tristan Marshall*, is plastered big as life on the side of that hut. On a wanted poster. But since you're so ungrateful, I clearly should have let them haul you off to jail."

He stared down at her before saying softly, "So why didn't you?"

"I'm not sure"—although this was truthful, she regretted her candor immediately—"except that those telegrams would have gone with you. Anybody could have seen them."

His expression changed, hardened again. "Did the poster say what I was wanted for?"

"Murder."

"You believe that?"

"I don't know. What difference does it make now?"

He started to say something, then hesitated. Finally he muttered, "Won't be safe to send those telegrams until morning—maybe there won't be anybody watching for you by then. We better find cover for the night. Unless you're afraid to be with a murderer."

"Presumably you don't murder just anyone. Because if you did, you had plenty of opportunity on the train." Bronwen looked him straight in the eye, waiting for his reaction. Despite the confident words, her right hand hung at her side—toward the stiletto.

But the sound of voices coming around the hotel made them both drop low, knees bent, ready to spring.

"That stable behind you," he whispered. "Make for there."

Bronwen nodded. She backed out of the trees, watching over her shoulder as several men carrying water buckets appeared at the rear of the hotel. Pulling her cap visor down, she sauntered in the direction of the stable, expecting at any moment that someone would grab her and accuse her of starting the fire. The men, however, seemed to be paying her no attention whatever. They began to rewind the hose.

"Damn lanterns!" one of them said. "Gonna burn the whole city down someday."

Bronwen couldn't help but wince. It *had* been a crazy thing to do—on the other hand, it had worked. And as it wasn't the case that there had been no one close by to extinguish the fire, she absolved herself.

She glanced casually about her before slipping through the open stable door. Once inside, the well-known smell of horses and hay and leather gave her a measure of comfort, although the horses whinnied, moving restlessly in their stalls, undoubtedly still fearful of the faint odor of smoke. She peered into the darkness and, after her eyesight adjusted, spotted a ladder standing in the rear. She moved a little further into the barn and waited.

A minute or two later, she sensed someone coming through the door.

"There's the ladder to the hayloft," she told Marsh when he materialized beside her, holding a crumpled paper sack. "You go up first."

"And risk a knife in my back?"

"*My* face isn't on a wanted poster."

"It should be!" he said as he went up the ladder.

Bronwen waited until he had reached the loft before climbing up herself, then crawled on all fours to a back corner. Marsh was already scooping straw into a pile. He stopped long enough to reach into the sack and toss her a couple of hard rolls—the bakery shop's, no doubt—then flung himself with a groan into the straw. Above them a window opened on a black sky flecked with stars, and although the air was chill, Bronwen knelt for a moment to stare out while she ate the rolls. Then the cold made her dive for the straw.

As she burrowed under it, pulling the rough, dry stalks over herself, she felt acutely aware of her vulnerability, of her distance from all that was familiar. She curled up on her side with her back toward the motionless lump beside her, knees drawn to her chest, and in the quiet darkness she felt the sudden smart of tears.

She must have made some inadvertent sound, because he said, "What's the matter?" His voice sounded almost amiable.

"Nothing." Bronwen choked back tears, furious at herself for her weakness, more furious still for letting him see it.

She heard the rustle of straw beside her, and stiffened.

"You crying?" His tone was incredulous.

"No, I am *not* crying," she answered, although her choke gave the lie to this.

For a minute there was only silence. Then she again heard rustling and felt his arm reach around her shoulders, the palm of his hand coming to rest under her cheek. She lay rigid, waiting, but he did nothing more. And almost immediately she heard the soft steady sound of his sleep.

She inched backward into his warm side. At a later time she would recall thinking it bizarre to be comforted by the closeness of a relative stranger, and an accused murderer as well. And that if she had even remotely suspected what lay ahead of her, she could never have succumbed to such a deep and tranquil sleep. As it was, when she drifted off, the last thing she remembered was the curve of his fingers against her face.

16

My wife is as handsome as when she was a girl
and I a poor nobody then, fell in love with her and
once more, have never fallen out.

—Abraham Lincoln

Mary Lincoln lifted her face to the sunshine straining
through the train's dusty window. Although it warmed
with only the feeble strength of February, the sun made her
feel hopeful, safely distanced from the danger she'd come
to anticipate every waking hour. Four days previous, there
had been another suspicious incident: a freight train de-
railment on the way into Pittsburgh that had caused their
own train a two-hour delay while the track ahead was
cleared. There was some speculation that the rails had been
deliberately loosened, although to Mary's dismay, Mr.
Lincoln seemed to find this conjecture "fanciful." Subsequently, however, nothing untoward had occurred. And the
crowds, not only in Pennsylvania, but in Cleveland, Ohio,
and yesterday in Buffalo, New York, had been huge and
enthusiastic.

Thousands had jammed the streets of the western New
York city on the shore of Lake Erie when she and Mr. Lincoln climbed from the train to be met by former president
Millard Fillmore. The crowd was so large that the Buffalo
police had needed to make a passageway to the waiting car-

riages. Even so, Mary and Mr. Lincoln had been forced to fight their way through the crush of bodies, all wanting to shake the new President's hand, then rode to the American Hotel with a procession following.

At first Mary had been offended by the familiarity of the crowd, and thought the shouts of "Hi, Abe!" and "Good luck, President Abe," to be disrespectful. But the greetings were given with such exuberant good nature that she came to understand it was simple affection being offered; that her husband was viewed as friendly and accessible to the common man. She found herself caught up in the excitement, waving to the well-wishers lining the street and taking pride in the hundreds of American flags flapping in the brisk wind. Perhaps her melancholy had begun to fade. She knew she was changeable, always had been; her moods like "sunshine or storm," Mr. Lincoln frequently said, and "tempestuous as midwestern spring weather."

After the Buffalo mayor's welcoming address on the steps of the hotel, Mr. Lincoln spoke but a few words in a voice, Mary noted with concern, that had become increasingly hoarse: "We've had a fortunate and agreeable journey during the week, with nothing to mar the trip." Of course, he *would* say that.

At six o'clock this morning, as the train had chugged out of Buffalo, the streets were again thronged. In spite of the early hour, the atmosphere had been warmly festive, and what with that and the sunshine, Mary resolved she should look to the future with optimism—perhaps the worst lay behind them. After all, she was now the First Lady. It had taken a while for this fact to settle in, but she had finally begun to enjoy her new persona. The newspapers in the cities they passed through had commented approvingly on her "ease, grace, and fashionability," and the widely circulated *Home Journal* had conferred upon her the title of "Illinois Queen."

She glanced at Mr. Lincoln on the seat beside her, reading a Buffalo paper. He had not been entirely happy, the previous month, about her two-week shopping excursion to New York City. Not only had she purchased the latest in fashions—unavailable in Springfield—but invitations to her social teas held daily in the ladies' parlor of the Astor Hotel were much sought after. In fact, she had such an enjoyable time, she extended her stay; Mr. Lincoln had met the train for three nights running before she at last, reluctantly, returned to Illinois. Shopping always made her feel good, although the sense of well-being was invariably followed by the guilt of having spent too much. But given the recent newspaper accounts, the New York trip had proven more than justified.

In addition, the shopping had been an escape from the mail that began to arrive almost directly after the election: the anonymous letters decorated with skulls and crossbones, one containing a sketch of her husband tarred and feathered with a noose around his neck. Even their son Tad had received a fearsome black-faced caricature doll sent to "Master Lincoln" in care of the Springfield Post Office. After that episode, the arriving mail had been funneled first through a male secretary.

Now, with the train wheels clacking monotonously as they neared Rochester, Mary gazed through the window at the rolling landscape of western New York and the miles of snow-dappled pine and fir stretching beside the tracks. Sunlit frozen ponds resembled large silver platters serving up coveys of mallard ducks. After Rochester, there would be a short stop in Syracuse, then on to Utica, with arrival in Albany at mid-afternoon. A grand reception would be held there, to be followed by a cavalcade to the capital. An evening theater party had originally been scheduled, but the performance then canceled because the leading player had fallen on his dagger a few nights earlier; Mary regretted that she was not to see the celebrated young actor John Wilkes Booth.

Crossing the Genesee River railroad bridge, she recalled that their Springfield neighbor, Robin Tryon, had been born in Rochester, as had his sister; Glynis Tryon had spent a year in Springfield caring for Robin's failing wife before returning to her home in Seneca Falls. Her niece, Robin's daughter Emma, had gone with her. Dear, dear Emma. She'd recently written Mary that she now owned her own dress shop, which certainly came as no surprise. The young woman was talented beyond measure, and while still in Springfield had done much of Mary's dressmaking. Seneca Falls, Mary thought she remembered Glynis Tryon saying, was a small town somewhere between Rochester and Syracuse; a shame there was no leeway in their rigid schedule to stop there.

Mary reached over to smooth Mr. Lincoln's hair, forever unruly. He'd been dozing, but his eyes opened briefly and he took her hand to give it a firm squeeze, then held it clasped to his chest. "A long journey, Molly," he said with a slow smile. "A long journey indeed, from Springfield to Washington."

Mary knew he did not have in mind the present train trip.

The noon sun was slipping behind clouds when they stepped out onto the train's rear platform in Syracuse. Mary motioned for her husband to bend down, so that she could wrap his muffler more securely around his neck. As he straightened up, Mary kissed his cheek and tucked her arm through his. The crowd cheered, seeming to approve this display of affection, and she wondered if previous Presidents' wives had behaved thusly. But the past didn't much matter, she decided. This was *their* time, his and hers.

She heard a familiar voice call softly, "Mrs. President Lincoln," and looked down to see, standing directly below her, Emma Tryon.

Mary leaned over the platform railing and reached for Emma's outstretched hand. "My dear Emma, how lovely of you to come."

"Oh, I wouldn't have missed seeing you for anything, Mrs. Lin— . . . I mean, Mrs. President."

Emma blushed slightly and Mary laughed. "How are you, my darling girl?"

"I'm fine, thank you. If you'll forgive my familiarity in saying so, you look just . . . just regal, Mrs. President. What a beautiful gown that is. Watered silk, so very elegant."

"I'm delighted you approve, Emma. Do you remember the splendid times we had, you and I, when you made my clothes?"

"Of course I remember! And now, with your permission, I can say that I once sewed for the First Lady."

"You have my permission. And you must come to Washington with your aunt for a visit. How is Miss Tryon?"

"She's . . . she's fine. As a matter of fact, she's on her way to Washington right now."

"Emma, please write and tell her to come and visit . . ."

A shrill whistle from the locomotive covered her words. She blew the young woman a kiss as her husband took her arm. He smiled down at Emma, tipped his tall silk hat to her, then escorted Mary back inside the passenger car.

As they settled into their seats, he commented, "You liked seeing Miss Tryon again, and I reckon that made things better. You look happy, Molly."

She nodded, suddenly realizing that she *was* happy.

And why not? She was the President's wife. They were

on their way to Washington, where a great adventure awaited. And after that, after the history they would make, they could go back home to Springfield and grow old together.

Why shouldn't she be happy?

17

—m—

*I asked . . . what was the object of the Organiza-
tion. He replied, "It was first organized to prevent
the passage of Lincoln with the troops through
Baltimore, but our plans are changed every day,
as matters change, and what its object will be
from day to day, I do not know, nor can I tell."*

—from *Pinkerton's Records*, Baltimore office,
February 19, 1861

*T*he morning smell of coffee, frying bacon, and stone-
ground hominy grits permeated the dining room of Atlanta's
Hotel Olympus. One of three men seated at a corner table
was in the act of pouring red-eye gravy on his grits, and another was swallowing coffee, when a fourth man entered the
room. All three diners scrambled to their feet as the man approached them, although the one called Weasel glanced
with regret at the gravy already cooling on his plate.

"Well?" came the brisk greeting from the arrival.

Weasel shifted his feet. "We lost her." He raised his eyes
from the plate to meet the other's angry look.

"You damned fools! That's all you have to say—'We lost
her'? And you have no idea where she is?"

"We know where she *isn't*. Not in West Point, Georgia,
anyway. The man we left there is positive—said he tore the

town apart looking for her. And she's not here in Atlanta, not anymore—at least we don't think so."

"You don't think so? But you don't know so! Correct?"

The three men nodded. The black-bearded one volunteered, "We know she was here. Can't say where she hid on the train, but we found her dress in the baggage car—in a trunk that had been forced open. We figured she might try to wire her boss, so we been watching the telegraph office for the last twenty-four hours. And Joe's still posted there, just in case."

"If she'd changed her clothes, how would you know who the hell you were watching for?"

Black Beard risked a tentative grin. "That red hair stands out a mile away. We wouldn't have missed her. She must have cut out, left Atlanta. We think she could be heading north. Maybe for Chicago and the Agency."

"I don't think so. With what she knows, she'll make for Baltimore."

"But Pinkerton's in Chicago."

"Pinkerton's in Baltimore! That's the latest word we've had. Trouble is, nobody knows what he looks like—even if he's not in disguise. No, our little Miss Troublemaker will head for Baltimore. And I expect you to find her before she gets there! You understand what it is I'm saying?"

Black Beard and Weasel glanced nervously at the other hired killer, who nodded with extraordinary vigor. "Oh, yeah, we understand! But there's a lotta ways she could go to Baltimore from here. There's trains east to Augusta and Charleston, then short lines up the coast, or north to Raleigh and Richmond. She could even get there by way of Norfolk, then by steamboat up the Chesapeake."

"Then find the way! Split up, bring in other men and fan out, and search every route she might take. And for your own good, you damn well better track her down. The plan's

been made, it's ready—too late to change it now, and too many involved to call it off. So get her!"

As the fourth man strode away, Weasel sat down heavily, and eyed his congealed gravy with a distinct lack of interest.

In Allan Pinkerton's room at Baltimore's Howard House hotel, Mrs. Kate Warne sipped her lukewarm tea while waiting for the detective to arrive. He must have been held up at South Street, in the pseudo stock broker's office he'd opened there as a cover for his activities. It was unlike him to be late, but then, the present case was unlike any other she'd been involved in during her four years with Pinkerton's Detective Agency.

Mrs. Warne straightened on the uncomfortable cane-seated chair to glance at the mirror on the wall opposite, tucking errant strands of pale brown back into the large, smooth roll of hair at the nape of her neck. She gazed at the face Pinkerton had called "self-possessed and honest, which would cause one in distress to select her as a confidante . . ." and smiled to herself, thinking this assessment of his was characteristic. Other men saw her differently—many called her beautiful, or intelligent, or desirable—but Allan Pinkerton would always view her in the light of how useful she was to him as an agent.

She abruptly recalled the afternoon she had first met him at his Chicago office, having been recently widowed and in search of employment. She'd been completely candid with him: she wanted to be a detective. The look on his face when she had announced this was not one she'd ever be likely to forget.

"I've never heard of a female detective," he had said initially, but then leaned back in his chair, studying her with interest and, she'd later decided, apparently a somewhat open mind. "And why do you think you would be of value to me in that capacity?" he asked.

She had looked him straight in the eye and answered, "Because a clever woman can worm out secrets in many places to which it is impossible for male detectives to gain access."

At this, she'd been treated to one of his extremely infrequent smiles, and told to return the next day, as he "needed to think it over."

When she arrived the following afternoon, he told her he'd stayed up much of the previous night mulling over her idea. The more he thought about it, the better he liked it. Thus he would hire her as the nation's first female detective, and would assign her a case immediately. After she had completed that assignment, he had allowed her to read his report, which stated, "Mrs. Warne succeeded far beyond my utmost expectations."

She had been with him ever since.

Now she looked up as the door opened. Pinkerton removed his ubiquitous cigar before taking her hand. "My dear Kate, you made good time indeed. I met your train, but apparently it came in ahead of schedule."

"I caught an earlier one—it seemed speed was essential, as I received this wire directly after yours arrived." She reached into her purse and withdrew the telegram. "It's from Timothy Webster. He didn't want to risk exposure—his or yours—by wiring you here in Baltimore, so he sent it to my house in Chicago."

Webster was a Pinkerton agent in Perrysville, Maryland, who had succeeded in infiltrating a cavalry unit there. He'd recently been invited to a secret meeting in Baltimore, having become friendly with a unit commander and other officers in the company.

"Good," Pinkerton said, taking the wire Mrs. Warne

handed to him. "I've been expecting this." He read it silently, and Kate Warne waited in like silence. She knew the content of the wire: That sometime during, or directly following, the presidential inaugural ceremony, the Confederate cavalry planned to cut telegraph lines, blow up railroad bridges, and destroy the tracks leading into Washington to prevent Union troops from reaching the city.

"Yes," Pinkerton said, folding the wire and slipping it into his frock coat pocket, "this confirms the rumors I've heard ever since I've been here. Samuel Felton has every reason to fear for his railroad."

"They intend to isolate Washington," Mrs. Warne said, "but then what?"

"We don't know precisely yet, although it seems obvious that all the pro-Confederate factions here in Baltimore aim to disrupt the federal government. And force Governor Hicks to secede Maryland, which he has up to now opposed. But the means by which each group plans to do this varies— and some seem to be more immediately dangerous than others. Fanatical is the word."

Kate Warne nodded. "There've been reports in the Chicago newspapers of clashes already between Northern and Southern partisans here in Baltimore."

"Oh, this place is a political hot bed. I'm fairly certain that we don't yet have the whole story, but it's a potentially explosive situation. And I'm concerned about the police chief here in Baltimore, Marshal George Kane; I'm not certain he can be trusted."

"Forgive me for changing the subject," Kate Warne said, "but have you heard anything, anything at all, from Montgomery?"

Pinkerton's usual impassive expression turned decidedly grim. "That's the main reason I called you down here. Bad news is what I've finally heard from Montgomery. I'm very much afraid we've lost two agents down there."

"*Lost?*"

"The operative I just sent down has reported that both Ann Clements and Arthur Kelly are dead. Made to look like accidents, but undoubtedly killed. Don't know by who, or why—not yet. Must be, though, that the deaths are connected in some way to the South's railroads—after all, that's why they were down there."

"And the novice—Bronwen Llyr?"

Pinkerton's scowl deepened. "Bronwen Llyr has disappeared. Last seen by Thaddeus Dowling in West Point, Georgia—he was bringing her back to Chicago—she just vanished. Don't look so concerned, Kate. If anyone can land on her feet, it's Llyr."

"But she's so young. . . ."

"Young doesn't mean she isn't resourceful. She may be willful, reckless, a genuine pain in the a— . . . sorry . . . but she *is* resourceful, I'll give her that."

"If you didn't like her, why did you hire her?"

"Who said I didn't like her? Actually, I don't much, but there's a chance—just an outside one, mind you, but a chance—that she'll make a good operative. If she learns how to follow the rules! And if she lives long enough. But if she botches this one, she's through! One step out of line and she's finished."

Kate Warne looked away from him in a rare moment of anger. The girl never should have been hired—she was simply too young. And although Kate suspected—at least she hoped—that Allan Pinkerton was not as callous about Bronwen Llyr as he sounded, the girl was still his employee. But he could be a very hard man.

"Kate? You listening to me?"

"No, what did you say?"

"I'm sending you to New York City. I want you to meet up with Mr. Lincoln's contingent. See if you can find out what precautions they're taking to get him to Washington without incident. I don't like the fact that his itinerary has been made so public. I may come up to New York myself, depending on what you report. First I need to see Felton in Philadelphia—expand the strategy to protect his railroad."

Kate Warne rose and began to pull on her gloves. Two agents, people she had known for several years, were dead. Although she and every other Pinkerton operative knew there was always the possibility of danger in this work, she couldn't remember ever being so uneasy about an assignment.

III

Through blinding storm and clouds of night
We swiftly pushed our restless flight;
With thundering hoof and warning neigh,
We urged our steed upon his way
Up the line.

Afar the lofty head-light gleamed;
Afar the whistle shrieked and screamed;
And glistening bright, and rising high,
Our flakes of fire bestrewed the sky,
Up the line.

Adown the long, complaining track,
Our wheels a message hurried back;
And quivering through the rails ahead,
Went news of our resistless tread,
Up the line.

The trees gave back our din and shout,
And flung their shadow arms about;
And shivering in their coats of gray,
They heard us roaring far away,
Up the line.

The wailing storm came on apace,
And dashed its tears into our face;
But steadily still we pierced it through,
And cut the sweeping wind in two,
Up the line.

A rattling rush across the ridge,
A thunder-peal beneath the bridge;
And valley and hill and sober plain
Re-echoed our triumphant strain,
Up the line.

And when the Eastern streaks of gray
Bespoke the dawn of coming day,
We halted our steed, his journey o'er,
And urged his giant form no more,
Up the line.

   —Will Carleton, "Up the Line," from
     Farm Ballads

18

[Woman] . . . has but one right and that is the right to protection. The right to protection involves the obligation to obey. A husband, lord and master . . . nature designed for every woman.

—George Fitzhugh, 1854

*B*ronwen felt her body begin to slip sideways on the horse and jerked herself upright. Her thighs ached from riding bareback, and she had to struggle just to keep her eyes open; the Virginia sun, although low on the western horizon, shone warm on her shoulder blades, and the slow, monotonous pace made her drowsy. She would give anything for a bath and some sleep—not just a catnap, but real sleep. How long since she'd had any? The hayloft in Atlanta, but that must have been . . . two nights ago? Was that all? It seemed more like two weeks.

Marsh, on a sway-backed gelding plodding beside her own aged mare, leaned over to say, "How much farther do you think?" He looked none the worse for their journey north. If anything, he looked healthier than when they'd met, which also seemed weeks ago. He appeared to have put on a few pounds, and his eyes were somewhat less wary.

"I'm not sure," Bronwen answered. "The directions Aunt Glynis gave me, and it was ages ago, were a little vague on distance. But the James River is over there—" she pointed to her right "—and Riverain plantation is supposed to be on a bend of it. How long have we been riding east since we left Richmond?"

"Not long. Maybe a half hour."

"Then we should be there soon." Please Lord, let it be *soon*.

She hoped never to see another railroad car, unlikely as that hope might be. Since leaving Atlanta, they'd ridden hundreds of miles in various baggage cars, in unoccupied freight cars, and in—by far the worst—one well-occupied cattle car. They'd traveled from Atlanta to Augusta, Georgia, to South Carolina, and to North Carolina, and had finally reached Virginia. It hadn't been the most direct route, but clearly it had been the safest. They were still alive.

The telegrams had not been sent.

The morning she'd awakened in the hayloft in Atlanta, Marsh was just reappearing at the top of the ladder with fresh figs and buttermilk scones. Bronwen didn't inquire as to whether he had broken into the bakery shop; she did not want to know just how much she had corrupted his fundamentally honest nature. And he would have said it was none of her business. But he *did* consider it her business to know there were several men "just hanging around the telegraph station. They're not doing anything, not sending wires, just hanging around."

"What do they look like?"

"Like men. How're they supposed to look?"

"Like any of those in the train."

He shook his head. "I didn't get a good view from my belly position on the roof, if you remember. I heard them talking just now though, and one of the voices *did* sound sort of familiar."

"A deep voice?"

"Not especially. Just familiar. Think if you're smart, you'll stay the hell away from there. Forget the telegrams."

"I can't. The one to Pinkerton is too important. Maybe those men are just locals. I'll take a look myself."

When, peering around the corner of the hotel porch, she saw two men circling the telegraph office in seemingly aimless fashion, she felt queasy. Then she spotted two more of them, nearly hidden by bushes, lurking behind it. At least they looked to be lurking, hats pulled down over their foreheads and collars up around their chins. Plus they kept glancing about as if they were watching for someone. And two of them appeared vaguely familiar. She couldn't quite place them, but decided she'd seen them somewhere in Montgomery. It was more than enough persuasion to keep herself concealed.

She waited by the porch for over an hour. Frequently two or three of the men would saunter away, but they always left at least one there.

"O.K.," she said at last to Marsh, who was crouching behind her. "I guess they *are* watching for me. I don't suppose *you* would—"

"You suppose right! It's *my* face on the wanted poster over there, remember? Look, you can send the wires from somewhere else. Let's just get the hell out of here!"

Bronwen couldn't argue with this logic.

Since trains left fairly often, they thought it would be merely a matter of concealing themselves behind the station to wait for one heading north. When a conductor yelled, "All aboard—to Greenville, South Carolina," they started for it.

"We can get tickets on board," Bronwen called over her shoulder as they ran toward the passenger cars.

Halfway across the tracks, Marsh whispered, "Wait!" and grabbed her sleeve to stop her. He pointed to the platform where, through clouds of steam, one of the men from the telegraph office had materialized.

They waited another two hours before the train to Augusta made ready to leave. "Let's go," Bronwen urged.

"But Augusta's not north," Marsh protested. "Why should we go east?"

"We should go east because they're expecting us to go north," Bronwen said impatiently, pushing him along the track. But she stopped short when she spotted the bearded man who stood watching from the platform.

Waiting until the locomotive began to inch forward, they darted around the rear of the caboose, then, loping along the far side of the train, they grabbed the ledge of a baggage car's open door. Marsh easily hurdled up and climbed inside. Bronwen, now running as fast as she could, knew she'd never have the strength to jump aboard as the train was beginning to pick up steam. Marsh reached down, grasped her wrists, and dragged her through the opening just as the station house flew past.

"Do you think he saw us?" Bronwen panted.

Marsh shrugged. "Too late for them to do anything about it now," he said laconically. "But we better watch it in Augusta."

And indeed, the circumstances repeated themselves at the Augusta station, and again at Columbia, South Carolina. "One of these times," Marsh warned, "we won't be so lucky. Let's try something different."

"Right," Bronwen agreed. "We should take a circuitous route—and on freights." She'd learned, by then, to haul herself aboard by waiting for just the right moment to position her hands on the ledge and vault sideways into a car, using leverage rather than strength. And had felt childishly pleased with herself the first time she'd swung up into the train without Marsh's help.

Many short, zigzagging hops later, one of them aboard the cattle train, they reached Greensboro, North Carolina. Here, for once, they pulled into a fairly deserted depot. Bronwen yanked the wire messages from her coveralls pocket only to discover a station house too small for a telegraph. Her frustration was tempered by the apparent absence of any would-be assassins.

"Maybe we've finally lost them," she said, although not convinced of this. So, after hiding several hours, they again caught a freight car, this time to Petersburg, Virginia, and then another to Richmond, as caution and fear had combined to make them both leery of passenger cars.

And a prudent course this had proved to be. As they pulled into Richmond, Bronwen, peeking out from behind the freight car's sliding door, saw with astonishment that Cormac Quinn and Zoe Martin were just stepping down to the platform.

"I don't like this," she muttered to Marsh. "Why are *they* here in Richmond?" She liked it even less when she saw Thaddeus Dowling and Colonel de Warde also detrain.

"Maybe they're all on their way to Baltimore," Marsh offered in a grim tone. "If so, we better stay put right here as long as we can."

They'd waited until the station master announced that the train was leaving before jumping off, then hunkered behind the caboose until the last minute. After darting around the rear of the station house, they waited again before venturing out to lose themselves in the throngs of an adjacent public market.

A nearby livery rented them the horses, old but cheap. And although they had seen no one following, Bronwen found herself frequently looking over her shoulder. "But they're probably expecting me to head straight by train for Baltimore," she told Marsh as they started toward Riverain.

"Which is the last thing I should do. They've likely got a *dozen* Equus men watching the station there."

Now, as she fought to stay awake, the narrow dirt road began to curve beside a bend in the river. Above them, at the crest of a small hill, sat a well-proportioned, white wooden building with a columned portico that overlooked the James.

"It's Riverain," she said to Marsh. "Has to be."

After tethering the horses to a hitching post below the portico, Bronwen climbed the steps to hesitantly rap on the front door. A very tall, very stately Negro woman, who must have seen them riding up the long drive, appeared almost instantly. Bronwen, confronted with a stern expression on the ageless blue-black face before her, suddenly realized how disreputable both she and Marsh must look. The woman probably assumed they were hobos. Which wasn't too far from the truth.

"Ah . . . please excuse our intrusion," she said with elaborate politeness, "but is this the Dupont residence? The home of Mrs. Chantal Dupont? I hope it is," she added, aware that she sounded more plaintive than she'd intended. The strain of the past days, however, threatened to buckle her knees, and she prayed she wouldn't collapse on the elegant portico like one of P. T. Barnum's rubber-legged, circus clowns.

As the tall woman stared inscrutably down at her, a slender figure appeared in the doorway to ask, "Who is it, Masika?"

When this figure stepped forward, Bronwen immediately identified her from Aunt Glynis's description. The striking face, the curly, tumbled white-blond hair, couldn't belong to any other than the widowed mistress of Riverain. And the woman named Masika would be Zeph Waters's grandmother, once a slave but freed by Chantal Dupont upon her husband's death, as had been all the Riverain slaves.

"Mrs. Dupont? I'm Glynis Tryon's niece, Bronwen. My aunt said that I could come here. . . ."

"Yes, yes of course!" Chantal Dupont broke in, extending her hand. "I got a wire from Glynis just two days ago. Come in."

Bronwen was conscious of Marsh behind her shuffling his feet. "I'm afraid there's two of us," she explained. "This is . . . ah . . ." She felt a jab in her ribs as she said this, and spun around to him, responding tartly, "If *I* trust you, why shouldn't *she?*" Turning back to Chantal Dupont, Bronwen went on, "This is Tristan Marshall. He prefers to be called Marsh—and if you wouldn't mind, we can go into why, later. Because right now, if I don't sit down, I may pass out."

It was truly amazing, Bronwen thought sometime later, what wonders a hot bath could work. She now sat at an oak trestle table in the huge kitchen, her head wrapped turban-style in a thick white cotton towel.

"You expect to stay incognita with that red hair?" Chantal Dupont asked, while Bronwen and Marsh devoured a platterful of honeyed pork chops and yams.

"I told her to cut it," said Marsh in between mouthfuls. "She said she'd rather die."

"An unfortunate choice of words, perhaps," Chantal responded with a dry smile. "From the events the two of you have described, I think you should take every precaution. That is," she said to Bronwen, "unless I can persuade you to stay here until your aunt arrives. She was due in Washington, so her wire said, sometime today."

"I can't stay."

"Can't or won't?"

"Both," Bronwen answered. "There's no time to wait for Aunt Glynis, and besides, she'll try to talk me out of this—

at least she'll think she *should* try. But it won't work, and then we'll both of us feel guilty, and what good is that?"

Chantal Dupont looked somewhat bewildered, but Bronwen saw, to her surprise, that Marsh was nodding in agreement. Though he had a vested interest in seeing she got word to Pinkerton, thus earning the detective's approval.

Chantal Dupont sighed, but it sounded like a resigned one, Bronwen thought with relief. The woman then asked, "What is it you plan to do?"

"I have to locate the Pinkerton operative here in Richmond," Bronwen told her. "Telegrams are probably not much use at this stage. I don't even know if Pinkerton is still in Chicago, but the operative should know and could get my message to him. I'm convinced something disastrous is planned, possibly blowing up the Baltimore railroad."

"So you said," Chantal nodded. "How can I help?"

"I know there's a group of conspirators who call themselves Equus. And that someone will be murdered by them. I just don't know when or who. I need to get back into Richmond safely, and find the agent. Can you help me to do that?"

"Yes, although I hate to think what your aunt will have to say about it. Still, she's not led the most sheltered life herself, and she knows full well what it is you're doing. . . . *She does know*, doesn't she?"

"Oh, yes, she knows I'm with Pinkerton's," Bronwen said, hedging.

She caught the look Marsh shot her, but he said nothing to dispute her evasion.

"Right now you need sleep, though," Chantal said, "and there's no point trying to find anyone tonight in Richmond. In the morning I'll have Jonah drive you into the city. Do you have some idea where this operative is?"

"I have an address," Bronwen said, "but no name. Allan Pinkerton is very cautious."

"He probably has good reason to be, especially here in Virginia and in Maryland," Chantal stated. "These are, after all, becoming dangerous times."

Marsh, polishing off the last of a pecan pie, rose from his chair and announced he would like to get some sleep. Masika handed him a glass-globed lamp, then motioned toward the staircase.

"Thank you for the good meal, ladies," he said to Chantal and Masika. "I'm obliged to you for your hospitality." He gave Bronwen a look which she couldn't read, then mumbled something like "See you in the morning," and started toward the stairs.

Bronwen watched him until she felt Chantal Dupont's eyes on her.

"Nice lad," Chantal said, although there was a question in her voice.

Bronwen nodded. "He's O.K." She didn't add, despite Chantal's obvious curiosity, that she had no intention of getting too entangled with Tristan Marshall. Life was complicated enough without that.

Nonetheless, "You mentioned how you met," Chantal prodded, "but what do you know about him?"

Again, Bronwen hedged. "Not much. While we were traveling, he told me that he'd been sold into servitude by his stepfather, against his mother's will, to a shipbuilder in Mobile, Alabama. And that along with several other men he managed to escape from what sounded like horrible conditions. More like prison chain-gang labor than servitude."

"And now?"

"Now he . . . I'm not sure."

Chantal didn't look convinced of this, but did not press further. All she said was, "Be careful, Bronwen. Although," she added bluntly, "your aunt tells me that isn't one of your foremost concerns."

Bronwen smiled. "Aunt Glynis should talk. She's been involved in some pretty hair-raising things herself."

"They've not been things she sought out."

"No, but she didn't exactly avoid them, either. She's just more . . . more discreet than I am. And less stubborn."

Chantal did not seem inclined to disagree.

A few minutes later Bronwen followed Marsh up the stairs. She held a lamp in front of her as she started down the hallway, then paused before the door of his room. It stood slightly ajar. She wondered if he was feeling anywhere near as alone, as uncertain, as she. Not that it mattered, because although she'd become accustomed to curling up beside him to catnap, this was not the same. A secluded room with a soft feather bed would afford a very different atmosphere from the rumbling, dirty car of a railroad train. They'd grown closer, though, and she had begun, despite herself, to . . .

No. Allan Pinkerton constantly harped on her disregard for potential consequences. For once maybe she should pay attention to the inner voice that told her there definitely would be consequences here. For one thing, the tenuous alliance she and Marsh had hammered out would become more complicated. For another, she could hardly overlook the fact that, no matter the circumstances—and as yet she did not know precisely what they were—he remained wanted for murder.

As it was, she shuddered to think how Pinkerton would receive the news that she'd promised an accused killer the Agency's assistance. It didn't bear thinking about too closely.

In spite of that, she still felt unmistakable regret, sadness, and simple loneliness when she walked on to the next bed-room.

Rising softly against the morning's darkly overcast sky, the rounded hills of Richmond made for a particularly beautiful city, Bronwen conceded, though she was experiencing a certain amount of impatience while Jonah maneuvered the carriage through the crowded streets. She also felt a large measure of envy at the elegantly dressed people she saw on the sidewalks, since she herself was again wearing denim overalls—*clean* ones—bibbed over her chest, another loose shirt, and a sailor's hat with a turned-down brim. Marsh, seated beside her in unexplained sullen silence, also wore a clean shirt and trousers, no doubt the first in some time. Earlier, she'd noticed an unmistakable bulge in the right pocket of his trousers. She had not asked.

Bronwen might not have felt such a need to remain disguised if she hadn't seen the foursome from Montgomery detraining the previous day. It still struck her as odd. No, more than odd: suspicious. Why would Thaddeus Dowling be arriving in Richmond when he should be returning to Chicago? Unless he and Colonel de Warde had some business to conclude here. And that certainly didn't explain Zoe Martin, although Cormac Quinn *was* a news reporter and perhaps he had employed her as a photographer. This scenario was *possible*, even if it did seem extremely far-fetched. But if Guy Seagram should suddenly turn up, Bronwen decided, she would run straight to Baltimore. Granted that she hadn't yet figured out how to get there if not by train. However, Chantal Dupont had given her the name of an Elizabeth Van Lew, mistress of the Church Hill mansion, which was used by Richmond's Underground Railroad to hide slaves escaping to the North. And Van Lew herself was a devout Union sympathizer.

"Go to her," Chantal had urged. "If there's trouble, she can get you out of Richmond if anyone can."

At the moment, Bronwen would be satisfied just to find the Gee Street address of the Pinkerton operative. Even their Negro driver, Jonah, who had lived in and around Richmond all his life, seemed vague about where it might be.

"It's somewhere down by the docks, I reckon," he'd said when they started out.

Right now they traveled up a steep, cobbled street, the team of horses moving slowly but steadily until they came abreast of an iron-fenced space known as Capitol Square. Narrow stone walks wound under gnarled trees, some of which might have stood there for centuries. Then Jonah steered the team left, and they started down toward the river-front, with its rows of multistoried warehouses and low sheds. Crossing Main Street, they came to the corner of Eighth, where before them reared the recently finished, four-story Spotswood Hotel. Jonah slowed the horses to skirt the other carriages and omnibuses crowding the busy hotel entrance.

"Think the street you want might run off the Kanawha Canal," Jonah said to them over his shoulder from the driver's seat. "We'll take a look."

The Kanawha had been dug alongside the river, as had canals in Seneca Falls and Rochester, and for the same reason: to bypass the swift, falling rapids.

"Wait!" Bronwen called out. "Now I remember. Pinkerton said the street *was* near the canal. That it ran below this Spotswood Hotel."

Jonah nodded, the three of them looking right and left.

"There!" Jonah pointed his whip toward a narrow strip of cobblestones that appeared to be an alley running between a row of wooden warehouses. Painted on the side of a corner building was an arrow with the words "GEE STREET."

"You'd better wait for us here," Bronwen told Jonah, who immediately pulled his hat down over his forehead and slouched back against the seat.

Marsh gestured at the glowering sky. "We need to do this fast," he said as Bronwen climbed from the carriage. "What's the number?"

His sullen mood didn't seem to have lifted, but at least he was speaking to her. All at once she wondered if he'd heard her stop by his bedroom door the night before. Was he repelled by the thought that she had considered going to him? Or disappointed that she hadn't?

"Number eleven," she answered briskly, deciding once more to ignore his bad temper. "It's supposed to be an office, I think, but these all look like warehouses."

Marsh had already started down the alley, slowing to peer at each of the doors, only a few of which held numbers. He stopped, glancing around until Bronwen caught up with him. "I'm not real happy with this place," he announced, and gazed back at the carriage with yearning. "Looks like it could be a trap. It's too quiet. This is a city. So where the hell *is* everybody?"

"That it's isolated is probably exactly why it was chosen," Bronwen retorted. "And if there's no one around, what are you worried about?"

Marsh didn't answer, his eyes scanning both sides of the alley. "This must be it," he said, pointing ahead of him to a dingy, unpainted door. "There's no number, but the one back there is nine, and that one across the way there is ten."

Bronwen stepped forward and tried the door. It grated open with the creak of rusty hinges. Straight ahead was a steep flight of rickety-looking stairs, looped with cobwebs and dust. The rank moldy smell fortified the impression of a seldom-used structure.

Then, just as she stepped over the threshold, from somewhere above came a sudden rush of footsteps. A man's voice yelled, "No, wait! You've got the wrong—"

The words were sliced off by the bark of a revolver.

Marsh grabbed for the nearest door, and shoved Bronwen ahead of him into a musty closet, pulling the door closed behind them. Between the hinges and the frame a slim crack of light remained, almost immediately shadowed by someone hurtling down the stairs. The footsteps stopped directly in front of the closet door. Although she was crushed against the wall, Bronwen tried to reach for the stiletto, but Marsh seized her arm with fingers strong enough to cut off the circulation. She didn't protest, not with the possibility of a gun just a few feet away.

The door to the alley abruptly creaked open, followed by the sound of hurrying footsteps. Marsh quickly shifted his hand to cover her mouth and held it there. What did he think she was going to do? Scream? Recite the Lord's Prayer? Angrily, she pushed his hand away.

They waited one, two, three minutes, in absolute silence before Marsh gingerly pushed the door open and stepped into the short, gloomy hallway. Bronwen, right on his heels, caught a trace of gunpowder wafting down the stairs.

"Did you see whoever it was?" she asked.

"Just a glimpse. He had on a hat and coat—the collar turned up—looked like he was ordinary height."

"*He?* Are you sure it was a man?"

"Am I *sure?* What would a woman be doing in this rat-trap?"

Bronwen glared at him, but refrained from pointing out the obvious. Instead, she jerked her head toward the stairs.

Marsh looked incredulous. "You want to go up there? Are you crazy?"

"I have to find the Pinkerton operative."

"What you're going to find is a dead body. Didn't you hear that shot?"

"We don't know that it *hit* anyone. Or maybe he's lying up there hurt." She cocked her head to listen, then added, "There doesn't seem to be anyone else walking around. However, I'll be glad to go first." Instantly she regretted what she'd just implied.

Marsh swore softly and elbowed her aside. She tried to give him the stiletto, but he slapped her hand away. As he started up the stairs, he reached into his pocket and in the dim light struggling through grime-streaked windows she saw the glint of metal.

Bronwen reached out and gripped his arm. "Where did you get that pistol?"

"None of your business."

Had he raided the gun cabinet at Riverain? Or had Chantal given it to him, not knowing he was wanted for murder?

Bronwen followed directly behind him, her own weapon held ready. The stairs complained so loudly under their combined weight that if someone waited at the top, their coming might as well have been trumpeted. This could be a good thing, though, she told herself, as there would be time for whoever it was to get away. After all, she and Marsh *could* be the police.

She lowered her chin and made her voice deep. "Right up there, officer! I heard the shot just a minute ago."

Marsh half-turned on the step above and gave her a look of disgust.

When they reached the top stair, an expanse of raw wood planking stretched before them. The cavernous warehouse space looked empty except for a shoulder-high partition protruding some ten feet out from a side wall. This interior wall stood midway down the warehouse floor, as if an office cubicle had once been contemplated, then abandoned half finished. Marsh cautiously made for the partition, his revolver held straight ahead of him. Bronwen followed, then heard his intake of breath as he rounded the wall.

When she reached his side, she saw a man sprawled face-down over a desk. A thin trickle of blood ran from a bullet hole above his left ear.

"Not exactly a surprise," Marsh said slowly. His voice, though subdued, echoed in the empty warehouse. "Know who it is?"

Bronwen shook her head. She resolutely closed her mind to what lay before her, and stepped forward to riffle the few papers on the desk. Then she began searching the dead man's frock coat pockets.

Standing behind her, Marsh said harshly, "What in hell are you *doing?*"

"Looking for something. He should have a . . ." She stopped and withdrew a money clip. After flipping through a number of banknotes, she found it: a small card with a Chicago postal box number on it. All operatives carried the cards—Bronwen herself had one in the purse strapped to her thigh—as identification they could give to one another. And in the possible event of such as this.

"It's him, all right," she said to Marsh. "The Pinkerton operative."

"O.K., so it's him. So let's get out of here." He rocked on his feet, eyes darting toward the stairs.

"Just a minute!" Bronwen continued to search through the coat pockets. She stopped when, at the dead man's hip, she glimpsed a white edge of paper protruding from a trouser pocket. She withdrew what looked like a list or schedule of some kind. It contained columns of dates opposite which were city names and obvious timetables followed by words or just initials: "New York Central," "Penn-Central," "P, W & B," and "B & O."

"Railroads," she said, waving the list at Marsh.

He was standing with his back against the partition wall. "So what? C'mon, let's go! No . . . wait!"

Both tensed at a sudden odd rustle near the stairs. Bronwen felt her lower lip begin to quiver, and caught it between her teeth, while backing up against the wall. Marsh raised the revolver and started to move along the partition toward its outer corner in the middle of the warehouse space. Then he cautiously dipped his head around the wall.

Revolver explosions dropped him to the floor.

Dear God, was he dead? In a split-second that reached for eternity, Bronwen plunged to her knees to grab his feet and drag him back behind the partition. Stretching forward for his pistol she expected to see a muzzle appear around the wall.

Suddenly, a hand seized her shoulder. She nearly screamed before she realized it was Marsh pushing her backward. In a blur of fear, she heard him counting under his breath. *Counting?*

Again the revolver barked. One after another, bullets crashed through the partition wall above their heads. Shards of wood rained down. Then came a silence almost as terrible in its potential as the gunfire.

Bronwen chewed her lower lip, tasting blood. She could sense Marsh gathering himself beside her, and hoped he wouldn't try something stupid. Heroic, maybe, but stupid. Then another round slammed into the wall. Immediately, Marsh jumped up and disappeared around the partition, the revolver in his hand roaring. Bronwen could hear bullets splintering wood, and then a shout of pain. Followed by a strangely uneven rush of footsteps on the stairs.

"Marsh?" she breathed.

"Yeah." He reappeared around the wall, holding up the Remington revolver with its muzzle smoking like a blue-black cigar. "You hear him yelp? He grabbed at his leg, so I bet I winged him. Couldn't have been too bad though, 'cause he took off running. Maybe I should go after him."

"Are you *insane?* You're lucky to be alive. How could you jump out there in front of him, you crazy idiot?" Bronwen, to her contempt, felt her entire body shaking. She bit down again on her bleeding lip.

"Do you think I'm that stupid?" Marsh snarled. "I know a Colt when I hear one. He had to reload after six shots—I'd been counting! So who's the idiot?"

He sounded infuriated. Couldn't he see how relieved she was that he hadn't been killed?

"And stop biting your lip!" he shouted. "You're dripping blood all over the place. I'm getting out of here! Now c'mon!"

"How do we know he isn't waiting below?" she asked quietly with, she thought, admirable restraint given his outburst and her own desire to bolt.

"We don't know! Except I heard the door slam."

"Could be a trick. To make—"

"Yeah, yeah." He headed for a window on the far side of the building, and looked down.

"Can you see the street?" Bronwen came up behind him.

"I can see it. There's some people out there now, and one is a copper. Just what we need. . . . Hey, wait a minute!"

Bronwen edged in beside him and stared down. Jonah was standing beside the carriage, gesturing at the policeman and pointing vigorously in the opposite direction. The policeman suddenly took off toward the river at a run.

"C'mon," Bronwen said, pulling at Marsh's sleeve. "Jonah's misled him so we can get out."

As they clambered down the stairs, Bronwen paid attention to several large splotches of blood on the steps ahead of them. The gunman, she pointed out to Marsh, must have been more than winged by the Remington bullets. He nodded, then said irrelevantly, "How does Jonah know we aren't dead?"

"He doesn't. But he knew you had a gun, didn't he?"

By the time they reached the bottom of the stairs, a few hardy souls had tentatively started to push in the door.

Bronwen stepped forward and yanked it all the way open. "Upstairs!" she said to the frightened faces. "I think someone's been shot."

She and Marsh slipped out, then raced to the carriage, Bronwen hunching her shoulders against the bullet she expected might fell her at any moment. But apparently the gunman had also fled.

"Get us out of here!" she told Jonah.

Jonah, already back in the driver's seat, smiled broadly at them. "Y'all ghosts? I heard a lotta shootin'."

"Let's *go!*" Marsh yelped.

"Where you want to go?"

"Church Hill," Bronwen said, her voice trembling only slightly. "To Elizabeth Van Lew's place. Clearly we have to get out of Richmond fast."

19

—m—

*She risked everything that is dear to man—
friends, fortune, comfort, health, life itself—all for
one absorbing desire of her heart, that slavery
might be abolished and the Union preserved.*

—bronze headstone of Elizabeth Van Lew,
Shockoe Cemetery, Richmond, Virginia

"Y'all cannot send a telegram, not out of Richmond.
Wouldn't be safe," asserted Elizabeth Van Lew, sitting ram-rod straight on a brocade sofa in the parlor of her Church
Hill mansion. "Virginia's about to secede and tensions are
high, so any wire sent to the North by a Yankee could be intercepted. Doesn't matter anyway. I've heard your Mr.
Pinkerton is not in Chicago, he's in New York City." Elizabeth Van Lew's sharp blue eyes reinforced her words, convincing Bronwen that the woman would brook no further
argument about telegrams.

Given what Bronwen now suspected, it made some sense
for Pinkerton to be in New York. But she wondered how
Van Lew could know his whereabouts. Unless Chantal
Dupont had learned since this morning. That might be possible if she'd managed to reach Aunt Glynis by wire through
the Treasury Department. Actually, Bronwen now realized,
she should have thought of that herself, as Aunt Glyn's

friend Rhys Bevan was head of the Special Detective Unit at Treasury.

Marsh now said, having obviously missed Van Lew's intent, "But why couldn't someone send a wire *for* her?" he asked, motioning to Bronwen.

Elizabeth Van Lew's features rearranged themselves into a frown clearly meant to intimidate. Which, since she was a fragile-looking blonde of tiny stature, might have seemed ludicrous, except for an earlier glimpse Bronwen had caught of an iron substructure beneath the soft facade of a well-bred Southern lady. And she had already come to recognize this mythic softness characteristic of most women—white and free black—whom she'd met below the Mason-Dixon line. No matter their social class, they were far sturdier than they appeared, at least in public. It was a good thing; according to Elizabeth Van Lew's outlook on the immediate future, Southern women of every class and color would need their strength. But so many disguised it. Was it intentional, Bronwen wondered, or something of which they were not even aware? Or an illusion they adopted to conform to the ideals of Southern men? If so, they were not very different—only in their degree of compliance—from their Northern sisters. But a war, especially one fought on Southern soil, might change that.

The smell of cooked apples now brought Bronwen upright on the straight wooden chair, and she hungrily eyed, again, the blue and white delftware teapot and Dutch apple turnovers on the parlor table. But she could not ignore the fact that she was under the surveillance of thirty or forty cats. The cats draped themselves over every available surface—this included the table, on which lounged a brown-and-black-striped tabby, one white paw curled proprietorially around a cream pitcher—and these were but a small contingent of the cats that had skeptically watched the carriage when it had made its way up the mansion drive. There must be hundreds of them, Bronwen decided. Those in the parlor had been steadily regarding her with the classic feline stare of moral and intellectual superiority. She sensed that if she were to extend a hand toward their delftware teacup, she would be made to suffer.

Thus she kept her hands folded in her lap and said to their mistress, "As I told you earlier, Miss Van Lew, there is every reason to believe that Mr. Marshall"—she ignored Marsh's scowl—"and I are being tracked with deadly intent. We must leave Richmond quickly, but I must also get word to Mr. Pinkerton that there is something dangerous afoot of which he should be aware."

Bronwen knew she was undergoing a careful assessment. Since their arrival an hour ago, Van Lew had scrutinized her without any attempt to conceal it, obviously weighing every word and gesture. But weighing them against what? Bronwen had been almost completely forthright, as Chantal Dupont had said to be. She had omitted a few irrelevant details regarding Marsh—such as his status as a wanted man—and hadn't disputed Elizabeth Van Lew's apparent conclusion that the traveling pair were, more or less, affianced. Fortunately Marsh had been too busy coping with cats trying to scale his legs to hear this indignity.

"What is it that you fear will happen, Miss Llyr?" asked Van Lew. Bronwen glanced quickly at the woman to see if ridicule had been intended. She couldn't tell; Van Lew's expression was, as usual, unreadable.

"I'm all but certain there's a secessionist plot to destroy the railroad line into Washington. To prevent the movement of troops to the capital."

To Bronwen's astonishment, Van Lew nodded agreement. "Oh, I can believe that myself. And I also believe, as you said earlier, that this will take place in or around Baltimore. That's where the most radical activity has been centered."

Bronwen felt a warmth that symbolized as much gratitude as relief. The woman had accepted her seemingly unacceptable story.

"But you haven't told me all of it, have you." Van Lew presented this as a statement rather than a question.

"I'm not certain I *know* all of it," Bronwen answered truthfully, "but yes, I think there's more. Just the fact that we . . . ah, that I'm being hunted leads me to feel there is something more sinister—"

"What," Marsh interrupted, "could be more sinister than blowing up a railroad?"

Bronwen hadn't had opportunity to tell him of her recent discovery, one she'd made only in the past hour, or of the unavoidable reasoning that followed the discovery. Nonetheless, it seemed so monstrous that he would very likely mock it as some overblown imagining on her part. But would Elizabeth Van Lew? Bronwen had been afraid of that until just now, when the woman finally appeared to suspend her distrust. Not that Van Lew didn't have every reason to be wary: she supported the illegal Underground Railroad despite strong suspicion by the area's slaveholders—ever since her family had freed all their own slaves. On the other hand, Bronwen had felt there was no choice but to try to convince the woman to help her. Plus, she now saw how short the time remaining was.

She stared at the *Richmond Enquirer* lying on the marble-topped sidetable. "What could be worse than blowing up a railroad?" she repeated tersely. "Blowing up a train with someone on it."

The other two followed her gaze to the newspaper. "What are you talking about—someone *on* it?" Marsh said, rising to his feet and tumbling several cats off his lap. He picked up the *Enquirer* from the table.

Bronwen, watching him scan the front page, saw his eyes stop, move back, then slowly reread. At last he looked at her in disbelief. Rattling the newspaper, he shook his head, saying, "You don't mean *this?*"

Elizabeth Van Lew, who by this time stood beside him to read, made a small incoherent sound. Then, "They would do *that?* No, it's unthinkable!"

"Is it?" Bronwen asked. "Is it so unthinkable? Why else would they be trying to kill me? They could blow up a railroad *any*time—so what is it they think I overheard in Montgomery that makes me so dangerous *right now?* What could possibly have been worth the murder of three agents? And they're not done yet. They're planning to kill Lincoln!"

Marsh's face had drained of color, which meant he just might believe her. Elizabeth Van Lew continued to stare at the *Enquirer,* but when she finally looked at Bronwen she had likewise blanched.

"And there it is," Bronwen went on, pointing, "right there in that newspaper: Lincoln's itinerary. The scheduled stops, and the timetable his train has been following since he left Springfield. For instance, it indicates that today Lincoln is in New York City. And note," she said, turning to Marsh, "that it matches exactly—*exactly*—the schedule we found on the murdered Pinkerton agent, who might well have figured this out, too. We have no way of knowing, though, if he'd had the time or the means to contact Pinkerton. And his killer doesn't know either, if he didn't find the schedule before we arrived and surprised him."

She pointed again at the newspaper. "There's the date, February twenty-third, when the President—the President-elect—is supposed to arrive in Washington for his inauguration. But first, Lincoln *has* to pass through Baltimore!"

Elizabeth Van Lew strode to the parlor window and stood looking out over the city from which, because of her outspoken abolitionist convictions, she had become a virtual outcast. She, whose Dutch family had once been among Richmond's leading residents, who had attended school in Philadelphia, where her grandfather had been the mayor, now lived alone, except for the company of the former slaves who had remained with her after their manumission. And, of course, the cats.

She turned back to the room, clearly having made a decision. "If you compose a telegram to your aunt," Van Lew said to Bronwen, drawing herself up to her full five feet, "I will try to have it sent to Washington."

"But won't that put you in danger?" Bronwen asked.

"Oh, I'm already well-known here, but so far—to be blunt—my wealth and my family's former position have protected me. Virginians are, after all, gentlemen! It is extremely unlikely that they would allow me to be in any way molested. Frankly, young woman, at the moment my concern is for you. How can you be certain you've not been followed here? As I said, I am known and this could well be the first place they would expect you to come."

Marsh shot Bronwen an I-told-you-so look, which she tried to ignore. "I'll write the telegram now," she told Van Lew.

It took some time:

Red fox steaming to see Barbara Marlboro stop Urgent to divert Mary and family from seeing Barbara or all is lost stop

It might work, Bronwen thought, but only if Aunt Glynis were a genius. She'd figure out "Barbara Marlboro" as Baltimore, Maryland, all right, but would "Mary and family" make any sense to her? It was a long shot, but time ran short. And Bronwen felt she had to try something!

The wire, though, probably had small chance of getting through; they couldn't depend on it, not with what was at stake. She needed to go to Baltimore herself. At least there she could find some Northern sympathizers. She might even enlist the help of the Maryland governor. Her first idea had been to contact the Baltimore police chief, warning of the plot to assassinate Lincoln, but Van Lew immediately disabused her of this notion, saying that Marshal Kane was a rabid secessionist who might welcome the death of the Yankee President-elect.

"And who knows how many others are involved," Elizabeth Van Lew warned.

No, they agreed, Bronwen *had* to go to Baltimore!

An hour after nightfall had shrouded the city, a small, ordinary-looking buggy drew up in front of a barber shop located one block from the Richmond telegraph office. The muscular young Negro driver climbed down, tied the horse to a nearby hitching post, and, not lifting his eyes from the cobblestones, ambled down the street. He kept his head carefully averted from the gaslights. He walked slowly, so as not to draw attention. He did precisely what he had been instructed to do.

A short time later he came out of the telegraph office, walked around to its rear and, staying well behind the offices and shops, eventually made his way back to the buggy.

He could not have seen the white man who had followed him. Who had stealthily waited outside the telegraph office, watching through the window until wire and coins had been given to the telegraph operator. But after the Negro messenger slipped out the door, the white man entered the office.

*A few minutes later, when the white man emerged, he
clutched in his hand a small rectangle of yellow paper. He
walked into the night, as quickly as his limp would allow.*

The horses galloped through the city's early-morning dark,
the buggy they pulled jouncing over uneven cobblestones
until Bronwen thought her spine would splinter. But she
couldn't argue with the pace the driver maintained. The
Richmond Directory listed the Norfolk Steamboat Line's
departure as "half past 5, A.M." Which meant that the *Curtis
Peck* would leave Rockett's Landing in less than an hour.
The driver vowed they would make it in time.

This driver was none other than Elizabeth Van Lew herself, hunched over on the buggy's front seat, wrapped in a
black, hooded cloak. The cloak, flapping like bat wings
around her thin frame, made her look like a highwayman of
the past century; the difference being, Bronwen thought,
that there were no steamboats to catch in the 1700s. But
thank God for them now. The railroads, with their exposed
station houses, had become too dangerous to even consider,
and the trains no doubt were watched. The warehouse murder of the Pinkerton agent and the ensuing gun battle had
frightened Bronwen more than any other single thing that
had occurred since that terrible night in Montgomery. The
night when it all began. Death had now become too close,
and too real, for her to think it would somehow forever continue to pass her by. She had come to believe—she could
imagine her mother's belated relief—that she was mortal.

For the past three miles the buggy had swiftly traveled
past Hollywood cemetery, then beside the James River,
where, narrowed between high banks, the current churned
into foaming rapids and swirled around patches of islands.
The road seemed nearly deserted. Nothing approached from
the opposite direction, and Bronwen, looking out the rear,

saw only a dim swinging light, presumably from a carriage journeying some distance behind their own.

It was ten minutes to five and still dark when they reached Rockett's Landing, the head of the river's traffic, above which point no vessel of any size could navigate. Bronwen and Marsh jumped from the buggy's rear seat even as Elizabeth Van Lew pulled up the team. Several other carriages drew up alongside, as well as one that jockeyed in behind them. Those climbing down could be seen only in vague outline form in the gaslight filtering through veils of fog drifting off the river. Bronwen fought a fierce desire to examine these fellow travelers closely; she almost managed to convince herself that no one would be looking for her to board a steamboat at five in the morning. Which was specifically why they had chosen this ungodly hour.

As the fog crept to the shore, it brought the not unexpected smell of fish and seaweed. But there was more activity on the James than she could have anticipated. Beneath warehouses looming along the riverbanks, shallow skiffs edged the piers, small fishing boats were being rowed from the docks, and a few sailing sloops made ready to cast off. Although . . . maybe all this hubbub was fortunate; it would cover the two young "men" waiting in the shadows for a hooded figure to purchase their tickets.

Then, after surreptitiously passing them the tickets, Elizabeth Van Lew faded back to the cobbled street. Bronwen and Marsh waited again, dawdling until the last minute to board the steamboat. Now a pungent smell of burning wood overlay all other odors; the heat of the fire boiled the water that produced the steam that turned the paddle wheels. Bronwen and Marsh walked the short gangplank, both keeping their heads down until they reached the bow which appeared to be empty of other passengers. Bronwen only then risked a quick glance toward the shoreline. Through the thickening fog, she could barely make out the small buggy heading back in the direction of Church Hill.

It was then, from the corner of her eye, that she saw the man standing not ten yards down the deck. He stared at the roiling water under the paddle wheel, his face in profile, but Bronwen, seized with near-panic, recognized him in an instant.

She looked away quickly, praying she had imagined it. That when she looked again the apparition, merely a figment of her fearful imagination, would have vanished. She slowly turned back. The man still stood there.

It was, unmistakably, Guy Seagram.

20

Mrs. Lincoln . . . acquitted herself most gracefully and admirably. She was dressed plainly but richly. She wore a beautiful full train, white moire-antique silk, with a small French lace collar. Her neck was ornamented with a string of pearls. . . . She displayed but little jewelry and this was well and appropriately adjusted. She is a lady of fine figure and accomplished address and is well calculated to grace and do honor at the White House.

—a February 1861 item from the *Missouri Democrat* newspaper

No matter that she adored New York City. Or that much of New York City clearly adored Mr. Lincoln. Or that their elegant Astor House suite, blooming with thousands of flowers sent by admirers, resembled a terrace garden. Or that champagne frothed and sparkled; that fluted-glass bowls sat mounded with bluepoint oysters on blocks of ice shimmering in the gaslight; that silver platters lay heaped with lobster croquettes, *filet de boeuf* and mushrooms, Richelieu pears, Chantilly cheese, steaming pastries and bonbons, all of which looked and smelled divine and tasted even more so. Mary Lincoln no longer cared. She would have relinquished it all merely to sit down.

Her legs and feet ached. She had been standing for hours,

and the fashionable white satin shoes that slipped on so easily in the Fifth Avenue salon had by now become a pair of iron pincers. Her upper torso, squeezed to hourglass stylishness by a rigid corset, felt as if it might at any moment burst its bounds, exposing her bosom to half the politicians in Manhattan.

But then, still resolutely smiling, she glanced at Mr. Lincoln. Her own bodily discomfort vanished beneath a sharp sense of distress: her husband looked worn, pale, tired. He was talking very little. His voice had given out somewhere amid their tumultuous welcome at the cold, windy railroad station, the mounted police escort to the hotel, and the Astor House balcony where he'd been prevailed upon to make yet another speech. It had been a waste; the crowd below had been so noisy Mary hadn't heard a word of what he said, and the rawness of his throat mercifully made him cut it short. He'd smiled, and joked that he was "perhaps just a tad weary."

Still, Mary feared that what she saw in her husband's face described more than fatigue. He looked acutely troubled. Although no one but she would recognize it. To everyone else he would simply appear preoccupied, somewhat tired—certainly to be expected. But to Mary it signaled something else.

Although the New York crowds had generally been boisterous and friendly, there had been some in the sea of faces below the balcony who frightened her, their expressions surly and antagonistic. And afterward, no sooner had they gone back inside the suite than that strange man from Chicago arrived, either clenching his cigar between his teeth, or else brandishing it in his fingers like an unlit firecracker. This person had first requested to talk to Mr. Lincoln alone. When he'd been refused, he then insisted, and ultimately demanded it. Unpleasant little man. Mr. Lincoln had finally given in, as he always did to what he called "admirable persistence," and they went into the next room. And not alone. A striking woman, a Mrs. Kate Warne, joined the man Pinkerton and had been allowed access to the "private discussion." Mary had been excused. Pinkerton had all but shut the door in her face.

Since then, Mr. Lincoln looked not only tired but sorely affected by some unknown news the Pinkerton man must have brought. Not anxious or fearful—her husband never seemed afraid of anything, unlike Mary, who sometimes believed she was afraid of everything—but concerned in his quiet, melancholy way. The worst part was that he refused to tell her why Pinkerton had come.

"It's nothing to fret about, Molly," he'd said in that soothing tone he used with her.

"But *you're* fretting about it!" she'd argued.

"It's my job to fret. Doesn't mean you have to help me do it." He had smiled then, despite his sad eyes. "Now, Molly, you just go get all gussied up for this big shindig they're making us go through. You love parties, and I don't. I like worrying, and you don't. So we're a fine pair."

He had leaned down and kissed the top of her head. She would get no further. It made her angry, and she wondered if this was the way it would be now. Before, they had always shared everything; would she in future be made to stay on the outside? Excluded like a bothersome, feebleminded child, relegated to merely observing? Almost as disturbing was her contemplation of whether all eastern women were as attractive as Mrs. Warne.

She became aware of the smell of pipe tobacco, and heard a confusion of words. Mary tore her eyes away from her husband to respond to whatever the young, bewhiskered man beside her had just said. She turned to Frederick Seward, whose father, New York senator William Seward, her

husband had just appointed Secretary of State. "Please forgive me," she said to him with a rueful smile, "I'm afraid I
didn't hear you."

The young man motioned toward the door. "I said that
Superintendent Kennedy has just arrived, Mrs. Lincoln."

"I'm afraid I don't know him," she apologized, although
why she did she wasn't sure. How *could* she know this man?
She'd never seen him before.

"John Kennedy's the New York City police chief," Frederick Seward explained.

Mary experienced a frisson of apprehension, then told herself it was perfectly natural, indeed even obligatory, for the
city's chief of police to attend a party given in honor of the
new President. Furthermore, the man deserved her thanks for
maintaining order along their parade route to the hotel.

As she dutifully went toward the police chief, Mary recalled that in the morning Vice President–elect Hannibal
Hamlin was due to arrive from Maine. There would follow
interminable meetings—but this could be her one chance to
enjoy herself. She would go shopping, forget the fears that
assaulted her, the threats that caused her almost constant
dread. She would buy clothes to make herself look beautiful
for her husband's new position, and for her own, she remembered with delight; she would show these eastern
women they possessed no more style than she. They had
nothing that she could not buy. And Mr. Lincoln would be
happy if she was happy.

Smiling now with genuine pleasure, she reached the
handsome Irish police chief, who was already bowing gal-
lantly, and extended her gloved hand. Suddenly she heard a
voice, a man's voice somewhere behind her in the crowded
room, say, "Lincoln seems especially melancholy tonight.
Looks sad enough to be going to his death instead of to his
inauguration."

21

~~~

There's a certain Slant of light,
Winter Afternoons—
That oppresses, like the Heft
Of Cathedral Tunes—

When it comes, the Landscape listens—
Shadows—hold their breath—
When it goes, 'tis like the Distance
On the look of Death—

—Emily Dickinson, circa 1861

Glynis Tryon, seated in a slow-moving open carriage, stared with repugnance at the yellow Potomac River. A fetid smell rose from the water that moved sluggishly as if thick with muck, the contents of which she didn't want to contemplate. She could only hope with intense fervor that the river was not being put to use for drinking. When several bloated dead rats drifted past, she shuddered and turned away.

Although she'd not said a word, the attractive Welshman on the carriage seat beside her nodded with perception. One hand on the reins, Rhys Bevan gestured toward the river with the other, saying, "Looks not fit for man nor beast, does it?"

"No it doesn't. I expected something . . . well, more picturesque, I guess."

"It *is* picturesque until it gets to Washington. Up near

Harper's Ferry it's a beautiful river. But it's been ill-used here."

Glynis didn't miss the mention of Harper's Ferry. And she knew it was not simply a casual reference on the part of the Treasury agent. Immediately upon her arrival in the capital, she'd insisted on sending a wire to Jacques Sundown—who she prayed was still *at* Harper's Ferry—reasoning that in her experience if anyone in the world could locate her missing niece, Jacques would be the most likely.

Rhys Bevan, however, had seemed put out by her telegram. "What's some Indian scout from western New York going to do here in the South that I can't? You now have at your disposal, my dear lady, the best detective unit in the civilized world—Pinkerton's notwithstanding. We'll find your errant lass! If, in fact, she's lost."

"*If* she's lost? Meaning . . . ?"

"Remember that you've told me about your Bronwen. How can you be certain she's not off on a lark? Having herself a fine time while you're frantic with worry?"

"Because she *knows* I would be frantic! Bronwen may be a . . . a bit unbridled, perhaps somewhat imprudent at times, but she's not cruel. She would not callously allow me to worry, I'm sure of that! Something has happened to her, Rhys."

Glynis pressed her lips together against a growing anger she didn't want displayed. Both Rhys Bevan and Cullen Stuart persisted in this cavalier dismissal of her concern, as if she were some hysterical female with a long history of groundless fears. They should know her better. Or perhaps their reaction had nothing in particular to do with *her;* it took place simply from force of habit because she was female, period. But if one of the all-male Treasury detective unit suddenly dropped from the face of the earth, after sending alarming communiqués, would Rhys then so lightly dismiss *him* as being merely "off on a lark"?

"Better hold on!" he now directed, pointing ahead to a sagging, rotted wooden bridge.

"Do we have to cross that?" Glynis asked. "Isn't there some other in better condition?"

"The others all look exactly the same. Half of Washington is either unfinished or falling down. The retiring administration refuses to spend money on public works—and if you want to cross the Potomac, you have to take a bridge, unsafe or not."

While the carriage clattered across the swaying, decrepit span, Glynis held her breath. What Rhys had said seemed all too true. A tall lance of white marble, surrounded by scaffolding, rose uncertainly against the chill blue sky—an unfinished monument to the country's first President. At the end of wide, tree-lined Pennsylvania Avenue, structural supports enclosed the Capitol, and cranes hovered over its uncompleted dome. The Treasury Building, for which she and Rhys were bound, was likewise under suspended construction. And even though the main thoroughfares had mostly been cobbled, the side roads slanting from them were no more than dirt paths populated by rooting pigs.

There were a few recently completed structures; the Post Office at Seventh and F streets, across from the imposing, brick Patent Office, and a Gothic and Romanesque turreted brownstone, housing an institution founded by the bequest of an Englishman, James Smithson. One dramatic thing Glynis noted was the absence of the slave pens and auction blocks. They, mercifully, had been dismantled.

Rhys now drew up the carriage before one of a succession of low wooden structures squatted beside a huge, scaffolded edifice that was the new Treasury Building. After lifting Glynis from the carriage, then swinging her over an open drainage ditch, he guided her around piles of construction debris to the door of a surprisingly clean office.

"Home," he said, sweeping his arm over desks and wooden file cabinets neatly organized along four walls, which were covered with varicolored maps and what looked to be nautical charts. Two men stood at the far wall, studying a map labeled "The Southeastern Regions."

After being introduced to Glynis, an agent named Dan Morrow handed Rhys a clutch of telegrams. "These came in since you left, chief."

Glynis stepped forward, hoping against hope; but Rhys, riffling through them, shook his head. "Afraid what you're looking for isn't here," he said to her. He turned to the others. "When I met Miss Tryon's train, I told her we'd traced her niece as far as West Point, Georgia. Anything new since then?"

"No positive identification after that," Dan Morrow said. "We've wired all our contacts along the rail lines, and they're watching for her."

Glynis could feel her body sag, not only with worry but fatigue, and she lowered herself into a nearby chair. "There's been no sign of Bronwen since three days ago?"

The other agent, whom Rhys had called Timothy Burns, said, "We did get a subsequent report from Atlanta, but it turned sour—that is, your niece wasn't traveling with anyone, right?"

"Yes, she was with a Mr. Thaddeus Dowling."

"We're aware of Dowling," Rhys said. "Who was the report about?" he asked Burns.

"Oh, just a young fellow wanted in Atlanta for breaking into a bakery shop. Somebody reported seeing him the night before with another boy. Boy's cap started to blow off near the rail station, and a witness said he saw red hair."

"Bronwen has red hair!" Glynis said tersely.

"But she's not a boy," Rhys pointed out with such unarguable logic that Glynis, after a first flush of anger, felt silly.

She recovered quickly. "No, wait!" she said. "Maybe Bronwen is in disguise. With trousers she'd be slim enough to pass for a boy, and she might have tucked her hair up under the cap."

"Then who's the fellow she's with?" Rhys asked her. "Apparently he's too young to be Thaddeus Dowling, and at any rate, I doubt Dowling would be robbing bakeries. Now don't worry, we'll keep at it until we find her."

But find her in what condition? thought Glynis, and then scolded herself for yielding to despair. Still, Bronwen had been missing for days. "Rhys, how do you . . . you *know* you'll . . . find her"—she stumbled over the words, but felt she had to say them if only to show her seriousness—"find her alive?"

Rhys started to answer, then shook his head. "We'll find her alive, Glynis."

"But how do you *know* that? You can't."

Rhys turned back to the telegrams he'd thrown on the desktop, and began to go through them singly. He suddenly looked up, handing one to Glynis. "Here, I didn't see this. It's for you in care of this office."

Glynis seized the telegram. "It's from Chantal Dupont in Virginia," she said excitedly. "I wired her earlier, telling her where I'd be." Glynis broke off, reading. "Rhys, she's seen Bronwen! Chantal says she was *there*, in Richmond."

"When? When was she in Richmond?" As Rhys asked her this, he threw the other agents a frowning look of rebuke.

"It would have been just yesterday! But . . . oh no! Bronwen told Chantal she was being followed. And she *is* traveling with someone—a Tristan Marshall."

Movement caught Glynis's eye and she glanced up to see

Rhys gesturing, and mouthing something to the other men, both of whom then dashed to the door, pulled it open and disappeared through it.

"Anything more?" Rhys asked, ignoring the perplexed look Glynis sent him.

"Just that Bronwen left Chantal's in the morning—that would have been yesterday—to go into the city. Chantal hasn't seen her since. That's all. But why, in that case, haven't I heard from Bronwen? She should have been able to wire from Richmond."

"But she doesn't know where you are."

"Chantal would have told her I was coming here."

Rhys Bevan turned back to the wires and began to read another of them, a lengthy one. "This," he said at last, his voice sounding oddly strained, "is from your Constable Stuart in Seneca Falls."

"Cullen?"

"He says he finally heard from the Pinkerton Agency in Chicago. But from a Pinkerton associate, *not* from Pinkerton himself, who's apparently in either New York City or Baltimore."

"*Baltimore!* Why?"

"Doesn't say." Rhys Bevan looked at her with obvious concern, and Glynis felt her stomach lurch.

"What *does* it say? Tell me!"

He hesitated so long that Glynis snatched the telegram. He didn't try to stop her.

She scanned Cullen's wire, her blood chilling with every word. The Agency lost track of Bronwen after she left Alabama, it read. But during the time she was in Montgomery, two other Pinkerton operatives there had been killed.

Killed?

As Glynis got to her feet, she felt Rhys Bevan's hand on her shoulder. She walked away from him and went to stand at a window. Staring at the pane of glass, she saw her sister's face; a face drawn with anxiety, and at the same time ashen with rage. And she saw Bronwen as a small child, climbing down a rocky embankment in search of wildflowers, despite being warned by Glynis that the slope was too steep. The child slipped and fell, trapping an ankle between jagged boulders. She tried to yank herself loose, retorting to her aunt's concern with, "No! I don't *need* help." A few more futile attempts to free herself brought a change of heart. Bronwen's lower lip had trembled when she whimpered, "Come get me, Aunt Glyn. My ankle really hurts. Please come get me."

Please come get me.

Glynis let out her breath with a shudder. "I would come get you, Bronwen," she whispered, "if I only knew where you were."

Reflected in the window glass, Rhys Bevan stood behind her. Again his hands reached for her shoulders, and Glynis did not move away.

"There's something else," he said, quietly. "Something you asked when you wired from Seneca Falls."

"I asked about Colonel Dorian de Warde. If you knew why he was here in the States. Do you? And do you know where he is now?"

"Yes, at the moment he's in Richmond."

Glynis whirled to face him. "Richmond! Where Bronwen is? Rhys, why would he . . . ?"

"We don't know why," he broke in. "But since he's been here he's stayed mainly in the South. Among other things, he's negotiating new contracts with plantation owners. As insurance of sorts, that the cotton flow to Britain won't be interrupted if there's war."

"So what he's doing doesn't at all involve Bronwen?"

"We can't say that with absolute certainty, but I wouldn't

think so. De Warde's shoring up alliances, probably making promises of British aid to the Confederacy. Can't see how that would concern Bronwen or Pinkerton's. But just in case, Glynis, I've ordered that de Warde be picked up and brought here for questioning. Timothy Burns is seeing to that now."

"De Warde won't tell you anything, Rhys. And you know from our last encounter with him that he hires others to do—as he would say—the 'unpleasantries' for him. And then he just walks off, scot-free."

"He won't walk anywhere this time," Rhys said grimly, "until we find Bronwen."

"If he even knows where she is."

"He might tell *you*," Rhys said with a slight smile. "De Warde liked you, remember?"

"That was then—in Seneca Falls. We don't know if—"

She stopped as the door flew open. Dan Morrow rushed in, and Glynis saw with dread the perspiration from running. Please, no more bad news.

"Just came from the Post Office," Morrow said, panting. "Afraid you were right, chief. That guy *is* wanted."

Rhys turned to Glynis. "That wire from Atlanta, the one that said the redheaded boy's companion was wanted for robbery—"

"He broke into a *bakery shop*, Rhys!" interrupted Glynis. "Not the United States Mint."

"It could indicate a pattern. Criminals *have* patterns, Glynis—that's why they occasionally get caught. And, unfortunately, it seems to be the case here. What's this Marshall wanted for, Dan—grand theft?"

Dan Morrow shook his head. He shifted his feet several times before saying, "I'm sorry to have to tell you this, Miss Tryon, but there's a handbill on him at the Post Office. Tristan Marshall is wanted for murder."

22

It is best not to swap horses while crossing the river.

—Abraham Lincoln

Between dark overhead clouds and the horizon, a narrow strip of sky above the eastern shore of the James had just begun to pale. This light, however, had not yet stretched to where Bronwen huddled beside Marsh under a heap of tarpaulins near the bow of the steamship *Curtis Peck.* Despite the dampness slicking the deck, the space beneath the oily-smelling canvas was quite tolerably warm.

After spotting Guy Seagram, she'd hauled Marsh to the far side of the forward cabin and then, in a rush of words, explained her anxiety.

"That's just dandy!" had been Marsh's reaction as they crawled under the tarps. "Is there *any*place that's safe with you around?"

"Look, that I accidentally overheard something in Montgomery is not my fault and I resent—"

"Oh, yeah?" he interrupted. "Then why is everybody in the goddamn world after you? Because you let yourself get caught snooping. That *is* your fault!"

Bronwen started to retort, but stopped herself. There was no point. Besides, she conceded that Marsh did have reason to be agitated. But then, for different reasons, so did she.

"Ah, Marsh?" she began now, leaning against his shoulder and drawing her knees up under her chin. "Marsh, I think it's time."

"For what?"

"For you to tell me why you're wanted for murder."

He pulled away from her. The morning light was still murky, but a swinging lantern some yards away showed her the look of surprise on his face. His dark eyes, though, were shadowed.

"What brought that on?" he asked, his voice distant.

"I like to know who and what I'm dealing with."

"You've been dealing with me for a while now—"

"Yes," she interrupted, "and you still haven't told me. And don't say it's none of my business, because it is!"

"I don't see why. It doesn't concern you."

"As long as I'm with you, it concerns me. We've got more than a hundred miles to Norfolk, but by then I need to decide what to do. And whether I have to do it alone."

"Thought you were going to pick up another steamer to Baltimore. Powhatan Line goes up there."

"I can't take that if Guy Seagram does. I doubt it's coincidence he's showed up here, so he could well be the one who's been following me—or at least one of the ones—and it's reason enough to distrust him. But that's not the only important thing—not right this minute, anyway—so don't try to divert my attention. I want to know why your picture's on a wanted poster."

"Because I'm a murderer—isn't that what you think?"

He sounded angry, but even so, Bronwen realized, she wasn't afraid of him. Not remotely. "As a matter of fact," she answered, "no, I don't think you're a murderer. When I first saw the poster in Atlanta, I didn't think so—and even though I watched how easily you handled that gun yesterday, I still don't think so. My initial reaction was that you'd been falsely accused, or else you'd killed someone in self-defense."

"You got that right," he muttered.

"*What* right? Which part?"

"The falsely accused part. I didn't kill anybody."

"Then tell me why your face is on a—"

"All right! I still don't think it's any of your business, but O.K., I'll tell you just to shut you up about it." Marsh glared at her, then turned to watch the river being slapped by the steamship paddles. The sun had moved higher and its light now caught the ship's spray, changing it to a sparkling crystalline mist. The smell of burning wood drifted over lightly ruffled water.

Bronwen waited. Finally she demanded, "So?"

"O.K.! I already told you things were bad, very bad, in that Mobile shipyard," he began, still looking at the water. "And after I escaped the first time—and got caught and taken back—it was a lot worse. Shipyard owner had me whipped, then chained my leg to a pier. You want to imagine what it's like having to work with a back like raw meat, and an iron shackle around your leg dragging pounds of chain?"

He stopped and glanced quickly at her before turning again to the river. In that glance, though, Bronwen saw as much pain as rage. Hardly aware she was doing it, she reached out and touched his back. When he winced, she drew her hand away.

He shook his head, then went on, his voice sounding somewhat calmer. "After a couple weeks of that, the owner started getting careless. Leaving tools around, 'cause he forgot about me. One night at quitting time he left a hacksaw a little too close. Took me two nights, but I cut through that shackle. I was sneaking away, and two other men—they'd been sold to the shipyard, too—came up and said they were going to leave with me. They were a rough breed, those two, and I didn't like it, but didn't see as I had a choice. We'd made it to the town side of the yard, past the night guard, and I thought I was free. Then one of these men says something like, 'I hate that bastard guard. I'm gonna get him!' I told him it wasn't worth it, to leave the damn guard alone, but the guy went crazy. So I ran."

Marsh broke off, looking at Bronwen. She said nothing, not wanting him to stop. But she glanced around because his voice had been rising; he must have understood, as he lowered it before he went on. "The guy really did go berserk. I looked back over my shoulder just as he jumped the guard and grabbed his gun. Guard started yelling. And the guy shoots him. Just shoots him. Then the owner appears and he gets shot, too—no grief on my part about *him*—but then all hell broke loose. Madman with the gun, he kept on shooting until the bullets gave out. By then, police were closing in on him and his pal. But I kept running. Found an old burned-out shed near the railroad tracks where I could hide. Train came by a few minutes later. And that's about it."

"But you didn't shoot anyone, so why are they hunting *you* for murder?"

"I was *there,* that's why. And the Southern shipyard owners aren't going to let this drop. They've got too much at stake to have their cheap labor start getting ideas; South's got a powder keg waiting to blow, what with the whites forced into servitude and the blacks who are slaves. If they ever banded together . . . but they won't. No matter how bad off or low down a white man is, he can always look around and see a Negro he can feel he's better than. . . ."

Marsh's voice trailed off as he shook his head. Then he turned again to Bronwen, saying, "But I figure that somebody at that shipyard saw it wasn't me did the shooting.

That's why I need to hire Pinkerton. To find an eyewitness without going back to Mobile myself."

"Why wouldn't you tell me this before?"

Marsh shrugged. "Didn't know if you'd believe me."

"I believe you. And—"

She broke off, hearing an ominous clicking sound directly behind them. But it wasn't the click of a gun. It was the creak of the deck's wood planking, followed by a deep voice saying with a chuckle, "Now that's one fine story! And I don't believe a word of it."

"Seagram!" Flinging the tarps aside, Bronwen scrambled to her feet.

"Red, don't tell me you believe that yarn of his." Guy Seagram flicked his cigarette over the side of the ship, gazing at Bronwen with the sleepy, hooded eyes she remembered.

She could see Marsh crouching as if ready to spring, and she shook her head at him. "He won't do anything, not here. Will you, Seagram? You'll wait and play a bit more, like a cat with a mouse. Why didn't you kill me in Montgomery when you had the perfect opportunity?"

"I don't want to kill you, Red. You're right, I had the chance—if I'd wanted it. I do want to talk to you, though. Without your chum, here."

"No!" Marsh's tone allowed little room to maneuver.

It didn't discourage Seagram. "Tell him, Red, that my intentions are honorable. I wouldn't dream of violating you on the deck of a steamship. After all, we had that cozy bed in Montgomery. . . ."

"Just what is it you want, Seagram?" Bronwen broke in, seeing Marsh's sudden confusion. And to him she said, "Just ignore this man, Marsh. He will say *anything*—anything he thinks might get a reaction, so please don't indulge him!"

"She's right." Seagram nodded. "And I really don't intend to harm her—or you either. But," he said now to Bronwen, "if you want to know what Equus is, you'd better send your friend elsewhere."

When Marsh took a step toward him, Seagram added, "You don't have to go *far*. Just down the deck a ways, so you can keep an eye on things, and Red and I can talk in private."

Bronwen, despite her misgivings about Guy Seagram, couldn't resist the reference to Equus. "Yes, Marsh," she said hurriedly, "you can watch from there in the bow. Please," she said, sending him a long look of appeal.

Marsh muttered something mercifully unintelligible, and moved off. A few yards away, he leaned back against the rail, arms crossed over his chest.

"You know, Red, he wouldn't be half bad if you cleaned him up some. So, what are you doing with him? As if I couldn't guess."

"Seagram, what about Equus? And what are you doing here?"

"Trying to save your life, you little fool!" In spite of the words, Seagram's voice was soft. Bronwen had to lean toward him to hear, and she saw Marsh take a step forward. She shook her head at him. When he moved back, it was with obvious reluctance.

"Regular bodyguard, isn't he?" Seagram smiled grimly. "Maybe the reason you've made it this far—either him or dumb luck. They're after you, my appealing young agent."

"Who are 'they'? And you know it's Equus I mean."

"A Maryland brotherhood that wants secession. A few of the more radical ones were in the state delegation that went to Montgomery. The others are in Baltimore, under the sway—so to speak—of a fanatic named Cypriano Ferrandini, who fancies himself the savior of the South."

"What do they intend?"

"They intend to go their own way without interference from a Yankee President."

"They may not have that choice," Bronwen said, trying to keep him talking until he tripped, unlikely as it was, and gave her a forecast. "And if they don't, what then?"

"They aren't going to wait and see. They want to throw the United States government into disarray—and they think the way to do it is by assassinating your new President."

Bronwen was torn between feigning ignorance and allowing him to know she'd figured this out. Unsure as to which would produce the most information, she opted for silence.

"You don't seem surprised, Red. But then, the way this bunch operates, I doubt there will be anyone in the state of Maryland who won't know about their intrigue."

"And how do you know, Seagram? Are you one of them?"

He laughed, not a particularly cheerful sound. "Oh, they think I am. So, what have you informed Pinkerton thus far about this?"

Why should she tell Seagram anything? "How do they expect to accomplish this scheme?"

"They plan to kill Lincoln next Saturday, the twenty-third, when his train stops at Baltimore's Calvert Street Station. It'll be sometime around noon. At least one assassin, possibly more than one, will be in the crowd."

"So why are you telling *me* this?" she asked, not expecting a frank answer, but nonetheless curious. "Why?"

"Because while Pinkerton has sent agents into Maryland to investigate the inevitable rumors—inevitable because the plotters are so widespread—he's still operating in the dark. They intend to keep you from enlightening him."

"*Who,* Seagram? Who is after me?"

"They think I am. I volunteered for this jaunt, but somehow I'm going to slip up. Unfortunately, since you've so successfully eluded them thus far, they've taken that possibility into account. There will probably be a few of them waiting for you in Norfolk."

Bronwen couldn't keep her fright at bay much longer; if it caught and held she wouldn't be able to think straight. Then, from the tail of her eye, she saw Marsh regarding her intently, concern creasing his forehead. It helped her, his watchfulness, to focus on other than fear. "Who *are* these people?" she asked again.

Seagram shook his head, not answering. But she hadn't really expected him to; it might reveal his own mysterious role in this.

"All in all, Red, I think you better find another way to Baltimore other than those you've used in the past. Baltimore is where you're headed, isn't it? The railroads will be watched, as well as the steamships out of Norfolk."

"But why tell me this, Seagram?"

"I like you. I don't want to see you killed. Forewarned is forearmed, as they say. So, *if* you somehow make it to Baltimore, where are you meeting Pinkerton? At the hotel where he's gone to ground?"

Pinkerton was in Baltimore? Bronwen hoped she didn't look as stunned as she felt, once again desperately wishing she could trust Seagram. Why shouldn't she? The man was obviously attempting to keep her alive as, she reminded herself, he had in Montgomery. Yet . . .

"I don't know if I'm going to Baltimore," she lied.

"C'mon, Red, this is *me* you're talking to, remember?"

"Just a minute, here!" Bronwen said. Her sharpness of tone was unintentional, and brought Marsh a step closer, but she needed to verify what Elizabeth Van Lew had suggested. "Seagram, what about the Baltimore police? Why can't someone tell them about the plot to kill Lincoln?"

Seagram laughed harshly. "The Baltimore police? They're *in on it!* Marshal Kane is hand in glove with Ferrandini."

"That's . . . that's monstrous!"

"Now there's a straightforward reaction. But you're still too naive, Red, and that's dangerous. This isn't the first time I've warned you about it. Don't trust *anybody!* You better learn that fast."

Bronwen fixed him with a steady gaze. "I'm learning."

"We need to decide about Norfolk," she told Marsh, after Seagram had sauntered toward the bar located inside the steamboat cabin.

" 'We'? What's this *we* mean?"

"It means what it sounds like. I have confidence in you." She yanked up the bib of her drooping, masculine overalls which threatened to reveal what they were meant to conceal. While she retied the shoulder straps, she could avoid his eyes as she said, "And from the way you acted with Seagram just now, I think you care what happens to me."

"I care about getting to Pinkerton," he said, but flashed a grin when her face fell. Then, to Bronwen's astonishment, he swung an arm around her shoulders, and pulled her to him. The kiss was of necessity hurried, but its meaning came through clear enough.

"You are insane!" Bronwen whispered, pushing him away and looking frantically around. "What if somebody saw you?"

He shrugged. "There's nobody here. But so what?"

"So *what?* You'll be wanted for more than murder, that's what—kissing a *boy!* Just remember who you're with, mister." She gave the brim of her cap a flick.

At least she got a blush along with his grin.

She lowered herself to the deck and dangled her feet over the side. February, but the air smelled spring-like, and the sun felt warm—as warm as April's would be back in Rochester. It made her homesick. And she couldn't afford it.

Marsh squatted beside her, toying with the end of a rope coiled around a cleat. Bronwen watched his fingers, compact and deft, tie a knot in a figure eight, and seconds later a square one; then, with spare, skillful movements, a more complicated bowline. It made her suddenly remember: he'd worked in a shipyard. Which meant . . .

"Marsh, you can sail a boat, can't you?"

"Of course."

"Then that," she whispered, glancing around to be sure they weren't overheard, "is how we'll get to Baltimore."

"*Sail* . . . up the Chesapeake . . . in *February?* You're crazy. Have *you* ever sailed?"

"Not . . . exactly."

"What's that mean? You've either sailed or you haven't."

"I was *on* a sailboat once. On Lake Ontario."

"What kind?"

"A large one."

"How large?"

"Very. It looked as big as a city block, that boat."

"That wasn't a boat, it was a ship, and no! I've sailed that Bay before, but in summer. You're not talking me into going up the Chesapeake in February—and for sure not with a landlubber!"

"Why not? If you tell me what to do, I can follow instructions."

"Oh, right. And when was the last time you followed instructions? Anyway, this time of year the weather's too unpredictable."

"Unpredictable? It's sunny. And warm. Marsh, there isn't another way to—"

"No!"

Bronwen smacked her palms on the deck and turned her back on him to watch the land move past. They had rounded a deep bend in the river, and above the shore, spans of green stretched to Georgian plantation houses. They grew tobacco here, Bronwen recalled her aunt saying. Aunt Glynis! She'd be in Washington now, and must be wondering why she hadn't received a wire. At least she'd undoubtedly heard from Chantal Dupont, and so wouldn't be worried.

"Look there!" Marsh pointed to a diamondback terrapin that had surfaced at the water's edge, then swam along a shoreline retreating from the steamship. The river had grown wider, and the current flowed more swiftly toward the Chesapeake and the sea. They should be in Norfolk by late afternoon.

The questions that now confronted Bronwen seemed unanswerable. How could she evade those Seagram warned her would be waiting? Reach Baltimore with her crucial information and, moreover, get there in time? Even if she did, could Pinkerton and his agents stop these faceless assassins? From what Seagram had said, some were apparently ready themselves to die in order to murder Abraham Lincoln.

Then she recalled something else. When she'd asked Seagram who was waiting for her in Norfolk, he hadn't answered; it now occurred to her that it must be the killer of the other three agents. But which of the five persons she suspected? By a process of elimination, one had begun to seem more probable than the others.

Bronwen shivered in the warm sunshine and, in spite of her sense of urgency, wished the *Curtis Peck* wasn't steaming quite so efficiently toward Norfolk.

23

Once more upon the waters! Yet once more!
And the waves bound beneath me as a steed
That knows his rider. Welcome to the roar!

—Byron

*L*arge flat portions of island spewed in all directions from the mouth of the James River and two other tidal estuaries. At least it seemed so to Bronwen, peering with Marsh from under tarpaulins while the *Curtis Peck* rocked, backing and filling from the operation of its paddles, beside one of the scores of bustling docks in the Hampton Roads Harbor above Norfolk. The harbor held all the commotion and noise of a city. Perhaps they could manage to lose themselves in it.

"Marsh, look!" she whispered, directing him to a finger-like projection of land. "Look over there to the east—all those little sailboats."

"Sloops," he said, "and no, we're not taking any of them, so forget about it."

Bronwen wondered just how hard it would be to sail one of those boats—*sloops*—by herself. Beyond, in the magnificent harbor, she could see any number of small boats being piloted by a single person. Still, from her sole experience aboard a sailing ship, she recalled there being a great deal of energetic activity. While she hadn't understood its purpose, it must have *had* some, so clearly sailing was more complicated than she'd guessed. She needed Marsh. Not that she had gotten far trying to talk him into a Chesapeake voyage. But she didn't think he would simply abandon her; not after that kiss, she didn't. She'd just have to bide her time. If, when they got off the steamship, there would *be* any time.

She felt Marsh nudge her. "There's your friend," he said, pointing.

Guy Seagram was walking down the gangplank to the pier alongside which the steamship had docked, his frock coat flapping in a brisk wind. He looked back several times, but Bronwen and Marsh had dragged some of the tarps to a different site, so Seagram couldn't know—not exactly, at least—where they were hidden.

Small clutches of people stood on the pier to greet those disembarking. Some steamboat passengers then boarded a scow to presumably ferry them to another pier, where they could pick up a carriage into Norfolk. Bronwen didn't recognize anyone. "That doesn't mean no one is watching for us, though," she told Marsh. "We'd better wait. But we have to find someplace where we can hide. Until we decide what to do next."

"O.K. Can't just go waltzing off the ship now—it's still daylight."

"But it won't be for long. Look at that sky."

In the southwest, streaks of red cloud whipped across the face of a dark-gold ball of sun. The entire sky had begun to flame with color, and beside Bronwen, Marsh's face held an unnatural copper glow. "You look like Jacques Sundown," she whispered, smiling—although smiling in their circumstances made no sense.

"Who?"

"Jacques Sundown. Most beautiful man in the world."

"*Beautiful!* What kind of man is that? He a milksop or something?"

Bronwen almost laughed before clapping a hand over her mouth. While Marsh scowled fiercely, she whispered, "No, believe me, he's not a milksop! Far from it."

"So, who is he?" Marsh still scowled.

"A friend. Actually, he's originally my Aunt Glynis's friend—sort of."

"Sort of?" Marsh echoed, although the scowl receded.

"Well, when I would see them together, they appeared more than friends. Nothing obvious—not Aunt Glynis!—but just the way they looked at each other."

Marsh didn't comment, but the scowl had disappeared.

Melancholy cries above her brought Bronwen's head up to watch black shapes riding the wind. Silhouetted against the red-and-gold-streaked sky, hundreds of large, long-necked birds winged home toward the Chesapeake. "What are those?" she asked Marsh.

"Whistling swans—you ain't seen them before?"

She shook her head, staring at the birds in wonder. "No, I ain't." She turned to look at him. "Why do you say things like that, Marsh—like 'ain't'? You don't do it all the time, just now and then."

"I forget every once in a while. Had to learn to talk like the dockworkers and the rest in the shipyard, or else I'd stand out. You don't *ever* want to stand out in a labor camp! So I'd practice at night, over and over, 'ain't,' 'hain't,' 'ain't got none.' I've had schooling, you know," he said somewhat defensively.

"I was just curious, that's all. I sometimes wonder if you're really what you seem to be. You're obviously educated. So why hide it?"

He gave her an odd, sideways glance. "You're too curious for your own good." Then he added, "Look, no one else's getting off the ship. And the pier is pretty much empty. There's some old shacks along the shore. Want to make a run for it?"

Bronwen scanned the sky. It neared twilight, and the distance between things had begun to blur, making it difficult to figure how far away the shacks stood. But they couldn't stay on the steamship much longer. The crew would begin swabbing the deck soon. In fact, she saw unlit lanterns being brought forward from the hold; as soon as they were filled with kerosene, the deck would shine revealingly with light.

"Yes, I guess we'd better do it now," she agreed with reluctance. Once off the ship, they would be so exposed, vulnerable to whoever might be waiting. True, they'd been warned. But how many were there? And where was Seagram at this point?

"O.K.," Marsh said, "we'll head for that shack to the left, the one next to the water. That way, if things get tight, we can always jump off the far pier and swim under it." He paused, then said doubtfully, "You can swim, can't you?"

"Like a fish."

"The way you sailed? *Once?*"

"No! I can swim very well, so just don't you worry about me. I assume *you* can swim?"

"I worked as a shipwright!"

"But can you *swim?*"

"Like a fish. Better hope we don't have to—that water's gotta be cold!"

They crept cautiously from beneath the billowing tarpaulins and, after looking around, casually stood up and walked down the gangplank to the pier. At the next pier another steamboat was docking, disgorging passengers who, even though their number was small, Bronwen hoped might afford some protection. Surely no one would start shooting at them with people nearby. Still, her stomach was churning, expecting, as she did, that any moment someone would attack. When they rounded the end of the pier and started toward the shack, they were walking so fast they nearly jogged. And should be running, Bronwen fretted, but they feared drawing attention to themselves.

Thus their pace wasn't fast enough.

Halfway to the shack, Bronwen saw him. A dark figure circling the end of another pier with an object in one hand that glinted in the windy twilight. The figure was a man of average height, and as he stepped out of the pier's shadow, and Marsh's hand suddenly gripped her arm, she saw what she expected to see. The man had a limp. Even before she could make out his face she knew who he was: the person she hadn't seen leaving the train in Richmond. The person who needed to remain concealed—because he had yet another agent to murder.

They'd stopped some distance from where the man stood, and Marsh kept trying to thrust Bronwen behind him despite her efforts to resist. She should stay in front of him! He needed to get his gun from his jacket pocket without being seen—didn't he realize that? If he'd just stop trying to be a hero and *think!*

The wind was now blowing strongly enough that any sound became distorted; still Bronwen thought she heard voices behind her, which might explain why the man wasn't firing at them. With a half-formed prayer, she searched for the source of the sounds. And found their means of deliverance.

Just yards away, some dozen of the newly arrived steamboat passengers were boarding a scow, most likely the ferry to another pier. Although initially Bronwen didn't care in the least where the boat was going, she did notice that its prow pointed east. The sailboats!

"Marsh, over there!" she whispered, pulling at his sleeve.

He saw immediately what she meant. Words not necessary, they ran to join those in the scow, and scrambled over the side to crouch in the flat-bottomed hull. They received a few startled glances, but no one protested. No one objected. Most Southerners were so courteous, Bronwen reminded herself, that even when confronted with blatant rudeness they usually didn't respond in kind. In fact, one elderly gentleman asked if they wouldn't join him on an already crowded plank. Marsh frowned when Bronwen said, "No thank you, sir."

"Why can't we sit up there?" he muttered to her. "No one's going to shoot at us now. This bottom's hard, and cold!"

"We have to get out at some point, remember?" Bronwen whispered in his ear. "We need to stay hidden as long as possible," and she nestled openly against Marsh's side as if they routinely traveled in the bottom of boats.

But when she glanced up, those seated above were now observing her and Marsh with obvious reservation, and Bronwen abruptly recalled she was dressed as a boy! She immediately whipped off her cap to let the long braid fall over her shoulder, and drew out a few softening wisps around her face.

"We're just married," she quickly explained, ignoring a loud gasp from Marsh. "And we're hiding from some friends who insist on playing nasty practical jokes. That's why I'm disguised," she added.

The solicitous smiles then bestowed from those above were accompanied by distinct relief. And although she didn't dare look at Marsh, Bronwen realized she'd just fallen into a charade that could be useful.

The scow did indeed head east, and the fleet of sailboats became visible after only a few minutes. Bronwen nudged Marsh and pointed silently.

"No!" he snapped, lifting a few of their fellow passengers' eyebrows.

"But dearest one," Bronwen murmured, difficult to do between clenched teeth, "I've always wanted to take a moonlit sail. And you're so accomplished on the water."

The look on Marsh's face made it all she could do to keep from laughing.

"Not a good night for a sail," he growled, bringing frowns of concern from their companions. "That is," he quickly amended in a more benign tone, "another time would be better."

"But perhaps there won't ever *be* another time," Bronwen said with sweetness, while furtively jabbing him in the ribs. "Our *friends* might prevent that!"

The face he turned to her showed sudden understanding. And a good thing, as the scow was approaching a pier, directly beside which the numerous sailboats clustered.

"I'm sure," Bronwen said rapidly, "that your brother would find it agreeable if we borrowed his boat over there"—she gestured in a vague arc—"especially if it meant avoiding any more unpleasantness."

She jabbed him again. "Oh, no," Marsh said lightly, but with what to Bronwen was unmistakable sarcasm, "no doubt the good fellow wouldn't even notice it was gone." He sent her a protracted, if covert, glare.

"I'm certain he won't be planning to use it tonight, my dear husband," she said, disregarding the glare and the sharp elbow in her side.

As she saw the pier draw closer, she looked up at the others in earnest appeal. "I wonder if we might ask y'all a very great favor?"

Bronwen paused for the reaction. The sympathetic expressions led her on. "When we dock," she said with teeth-aching sweetness, "my husband and I would be so grateful if y'all could just sort of, well, conceal us in your midst. That's in case some of our friends . . . No, I must be truthful with y'all," Bronwen improvised, warming to the role and the receptive audience. "Those people are ruffians. One of them demanded that I marry *him,* even though I was in love with my dear Mar—Martin here. So that brutal man and his brothers have vowed revenge. I'm really very afraid of them," she said, miraculously winding up with the truth.

"Oh, my dear child," said a round-faced, ample woman who sat balancing a square wicker basket on her knees, "how dreadful. And you just married! Of course we will help, won't we, Albert?" she addressed the man next to her. Albert inclined his head with some hesitation, unlike the elderly man and the others, who nodded with vigor.

Marsh leaned over and in the process of nuzzling the hair above her ear, softly proclaimed, "You're crazed! A genuine loon. We'll never get away with this."

"We'd better! So pick a good boat," Bronwen whispered, her lips brushing the skin just beneath his earlobe. "Lovely night for a sail—much more romantic than being murdered, don't you agree?"

When she searched the shoreline, Bronwen couldn't see anyone watching from the pier. Everything would depend on how long they could keep their new acquaintances as shields, and how quickly Marsh could find a boat.

As the scow bumped against the dock, Bronwen grabbed Marsh's hand, and looked up at a blackening windswept sky flecked with emerging stars. And gave silent but ardent thanks for a clear night.

The North Star could guide them to Baltimore. But only if they kept their wits and attracted from the heavens exceedingly good luck.

24

—⁓—

. . . a faire Bay compassed but for the mouth with
fruitful and delightsome land. Within is a country
that may have the prerogative over the most
pleasant places of Europe, Asia, Africa, or Amer-
ica, for large and pleasant navigable rivers.

—Captain John Smith, 1607

Now that they'd cleared the harbor and had set sail north,
the little sloop was, as Marsh termed it, "running with the
wind."

"Hallelujah!—" he laughed "—as the Alabama preachers
would say. Just you look at those sails!" Marsh perched on
the gunwale, smiling broadly at what must have been Bronwen's incredulous stare; she'd never have believed him capable of such high spirits.

"So far so good," he went on. "There's a fair wind from
the southwest, and it's almost warm. Lord Almighty, have
we been *lucky!*" he said with evangelical fervor, eyeing with
satisfaction the wind-filled sails. "Somehow, everything's
gone right."

Bronwen felt an unpleasant sensation dart up her spine,
which she recognized with disgust as superstition; she could
scoff all she liked at these absurd heralds of doom, learned
at her grandmother's knee, but they persisted. And Grandmother Tryon used to say: "A bad beginning makes a good

end." Bronwen had always wondered if the reverse might also be true. So now she tried, with meager success, to shake off visions of a catastrophic finale. She did, however, resist the temptation to knock on the wooden hull.

The real question was, Would their good fortune hold?

After they'd scrambled from the ferry scow, Marsh had taken forever to locate what he considered a "trim ship"—whatever *trim* in the context of boating meant. This while Bronwen had waited impatiently inside the circle of their newfound friends for what seemed an eternity, while her "husband" inspected boats that to her all looked closely alike; single-masted, shallow, and about twenty-five feet long. He'd insisted, for some arcane reason, in finding one with a centerboard rather than a fixed keel; but she, being in his words an "ignorant lubber," had been forced to trust his judgment. In the meantime, she'd kept up a nonstop conversation to distract those around her. She didn't want them wondering why her beloved was taking so long to find his own "brother's" boat.

"*Husband,* do you think you might please hurry?" she had finally pleaded in servile wifely fashion, and smiled at him gamely while gritting her teeth. But once he found his vessel—the name *Cascade* painted on its stern—he took so long fussing with charts and inspecting the bewildering amount of ropes, that she expected at any minute to see the boat's real owner come dashing down the pier with the entire United States naval force behind him. To say nothing of the treacherous Equus assassins. Were they just standing idly by, watching the charade play itself out until they could strike?

Bronwen now sat, her feet braced against the interior hull as the sloop heeled to starboard, slicing through water just inches below its gunwale, while she inspected the contents of a large wicker basket. At the last minute, the kind, round-faced woman had insisted Bronwen take it. "Y'all need to eat, honey. Got to keep your strength up," she smiled knowingly, "to make that good-lookin' young husband of yours happy."

As it turned out, the basket held food enough to make several men happy: cheeses and Sally Lunn yeast bread, corn muffins, salt pork, six corked brown bottles of beer—guaranteed happiness—and squares of gingerbread. They had indeed been fortunate so far.

"I'll have some of that gingerbread," Marsh said, letting out a line.

Line, not rope, Bronwen had been informed curtly when they'd cast off from the harbor pier. Admittedly she had not been much help, tripping over everything, tugging at the wrong lines, and nearly being swept into the harbor as the swinging boom clipped the side of her head.

Marsh had yelled, "Just get down—and stay down!"

"But—"

"No 'buts'! There's only one captain here and I'm it, so you do what I say! No arguing!"

He'd sounded dangerously serious. Bronwen got down and stayed down.

Then as they'd moved out into the harbor, Bronwen scanned the shoreline, but the night had grown too dark to disclose any watchers. She knew they were there, somewhere. But what now? Even if Guy Seagram weren't one of them—and Bronwen had sincerely begun to doubt that he was—the Equus men would surely have guessed that the *Cascade* was bound for Baltimore. So, would the conspirators go there by rail and wait for her to arrive, or would they decide to chase the sloop? Not an attractive speculation.

Now Bronwen again glanced to the south as she had done constantly since they'd left Norfolk. "How fast are we going?" she asked Marsh, handing him up a square of the gingerbread.

"Hmmm . . . about seven knots, maybe. It's a good stiff breeze we've got. But you have to understand, speed is relative to the tide. We've got a flood tide now, so we're moving right along. Things will change, though, when the tide turns, and when we get farther up the Bay."

He didn't sound like the person with whom Bronwen had struggled in the train's baggage car. And he didn't look the same. Ever since he'd first hauled the sheets up the mast, it was as if he'd begun to shed an outer shell, moulting like a Chesapeake crab. Initially the sails—a mainsail and a smaller jib sail—had fluttered alarmingly, like limp pieces of laundry on a clothesline, but when Marsh had headed the *Cascade* at an angle to the wind, the sails filled and the sloop picked up speed. Following this, the altered Marsh had fully emerged. A broad smile warmed his features, and even now in the darkness she could see his eyes shining like sunlit pools.

For a time neither of them spoke, the only sound being the slap of water against the *Cascade*'s plank frame hull. Since sailing represented their escape—why else would she be on Chesapeake Bay in February?—it shouldn't have encouraged a sense of calm, but for the first time in days Bronwen felt safe, even if it lasted only for the moment. She could finally unbraid her hair, damp with spray, and let it dry in a wind the warmth of which surprised her. Chantal Dupont's borrowed pea jacket hadn't even been buttoned yet. And as the moon stood high over the Eastern Shore, Bronwen became aware of something she guessed might be contentment—*might be,* because it was so mysteriously foreign to her.

The contentment proved short-lived. "Marsh, can't a large ship travel faster than a small one?"

"Yeah. And if you mean could those killers outrun us, well, sure—all things being equal. But they're not equal. For one thing, most of the Chesapeake is shallow, about twenty feet deep on average, and there's places along the Eastern Shore that're only three or four feet deep. That will help if they come after us. A big ship needs deep water, so it's pretty much got to stay in the channel that runs down through the middle of the Bay—I've heard tell it's an ancient bed of the Susquehanna."

"The Susquehanna *River?*"

Marsh nodded. "It empties into the Bay north of Baltimore at Havre de Grace."

"But how can that be? The Susquehanna begins as a stream spilling out of a little lake, up at Cooperstown in central New York State! You mean it comes all the way down here?"

"It's a mighty long river—longest in the East. Anyway, we don't need the depth of the channel. That's why I wanted a centerboard, which I can haul up if need be. Besides"— and Bronwen caught a flash of white teeth—"I'm a pretty good sailor, and that counts for a lot in a race."

"A *race?* Is that how you look at this?"

"How do *you* look at it—a nice moonlight sail? In February? Yes, it's a race, a serious one, dammit, but still a race! And I intend to win it!"

Men were so competitive. Wouldn't it be enough just to make it to Baltimore? *Alive?* Then Bronwen remembered the times she herself had wanted, wanted desperately, to win: a horse race, a shooting match. . . . Most other women didn't seem to be that way, though, so maybe she was as peculiar as her mother said. Or, as Aunt Glyn put it a bit less critically, maybe she was simply "different."

"Hey, are you listening?" Getting her attention, Marsh

went on. "I meant what I said back there in the harbor. You *cannot* argue with me . . ."

"Now, just a minute—"

". . . because I know what I'm doing and you don't. Now those are the rules. Take them or . . . or swim!"

"I think your attitude is rotten, *Tristan!*"

He grinned. "You want to get off now?"

"You only order me around because you're a man and bigger than I am."

"I'm 'ordering you around' because I'd like to get to Baltimore in one piece. And the rules of the sea say there's *one* captain per ship. You ever hear of a woman captain?"

Bronwen glared at him, searching for a scathing rejoinder. Of course he knew more than she about sailing. But he didn't have to be so overbearing about it.

"Tell you what," he said, his voice holding a suspiciously agreeable quality. "I'll let you be first mate."

Bronwen had no idea how long she'd dozed, curled up on a narrow bunk in the forward cuddy cabin. The enclosed space near the mast was small, but it afforded shelter. It held several cupboards containing wool blankets, oilskins, some lanterns, a spyglass, a compass, and the charts Marsh had been so interested in—although now that he'd explained about water depth she understood why the charts were crucial. The shelter also held a covered chamber pot.

She'd awakened wondering who owned the *Cascade,* and how it could be returned to Norfolk with compensation. Marsh appeared to feel even guiltier about stealing—Bronwen preferred the term *borrowing*—the sloop than she. Which wasn't surprising when she recalled the gold eagle they'd found in the train. She still had it. But once they reached Baltimore, surely for a price someone would sail the sloop back south. And Marsh could have been right, even if he was being sarcastic, when he said the owner might not even miss it. Who, after all, would expect a boat to be commandeered in winter?

She crawled to the end of the hard bunk and stuck her head out of the shelter. Marsh sat hunched on a gunwale, silhouetted against a pale, rose-colored dawn sky. His eyelids fluttered, opened and closed, but his shoulders and hands did not have the relaxed look of a man asleep.

"Marsh?" she whispered.

When his eyes flew open, she saw that the ebullient sailor of the previous evening had mellowed considerably. He had circles under his eyes, and his face looked drawn with fatigue. Bronwen also intuited a certain tenseness in him, although he plainly tried to conceal it under a wan smile. Which meant he'd tell her, if she asked, that whatever was bothering him was none of her business.

"Where are we?" she asked instead.

"We've had a good steady wind, so we're a fair distance up the Bay—we should be crossing the Virginia-Maryland line right about now. Over there to the east is Smith Island, and up ahead, to the west, will be the mouth of the Potomac and a lighthouse on Point Lookout."

"We're still going straight up the middle of the Bay, then?"

He seemed to hesitate before answering, "For now. You slept pretty good for a lubber's first night out," he added, as if to change the subject. "Couple times I looked, you were dead to the world." He stopped.

"Not the best choice of words," Bronwen agreed, "but yes, I slept. You didn't, though. The water seems calm—could I try to handle the tiller so you can rest?"

"No!" Then, as if to explain his harsh response, "We've got a . . . a few problems. It seems calm because the tide's turned and we've slowed down. Seriously slowed down. And I don't much like the look of that eastern sky. Too red."

Bronwen, still kneeling on the end of the bunk, stuck her head out farther and faced east, where the sun's light was still a mere glow on the horizon; the sky had, as Marsh said, taken on wide bands of brilliant crimson and violet. "The colors are beautiful! Why on earth are you complaining?"

"Could be bad weather coming, that's why. In any case, we're going to try tacking toward the east." His eyes went over her shoulder. "You'd better take a look behind us."

Bronwen edged uneasily off the bunk and followed the direction in which Marsh pointed. Then she sucked in her breath, straining to see more clearly. A ship, its several masts and multiple sails outlined against the horizon, appeared to be coming on fast.

"It's a good-sized one," Marsh said evenly. "Looks to be rigged like a schooner. It's been out there for some time, and last I checked it was back somewhere around Tangier Island. So I didn't start to worry until just now, when it tacked and began to pick up speed. Get the spyglass."

Bronwen leapt into the cuddy and yanked open the cupboard door. Back out on deck, before she had time to lift the glass, Marsh snatched it from her. She was just as glad—not only was she afraid to look, but she wouldn't have known what to look *for.*

Marsh hoisted the small telescope, and for several minutes said nothing. Bronwen, fidgeting with impatience, at last could stand it no longer and blurted, "What *is* it?"

"It's a frigate—and rigged like a schooner all right. The flag it's flying could be Virginian—that's just a guess, because I can't see its color. Might mean the ship's from Norfolk, or it might not, but we can't take chances. We'll get the hell out of here."

"To where?"

Marsh swung the spyglass to the east, then glanced down at the chart beside him. "Over there, seven or eight miles I figure"—he pointed—"is the northern part of Smith Island. There's plenty of coves and creeks to hide in, and not enough depth for the schooner to follow us. Like I said before, it'll have to stay in deep water."

"But wouldn't those men have known that when they started out? If they're after us, I mean?"

"Sure, but what they couldn't know is that I've sailed this Bay before. Now, farther up—because we can't outrun them—we could have real trouble where the Bay narrows between Kent Island and Annapolis. But maybe that ship back there is nothing to worry about. We'll find out pretty quick now, I'll bet. You can help work the lines. Just follow directions without any lip, O.K.?"

Bronwen frowned.

"Did you hear me? I said 'O.K.?'" Marsh repeated sharply.

"Aye, aye, *sir!* Now are you happy?"

"Haven't got time. I'll be happy later."

Some minutes after they swung east, the wind, which had been diminishing, died altogether. The *Cascade*'s sails hung slack without so much as a flutter. Bronwen could hardly bear to look back at the schooner, but although Marsh mostly watched the sky, he frequently turned to scan the schooner's path. The larger ship still seemed to be moving toward them, although more slowly.

"They've got some wind out there," Marsh muttered as if to himself. He kept glancing down at one of the charts, while his lips moved soundlessly.

Bronwen, watching the sails and Marsh with almost equal frustration, finally yipped, "Marsh, why are you talking to yourself?"

When he didn't answer immediately, she had a terrifying thought: the strain might have driven him insane. After all, what exactly did she know about this man's stability? He might be subject to episodes of madness, and maybe they came periodically. During certain phases of the moon.

"What did you say?" he asked at last, bringing to Bronwen a rush of relief.

"What are you doing that requires muttering?"

"Figuring the tides and currents. They're the most important allies we've got right now. I think," he said, "it's time to stop fiddling around and head for shore."

"But there's no wind!" Bronwen protested.

"I've got a hunch I'll find some in toward the shoreline. Have to try, otherwise we'll start drifting backward on the ebb tide. And *you* are supposed to carry out your duties as first mate—which do not include second-guessing your captain. Now bring out the oars!"

Thirty minutes or so later it became all too clear that the schooner was intentionally bearing down on them. The sloop, however, seemed no nearer the east shoreline, and Bronwen decided her shoulders would be permanently dislocated if she had to pull her oar much longer. She felt like a galley slave. Perspiration ran into her eyes, and she couldn't even stop rowing long enough to wipe her face. Marsh, the slave driver, yelled every time she let up the least bit, but she'd be damned if she'd beg for rest. In any case, she didn't have the breath for it.

She glanced back to see the schooner not a quarter of a mile away. And now, when she looked at Marsh on the other oar, his face wet with sweat, grim with determination, she experienced an acute sense of guilt, the strength of which made her cringe. It was her fault he was caught in this deadly chase. A consequence of her own making. And inappropriate as the timing for it was, she understood that she cared for him.

Gasping for air, she pulled harder.

She focused solely on the rhythm of their oars, and so at first hardly noticed the peculiar sounds. Then she heard a noise that vaguely resembled soft spitting.

Marsh's voice sliced through her concentration. "The goddamn bastards are shooting at us!"

"They're too . . . far away," she panted, "to hit us. Just trying . . . to scare us."

"It's not working!" Marsh shouted, his lungs clearly not as compromised as her own. "I don't plan to surrender—do you?"

"Hell can freeze over before that!" Bronwen screamed. "Keep rowing!"

Then it happened. Her oar skipped over the water as the little sloop jumped forward. And Marsh let out a whoop that could have been heard in Norfolk.

"It's wind!" he yelled. "Stow your oar. It's wind from the northwest!"

Was that good? She didn't dare ask, as Marsh was bellowing orders, while she frantically tried to recall what he meant her to do.

Only a short time passed before they could see the schooner dropping back. "This wind's pushing us east toward shore," Marsh explained, the look in his eyes making them glitter like jet in his drawn face. "But that schooner," he went on, "has to tack west toward deeper water."

Bronwen rubbed her upper arms and shoulders. "Just please don't say anything about . . . about 'luck.'" She whispered the word.

Marsh shot her a grin; then, with one hand on the tiller, he reached with the other into the wicker basket. "This calls for some celebration," he announced, withdrawing a bottle of beer. Pulling out the cork with his teeth, he took a long draft, and handed the bottle to Bronwen.

When she hesitated, never before having had beer, he said, "C'mon, you deserve it."

She guessed she did.

The *Cascade* slipped through the shallow water north of the fingers of land that Marsh called Smith Island, but which were actually a tight cluster of small islands. Just before this, Bronwen had learned that the sloop could heel over at an alarming angle without capsizing, if she and Marsh clambered up the opposite side.

"But what if it *does* tip over, uh, capsize?" she asked.

"We get wet."

When he said, finally, "We're going in there," and pointed to a narrow inlet, Bronwen slumped with relief. It was too late for her shoulders, though; they would never recover.

The *Cascade* moved sluggishly through sparse cord grass into a stream before Marsh pulled up the centerboard and the sloop nudged the soft, mud bottom. "I've got to get some sleep," he told her. "Keep an eye on that schooner."

"What am I supposed to look for?"

"See if it keeps going, or if they drop anchor in the channel opposite here, which means they're going to wait us out. Or if . . . Look, I'm so tired I can't even think straight." He started toward the forward cuddy.

"Marsh! Aren't you even worried?"

"I'm too worn out to be worried. You're in charge—just like you wanted to be. Wake me up if something looks dangerous."

He threw himself on the bunk and pulled the blankets around him. Bronwen could tell from the even sound of his breathing that seconds later he was asleep. Just like that, he deserted her; left her to fret alone. Without even a word about how she'd obeyed his every order perfectly, almost. He might have said *something!*

After eating several pieces of gingerbread, more for comfort than for hunger, she grabbed the spyglass and started north along the stream to find a lookout site. The sky overhead was scattered with gray clouds, and an occasional sprinkle of rain fell. The bare-branched trees whose bark looked like that of oak and birch and sweet gum were fairly sparse along the narrowing stream, although one thick trunk provided cover while she stopped to watch a spindle-legged blue heron pick its way through marsh grass. Quail and wild turkeys rustled through the underbrush, seeming to ignore her presence.

Finding not even a slight elevation, she kept walking until she could see west to the Bay. When she lifted the spyglass, the schooner hove into view immediately. It appeared to be in the easternmost part of the deepwater channel.

Although she couldn't see anything specific on board, she did note that its flag had the colors Marsh had mentioned as likely to be Virginia's. She watched the schooner heave to, trimming its sails and bringing its head into the wind, thereby all but stopping its passage through the wide channel between Point Lookout and Smith Island.

Bronwen dropped to her knees. Even though the schooner must have been seven or eight miles distant, she could almost feel spyglasses trained on her. Impossible, she told herself, but terrifying nonetheless. Marsh had said the channel was some hundred or more feet deep out there, while the depth around Smith Island where the *Cascade* rested was only four or five feet. Presumably, then, they were safe for now.

Unless . . . might the schooner be trailing a smaller boat, one that could be rowed to the island? Surely they wouldn't row seven miles, though, when all they had to do was wait right where they were now. And in fact, that's what the schooner seemed to be doing. Its sails drooped like the folded, unspread wings of a giant bird of prey waiting for its defenseless quarry to show itself.

Bronwen herself waited. With the sun obscured by cloud cover, time advanced with no way to measure its passing. A doe came out of the trees, saw her, and with flick of tail went leaping off to safer ground. The unseasonable warmth seemed to be changing; Bronwen turned up the collar of the pea jacket, and hearing a growl of hunger in her stomach, wondered how long she'd been kneeling there. Always, hovering over her like the sword of Damocles, was the urgent reminder that she must reach Baltimore well before Lincoln's train arrived on Saturday. So little time. They had to keep moving north, but how, with the schooner menacing? If the sloop were to try and dodge the ship, she wondered how far a rifle shot would be accurate; that it was probably no more than one hundred yards at the most did not prove as comforting as she would have liked.

A sudden, shrill *ha-ronk, ha-ronk,* instantly magnified tenfold, made her heart stop. This was followed by the thunderous flapping of thousands of wings, as nearby a huge flock of Canada geese took to the air for no apparent reason. That was, unless something was approaching.

Bronwen fearfully hoisted the spyglass, expecting to see a rowboat or, worse still, a sloop. Instead, she observed the schooner's sails beginning to fill as it appeared to be making ready to leave. All at once a rustle behind her brought the stiletto whipping out of her boot, and she spun on her heels, then sprang upright. A tall stag paced elegantly and unperturbed through the woods just yards away. Bronwen watched him, feeling an inexplicable sadness, or perhaps it was envy. By the time he disappeared into a stand of pine, a soft rain had begun.

She tucked her chin into the pea coat collar and waited until the schooner began sailing due north. Groaning at the dampness, the cramps in her legs, the ache in her shoulders, she started back to the *Cascade* and its sleeping captain.

When she reached the sloop, the captain was not asleep, although he looked groggy. He sat in the cuddy at the edge of the bunk, poring over charts spread on the blankets. Bronwen climbed into the sloop and wrapped herself in the oilskin he tossed her. She stayed out on the deck, however, while he remained inside the shelter.

"Did you sleep long?" she asked a bit waspishly, finding herself still annoyed—even though she knew it was unreasonable—to have been cast aside, afraid and alone, while he slumbered blissfully unawares.

"Just woke up. Anything happening with that schooner?" He gestured toward the Bay.

Did he even notice that she was standing in the rain? Bronwen was tempted to announce that she'd been ravished by pirates, for which he would probably blame *her,* but her generally unreliable maturity this time prevailed and she said, "Yes, they stopped for some time."

"No wind?"

"There seemed to be wind. The water was ruffled." She looked at him to see if this was what he meant.

He nodded somewhat distractedly, and glanced at a chart. "They still out there, then?"

"They moved on north just before I started back here."

"How long ago was that?"

"Maybe twenty or thirty minutes. So maybe we don't have to worry"—Bronwen knew this was false hope even as she said it—"about that schooner anymore, right?"

"Wrong! We have to worry a lot. They probably stopped

on purpose, just long enough for us to see them. Then they went on north so we'd think they'd given up!"

Bronwen nodded, bringing unexpected attention from Marsh. "I guess you already thought of that," he said.

"I was afraid of it. I hoped you'd tell me I was crazy."

"I've already told you *that*."

Bronwen started to retort, but instead, surprised herself by smiling, and even began to laugh. She was more surprised when Marsh smiled. What with their lives in serious jeopardy, this mutual reaction—while unquestionably intriguing—she did not view as reassuring. They *both* must be crazy.

His smile held her, both of them silent until, attempting to distract them from the obvious, she said without forethought, "We'd better decide what to do."

When he laughed softly, she murmured, "That's not what I meant," but found herself still smiling.

"I think it was," he said evenly.

"Marsh, we have to find a way to Baltimore." That was hardly a revelation, much less pertinent, since she *should* tell him to forget what was so clearly on both their minds. She didn't, however.

"We can't leave yet, on any account," he said, "not with the schooner still near at hand. We'll wait a while, then tack north along the Eastern Shore and see what they do. This rain is an advantage," he added, looking not at the sky but steadily at her.

"And in the meantime?" She stopped, reminding herself how much she disliked coyness. The direct approach left far less room for misunderstanding. "Now look, Marsh. If we stay here any longer, I expect we . . . we will do something reckless," was as plain as she could make it.

"I expect you're right. So why are you standing out there in the rain?"

25

*[Said Ferrandini] . . . we shall show the North
we fear them not. The first shot fired, the main
Traitor (Lincoln) dead, and all Maryland will be
with us, and the South shall be free, and the
North must then be ours. . . . Lincoln shall die in
this City.*

—from *Pinkerton's Records*, Baltimore office, 1861

When Seagram alighted from the train at Baltimore's
North Central Railroad Depot, more commonly known as
the Calvert Street Station, the wind felt warmer than he
would have predicted when he left Norfolk. So maybe Red
wasn't freezing to death on the Chesapeake Bay after all.
Admittedly, compared to other possibilities, freezing wasn't
the worst that could happen to her.

He had known without question that nothing could divert
her attention from Baltimore. Not even her rugged young
white knight, or more likely he was a lover, which would
sadden but not surprise Seagram. No, nothing short of lethal
means would even have slowed her down, not more than
temporarily.

When Seagram rounded the corner at Fayette Street, he
encountered more than a dozen other men silently intent on
entering Barnum's Hotel. The doorman, whom Seagram
recognized as one of the *Equus* conspirators, made a mute

gesture toward the rear of the lobby. Seagram went through a swinging door, then up a flight of stairs to enter a darkened chamber where others had already gathered and had seated themselves in a circle. He was struck by the forbidding quiet in this room of waiting men. No one spoke aloud, only in sporadic whispers, the air permeated with a near soundless pulse of expectation.

When "Captain" Cypriano Ferrandini swept in, long black topcoat swirling round him like that of a villain in a Dime Novel, Seagram nearly grinned. He restrained himself with a reminder that this puppet master and his marionettes, however inept and theatrical their performance, were deadly serious.

The meeting did not begin immediately; unquestionably they were awaiting the Horseman, who, Seagram was well aware, had first been detained by his leg wound, then by the necessity of hiring a schooner in Norfolk. Seagram had maneuvered to catch the same train as he, north to Baltimore, but now the Horseman had undoubtedly been further delayed by posting men here at Fell's Point in the harbor. He was not one to again trust chance, the Horseman; unlikely though it was, his hired killers aboard the schooner just might slip up. He could not afford any more costly blunders at this late stage of the game.

And game it was, Seagram thought with distaste. Ferrandini, apparently believing the hour late enough, began to discuss the plot in his mesmerizing voice. Seagram granted that the large crowd of secessionists who had been urged to wait for Lincoln's train would have no knowledge of what was intended for the President-elect. They would be there to create a furor. To disrupt any ceremony, although in keeping with Maryland's ambiguity about Lincoln, no ceremonies to Seagram's knowledge had been planned. And, he conceded, even in this volatile city very few would counte-

nance murder. But the confusion produced by a crowd encouraged to agitate would allow the assassins to strike. And not only to strike, but to get away with it.

Ferrandini was now asking for the man, the man of exemplary valor, who would free the South from the tyranny of a Yankee President. Seagram knew this to be a farce. Ferrandini, Marshal Kane, and the Horseman had already resolved this matter. And yet it was fascinating to watch Ferrandini's manipulation of near twenty men; they were soon convinced that they themselves had decided to draw lots for what had taken on the aspect of a holy mission.

The drawing, however, was rigged. Each man there would blindly withdraw a slip of paper concealed within a box. All the slips were white but one; thus the man drawing the single red ballot would "win" the role of assassin. Or so these men were made to think. In reality, the Horseman had told Seagram, there would be not one red ballot, but eight! Since the ballot winner, for his own future protection, was to remain unknown to the others, each of the eight men drawing red ballots would think theirs was the sole assignment. Each would feel the responsibility to carry out the deliverance of the South. This because the Horseman couldn't afford any more unexpected, random problems. Like the one, Seagram thought wryly, now somewhere in the middle of the Chesapeake Bay.

The fact remained, however, that when this meeting adjourned, the coming Saturday would find eight potential assassins of Abraham Lincoln, along with scores of others who knew what to expect, prowling the Calvert Street Station. With such high stakes, it was supremely unlikely that the Horseman and his cohorts would allow to survive a courier who would announce their intentions. Hence, Seagram thought with sincere regret, his long-legged, ginger *filly might not live to see the battleground that was Balti-more.*

But hers was a contest of wits and of luck. And if, as he'd gambled, she somehow finished the run up the Chesapeake, then he himself would have to stalk her.

26

Ships are but boards, sailors but men; there be land-rats and water-rats, land-thieves and water-thieves.

—Shakespeare

The rain came with no great force, and occasionally dimpled the Bay waters with soft, fat droplets that Bronwen could almost count. The accompanying northwest breeze allowed the *Cascade* a steady, if zigzagging, passage that skimmed the western edges of South Marsh, Deal, and Bloodworth Islands. Then, keeping eyes peeled for the schooner, they sailed on north, hugging the shallow eastern shoreline, past the mouth of the Little Choptank and the wide-mouthed Choptank River itself toward Tilghman Island. And Marsh, to Bronwen's irritation, began to boast again about luck.

"Don't, please—you'll tempt the gods," she said, covering his mouth with her hand.

"Superstition!" He grabbed her hand and held it.

"Yes, I guess I am a little . . ."

"A *little?*"

". . . superstitious. It's like tradition," she retorted, "passed down through generations, so don't mock *it* or my ancestors. Or else do it without me around."

"Now what would I be doing on this Bay, in this weather,

without you around? Other than trying to clear myself of a murder charge."

Bronwen lifted the spyglass, and scanned the misty horizon. "Nothing there. Where do you suppose that schooner went?"

Marsh's face took on the expression she'd come to recognize as the equivalent of "none of your business."

"You think they're waiting for us somewhere, don't you?" she asked. "And don't give me some evasive gibberish."

"For a first mate, you're close to mutiny with your continual orders. And why d'you want to worry about something that might not happen?"

"I like to be prepared. Not caught off guard by the unexpected."

"Since when? In the time I've known you"—he smiled slowly as if reviewing a parade of recollections—"not a single thing's happened that *has* been expected. We've done nothing but improvise. So maybe you're in the wrong business, Detective Llyr."

"I *intended* to be detecting railroad theft, not fleeing assassins," Bronwen replied with passion. "And if you think I've enjoyed being hunted, you're wrong! I'm scared unto death."

Marsh looked at her with surprise. "How was I supposed to know that?"

"You could have asked!"

"I didn't know the question! You don't act as if you're scared. Not much, anyway."

"Would you like it better if I whimpered and cried and carried on? Maybe, but I doubt it. I also think that in some twisted way you're enjoying this—this cat-and-mouse game."

"It beats being chained to a pier in Alabama."

"You still haven't answered my question. You think they're laying a trap for us, don't you?"

"O.K.," Marsh sighed. "Yeah, I think they're going to try and nail us up around Kent Island—where the passage is only about three miles wide between the island and the western shore at Annapolis, and where the water's deep. So that's why I'm not worried *yet*. Plus, the tide's changing, and if the wind keeps steady, we can make good time tonight. That way maybe we can creep past them while it's still dark."

"But after Annapolis we still have to go north to Baltimore—and Lincoln's train is due on Saturday, Marsh! We've only three more days!"

"I know that! But once we get to Sandy Point, north of Annapolis, it's only about twenty-five miles to the Baltimore harbor. I think we can do it—*if* the wind holds!"

As they neared the southern tip of Kent Island, Bronwen found herself increasingly uneasy; Marsh's heightened tension had become contagious, and twice he snapped at her for not responding quickly enough. "It's *shallow* here! We're gonna run aground if you don't act fast!" he barked.

"I can't see anything," she retorted, although that was not completely true. The rain had stopped, and the wind had risen some, blowing clouds across the face of the moon. But once or twice the moon broke through to make the light off the water almost as bright as that at twilight. It was simply "bad luck"—Bronwen hoped with this phrase to appease whatever water spirits Marsh might have offended—that his maneuvers never seemed to coincide with these moonlit moments.

It didn't make her any less uneasy when Marsh began throwing frequent glances toward the eastern horizon.

"What are you looking for?" she asked finally.

"Dawn! It's still way too early for it, but we have to cross the Bay to the western shore long before the sun even starts to show. In case you haven't noticed, the water's getting deeper, and we'll be sitting ducks for that schooner if we can't reach the western shallows. There's a region of the shore south of Annapolis—near the mouth of the Severn River—that's riddled with small streams and coves. We'll set sail for that now while it's still good and dark. The schooner, if it's at anchor, is supposed to have a white light hoisted—but I doubt those killers are too impressed with rules of the sea. If they're waiting for us, they'll keep the ship darkened, out of sight."

He looked again at the eastern sky, then directly over-head, and checked the compass. "No stars, no moon. So pray the cloud cover lasts. And don't talk loud—sound carries a long way over water. O.K., let's make sail. Ready about!"

They stayed on one tack, heading across the Bay at what seemed a fair clip. Bronwen kept raising the spyglass to scan what little she could see through the darkness, terrified that the schooner would suddenly rise up before them.

She jumped with a gasp when Marsh touched her arm to whisper, "We're about three-quarters of the way there. We can make it easily if our luck holds."

Bronwen shuddered, vowing prodigious sacrifices if only her captain's arrogance would be overlooked. These good intentions were not enough. Marsh grabbed her shoulder, his arm swinging in an arc. The windswept clouds were thinning, the moon was visible, and its filtered light began to dance off the water.

And bearing down on them from the north loomed the three-masted schooner.

Softly, but succinctly, Marsh said, "Shit."

The schooner looked to Bronwen like the great white whale of that book Aunt Glynis had tried to make her read.

"Ready about!" Marsh yelled. The *Cascade* heeled to port, nearly casting Bronwen overboard, just as something spattered the surface of the water, although a considerable distance away.

"They're shooting at us!" Bronwen screamed over the sound of the sails whipping, and she clung to the gunwale like a barnacle. Water sprayed over her as the sloop canted dangerously. She cursed Marsh roundly before she even started on the Equus conspirators, since he seemed determined to either toss her off, or capsize the *Cascade,* or both.

Another spatter followed by an ominous *crack* told her the guns were closer, and the sloop suddenly lurched to starboard. Bronwen yelped, then realized Marsh was letting out the mainsail and jib so they were at right angles to the wind, and the little sloop leapt forward as the sails filled.

"Hang on," Marsh shouted, "we got to stay abeam of the wind. Their draft will keep them from going much farther if I can stay in this air current that's bouncing off the shoreline. And look at the water! You can tell from the surface that it's shallower."

Again came the *crack*s of rifle fire, bullets striking the water near the sloop with menacing spits of sound. Bronwen, scrambling constantly with the *Cascade*'s lurching, and clutching at anything that seemed nailed down, couldn't think why the bullets continued to miss them. By sheer number alone—although there might have been fewer than the thousands she imagined—one should have hit its mark. Except that Marsh kept the *Cascade* zigzagging, an erratically fluid target. And then, all at once it seemed, the distance between the schooner and the sloop increased. The gunfire sounded more distant. And Bronwen, looking west, saw trees coming closer while Marsh, looking over his shoulder, let out a whoop.

"Bastards are stuck out there," he chortled, "they'll have to tack toward deeper water. Hey, mate, salute your captain! Praise his outstanding skill."

"I shall sing his praises forevermore," Bronwen promised, "if he can simply get us to land before I throw up."

She smiled at him, though, in spite of her queasiness. "Guess I'm not much of a sailor," she said, putting her head down on her knees.

"No, I *did* have to toss us around some, mostly to keep them from getting between us and the wind. We'll head up that stream there, then put in to shore."

"What's to stop them from following us in a smaller boat?"

"Why should they?" he said, pointing at the eastern sky. Pale bands of gold were widening, brightening, as Bronwen watched with relief and felt her stomach settle.

"They won't follow with a boat," Marsh said. "They'll just wait it out with the schooner again."

Bronwen then thought she truly would vomit. She'd managed to forget they would have to return to the Bay to reach Baltimore. What could they do to evade the schooner? It could outrun them. And time itself was running: toward Lincoln's deadly arrival in Baltimore.

They beached the sloop along a graveled shore just a few yards from a wide stand of pine trees. After climbing out, at first staggering slightly, they collapsed on a thick, fallen tree branch, and Bronwen explored the bottom of the wicker basket. Somehow it had survived the wild ride, and in better shape than herself, she thought, until she pulled out the sodden bread. Although the beer tasted bitter, they drank it anyway, and bolted down the remaining cheese.

Up the shoreline a short distance, Bronwen now saw an

isolated pier to which were moored several odd-looking vessels. They resembled hollowed-out logs with a single mast.

"What are those?" she asked Marsh.

"Hollowed-out logs. Sailing canoes," he said. "Chesapeake watermen swear by those things. That one right there is a two-log-wide one."

"Why do the sails look—well, not exactly dirty, but certainly not white."

"They're tan-bark, treated with oak, hemlock, that kind of thing, so they last longer in the sun. That's why they're brown. Some say the pirates who sailed this Bay and its rivers used them for camouflage . . ."

His voice trailed off, and they stared at each other.

"Then that's it!" Bronwen said. She made no attempt to quiet the excitement in her voice. "It's perfect! If we substitute the sloop for that log boat, the schooner crew won't ever recognize us. We can sail right past them. And then get lost in all the boat traffic around Annapolis. You said yourself we'd likely be safe going through there."

His face took on an expression she didn't like. She'd seen it before and knew an argument would follow.

"What are you," he said, "some kind of kleptomaniac? You just go around stealing things because they're there?"

"Kleptomaniacs steal things they don't need," Bronwen said archly. "We *need* a log boat. Besides, I was thinking more in terms of a trade."

"The sloop for the boat, right?" Marsh's voice had a sharpness Bronwen also disliked. She nodded even though she knew what was coming.

"Do I have to remind you," he said, "that the sloop is not yours to trade?"

Bronwen sighed and got to her feet. "Listen," she said in as reasonable a manner as she could muster, "if you were the

owner of that log thing, wouldn't you like to find a nice little sloop in its place?"

"And the owner of the sloop?"

"Well, I suppose we could send him money."

"We don't know who he is, remember? Because we stole
that, too."

"Marsh, haven't you ever heard the saying 'virtue is its
own reward'? So don't you think that sloop owner would be
rewarded beyond measure to have helped save his President's life?"

Marsh groaned loudly, then said, "And what if he's a secessionist?"

"Then to lose his sloop serves him right!"

Bronwen walked toward the pier, and had just begun to
check the mooring of the canoe when she heard behind her
several distinct and unpleasant sounds. She whirled to find
herself in direct line with a shotgun, while a large white dog
of indeterminate breed growled as if he meant business.
From the corner of her eye, she saw Marsh spring to his feet,
but the shotgun turned on him.

"Just what the hell you think y'all're doin'?" came a
voice as gravelly as the shoreline. Its owner was possessed
of enormous girth and unusual paleness of skin, what small
amount of skin was visible. That ghostly white whale was
haunting her, Bronwen decided; she *should* have read more
than just three pages of her aunt's book. Since the gun toting figure wore a hat pulled down over its ears, a long coat
covered with patches of every hue of red and brown imag-
inable, and enormous leather boots, it was difficult to make
a gender assessment. But Bronwen began to guess female.
Maybe it was a certain roundness of the girth; mostly it was
because some dozen or more pale, unkempt youngsters of
random ages came bursting out of the pine trees, confirmation coming eagerly from one of them.

"Are you gonna shoot 'em, Ma?"

Although trying to remain completely still—so as not to appear a threat to this large woman, her large brood, and her large dog—Bronwen risked a glance at Marsh. His mouth hung open. The youngsters began to surround him, inspecting him as if they'd never seen a grown man before. And perhaps, Bronwen speculated, surveying Ma and her shotgun, most of them hadn't. At least not often.

The dog's continuous, threatening growl had become nerve-racking, and apparently not only to Bronwen.

"Shut yer trap, Spike Monster," Ma said offhandedly to the dog, who, as if happy to be relieved of a burden, immediately began to wag his tail. "I asked y'all a question?" reminded Ma, although she didn't sound particularly impatient.

"Ah, well, you see," Bronwen began, "ah, we were . . . we were admiring your boat. Yes, that's what we were doing. In fact, we admire it so much we were thinking of offering to buy it."

Over the children's heads, she shot Marsh a look he couldn't mistake. He said not a word, having suddenly turned almost as pale as the clan. Perhaps, Bronwen deduced, this was because his leg was being intently sniffed by Spike Monster.

"Why'd you think I want to sell it?" The woman shifted herself and Bronwen saw the gun muzzle lower slightly.

In the meantime, Marsh was attempting to extricate himself from the dog and the mob of youngsters. He stumbled from their midst and came forward with his hand extended, and smile flashing. Ma proved highly susceptible to this gambit: she instantly planted the butt of the gun on the ground and grabbed his hand. Bronwen saw Marsh wince.

"My name's Tristan Marshall," she heard in amazement,

although it did seem unlikely there would be wanted posters nearby. "How do you do, ma'am."

"Well, now, I do just fine, I thank you. Name's Gert— Gert Sachs." She shoved up the brim of her hat to reveal more of the curious paleness—pale greenish eyes like anemic seaweed, and pale hair.

She ventured forth also offering her hand. "I'm Bronwen Llyr, Mrs. Sachs."

"Call me Gert. There's ain't no Mr. Sachs. Least not in recent memory." She laughed heartily, and not at all maliciously, and gestured toward the children. "These young-uns ain't all mine," she said. "Not the lil' young-uns, no how."

Bronwen couldn't see any that didn't look young. Although several of the older girls who were carrying infants could be Gert's daughters—with *their* children—since they nearly all had the pallid complexion and seaweed eyes of Gert.

"You two just wanderin' around in this river?" Gert asked. She'd by this time swung the shotgun over her shoulder, regimental style.

Marsh, his tone suddenly firmer than it had been, said to Bronwen, "I think we owe Mrs.—Gert, an explanation."

Bronwen would have preferred to think about this "explanation" somewhat longer, but since her hand had been forced, she asked, "Gert, how do you feel about secession?"

"Beg pardon?"

"Well, about the United States of America, then?"

Gert stared at her. The youngsters giggled, most of them, but one boy who looked about thirteen said soberly, "We got ourselves a flag. It's over the woodpile—" he paused, deep in thought "—I guess so's it don't get wet. The wood. That what you mean?"

"Yes, it could be," Bronwen said cautiously. "What color is it?"

"It's . . . well, it's wood color."

Give me strength, Lord. "No, I don't mean the wood, I mean the flag. Is it striped? Red, white, and blue?"

"Sure it is," Gert said now, although it was obvious she didn't think this a matter of great consequence. "Why didn't ya ask that in the first place?" She turned to Marsh, giving him a broad smile which displayed startlingly healthy teeth.

Bronwen threw Marsh a look. He was clearly the favored one here, and should proceed with his advantage.

"Gert," he said, smile outshining the rising sun, "there's something we'd like to talk to you about."

"Well, sure. Y'all come inside and have some drink." Gert motioned to an unseen "inside" and lumbered in that direction, with her long, patched coat swinging and young-uns scampering at her heels. Then she suddenly stopped, looked over her shoulder at Marsh, and said, "You married?"

Bronwen wondered if she had suddenly become invisible. Marsh's expression made her think she should consider herself fortunate. And Spike Monster stuck his large, cold nose in her hand.

"Inside" proved to be a huge wooden cabin of uncertain structural soundness, with more colorless Sachses of sundry ages milling around seemingly without purpose; although some of the males, most of them not pale, appeared to be mending nets. They glanced at Bronwen, their interest in her fragmentary. This apparently because she overheard several state emphatically, "Way too skinny." Marsh, on the other hand, was subjected to lavish attention from the female Sachses. Bronwen revised her earlier opinion that they were without purpose; they spent a great amount of time grooming—with combs made from what looked like animals' teeth—their long, white-blond hair. To Marsh's credit, he appeared as if he were actually enjoying himself.

It took gallons of bitter chicory coffee and some kind of doughy loaf-like objects, which Bronwen politely refused— not that Gert cared, so long as Marsh accepted them—to explain and convince and coax and barter. Finally, though, as Marsh put it, "They'd made a deal."

The log canoe with its tan-bark sail would be loaned to Marsh; said canoe to be retrieved at the Baltimore harbor by a Sachs in two days' time. For this "loan," Bronwen went outside to retrieve a silver half-dollar from the purse tied around her thigh. Except for Spike Monster, who accompanied her at a cheerful, tail-swinging trot, no one looked interested enough to even watch her leave the cabin. So she took a minute to count her remaining money, relieved to find there was still a fair amount. She did not include the gold eagle in her count. She had a feeling it might figure rather weightily in Marsh's negotiations.

Once back inside the cabin, however, she found that Gert had effected a stunning reversal. She'd determined that Marsh must promise to return the boat *in person*. Bronwen chewed her lip while the deal floundered, debating whether it would help or hinder to resurrect her and Marsh's "marriage." He, however, as if reading her mind, kept shaking his head at her.

Then, miraculously, one of the Sachs males proved to be made of even stronger stuff than his mother, or was it grandmother, or maybe mother-in-law—Bronwen had no desire to sort out the Sachs genealogy—and persuaded Gert that money in the hand was better than Marsh on the run. And, in return for the gold eagle, this unlikely entrepreneur agreed to sail the sloop back to Norfolk.

An expensive bargain, but plainly the best that could be

done in less than a month of negotiation. Short of marrying off Marsh to one of the long-haired Sachs girls. Or to possibly Gert herself.

Bronwen could relinquish the gold eagle without a second thought. But she sadly regretted giving up the game little *Cascade* that had brought them so far.

They sailed at twilight, leaving behind the blanched and fruitful Sachs menagerie. During their departure, Spike Monster had yelped incessantly, at one point leaping into the log canoe, with the obvious consequence. But once they had righted the vessel and bailed out the water, they took their leave swiftly. Marsh, Bronwen noticed, looked almost wistful.

Now the two-log canoe with its tan-bark sail hugged the western shore, and through the spyglass they watched the schooner riding at anchor in the deeper water. Waiting for a small, vulnerable sloop to appear. The canoe slipped past without incident, without a shot fired, but with a breathtaking release from apprehension on the part of the captain and his first mate.

As Marsh had predicted, the naval harbor at Annapolis was well trafficked, even at that time of year, providing them anonymity until they were well north, and within an hour or two of their goal.

A Fresnel oil lamp with glass prisms and cylindrical wick shone brightly from the squat, white-stoned Seven-Foot Knoll lighthouse that signaled the turn into Baltimore's harbor. Clouds scudded over the moon as the canoe rounded the Patapsco River's jutting peninsula, on which was located Fort McHenry, where bonfires burned and Union ships stood guard, their masts thrust into the sky like bayonets.

"This is more like it," Marsh muttered as they headed northwest into Baltimore's natural, sheltered Inner Harbor, gradually encountering more ships than Bronwen had ever before seen in one place. The moonlit port resembled a city—albeit a floating one—especially since the vessels had white lights hoisted, as required when they rode at anchor. In the distance, the gaslights of Baltimore glowed, and those atop Federal Hill flashed their traditional signals to the harbor traffic. Bronwen didn't say a word while Marsh maneuvered the canoe around the comparatively mammoth three-masted clipper ships.

"Beautiful. Damn, they're beautiful," he said frequently, and Bronwen caught the reverence in his voice. "Ships were being built here in this harbor before the town was even founded," he said to her. "You ever hear of the *Baltimore Clipper,* fastest ship ever designed?"

"I think I read in the newspaper about one called the *Flying Cloud,*" she answered.

"Yeah, that's the one made the news because it was the first to fly over the water—in '51 the *Cloud* sailed from New York to San Francisco in ninety days. Ninety days! But there's not many of those beautiful sleek ones left. Nowadays merchants don't care as much how ships look. They're more interested in how much coffee the ships can carry from Brazil than how fast they can carry it. Same with sugar from the West Indies." He shrugged, as if it weren't important. Bronwen sensed the beauty of a clipper would be very important to a man who was a shipwright.

"O.K.," he said curtly, "ready about! We're going in to Fell's Point."

Bronwen noted with some pride that Marsh didn't even check what she was doing, or whether she was doing it right. They came in against the wind, moving between several docks before tying up at the agreed-upon pier. The Sachses should have no problem finding their boat.

"You're beginning to make a fair sailor," Marsh said to

her. She knew this would be the most she could expect in the way of praise, but from him it was quite a lot.

"O.K., so now what?" he asked her after they'd hauled down the tan-bark sail, and climbed out onto the pier.

Bronwen carefully looked around them, although the only movement she could see were the lighted ships that rolled on the harbor's gentle swells. She wished she could shake the eerie sense of being watched; it must be a result of over-wrought nerves and fatigue. And she couldn't give in to weakness now—too much was still to be done.

"We need to find out how to get to South Street and Pinkerton's office," she told Marsh as they walked, and she glanced around again. "See that tavern down a ways?" She stopped and pointed. "We could try asking there."

They stood under a gaslight on a narrow, cobbled road whose warehouse signs said George Street, and Bronwen, when she realized how visible they were, moved into the shadow of nearby trees. Their skinny trunks seemed woe-fully inadequate, and while she kept reassuring herself that they'd left any peril south of Annapolis, the prolonged period of danger had taken a toll.

"You can't go into a waterfront tavern," Marsh an-nounced now as they walked toward the brick-front struc-ture. "I'll go in and ask—you wait out here."

"Alone? I don't think so."

"Well, you're not going in there! And I'll only be a minute. Look, there's a house next door with a porch and iron railing. It may be attached to the tavern."

"Probably a house of ill-repute."

"No, it doesn't look like . . . How would *you* know about those?"

"How would *you?*"

Marsh ignored this, saying "Just go stand in the shadow of that porch. You can yell or duck inside the house if someone looks suspicious. No one's going to assault you in *public*—this is a civilized city. We're in Baltimore!"

Exactly, Bronwen thought, but needed to find Pinkerton more than she needed to argue Baltimore's drawbacks as a safe haven. "Go ahead, Marsh. Just hurry."

He went through an archway with a wrought-iron gate and, swinging it open, stepped inside the recessed tavern door. Bronwen, checking the stiletto in her shoe, moved quickly into shadow to the side of the house. She leaned a shoulder against the brick wall and shivered with the cold of fatigue, uneasily aware that tiredness was fast overwhelming wariness.

The raucous noise from the tavern gave her concern, but after a few minutes she became accustomed to the boisterous shouts, the unrestrained laughter. Thus the sound of uneven footsteps were covered; the limp that should have warned her. As it was, she didn't hear it, didn't hear anything until a leather sleeve brushed against the brick. Only then did she know that behind her hovered something dangerous.

It was too late.

27

The arm swung around Bronwen's throat before she could even turn. "One scream from you," he said, right hand gripping a dagger with a blade that glinted in the gaslight, "and I'll cut your throat right here."

Even more than the words, the suddenness of the attack made her knees buckle. She slumped against him, and he maliciously yanked her upright. The dagger barely grazed her neck, but the pain straightened her back and cleared her head. Then came the jolting stimulant of anger.

"What good will it do to kill me now?" she whispered hoarsely, mostly to delay, not because she expected an answer. How badly she had once misjudged this man.

"Partly because you know who I am, don't you?" The arm around her neck tightened.

"The Horseman," Bronwen choked, calculating that to lie would enrage him, and praying that cooperation might slow his hand. If she could make him talk it might distract him, and flattery had worked before. "Is that why the code name of your group is *Equus?*"

She knew she'd erred when his arm squeezed her throat again, this time making her gag, and the dagger quivered in his hand. She could barely whisper, "You don't have to kill me. I can't stop you now."

"You might create a few problems if you run to Pinkerton," he said almost offhandedly. "But you're right, it can't be stopped now." Then, for a moment, he was quiet as if thinking about something else entirely.

Where was Marsh?

"But why?" Bronwen asked hesitantly. "Why kill Lincoln? The South's already seceded. Isn't that what you want?"

"I want to make certain there's war!" he said with a fervor that frightened Bronwen almost as much as the dagger. "I want British money for Southern cotton, shipped on *my* Southern railroads." He paused momentarily for breath, then said coldly, "And I want the North to keep their goddamn hands off states' rights."

She had heard this often these past weeks: that the South thought it had a constitutional basis for secession. She had not listened carefully enough. "But why kill Lincoln?" she asked again, hoping against hope that Marsh would appear, and that this man's greed bolstered by political self-righteousness would keep him talking.

"You Yankees and your buffoon of a President don't understand," he said abruptly. "You think we're going to sit back and let you damn abolitionist meddlers threaten us. Our whole way of life!" His grip tightened.

His pitch had escalated to the shrillness of a zealot. Bronwen realized with terror that, in a sense that made no sense, she had become to him *the* Northern abolitionist. And this was a man she'd dismissed as an ordinary, if rather tedious, rich man's son. If *he* could twist from the rational, how many others were there like him?

He began to tug her backward. She tried to dig her heels into the cobblestones as he pulled her, muttering, "One body more or less along the waterfront won't be a surprise."

"Mine will," Bronwen said, sweat seeping from every pore. "There are people interested in where I am." Time, she needed time. *Where was Marsh?*

Did she imagine it, or did the killer's grip loosen ever so slightly? Maybe she had given him grounds for doubt. "It would be foolhardy to kill me here, and you are not a foolish man," she cajoled, trying to keep the trembling of her body from agitating him, from letting him know she was readying herself. She knew escape wasn't likely, not with the dagger at her throat. Yet she had to try. She couldn't just stand there and let him kill her as he had three others. Keep talking, she told herself.

"They'll find my body right away," she said. "And since you've obviously been watching for me, you know that a man will come out of the tavern any second now."

"Then he can watch you get your throat cut before he finds a dagger in his own gut."

"He's got a gun."

"Fine, he'll shoot *you* then," he said, now pushing her forward into the gaslit street and positioning her between himself and the tavern door. "It'll save me the trouble. And you *have* been trouble. I should have taken you out of the way in Montgomery."

"Why didn't you?" Although desperate to stall him, Bronwen also felt a perverse curiosity.

"So you could lead me to other agents. Why do you think I made damn certain you left Montgomery? I wasn't sure then how much you knew. Or if you'd somehow managed to reach Pinkerton. But now I know you haven't told him anything yet."

His voice broke off as the tavern door swung open. It wasn't Marsh who emerged, and Bronwen's dismay nearly made her cry out. A disheveled man stumbled out into the road and rocked back and forth on his heels several times. Then he looked toward Bronwen. "Hey, honey, watcha doin' out here? C'mon in—I'll buy ya' a drink myshelf—I sure will."

He staggered toward her, but memory obviously failing to register his offer, he stumbled past and on into the night. The arm around Bronwen's neck tightened.

As if suddenly aware of his exposure, the killer said, "I can't waste more time here."

From the corner of her eye, Bronwen saw the dagger flash in his hand as it came around to slit her throat from ear to ear.

At that instant, she fell face forward. Instinctively she thrust out her hands to break her fall, but at the same time she hit the cobbles a sudden weight landed on her back, knocking the breath from her and flattening her against the stones. She smelled the metallic odor of blood and wondered if it were her own. Already squirming out from under the body sprawled on her, she saw the carved handle of a knife protruding from the dead man's back, just under the left shoulder blade. The blood she'd smelled ran from his gaping mouth. Bronwen, so numb she felt disembodied, crouched there in silence and looked down at what had been done. For the knife to have pierced the Horseman's lungs instantly, leaving him not even the strength to sweep a dagger along her neck, had required aim of extraordinary accuracy. Even so, unless she were in shock, there should have been *some* surprise when she saw the tall, lean man who came striding out of the harbor mist.

But there was only one person who could have hurled a knife with that precision. The man who had taught her.

He came forward, footfalls silent as those of a stalking wolf, black hair falling almost to his shoulders. Bronwen shakily climbed to her feet.

When Jacques Sundown reached her, his face was without expression. Characteristically so. "Cold night," he said, voice even and taciturn. He might be, as Bronwen had thought for years, one of the most sensuous men alive, but he was also one of the most dangerous-looking. Aunt Glynis once said that Jacques reminded her of a powerful, golden-eyed wolf; free, alert, always poised for action. And in the event he did act, he could be swift and deadly. Yes.

"It's a cold night?" said Bronwen. "Is that all you've got to say?"

"Your aunt's worried."

"I expect she is. A few minutes ago I was pretty worried myself. I imagine Aunt Glyn sent you to find me, didn't she? And thank God!" she added with feeling. She didn't ask exactly how Jacques Sundown had found her. There might be a simple, logical explanation. The Baltimore harbor, after all, would be the obvious place to look, if he knew she'd sailed from Norfolk. But something fey existed within Jacques; a prescient spirit that revealed itself rarely. He was half-Seneca, his mother born of the Wolf clan.

He was now leaning over the body to withdraw his knife when the tavern door burst open, attended by a cacophony of shrieks and curses that turned the air blue. Marsh appeared, silhouetted momentarily in the doorway, then he tore out of the tavern as if pursued by demons. More cursing followed him before the door slammed shut.

When he reached the road, he took one look at the body on the ground, then at Bronwen with Jacques Sundown beside her, and whipped the revolver out of his belt.

"Marsh, no!" Bronwen's yelp was overlapped by Jacques's "Put it down."

Confusion streaked across Marsh's face. Jacques held his knife poised with deceptive casualness as Bronwen took several steps toward the doubtful young man, holding out her hands to show him she was unhurt. He continued walking toward her then, but watched Jacques with distrust. Gesturing at the body with his gun, he asked, "Who is it?"

"Put the gun away," Jacques said. Marsh looked up, met the flat eyes, and stuck the gun back in his belt.

"Ah, Marsh . . . Jacques Sundown," Bronwen stammered. "Jacques, this . . . this is Tristan Marshall."

The two men merely looked at each other, then Marsh turned to Bronwen and said again, "So, who's this dead man? The killer, I hope. So we can stop running."

"You *might* have some idea who he is," Bronwen snapped, shock wearing off to be replaced by sudden anger, "if you hadn't been in that tavern doing God knows what all this time! And yes, he's the killer." She restrained further invective, as Marsh *did* look gravely upset. "His code name's the Horseman," she went on. "I assume it's because he is . . . was . . . involved with railroads. His real name is Jules Falconer."

Jacques said nothing, and Marsh stared at her, then said, "This is the guy I winged when he tried to kill us?"

"This is the one. I suspected him in Richmond when he didn't get off the train with the others from Montgomery. I also remembered that he was the one with the best opportunity to kill Ann Clements. I didn't see him at the ball immediately before, or after, she went over the railing. He must have gone up to the second floor and pushed her."

"Why would he do that?" Marsh asked, having reluctantly pulled the trouser up Falconer's leg and confirmed a calf wound.

"He could have thought she'd learned about the Equus conspiracy. And maybe she had. Arthur Kelly as well. They'd both been operating in Montgomery for some time, and Falconer could well have known they were Pinkerton agents—especially given the railroad connection among them."

"So what now?" Marsh asked.

"We need to get out of here. That schooner could dock any time. And we have to find Pinkerton fast. Jacques, can you help us? Falconer was a member of this conspiracy to assassinate Abraham Lincoln—maybe even a leader of it—but there are others. They're planning to kill the President when his train comes through the city on Saturday."

Jacques, true to form, didn't look at all surprised. "I know where Pinkerton's office is," he said, laconically. "It's in a house on South Street."

Bronwen gaped at him, but followed quickly as he started walking toward a livery at the corner of George and Broadway. Marsh fell into step beside her, and she turned to ask, her voice again sharp, "What *were* you doing in that tavern? While I nearly got killed!"

At least, she thought, he had the decency to look sheepish. "I was trying to get away from some women. They had me jammed into a corner."

"*What?*"

"You were right about that place." He said this with obvious chagrin. "At first, I thought those Baltimore ladies were just being overly friendly, and I tried to be civil and not create a scene. But they were pretty determined to get me upstairs. So then I made a scene. You only caught the tail end of it."

Without a word, Jacques turned around and gave them both a long, level look. Speaking volumes.

• • •

Bronwen, being forced to sit in silence in the bogus brokerage office on South Street, had become so wild with impatience that she couldn't remain still on the chair but began to twitch. This while one of Pinkerton's Baltimore operatives, Charles Williams, told her the Agency was already aware that an assassination attempt on President-elect Abraham Lincoln was to take place. *Somewhere* between Harrisburg, Pennsylvania and Baltimore, and *sometime* in the next two to three days.

"This plot," the gaunt, balding Williams announced, peering at Bronwen over spectacles that kept sliding down his narrow nose, "has not been one of the best kept of secrets—mainly because there have been too many fanatics involved."

So far Williams had not allowed Bronwen to say a word; she was, he informed her, in Pinkerton's bad graces—for having disobeyed orders in Georgia by leaving the Agency's client Thaddeus Dowling. She tried, repeatedly, to interrupt Williams with an explanation of *why* she'd had to leave, or rather, run for her life, but with no success. Meanwhile, time was running out while Williams persisted in telling her what she already knew.

Finally, beside herself with frustration, she hurled herself off the chair, shouting "For heavens' sakes, stop talking and *listen* to me!" and threw Jacques Sundown, standing with Marsh beside the office door, a frantic look of appeal.

Jacques stepped to Williams's desk and stared down at the operative. When Williams looked up in surprise, his expression changed from one of skepticism to uneasiness. Jacques dug into an inside pocket of his fringed, buckskin jacket to remove a document, and handed it to the agent.

Williams, after reading it, looked up and nodded at Jacques, saying, "O.K. Hope you can understand why I was doubtful. But if the Federal Treasury Unit has sent you, and they're willing to verify Miss Llyr had good reason to disregard Pinkerton's instructions, I guess that's another thing." He glanced at the document again. "Rhys Bevan says here—" Williams waved the document at Jacques "—that you're a scout for Major George McClellan. That right?"

As Bronwen expected, Jacques ignored the question. He said simply, "Your agent," he pointed to Bronwen, "has something to tell you. If I were you I'd let her tell it pretty damn fast."

Bronwen put her palms flat on Williams's desk and leaned forward to say, "I already *know* about the assassination conspiracy. This man," she said, motioning to Marsh, "and I have just sailed the Chesapeake all the way from Norfolk to get more information about it to Pinkerton. Now listen! Please!"

She paused for breath, watching Williams. He'd half-risen, but sat down again after a glance from Jacques. "All right," Williams said, settling back behind his desk chair, although again with obvious skepticism. "Go ahead."

Bronwen began with an account of the Equus conspiracy as she'd first overheard it in Montgomery, and went on from there as briefly as possible. Marsh was mostly silent, confirming or adding just a word here and there. She ended with Jules Falconer's death, saying, "The Equus conspirators plan to assassinate Lincoln at the Calvert Street Station when his train comes through here around noon on Saturday. That's the day after tomorrow!"

Somewhere in the midst of her story Charles Williams had abruptly sat forward in his chair. Now he continued to stare at her as he had during her entire recitation. Bronwen began to think that either he did not believe her account or he believed her to be insane; but suddenly he leapt to his feet, saying "Judas bloody Priest! It's true then. Pinkerton heard a similar rumor—from some military officers whose group he'd infiltrated—but we discounted the railroad station plot; first, because it would be broad daylight, and second, because the chief of the Baltimore police force assured us any crowds could be kept at a distance and that Lincoln would be well guarded. Now, admittedly, Pinkerton's been uneasy about the police."

"With good reason," Bronwen said. "The Baltimore police chief Kane is involved in the conspiracy."

At this point, Williams threw on a jacket and made for the door. "The Western Morse Line telegraph office is just up South Street. Pinkerton's in Philadelphia, and I can wire him there."

With that, Williams lunged disjointedly through the office doorway. Jacques Sundown followed him with effortless grace.

Throughout the night, Williams went back and forth to the telegraph office, waiting for telegrams from Philadelphia. Jacques left for a longer period, presumably to wire Washington, and didn't return, while Bronwen and Marsh dozed on the uncomfortable office chairs. When Jacques finally did come back, he carried a valise under his arm that he handed to Bronwen.

She looked at him with question, then opened the clasp. "Oh, dear Lord—clean clothes! Jacques, where ever did you find them at this time of night?"

She pulled out a gray wool cloak, a long skirt and a blouse, and stockings and boots, stopping when she got to a petticoat and chemise. Beneath those were clothes for Marsh.

"But where did you get them?" Bronwen asked again.

Jacques, who'd been looking at a map of Baltimore

pinned on a wall, said over his shoulder, "Pinkerton agents. Williams said we should get you cleaned up. He was right."

"Yeah," Marsh nodded. "I guess we're both kind of gamy by now. Thanks."

"Bathtub back there," Jacques said, tilting his head toward a side door. "Expect there's soap you might want to consider."

Periodically one of the men would go out to eat, but Bronwen couldn't bring herself to leave for fear of missing something. And while grateful to be clean again, she resented the change back to women's garb, vowing that if ever she emerged from this nightmare, she would begin to agitate on behalf of skirt prohibition.

On two occasions Marsh brought her freshly fried oysters in buttered French bread, and what must have been several quarts of coffee, which she managed to force down. But it wasn't until late afternoon of the following day that Charles Williams returned to the office and announced, "All right. There's a plan in place."

"What's being done to protect Lincoln?" This from Jacques Sundown; always one, in Bronwen's experience, to cut straight to the heart of the matter.

"The strategy," Williams said, "is to bring Lincoln secretly through Baltimore ahead of schedule. It will be sometime after midnight, tonight. He'll travel from Harrisburg— where he is now—back to Philadelphia and then south on Samuel Felton's Philadelphia, Wilmington and Baltimore Railroad. Then Lincoln's sleeping car will connect up to the Baltimore and Ohio line, here in Baltimore, for the last leg to Washington. But it's not as simple as it sounds."

"No, I don't think so," Jacques Sundown said. "You've got trouble spots there along the rail line north of Baltimore."

"Right," Williams agreed. "We've positioned agents at the bridge over the Gunpowder River—they've just located a cache of explosives planted under the bridge pilings."

"How about at Havre de Grace, where the Susquehanna empties into the Chesapeake?" asked Marsh unexpectedly. "I've been up there and it's too wide for a bridge—don't the train cars have to be ferried across the mouth of the river?"

"Yes, but we're not overly concerned with that location. There's a small town there, a railroad crew to keep watch, and a maximum amount of gas and lantern light, so it's not vulnerable to sabotage by this band of conspirators. Not like the Gunpowder bridge, which is in a woods in the middle of nowhere—even if it is just ten miles north of Baltimore."

Bronwen felt a sharp pang of disappointment. Everything had been planned, everyone had an assignment. All she could do now was sit on the sidelines. "So Lincoln has agreed to this?" she asked.

"Not without argument," Williams answered. "Pinkerton's had the devil's own time convincing the President there's an actual, planned conspiracy to kill him. Apparently since the election Lincoln has gotten frequent death threats. But Senator Seward had some similar information about a conspiracy from another source, and together with your report"—he nodded at Bronwen—"and its explicit details, Pinkerton and Seward finally managed to persuade Lincoln to take precautions."

"What happens here in Baltimore," said Jacques, "when you have to move Lincoln from one station to the other?"

Charles Williams frowned, and Bronwen, looking from him to Jacques, said, "*What?* What do you mean from one station to . . . ?"

"The Philadelphia, Wilmington and Baltimore line doesn't link up to the Baltimore and Ohio at the Calvert Street Station," Williams told her. "It *could* do it, but entire trains aren't allowed to move across the city of Baltimore. First the cars have to be uncoupled, and then teams of horses pull them through the streets to the Washington Branch Depot over on the south side."

Williams must have seen the disbelieving looks on Marsh and Bronwen's faces, as he added, with a sardonic look of his own, "Baltimore's teamsters need the work."

"That's the craziest thing I've ever heard!" Bronwen blurted.

"Agreed!" said Williams. "But that's the way it is. If we try to bypass the teamsters we'll gather attention we don't want. And this transfer will happen in the wee hours of the morning—if all goes well to that point."

He got up from behind the desk saying to Bronwen, "And now that most of the details have been discussed, there's some folks outside who want to see you."

Williams pulled open the back door of the office. While Bronwen's jaw dropped in astonishment, Zoe Martin entered, followed by Thaddeus Dowling.

"Thank God you're all right!" Dowling said with unmistakable relief.

Zoe nodded vigorously. "Y'all really had us frightened," she said to Bronwen, graciously including Marsh in her words. Zoe then gave Thaddeus Dowling an eloquent smile that told Bronwen exactly the form of their association, hard as it might be to understand an attraction between the lovely young photographer and—in Bronwen's opinion—a middle-aged, rather stuffy investor. But it explained why, in Montgomery, Dowling had kept his evening "airings" private. And why Bronwen had just happened to come upon Zoe Martin that one night. She'd probably been waiting for him and, in fact, Bronwen recalled, had specifically asked the whereabouts of Dowling.

"We've been extremely worried about you, young lady,"

Dowling said gruffly, surprising Bronwen with his obvious sincerity. "Cormac Quinn, too," he added.

"Really?" Bronwen said innocently. "Is *he* here in Baltimore as well?"

"He and Colonel de Warde," Dowling answered.

"My, my," she said speculatively, "a virtual Montgomery reunion, isn't it?"

Dowling gave her a puzzled look, and nodded rather uncertainly.

Jacques said now to Williams, "Seems like things are under control here—as much as they can be. I'm going back to Washington. Like to take her with me"—he motioned to Bronwen—"to her aunt who's there."

Williams shook his head. "Sorry. Pinkerton's orders are for all his operatives in Baltimore to stay put. Could still be something we don't know—an attack before or when he comes through." Bronwen noticed he didn't use a specific name. Perhaps Dowling wasn't entirely aware of the situation involving Lincoln.

"Pinkerton wants everybody ready in case there's trouble," Williams added. "And anyway, he's going to want to see her." He inclined his head toward Bronwen.

Jacques also looked at Bronwen, who guessed his unspoken question.

"Assure Aunt Glyn that I'm fine," she told him. "And that there's good reason why I can't leave. Besides, I don't *want* to leave before . . . before everything's done." She had a sudden inspiration. "But Jacques, maybe you could take Tristan Marshall with you."

"No!" came Marsh's expected response.

It took prolonged effort to convince Marsh that Rhys Bevan's detective unit could very likely help to clear him of the murder charge. "That's much more their kind of case than Pinkerton's," she explained.

In the end, Jacques had to all but drag the reluctant Marsh from the office. Bronwen followed, and caught hold of his sleeve, while Jacques went to untether the horses of their rented carriage.

"I'll be in Washington in just a few days," she said.

"I think before then you'll be in more trouble," Marsh argued, his voice once again as gruff as when they'd first met.

"How can I, with agents all over the place?" she asked him with a grin. "And Pinkerton will give me the boot if I do anything more out of line. Williams didn't have to spell it out. I'm in big enough trouble for not following orders in Montgomery."

"I don't guess I can make you promise not to act crazy?" Marsh said, attempting to sound offhand and not succeeding.

"I'll try." Bronwen forced a laugh she didn't feel. "Now go on to Washington, and next time I see you maybe you won't be wanted for murder."

They both saw the carriage coming toward them. Marsh started to say something more, but then just swung an arm around Bronwen's shoulders and held her tightly against his chest. When he released her, he walked to the carriage, looking back only once.

The force of Bronwen's sadness startled her; she supposed it shouldn't have, given that she questioned whether she'd ever see Marsh again. Despite their close, turbulent time together, she really knew little about him; his past, before the shipyard servitude, remained a blank. He might well just disappear back into that blankness. Although he had once mentioned that if cleared of the murder charge he would try to see his mother who, Bronwen thought she recalled him saying, lived somewhere near Gettysburg, Pennsylvania. He'd also said he intended to horsewhip his stepfather; if the bastard was still alive, he wouldn't want to be, after Marsh got through with him.

And who knew, Bronwen thought, where she herself might be by tomorrow? Provided Pinkerton didn't fire her.

While the carriage clattered up South Street in the direction of the Washington Branch Depot, she stood looking after it until it was well out of sight.

The wind began clearing away earlier clouds and, as she watched the sun sink low on the western horizon, she recalled moments aboard the *Cascade*. If she hadn't delayed her return inside, she wouldn't have caught the slight blur of movement from the corner of her eye. It occurred so unexpectedly, and seemed so surreptitious, that she stepped back into the shadows to look further without being observed herself. She watched as someone who had just slipped out a side door of the South Street house, carrying a leather valise, now moved in haste toward the road.

The sunlight being so dim, she couldn't be absolutely certain, but believed she knew who it was. Why would *he* be there? He now walked so fast as to be nearly jogging in the opposite direction the carriage had taken. Almost as if he was hurrying toward the Calvert Street Station—whose rails ran north of Baltimore. But why?

Bronwen wasn't aware of making a decision. The question she'd asked herself just seemed to propel her forward without volition. Later, when it became important to understand, she guessed she had followed him at first out of curiosity, and because she'd been restless from hours of inactivity and simply wanted to walk. Due to Pinkerton's "stay put" command, she'd intended going only a short distance, just far enough to work out the kinks in her legs. She supposed it *possible* that a grain of intuition began to take root in her mind, but at the time she had not been conscious of it.

IV

> *. . . and I heard, as it were the noise of thunder,*
> *one of the four beasts saying, Come and see.*
> *And I saw, and behold a white horse: and he*
> *that sat on him had a bow . . . : and he went forth*
> *conquering, and to conquer. . . .*
>
> *And . . . I heard the second beast say, Come and see.*
> *And there went out another horse that was*
> *red; and power was given to him that sat*
> *thereon to take peace from the earth. . . .*
>
> *And . . . I heard the third beast say, Come and see.*
> *And I beheld, and lo a black horse; and he*
> *that sat on him had a pair of balances in his*
> *hand. . . .*
>
> *And . . . I heard the voice of the fourth beast say,*
> *Come and see.*
> *And I looked, and behold a pale horse:*
> *and his name that sat on him was Death,*
> *and Hell followed with him.*

And power was given unto them over the fourth part of the earth,
to kill with sword, and with hunger, and with death, and with the
beasts of the earth.

—Revelation 6:1–8

28

I have never had a feeling, politically, that did not spring from the sentiments embodied in the Declaration of Independence . . . that in due time the weight would be lifted from the shoulders of all men and all should have an equal chance. Now, my friends, can this country be saved on that basis? . . . But if this country cannot be saved without giving up that principle . . . I would rather be assassinated on this spot than surrender it.

—Abraham Lincoln, Philadelphia, February 22, 1861

ℳary Lincoln, shivering in a wind blowing across the bunting-shrouded platform in front of Independence Hall, watched as her husband raised the red, white, and blue banner to the top of the flagpole. Thus bringing a thunderous roar of approval from the thousands of Philadelphians who had risen at dawn on this, George Washington's birthday, to meet their newly elected President.

Mary found herself only half-listening to Mr. Lincoln. She'd seen his notes and knew the speech was geared to the upcoming eighty-fifth anniversary of the adoption of the Declaration of Independence, in the same red-brick building that stood directly behind her.

But her husband shouldn't even be here. He should be moving quickly out of the path of danger. Every single one of the men involved in protecting him from this monstrous

Baltimore plot—of which she had just learned, minutes earlier, before leaving the Continental Hotel—all had urged
him to leave for Washington immediately. But no; he was
scheduled to be at Independence Hall in Philadelphia this
day and so he was there, as promised.

Mary hadn't realized, not until that very moment, how
angry she had become. Terrified, yes; she'd known that. The
anger, however, came unanticipated. But why should her
husband's life be put in jeopardy just so a crowd of anonymous people could say they'd seen the President? And why
should he risk being murdered—leaving her and their children alone in the world—just because he'd earlier vowed to
be in Philadelphia on this particular day? Why, when there
were despicable people out there who wanted to kill him?
Maybe some of them were standing in the crowd right now.
Watching him, waiting for the opportunity to strike him
down.

The anger was making her head pound. Dear Lord, no;
she couldn't have one of her terrible headaches, not now.
She had to preserve every ounce of strength to battle those
who would keep her from traveling at his side to Washington. Her struggle so far had been a short and futile one. She
now believed there was a conspiracy by the men surrounding Mr. Lincoln that was every bit as real as the Baltimore
plot. They had contrived to make her go through that dangerous, divided city alone. And if she survived the predicted
howling mob at the Baltimore train station, then she would
arrive in Washington alone. They had intrigued to separate
her from him, so they could exploit him for their own pur-
poses.

Mary looked up at her husband, and was suddenly buffeted by a deep sense of shame. Mr. Lincoln might be
unsophisticated, but he was not ignorant; eager to trust, but
not easily deceived. In time he would recognize the ex-

ploiters. Already he had been disillusioned by some seeking cabinet appointments, those like the scurrilous Simon Cameron. Mary had managed to shield him on occasion—which is why they wanted her out of the way. She knew full well that behind her back they called her interfering; an interfering, meddlesome hellcat who would be an ever-watchful obstacle in their path to the President.

Her attention was now drawn back to her husband's voice, hoarse and rather shrill, referring to something about the country being saved. And then he said, "I would rather be assassinated on this spot than surrender . . ."

Mary stopped listening. She swayed forward with the sensation of drooping, as if she were about to wilt; a blown, vulnerable rose shriveled by sun and lashed by wind from which there was no shelter.

She barely remembered their uneventful train ride from Philadelphia, or their tumultuous welcome in Harrisburg, followed by a formal reception at the State Capitol. For the duration of the journey and tiresome ceremonies, Mr. Lincoln had been engaged by Norman Judd, Ward Lamon, and others who insisted on endlessly rehearsing the clandestine plan to evade the Baltimore assassins. There was vehement and jealous argument about who should accompany Mr. Lincoln to Washington. No mention was made of her. She wasn't significant enough to even merit dismissal. Mary's dread grew mile by mile until it assumed the dimensions of a gigantic, unrelenting nightmare. And her husband appeared to be so indifferent to the circumstance as to make jests about it. He sat and told stories. And joked!

Now she perched on the edge of an overstuffed sofa in the Jones House hotel suite, watching him dress for dinner. "It's my *right* to go with you, my duty as your wife," she continued to argue.

His deepset eyes turned to her in weary appeal. "Molly, that dog just won't hunt this time. Now we have been over it, and it cannot be. Bad enough that I have to sneak into Washington like a thief in the night. Now let's have one member of this family—and by any reckonin' the handsomest one—sally forth with some self-respect."

He chuckled, and relenting she smiled in spite of herself. His hand stroked her hair, then, after glancing at a clock on the mantel, he went to stand at the window and stare out, closing himself away in a place she could not follow, as he did more and more of late. Mary pressed her fingers against her aching forehead, afraid she might again faint, as she had in Philadelphia. To her everlasting fury, she'd overheard two military officers imply she had deliberately made a scene to gain attention.

But her pain and her fear had been real. They still were, as in her mind's eye she saw the plans for her husband's flight; plans from which she had been excluded. At 5:45 a carriage would be waiting at the side of the hotel. Mr. Lincoln would excuse himself from dinner, come here to their suite to change clothes, then covertly enter the carriage to be driven to an isolated railroad siding at the edge of Harrisburg. From there he would travel back to Philadelphia to be met by the bewhiskered Pinkerton, who would accompany him to Washington. Thus, that short, cigar-smoking popinjay would be awarded more privilege than the President's wife!

In the meantime, she was expected to graciously continue to entertain Harrisburg dignitaries, while word would be given out that her husband was "resting in their hotel suite." And no one in the outside world could be the wiser—or so it was supposed—because the telegraph lines around Harrisburg would be cut; all of them, except for a single wire open to Pinkerton.

She and the boys would then be "allowed" to leave Harrisburg the following morning according to schedule.

There was nothing she could do about it that she hadn't already tried. Arriving at the hotel she'd been overwhelmed by panic, and, desperate for *someone* to listen to her fear, she'd made a terrible scene of weeping, pleading to accompany her husband. Those surrounding Mr. Lincoln said she simply suffered from exhaustion; that she'd become emotional, nervous, hysterical—all the usual words trotted out to make her feel humiliated. A disobedient child who, behaving badly, had caused the grown-ups needless discomfort. Worst of all, she had clearly embarrassed Mr. Lincoln.

Mary turned this over in her mind as she rose from the sofa to accompany her husband to the staircase of the Jones House, to descend into the midst of the smiling people below. At least Mary supposed they *must* be smiling, although to her the upturned faces took on the guise of hideously leering gargoyles. And one of those gargoyles might at this very moment be plotting to murder her husband.

No! She would not allow herself to be humiliated again. Determinedly, she smiled up at Mr. Lincoln. He tucked her hand inside the crook of his arm, and they started down the stairs.

29

Thou didst trample the sea with thy horses, the surging of mighty waters.

—Habakkuk 3:15

Bronwen kept her eyes trained on the cream-colored mare ahead. Although she didn't want to lose sight of it, at this point she would willingly wager it was headed toward the Calvert Street railroad station.

A short time earlier, when the man she followed had stopped at a German Street livery to rent the horse, she ducked out of sight behind the nearest tree, wavering as to whether she should continue on this questionable path. She was already in trouble with Pinkerton; to defy him again by leaving the South Street office would almost certainly spell disaster. Unless it could be proved that she'd left for a crucial reason. But had she? Her present pursuit could be for no reason whatsoever!

Except that by now she believed something to be markedly odd about this particular man's determined attitude: a certain urgency to his pace, a disregard of his surroundings that made him look neither right nor left but straight ahead, seeming to concentrate solely on his destination. Added to this was his stealthy exit from the South Street house—where no one had been aware that he'd entered. Bronwen felt fairly sure of this; she'd explored the house, although not every nook and cranny, while waiting interminably for Williams and news from Pinkerton. So *where* in the house had he been, and why had he been there at all? She now wondered if, when he had crept out, he assumed she'd left with Marsh and Jacques. The house stood surrounded by trees, and he might not have seen her remain behind. If she *had* gone with them to Washington, that would have left only Charles Williams to man the office. As was now actually the case, with her traipsing the streets of Baltimore with no one's knowledge, to say nothing of consent.

Thus she'd stood behind the tree near the livery, debating with herself. Now, when she *really* needed a captain to tell her what to do, she was forced to decide alone.

When the moment to act came, however, she simply acted; she needn't have bothered with all that deliberation, as her response was characteristic, bred in her bones. As soon as the man rode out of the livery, she had darted inside and rented a horse herself.

Now the mare ahead slowed from a canter to a trot as a train whistle sounded in the near distance. A few minutes later, horse and rider halted at a hitching post beside an elaborately designed, two-story building with a myriad of arched windows and doors as well as two four-story turrets. A large brass plaque over the entrance read "CALVERT STATION."

Bronwen held back, waiting until her quarry went through a three-arched entrance, then tethered her own horse and followed him inside. For an anxious moment she thought he had vanished into the fair-size crowd, but then spotted him at a ticket window under a sign that said "PHILADELPHIA, WILMINGTON & BALTIMORE LINE. TO NORTH."

This time she didn't debate. She merely delayed unobtrusively until he went toward a boarding platform before she then moved quickly to the ticket window.

"Excuse me," she addressed the ticket agent, a kindly looking man of ripe age, "but I'm afraid I've missed my . . . my husband." While this husband ruse had become habitual, it seemed to work. She clutched a handkerchief to her breast and gave the agent a look fraught with concern, saying, "I was to meet him here—and I'm afraid we had a misunderstanding about the time." She embellished this last with a catch in her voice, and dabbed at her eyes with the handkerchief. Then, gesturing vaguely in the direction of a steam-belching train, she asked, "Has he possibly already purchased his ticket? It would have been only in the past few minutes, I'm sure."

"What does your husband look like?"

"Oh, he's . . . he's distinguished looking. Such soulful eyes, he has." She tried to blush here, and, in case she'd failed, again applied the handkerchief.

"A well-dressed man, and I guess you'd call him distinguished," the agent answered, "bought a ticket here just a minute ago."

"Oh, thank goodness." Bronwen sighed. She opened her hand—the one without the industrious handkerchief—and placed coins she had ready on the counter.

The agent looked at her as if something obvious were missing. When he finally asked, "Where to?" Bronwen nearly lost her nerve, this whole charade having been prompted by the unknown destination. But then the agent added, "Oh, that's right—same as your husband?"

"Yes. Yes, of course."

He wrote *"Philadelphia"* on a yellow rectangular card, and handed it to her. "Good trip, young lady."

Bronwen shot him a swift smile then turned away quickly, needing to remain wholly alert to the heightened clouds of steam that would signal the train's imminent departure. After dodging behind other passengers for cover, she concealed herself at the side of an archway, her eyes locked on the Philadelphia-bound Guy Seagram.

Something unquestionably strange was going on here. Why would Seagram be heading north when Abraham Lincoln would have just boarded a train to come south, and into Seagram's own Maryland baliwick? It didn't make sense. Unless . . .

Of course! The answer struck her as being breathtakingly obvious. Why hadn't she seen it sooner? Guy Seagram was very probably an undercover member of the Treasury Department's Special Detective Unit. And that *did* make sense.

Early on, the rumor about a plan to destroy the railroad line into the capital must have reached Rhys Bevan in Washington. In response, Bevan would have directed Seagram to investigate, which he had done by feigning alliance with the Equus conspirators just as Pinkerton had done. And Seagram, as he had truthfully told Bronwen, suspected who *she* was after seeing her with Pinkerton agent Ann Clements in Montgomery. No wonder he had made such effort to protect her.

And now, at some stop between Philadelphia and Baltimore, he was undoubtedly going to board the unscheduled train to assist in escorting Lincoln, not only safely past Baltimore, but on through to Washington. Especially since the decision had been made to release the four officers from the War Department; their uniformed presence would invite too much attention. All of this explained why, at the South Street house, Seagram had not intruded. He had needed to learn the details, but knew Pinkerton would be outraged to think Treasury didn't trust *him* to get Lincoln unharmed through Baltimore.

Bronwen eagerly started forward to where Seagram waited for the "all aboard" call. Then, after just a step or two, she stopped cold. He would never allow her to take part in this. Never. And she, with like obstinacy, would never allow herself to miss it: the opportunity to see—as very few others now would—Abraham Lincoln's clandestine entrance into the nation's capital. But if she were careful, and stayed out of sight, she might well end up on the same train as the soon-to-be President. For whom she had already risked her life; surely she deserved to take part in this historic ride.

And at the same time, Pinkerton would have to acknowledge, if not in fact reward, her resourcefulness.

Bronwen, now seated beside a train window in the car behind the one Seagram had boarded, looked back at the receding city. The third largest in the country, its thousands of gaslights made glowing amber of the southern night sky. She had barely even seen Baltimore, widely regarded as one of the most cultured and beautiful cities in the nation, with a colorful if considerably volatile political history; its present unrest was not without precedent. She pressed her face to the glass to see the bright lights atop an observatory on Federal Hill, signals of passage for the thousands of ships that made up the harbor traffic. Ships that carried cargoes not only into and out of southern United States ports, but traded goods with the West Indies and South America and Europe as well. What would happen to that commerce if there was war? Some said there was talk of a blockade of southern ports. In which case, Baltimore could suffer greatly.

Bronwen, put in mind of the Chesapeake voyage, found herself missing Marsh considerably more than she had expected. She tried to explain it away as loneliness, her sense of isolation—which she should have predicted. However, she'd been told often enough that her choice of employment, and her employer, did not encourage singular attachments. It stood to reason; what man in his right mind would want a woman who with regularity left him for a railroad?

The night sky above the steel track running roughly parallel to the shore of the Chesapeake was not completely clear. A waning moon, still more than half-full, disappeared now and again behind large, billowing clouds. From the window, all that Bronwen could make out, even when the moon did emerge, was mile after mile of forest. Not the thick evergreen stands of western New York, but what looked to be oak trees with thick, ancient trunks and wide-spreading branches. When, some ten miles north of Baltimore, the locomotive slowed to approach the bridge over the Gunpowder River, Bronwen did not need a moon to see lantern lights ahead. And as the train reached the southern edge of the bridge, she could also see scores of men. They stood in a line along the riverbank, holding the lanterns and swinging them all in the same direction, right and then left. The waves of light surged backward and forward, signaling to the engineer that the bridge was secure. Bronwen tensed nonetheless.

The train clattered across the river and continued on north toward the town of Havre de Grace.

More miles of trees, occasionally punctuated by flashing lights she knew to be the lanterns of Pinkerton agents stationed at intervals along the track. The lights meant all went as arranged. Despite her best efforts to remain calm, Bronwen could feel excitement building, a lone excitement, since her fellow passengers had not the slightest idea what momentous undertaking was in progress. After she asked the ticket collector the time—close to one A.M. he told her—Bronwen calculated the train had traveled nearly twenty miles from the Gunpowder bridge. Which meant that shortly she could expect to see the Havre de Grace train yard on the southern shore of the Susquehanna.

Although she couldn't actually view the maneuver, when Bronwen felt a grinding jolt, she knew that her passenger car, pushed from behind by a small yard engine, had been thrust from the railroad track onto the track of the ferry boat. This followed by the rasping sounds of the car being locked into place. The sky at last clear of clouds, moonlight showed her that the huge Baltimore engine had already been uncoupled. Since its thirty-some tons could not be ferried across the river, the locomotive now was chugging on a side track toward the roundhouse to be turned back south toward Baltimore.

The sidewheeler ferry, the *Maryland,* looked perilously gargantuan; it was more than a thousand feet long, with a two-hundred-foot beam—or so the conductor had said—and Bronwen couldn't imagine how it ever stayed afloat. Moreover, its expanse obviously could accommodate far more than the three cars now being loaded. After the *Maryland*'s stern had been unlocked from the railroad track and the ferry was steaming toward the northern shore, she could see better from her window the broad span of the Susquehanna's mouth. What began as a stream in New York State grew to a mighty river as it wound its way south to the Chesapeake Bay and, at last, home to the sea.

Bronwen stood at the passenger car window in the north shore train yard, searching for Guy Seagram in the scant light provided by lanterns. The three passenger cars were now being recoupled to the north-bound locomotive, which would soon pull out. She went to the conductor positioned at the car's rear exit and again asked the time: two A.M. So although she hadn't seen him do it, Seagram must have left this train, and the locomotive bearing Lincoln's sleeping car from Philadelphia must be nearing at this very moment.

Bronwen went down the train steps to a wide wooden platform—and into rank confusion. The river ran behind her, the ferry boat's stern abutting the railroad track, while the station house, no more than a small hut, stood some small distance ahead. The train yard itself appeared more jumbled than any of those she and Marsh had encountered, primarily because of its small area, the large amount of equipment, and there being only two sets of main track. And *this* constituted the sole route from the north into Baltimore? Empty railroad cars stood on sidings to keep them out of the way of trains moving on the principal tracks running north and south. Lacking design, the yard, thought Bronwen with impatience, was an obstacle course in the midst of a maze. And now she heard the first rumble of an approaching train.

How would she find Seagram, especially in what was relatively dim light? When she did find him, she had decided to show herself. At this point, since he'd failed to divert her, what could he do? Make her stay behind while he boarded Lincoln's train? He'd know that wasn't possible short of tying her up. No, she'd made it this far; just let Seagram try to keep her from riding back to Baltimore on the presidential train!

And then she had another, less pleasant thought: Pinkerton would also be on the train. At least that had been the plan. Now that she'd actually gone and done this, she did not have quite the same earlier confidence that Pinkerton would view her actions with favor. Yes; Pinkerton, she should avoid.

The oncoming train from the north was one notably without a bell clanging or whistle shrieking, and as she peered down the track Bronwen could see its lights appear. And from behind her a whoosh of steam made her suddenly realize that the first train, the one in which she had arrived, was just pulling out *now*. She was trapped there on the platform between the trains and their two sets of track. Looking wildly around for cover, she saw a rickety baggage cart piled with unlabeled crates. Not good, she thought fleetingly as she dashed toward them, since the crates might be loaded with explosives—which was too far-fetched for even *her* to consider. Surely the entire yard, on Pinkerton's orders, would have been gone over with a fine-toothed comb.

She reached the baggage cart and, panting more from dread of Pinkerton's reaction than from her own exertion, hunkered down behind it, watching the Philadelphia-bound train finally pull out. The meager station depot with its few lanterns was nearby, but the crates shielded her from the view of anyone who might emerge. When the Baltimore-bound train actually pulled in—any minute now, as its thunder was already deafening—she might have to slide on her belly under the cart. Or, lacking the will to do that, she would have to give herself up to Pinkerton's wrath. Except that if she were to simply stand up, before she had a chance to identify herself, Pinkerton might conceivably shoot her. She'd better stay concealed. In the meantime, where was Seagram?

The platform shook as the locomotive from Philadelphia ground to a stop. It hauled two sleeping cars, but shades covered only the first car's windows. So Lincoln was *there,* only a dozen or more yards away.

There seemed to be very few trainmen around. Perhaps they'd been ordered to stay inside the station depot for security reasons. But it gave the scene an eerie lack of activity.

Bronwen heard the uncoupling process, then the locomotive immediately chuffed onto a side track. At the same time, a small yard engine prepared to approach from another siding to push the sleeping cars onto the ferry. Bronwen knew she probably had no realistic chance to enter either car now without being seen by *someone.* She would have to wait, and at the last minute, jump onto the boat before it started across the Susquehanna. Then there might be opportunity once the ferry got under way. It wasn't as if the cars were loaded with Pinkerton agents. She knew, in fact, of only one, other than Pinkerton himself: Kate Warne. The plan had been for Kate to pose as "a sick man's" nurse, accompanying a shawl-draped Lincoln into the sleeping car at the Philadelphia station. A mob of operatives—even if there had *been* that many in Philadelphia, which there weren't—would have created too much attention. A handful of Lincoln's friends and aides were aboard, but they could well be asleep; it was after two in the morning and no trouble was anticipated until Baltimore. And certainly not here in a small yard where no one even knew this train carried Lincoln.

Bronwen thought her plan would be worth a try! When Kate Warne recognized her—if Kate even saw her—she might relent enough not to tell Pinkerton.

Her plan in place, Bronwen relaxed slightly and looked around her. But then, seeing movement to the side of the depot, she quickly shrank back behind the crates. And it was not who she saw, but what she saw him do that made the breath catch in her throat.

Guy Seagram, standing now at the near edge of the station house, had just withdrawn a revolver from the brown valise. The first thought racing through Bronwen's mind was that Seagram had armed himself to guard Lincoln while passing through Baltimore. But why the revolver *now?* And he then did something that for Bronwen created sheer terror. He bent over and shoved the valise down behind some trash barrels, straightened, and concealed the revolver inside his coat. He then crept, stealth undeniable, toward the first sleeping car.

And Bronwen, with chilling clarity, understood. Guy Seagram was not a Treasury agent. He had not protected her life because of concern for her, but because he *needed* her. He needed to track her to Pinkerton's Baltimore agents; needed to learn what alternatives would be planned to evade the assassins—*after* she supplied her information. The information that *he* had given her. And why not give it to her? He knew very well, Seagram did, that the Equus conspiracy as it stood would be exposed. Thus it would fail. He'd said as much to her on the steamship out of Richmond; there were too many involved. Too many rumors, too many fanatics. It was only a matter of time before everyone in Baltimore would learn of the plot, just as he had learned of it. So he had donned the mask of sympathizer, pretending his allegiance solely to track Equus activity. As he had tracked her. Because if a Lincoln assassination were to succeed, *he* would have to do it. He alone.

There was no time for Bronwen to question why? The question was how to stop him. The worst of it was, she liked Seagram! Her instinct told her to plead, scream if need be, to make him give it up! But rationally she could not. A man who planned with such determination the murder of a President would hardly spare *her*.

He was just nearing the foot of the sleeping car steps as she pulled the stiletto from her shoe. Then a figure appeared on the top step, and for a blessed moment Bronwen thought it was over. Either Seagram would turn and bolt, or Pinkerton would shoot. But it wasn't Pinkerton on the step. It was Kate Warne. Bronwen recognized her voice. Heard her ask softly, "Is that you, Charles?"

Kate thought it was Williams. And when she realized her mistake, Seagram would shoot her, be up the steps gun exploding, killing anyone caught in his path until he reached his true target.

Bronwen had already slipped out from behind the crates. She lightly hefted the stiletto to test her equilibrium, ticking off in her mind each lesson Jacques Sundown had taught her. She could not bring herself to kill Seagram. But she could disable him, pierce the arm that would reach for the revolver.

She inched forward just behind and to his right; stopped, crept forward again, relying that he focused only on the one who stood in his way. She moved as close as she dared, flexed her calves and arms made hard by jumping trains and hauling sails, everything secondary now to Jacques's voice inside her head.

"Stand aside!" Seagram ordered Kate Warne. "Do it now!"

Kate gave a soft cry. In rapid succession, Seagram reached into his coat, pulled out the revolver and cocked the hammer while simultaneously raising his arm. Bronwen took aim—and she hurled.

At that exact instant, Seagram spun toward her. Had he seen her blade glint? It mattered not. The stiletto didn't pierce his raised arm, but flew past, straight and strong as an arrow into his chest. The impact sent him staggering backward, the revolver discharging harmlessly into the air.

He collapsed slowly, sinking to his knees before toppling. Bronwen had already reached his side by the time voices came from inside the train.

"Don't die," she heard herself say, not really aware of saying it. "Seagram, stop dying!" She squatted beside him, wanting to explain. "I didn't mean to kill you."

She stopped because he coughed; blood, not a lot, just a thin rivulet, ran from the corner of his mouth. He coughed again, and strained for air to say, "Told you don't . . . don't trust anyone, Red . . . can't you . . . *learn* that?"

"Why? Just tell me why you did this?" Bronwen refused to look up at those gathering. She didn't care about them. She wanted an answer. "Tell me, Seagram! Why?"

Someone standing next to her gripped her shoulder. She swatted the hand away. "Damn you, Seagram! Tell me why I had to kill you!"

"He's . . . dangerous." Seagram coughed more flecks of blood, then went on. "He knows nothing . . . nothing about war. Too trusting . . . unsure. Someone will get him . . . someday . . . better now before . . . before he blunders into war. It will . . . terrible . . . war."

His face was ashen, his breathing harsh, stopping and starting and stopping. He tried to raise his right hand, but it fell back to his side. Bronwen lifted and held it. Somewhere in her mind she registered that around them were silent people. Listening; totally silent.

Seagram's head rolled toward Bronwen, and someone reached down, put fingers on his neck, searched for a pulse. Bronwen, whose eyes had been fixed on the erratic, slowing, fluttering throb, knew it had stopped.

She again felt a hand on her shoulder. It was Kate Warne's hand. And then Bronwen dimly heard behind her, lifting over the murmur of voices, the sound of water splashing, followed by the grating of a boat being clumsily beached. Moments later footsteps pounded forward, then stopped directly in front of her. She thought she should be curious about this, but couldn't take her eyes from Seagram's lifeless form.

A long blank quiet was broken by a man's voice. "Are you Bronwen Llyr? Glynis Tryon's niece?"

Bronwen looked up, relieved at the prick of awareness her aunt's name brought. Perhaps it was a slight Celtic lilt in the man's voice, or the concerned, intense blue eyes, but she knew, or thought she knew, who he was. "Rhys Bevan?"

He barely nodded, his eyes never leaving her. The sound of other voices now grew louder. The Treasury detective took Bronwen's arm and drew her to one side of the small group around Seagram.

"I didn't want to *kill* him," she told Rhys Bevan, desperate for him to understand. "I didn't *mean* to."

"He meant to kill the President," Bevan responded, his voice so gentle perhaps he did understand.

"Do you know who he was?" Bronwen asked. "Who he *really* was?"

"Don't know much. There doesn't seem to be much to

know. We finally traced him—obviously not soon enough—through the War Department's military records. He'd enlisted some years ago, and the records show a surprising number of promotions in what was a short tour of duty. After his discharge, the department records led us to New Jersey, to a college there. Where he'd taught military history."

Bronwen sighed with what she felt as mourning. The enigma that had been Seagram began to emerge.

"He resigned from the faculty some months ago," Bevan went on. "In November, to be specific."

"The election," Bronwen said with certainty. "Lincoln's election."

"Yes, then. We haven't found much else, except for one other item. It seems Guy Seagram's father and uncle both died at the battle of Vera Cruz, Mexico—died rather horribly, according to War Department records. That may have some bearing on this."

It had much bearing. A reason Bronwen could grasp. "Why were you looking for him—Seagram?"

"Because we'd already been looking for you, and after your friend Marshall reached me and told his story, we became very interested in Mr. Seagram. It seemed to me he was crossing your path entirely too often. Finally, traced you both to the Calvert Station—and the ticket agent who remembered you. I only regret I didn't get here before . . ." Bevan gestured at the river he had just crossed, and then at Seagram.

"Miss Llyr!" The sudden gruff voice came from the direction of the train. Allan Pinkerton stood halfway down the sleeping car steps. "Miss Llyr, I want to see you. Right now!"

Kate Warne took a step toward the train, then stopped and shook her head before she turned to give Bronwen a look of compassion. Bronwen knew then that Pinkerton had found the excuse to discharge her. The Scotsman's self-importance was large and his word was law, and no matter what else she had done, she had disobeyed him. Under the circumstances, though, he wouldn't do it here, not in front of everyone. He was demanding she come forward, so he could fire her in private.

Well, she wouldn't let him fire her. Before he did, she would quit. She pointedly ignored his demand, looking back at Rhys Bevan, who had been studying her closely. But Kate Warne touched her sleeve. "Miss Llyr," she said, "please turn around. *Turn around!*"

Bronwen turned. At the top of the steps behind Pinkerton, a tall silhouette had appeared, and she heard a short, indistinct exchange take place. Pinkerton immediately hurried the rest of the way down the steps to the platform, then moved some distance away.

Bronwen, meanwhile, felt herself being nudged forward by both Rhys Bevan and Kate Warne. The tall figure had remained at the top of the steps. Bronwen went forward to within a few feet of the train car. Her numbness was mercifully fading. She needed to be alert; to clutch this moment, as here was the reason she had killed a man. It felt a little, she imagined, like being called to account by God.

However, the man who looked down at her from the top of the stairs did not remotely resemble Bronwen's notion of God. He did not look powerful; he looked tired. His eyes were grave, his face pale and drawn, and when he smiled at her it was a faint, weary smile, but it was there. Then he nodded and motioned to the stairs, his long fingers gesturing toward the inside of the car.

Her feet, as she went up the steps to meet him, felt heavier than she would have expected.

EPILOGUE

In your *hands, my dissatisfied fellow countrymen,
and not in* mine, *is the momentous issue of civil
war. The government will not assail* you. . . . You
*have no oath registered in Heaven to destroy the
government, while* I *shall have the most solemn
one to "preserve, protect and defend" it.*

—Abraham Lincoln, inaugural address, March 4, 1861

After a morning darkened by ominous black clouds, the
sky over Washington had been blown clear by the March
wind, and now Glynis had to squint against brilliant but welcome sunshine streaming over the Capitol. Bronwen, seated
to one side of Glynis, gazed solemnly up at the platform
where Abraham Lincoln stood at a podium, slowly and deliberately unrolling the manuscript he had just extracted
from a pocket of his black suit. Then his hand began searching in another pocket. His eyes, however, were on the manuscript, and his mind clearly on other than for what he was
hunting, because, when he withdrew his hand, he looked
with surprise at a pair of steel-rimmed spectacles. Glynis
caught the split-second smile that streaked across his face.
He would sorely need that self-deprecating humor.

Momentarily, he would begin to address the thousands
gathered near the Capitol's east wing, where the inaugural
platform had been erected.

Next to Bronwen, the young man Tristan Marshall also

gazed upward, but with not nearly so somber an expression. Glynis could well imagine that being newly cleared of a murder charge might account for his good spirits. When every so often he grinned, seemingly without volition, Bronwen would turn to him with a warning frown. "Marsh, this is *serious!*" But then she would relent and give him a fleeting smile.

And Glynis herself would have smiled at both of them had the circumstances been different; the surroundings not that of an armed camp. The assassination rumors persisted.

Rhys Bevan, seated to Glynis's other side, and ordinarily the most unflappable of men, had been shifting his position restlessly, turning this way and that, then twisting sideways. Ever since they'd arrived, his eyes roved continuously over the crowds spilling from the Capitol grounds into the cobblestone streets. And when Rhys wasn't scanning the crowds, he was looking up at the rooftops to either side of Pennsylvania Avenue, where scores of sharpshooters were positioned. On a grassy embankment near the East Plaza, artillerymen had assembled a row of cannons. Infantry patrolled the dirt side roads, as did units of cavalry, their horses picking their way nervously amid the noisy droves of celebrants.

To Glynis's mind, the inaugural celebration was a travesty, given the times. It included a full parade of waving flags, military bands, horse-drawn floats, double files of cavalry, and marching infantry. Presidents Buchanan and Lincoln rode together in an open carriage up a Pennsylvania Avenue lined with the stark skeletal trees of late winter. The festivities caricatured a normality which did not exist. And she imagined that, if offered a choice, Lincoln would have preferred a private, less circus-like ceremony. On the other hand, perhaps Lincoln thought a *display* of normality was important: the Union as solid, immutable, not to be swayed by the turbulent winds of politics.

Jacques Sundown, on a handsome, tall, black Friesian horse, was somewhere out there in the crowd. He was roaming undercover—only for *this* day, he made unmistakably clear—and only because the Treasury Department's Special Detective Unit had requested he stay for the inauguration. Strangely enough, the taciturn Jacques and the buoyant Rhys Bevan had gotten on fairly well; it reminded Glynis of the days when Jacques and Cullen Stuart had worked together. Days long, and sadly, gone.

Rhys Bevan's concern concentrated on Lincoln's safety. He had told Glynis several days before that the military could do only so much. Lincoln, or any President, needed a special security force whose primary job was to provide protection. That such a force did not exist had stretched the Treasury service to the limit. And, in fact, Rhys now apparently could sit still no longer. He excused himself to Glynis and swiftly vanished into the crowd.

Glynis glanced over the heads of three hundred or more dignitaries seated in the first rows; she and the others sat only eight rows back from the podium. Bronwen had at first been closemouthed about how this remarkable opportunity came to pass. It was she who had known exactly where their seats were located. And she, not Rhys Bevan, who had carried the stamped credentials that allowed them through the cordon of General Scott's troops surrounding the seated area.

"Your young Bronwen," Rhys had said, smiling when Glynis commented on this, "has acquired some rather . . . *influential* friends." He, like Bronwen, had not elaborated.

By that time though, Glynis knew to what he referred. Bronwen had told her, swearing her to silence. "We've all pledged secrecy," she'd said, "those that were there. Because the President doesn't want Mrs. Lincoln to know."

As if Mary Lincoln were a child, Glynis thought with some irritation, looking up at the woman on the platform. But a child was not the Mary Lincoln whom Glynis remembered from her stay in Springfield. Or even the one she'd seen a few days earlier at the Willard Hotel, the White House being still unfinished, when the new First Lady spoke at a morning tea. "Coming through Baltimore that Saturday afternoon with my children," she'd said, "was the most terrifying experience of my life. I truly believed that howling mob would pull us from the train and tear us apart limb from limb. They even forced the windows of our car open to shout their foul language."

Nonetheless, while she told of this, Mary Lincoln had sounded more angry than fearful. And now, as her elegant blue cloak billowed in the wind, Mrs. Lincoln pulled it around herself with a poised grace, but the gesture was, as well, typically one of determination. Seated at a far end of the platform, Mary Lincoln looked as courageous as any of those who sat between herself and her husband. She would endure. Glynis felt a certain sadness at this thought. Surely being the country's First Lady should be other than a trial of endurance.

And, Glynis supposed with somewhat less sadness, that her sister Gwen would also endure, when she learned that Bronwen had gone from the frying pan, so to speak, into the line of fire. Glynis recalled her own sense of relief when Bronwen announced she had left Pinkerton's—just before she would have been fired.

The relief proved short-lived.

"I have something to tell you, Aunt Glyn!" Bronwen's feline eyes, older and more guarded in the past weeks, yesterday had glittered with a familiar mischief. And Glynis had waited with a familiar apprehension.

"Pinkerton may think I'm *'undisciplined and not suitable material for a detective,'*" Bronwen had said, mimicking Allan Pinkerton's gruff tone, but with suspicious cheerfulness. "But Rhys Bevan doesn't think that. And, in fact, he thinks Pinkerton trained me well. So he wants to employ me—undercover, for the Special Detective Unit. In some situations a female agent can be more useful than a man, you know."

Glynis, somehow, had managed not to groan audibly. When she'd later confronted Rhys, praying her niece had distorted his enthusiasm, he confirmed his offer to Bronwen.

"Her Pinkerton training has made her of particular value. Unlike Pinkerton, however, I encourage ingenuity, the ability to make quick decisions."

"Rhys, she makes quick decisions because she's reckless."

"She'll learn caution. And she's as physically fit as any woman alive," he explained patiently, as if Glynis did not know this. "A smart woman in espionage work will be invaluable in time of war," he added, as if Glynis cared. "Besides, she *wants* to do this! Here I can keep an eye on her. And I doubt you—or anyone—can stop her."

Glynis could not begin to argue with that.

Now, hearing Lincoln clear his throat, she raised her eyes to the podium. The new President had been reviled without mercy in the Southern press for "sneaking like the coward he is" into Washington. The newspaper cartoons had been ruthless. And this noisy crowd, which undoubtedly included secessionists, seemed determined to disrupt his speech. Uniformed men on horseback moved in, efficiently isolating those who had become the most unruly.

Then Lincoln, after looking out across what must be wave

after wave after wave in the sea of upturned faces, began to speak.

He did so at some length. And what Glynis heard should discourage any of those remaining who had expected this man to retreat. To back away from his vow to defend and maintain the Union. It wasn't going to happen.

"We must not be enemies," he closed. "Though passion may have strained, it must not break our bonds of affection. The mystic chords of memory, stretching from every battlefield, and patriot grave, to every living heart and hearthstone, all over this brave land, will yet swell the chorus of the Union, when again touched, as surely they will be, by the better angels of our nature."

During this speech Glynis had glanced often at Mary Lincoln, who listened to her husband with a look of unabashed pride. As his wife, that was understandable. However, Glynis could not be the only woman there who experienced unease when hearing the new President's words "the better angels of our nature"; remembering, as she did, that it was not merely the "better," but the *best* of angels who had fallen farthest, precisely because of his nature.

She found herself scanning the Capitol grounds with increased misgiving, and it was then Glynis conjured a foreboding paradox; in a glassy, translucent light shimmering off banners and flags, four shadowy figures prowled. Four dark, hooded riders astride loosely reined horses of white and red and black and pale. Those shadowy riders could afford to bide their time: the few voices of men who still cautioned restraint were growing feeble, as stormclouds gathered over a tiny island in the harbor of South Carolina. And once those voices were silenced . . .

Glynis suddenly felt an overwhelming urgency, the need to leave this place, this biblical sea of glass about to be shattered. Rising from her chair, she searched the grounds for the tall black Friesian. But Jacques, as she might have known, was already directing the horse across the trampled grass. When he reached her, Glynis said, "Take me home. Please, Jacques, take me home."

As he lifted her up in front of him on the Friesian, Glynis gripped the horse's thick, flowing mane. They started north across the Capitol grounds, and Glynis took an unwilling look behind her to see, for what she hoped was the last time, bayonets and rifle barrels shining in the sun, spangled uniforms crisp and clean, black cannons gleaming on the hillock. Steam hovered above the railroad tracks, the smoky breath of iron horses champing at their bits.

And over it all, from a place too near, could be heard a ghostly drum of hoofbeats.

The Horsemen were coming.

HISTORICAL NOTES

—∾—

Baltimore Brigands

As historical confirmation of Samuel Morse Felton's fears regarding his Philadelphia, Wilmington and Baltimore Railroad: On April 19, 1861, railroad bridges to the north of Baltimore were burned by secessionist extremists to keep Federal troops from marching through the city. The troops were subsequently fired upon; the resulting battle fatalities are commonly accepted as having been the first of the Civil War.

Chesnut, Mary Boykin (1823–1886)

Born into an old, aristocratic South Carolina family, Mary Chesnut was present in Montgomery for the birth of her beloved Confederacy in 1861, and was an eyewitness to the anguish of its death in 1865. Her diary of the Civil War South has become an invaluable resource for historians, not least because of the societal vantage point from which it was written. For Chesnut was not a typical Southern woman: she was a member of the wealthy Southern elite, and as one reads her diary it becomes apparent that she was not even typical of the women within *that* confine. There are now in print several editions of the diary.

Historian C. Vann Woodward received the Pulitzer Prize for his *Mary Chesnut's Civil War* (1981). With all due respect to the exacting scholarship of the above, this author favors the first edition, *A Diary from Dixie,* published in 1905, and edited by Isabella Martin, who at Chesnut's written request was bequeathed the diary notes. To the cautious researchers this circumstance immediately hoists a red flag of warning: there will be selective omissions, an almost inevitable sanitizing. Moreover, the reader should be alerted that this edition is said to contain only half of the original material, and is believed to have excluded some items the editors thought, for one reason or another, might be inappropriate. Still and all, *A Diary from Dixie* offers a point of view that feels authentically female.

Dorothea Dix (1802–1887)

As is mentioned in the novel, Samuel Felton's information from Dix was one of the earliest-documented reports of guerrilla activities planned against the railroad leading into Washington, months before the actual onset of war. Dorothea Dix, however, is remembered primarily as a humanitarian, as a passionate crusader on behalf of the mentally ill, and as a pioneer in the campaign to improve the conditions of asylums for the insane. It is entirely likely that one of the Tryon women will in due time meet Miss Dix, as in June of 1861 she was appointed superintendent of army nurses for Civil War service.

Lincoln, Mary Todd (1818–1882)

Mary Lincoln is one of American history's most tragic figures. She was criticized during her lifetime (as have been many Presidents' wives), but that was as nothing compared to her posthumous malignment. It is well to remember that Abraham Lincoln's first biographers were male contemporaries, most of whom had a bone to pick with the late President's wife. For one thing, Mary was fiercely protective of Mr. Lincoln (as it appears she most often called him); she did not always suffer fools gladly, most especially those fools who, in her view, were not completely loyal to her husband. For another, Mary was well-educated, passionate, strong-willed, and outspoken—qualities in a woman that are not always viewed with favor even today. Imagine how they were viewed in the nineteenth century! Moreover, these qualities were described as something rather different by the contemporary male writers who engendered the myths of Mary Lincoln, and by subsequent historians who simply repeated them. Thus we read that she was *over*educated, hysterical (sound familiar?), stubborn, and opinionated.

If we rely on most of Abraham Lincoln's biographers, our view of the Lincoln marriage unquestionably must be: poor Abe. How did he stand it, *or* her? And yet, the words of Lincoln himself, in his letters and in comments recorded by others, give every indication of a man deeply in love with his wife. The signs point to theirs as a tumultuous love affair, until the Civil War drained Lincoln's strength and spirit, and left Mary adrift in a hostile political sea.

Finally, a woman who watched in anguish as three of her four children died from painful, drawn-out illnesses, saw a beloved husband murdered before her eyes, and was then committed to a lunatic asylum by her remaining son (she was released when no evidence of madness—other than compulsive shopping—could be documented), deserves from history far more insightful treatment than what she has received.

Pinkerton Operatives

The Agency operatives named in the novel are historically authentic, the exceptions being Ann Clements and Arthur Kelly, and young Bronwen. Allan Pinkerton *did* hire women operatives fairly early on, Kate Warne being the first, as related in the novel. Admittedly, the portrait of Mr. Pinkerton in *The Stalking-Horse* is perhaps overly harsh. But as indicated by his biographers, and deduced from his own records, the author imagines that his response to a young woman like Bronwen Llyr would have been as characterized. Allan Pinkerton definitely liked his women compliant.

Kane, George

The Baltimore police chief, Marshal Kane, was arrested on June 27, 1861, for Confederate activities, which in the eyes of the government amounted to treason. From the records available, there is every reason to believe that he was knowledgeable of, if not actually involved in, the Baltimore assassination plot.

Market Street

In 1884, the name of Montgomery's historic Market Street was changed to Dexter Avenue. However, even today (although the street is no longer unpaved), one can stand at the foot of the gently sloping hill and look straight up its broad expanse for an unobstructed view of Montgomery's magnificent Capitol building. And if one listens carefully, one might still hear the militia drums and the horses' hoofbeats of that February day when delegates voted to form a provisional government known as the Confederate States of America.

Mason and Dixon Line

Readers of previous Glynis Tryon mysteries have often asked about the Mason-Dixon line. Thus, and in brief: It is the boundary between Pennsylvania and Maryland, established by two English surveyors, Charles Mason and Jeremiah Dixon. The 233-mile line (marked with milestones from England), completed in 1768, was drawn to settle a long-standing controversy between the Penns and the Baltimores. The name was pragmatically shortened to the Mason-Dixon line and became popularly regarded as separating the North from the South.

McIntyre, Archibald C. (1833–c. 1890)

"20,000 Southerners captured on the spot!" This quotation is from a newspaper advertisement by A. C. McIntyre, Montgomery's leading photographer, who had "captured" the inauguration of Jefferson Davis. (The size of the crowd was most certainly exaggerated.) While none of McIntyre's original collodion prints seems to have survived, copies of the famous lithograph made from one of the inaugural photographs are familiar to Civil War enthusiasts. Given the infant stage of photography in 1861, McIntyre's photograph is remarkable; stunning in the vivid sharpness of its detail, right down to the spokes on carriage wheels, the ruffles on ladies' skirts, and the hands of the Capitol clock.

Spotswood Hotel

Erected in 1859 at the corner of Main and Eighth streets in Richmond, Virginia, the Spotswood would play a major role when the capital of the Confederacy moved from Montgomery to Richmond in May of 1861. President Jefferson Davis first stayed there, and during the war it housed General Robert E. Lee. After the war, Union generals Sherman, Sheridan, and Grant stayed there. It was destroyed by fire on Christmas Day, 1870.

Van Lew, Elizabeth (1818–1900)

This Richmond woman was unquestionably one of the Union's most effective spies (she called herself an "agent"). What is most surprising is that she got away with so much for so long in that she remained publicly loyal to the United States government. She even managed to hide escaped Union prisoners in her home. Her skill at maintaining a facade of mental derangement (which earned her the nickname of "Crazy Bet") no doubt contributed to the chivalrous Virginians' reluctance to arrest her. Although she became one of the most interesting characters in Civil

War Virginia, to say more about her in these particular "Historical Notes" would be a disservice to mystery readers; there can be little doubt that Elizabeth Van Lew and Treasury Agent Bronwen Llyr will meet again.

The Waterfront Hotel

The building at 15 George Street, Fell's Point, Baltimore, where Marsh made his inopportune scene, had been owned by shipbuilder Edward Fell. The original structure was of glazed brick (possibly the second-oldest brick building in Baltimore). It still stands on what is now Thames Street, a quaint picturesque building, presently a restaurant, whose historic charm has been restored by its present owners.

The Baltimore Plot

This term is the usual, facile label attached to the pre-inaugural attempt to assassinate President-elect Abraham Lincoln in the city of Baltimore. One reason the author chose not to use this label in the novel is the belief that this charming city has been more than sufficiently maligned for the doings of a handful of fanatics.

The event has been given rather short shrift by historians. The reader should be aware that at one time there was some doubt as to whether such a plot ever existed—some thought it was a Pinkerton advertising ploy. That doubt, for reasons beyond the scope of these notes, has since been put to rest. The author's research into Lincoln's train schedule and Pinkerton's activities relied primarily on a nonfiction work entitled *Lincoln and the Baltimore Plot 1861; From Pinkerton Records and Related Papers*. This was edited by Norma B. Cuthbert, chief cataloger of the Huntington Library in San Marino, California, copyrighted 1949 by same. The interested reader may come across this slim but informative volume in bookstores specializing in Civil War material.

History is frustratingly secretive to the point of silence about what eventually happened to the primary conspirators. It would appear that none were arrested. (See note on **George Kane.**) It is believed that Cypriano Ferrandini fled Baltimore in timely fashion, and apparently disappeared into the ether of the great historical unknown. One secessionist ("Hillard"), a conspirator familiar not only to Pinkerton but known as well to other agents, *was* ultimately called before a congressional committee; he testified that he had no knowledge of any plot against Lincoln or the federal government. While not unique, this unequivocal mendacity before a congressional body may come as some surprise to twentieth-century readers who are perhaps more accustomed to: "I don't recall."

The Stalking-Horse does not in any way alter the historical record *as we know it.* Samuel Felton did call on Pinkerton to investigate threats to his railroad (for which Felton was charged fourteen hundred dollars). Lincoln did receive numerous assassination threats following his election, and the near-disastrous track obstruction and grenade incidents did occur. Lincoln's time schedule and train stops were as they appear in the novel, and on Saturday, February 23, 1861 (between three-thirty and four A.M.), his sleeping car *was* pulled by horses through Baltimore, from one railroad station to another, to evade the assassins.

While nothing in the historical record indicates that an assassination was attempted at the Susquehanna railroad yard, nothing in the record indicates that it was *not!* And such, dear reader, is the stuff of which historical fiction is made.